Skulduggery Pleasant

Books 1 and 2

To be published in Great Britain by HarperCollins *Children's Books* in 2013
HarperCollins *Children's Books* is a division of HarperCollins*Publishers* Ltd,
77-85 Fulham Palace Road, Hammersmith, London, W6 8JB.

Visit us on the web at www.harpercollins.co.uk

Visit Skulduggery Pleasant at
www.skulduggerypleasant.co.uk

Derek Landy blogs under duress at
www.dereklandy.blogspot.com

7

ISBN: 978-0-00-752335-1

Printed and bound in England by Clays Ltd, St Ives plc

MIX
Paper from
responsible sources
FSC™ C007454

FSC™ is a non-profit international organisation established to promote the responsible management of the world's forests. Products carrying the FSC label are independently certified to assure consumers that they come from forests that are managed to meet the social, economic and ecological needs of present and future generations, and other controlled sources.

Find out more about HarperCollins and the environment at
www.harpercollins.co.uk/green

DEREK LANDY

Pages 5 – 369

Pages 371 – 719

HarperCollins *Children's Books*

Skulduggery Pleasant

This book is dedicated to my parents, John and Barbara.

Dad – this is for your bizarrely unwavering support and unflinching faith.

Barbs – this is for that look on your face when I told you the good news.

I owe you absolutely everything and, y'know, I suppose it's entirely possible that I feel some, like, degree of affection towards the two of you...

1

STEPHANIE

Gordon Edgley's sudden death came as a shock to everyone – not least himself. One moment he was in his study, seven words into the twenty-fifth sentence of the final chapter of his new book *And The Darkness Rained Upon Them*, and the next he was dead. *A tragic loss*, his mind echoed numbly as he slipped away.

The funeral was attended by family and acquaintances but not many friends. Gordon hadn't been a well-liked figure in the publishing world, for although the books he wrote – tales of horror and magic and wonder – regularly reared their heads in the bestseller lists, he had the disquieting habit of insulting people without realising it, then laughing at their shock. It was at Gordon's funeral, however, that Stephanie Edgley first caught sight of the gentleman in the tan overcoat.

He was standing under the shade of a large tree, away from the crowd, the coat buttoned up all the way despite the warmth of the afternoon. A scarf was wrapped around the lower half of his face and even from her position on the far side of the grave, Stephanie could make out the wild and frizzy hair that escaped from the wide brimmed hat he wore low over his gigantic sunglasses. She watched him, intrigued by his appearance. And then, like he knew he was being observed, he turned and walked back through the rows of headstones, and disappeared from sight.

After the service, Stephanie and her parents travelled back to her dead uncle's house, over a humpbacked bridge and along a narrow road that carved its way through thick woodland. The gates were heavy and grand and stood open, welcoming them into the estate. The grounds were vast and the old house itself was ridiculously big.

There was an extra door in the living room, a door disguised as a bookcase, and when she was younger Stephanie liked to think that no one else knew about this door, not even Gordon himself. It was a secret passageway, like in the stories she'd read, and she'd make up adventures about haunted houses and smuggled treasure. This secret passageway would always be her escape route, and the imaginary villains in these adventures would be dumbfounded by her sudden and mysterious disappearance. But now this door, this secret passageway, stood open, and there was a steady stream of people through it, and she was saddened that this little piece of magic had been taken from her.

Tea was served and drinks were poured and little sandwiches were passed around on silver trays, and Stephanie watched the mourners casually appraise their surroundings. The major topic of hushed conversation was the will. Gordon wasn't a man who inspired, or even demonstrated, any great affection, so no one could predict who would inherit his substantial fortune. Stephanie could see the greed seep into the watery eyes of her father's other brother, a horrible little man called Fergus, as he nodded sadly and spoke sombrely and pocketed the silverware when he thought no one was looking.

Fergus's wife was a thoroughly dislikeable, sharp-featured woman named Beryl. She drifted through the crowd, deep in unconvincing grief, prying for gossip and digging for scandal. Her daughters did their best to ignore Stephanie. Carol and

Crystal were twins, fifteen years old, and as sour and vindictive as their parents. Whereas Stephanie was dark-haired, tall, slim and strong, they were bottle-blonde, stumpy and dressed in clothes that made them bulge in all the wrong places. Apart from their brown eyes, no one would guess that the twins were related to her. She liked that. It was the only thing about them she liked. She left them to their petty glares and snide whispers, and went for a walk.

The corridors of her uncle's house were long and lined with paintings. The floor beneath Stephanie's feet was wooden, polished to a gleam, and the house smelled of age. Not musty exactly but... experienced. These walls and these floors had seen a lot in their time, and Stephanie was nothing but a faint whisper to them. Here one instant, gone the next.

Gordon had been a good uncle. Arrogant and irresponsible, yes, but also childish and enormous fun, with a light in his eyes, a glint of mischief. When everyone else was taking him seriously, Stephanie was privy to the winks and the nods and the half-smiles that he would shoot her way when they weren't looking. Even as a child she felt she understood him better than most. She liked his intelligence and his wit, and the way he didn't care what people thought of him. He'd been a good uncle to have. He'd taught her a lot.

She knew that her mother and Gordon had briefly dated ("courted", her mother had called it), but when Gordon had introduced her to his younger brother, it was love at first sight. Gordon liked to grumble that he had never got more than a peck on the cheek, but he had stepped aside graciously, and had quite happily gone on to have numerous torrid affairs with numerous beautiful women. He used to say that it had almost been a fair trade, but that he suspected he had lost out.

Stephanie climbed the staircase, pushed open the door to Gordon's study and stepped inside. The walls were filled with the framed covers from his bestsellers and shared space with all manner of awards. One entire wall was made up of shelves, jammed with books. There were biographies and historical novels and science texts and psychology tomes, and there were battered little paperbacks stuck in between. A lower shelf had magazines, literary reviews and quarterlies.

Stephanie passed the shelves which housed the first editions of Gordon's novels and approached the desk. She looked at the chair where he'd died, trying to imagine him there, how he must have slumped. And then, a voice so smooth it could have been made of velvet:

"At least he died doing what he loved."

She turned, surprised, to see the man from the funeral in the overcoat and hat standing in the doorway. The scarf was still wrapped, the sunglasses still on, the fuzzy hair still poking out. His hands were gloved.

"Yes," Stephanie said, because she couldn't think of anything else to say. "At least there's that."

"You're one of his nieces then?" the man asked. "You're not stealing anything, you're not breaking anything, so I'd guess you're Stephanie." She nodded and took the opportunity to look at him more closely. She couldn't see even the tiniest bit of his face beneath the scarf and sunglasses.

"Were you a friend of his?" she asked. He was tall, this man, tall and thin, though his coat made it difficult to judge.

"I was," he answered with a move of his head. This slight movement made her realise that the rest of his body was unnaturally still. "I've known him for years, met him outside a bar in New York when I was over there, back when he had just published his first novel."

Stephanie couldn't see anything behind the sunglasses – they were black as pitch. "Are you a writer too?"

"Me? No, I wouldn't know where to start. But I got to live out my writer fantasies through Gordon."

"You had writer fantasies?"

"Doesn't everyone?"

"I don't know. I don't think so."

"Oh. Then that would make me seem kind of odd, wouldn't it?"

"Well," Stephanie answered. "It would *help*."

"Gordon used to talk about you all the time, boast about his little niece. He was an individual of character, your uncle. It seems that you are too."

"You say that like you know me."

"Strong-willed, intelligent, sharp-tongued, doesn't suffer fools gladly... remind you of anyone?"

"Yes. Gordon."

"Interesting," said the man. "Because those are the exact words he used to describe you." His gloved fingers dipped into his waistcoat and brought out an ornate pocket watch on a delicate gold chain.

"Good luck in whatever you decide to do with your life."

"Thank you," Stephanie said, a little dumbly. "You too."

She felt the man smile, though she could see no mouth, and he turned from the doorway and left her there. Stephanie found she couldn't take her eyes off where he had been. Who was he? She hadn't even got his name.

She crossed over to the door and stepped out, wondering how he had vanished from sight so quickly. She hurried down the stairs and reached the large hall without seeing him. She opened the front door just as a big black car turned out on to the road. She watched him drive away, stayed there for a few moments, then reluctantly rejoined her extended family in the living room, just in time to see Fergus slip a silver ashtray into his breast pocket.

2

THE WILL

Life in the Edgley household was fairly uneventful. Stephanie's mother worked in a bank and her father owned a construction company, and she had no brothers or sisters, so the routine they had settled into was one of amiable convenience. But even so, there was always the voice in the back of her mind telling her that there should be more to her life than *this*, more to her life than the small coastal town of Haggard. She just couldn't figure out what that something was.

Her first year of secondary school had just come to a close

and she was looking forward to the summer break. Stephanie didn't like school. She found it difficult to get along with her classmates – not because they weren't nice people, but simply because she had nothing in common with them. And she didn't like teachers. She didn't like the way they demanded respect they hadn't earned. Stephanie had no problem doing what she was told, just so long as she was given a good reason why she should.

She had spent the first few days of the summer helping out her father, answering phones and sorting through the files in his office. Gladys, his secretary of seven years, had decided she'd had enough of the construction business and wanted to try her hand as a performance artist. Stephanie found it vaguely discomfiting whenever she passed her on the street, this forty-three-year-old woman doing a modern dance interpretation of Faust. Gladys had made herself a costume to go with the act, a costume, she said, that symbolised the internal struggle Faust was going through, and apparently she refused to be seen in public without it. Stephanie did her best to avoid catching Gladys's eye.

If Stephanie wasn't helping out in the office, she was either down at the beach, swimming, or locked in her room listening to music. She was in her room, trying to find the charger for her mobile phone, when her mother knocked on the door and stepped in. She was still dressed in the sombre clothes she had worn to the funeral, though Stephanie had tied back her long dark hair and changed into her usual jeans and trainers within two minutes of returning to the house.

"We got a call from Gordon's solicitor," her mother said, sounding a little surprised. "They want us at the reading of the will."

"Oh," Stephanie responded. "What do you think he left you?"

"Well, we'll find out tomorrow. You too, because you're coming with us."

"I am?" Stephanie said with a slight frown.

"Your name's on the list, that's all I know. We're leaving at ten, OK?"

"I'm supposed to be helping Dad in the morning."

"He called Gladys, asked her to fill in for a few hours, as a favour. She said yes, as long as she could wear the peanut suit."

They left for the solicitor's at a quarter past ten the next morning, fifteen minutes later than planned thanks to Stephanie's father's casual disregard for punctuality. He ambled through the house, looking like there was something he'd forgotten and he was just waiting for it to occur to him again. He nodded and smiled whenever his wife told him to hurry up, said "Yes, absolutely," and just before he was due to join them in the car, he meandered off again, looking around with a dazed expression.

"He does this on purpose," Stephanie's mother said as they sat in the car, seatbelts on and ready to go. They watched him appear at the front door, shrug into his jacket, tuck in his shirt, go to step out, and then pause.

"He looks like he's about to sneeze," Stephanie remarked.

"No," her mother responded, "he's just thinking." She stuck her head out of the window. "Desmond, what's wrong now?"

He looked up, puzzled. "I think I'm forgetting something."

Stephanie leaned forward in the back seat, took a look at him and spoke to her mother, who nodded and stuck her head out again. "Where are your shoes, dear?"

He looked down at his socks – one brown, one navy – and his clouded expression cleared. He gave them the thumbs-up and disappeared from view.

"That man," her mother said, shaking her head. "Did you know he once lost a shopping centre?"

"He what?"

"I never told you that? It was the first big contract he got. His company did a wonderful job and he was driving his clients to see it, and he forgot where he put it. He drove around for almost an hour until he saw something he recognised. He may be a very talented engineer, but I swear, he's got the attention span of a goldfish. So unlike Gordon."

"They weren't very alike, were they?"

Her mother smiled. "It wasn't always that way. They used to do everything together. The three of them were inseparable."

"What, even Fergus?"

"Even Fergus. But when your grandmother died they all drifted apart. Gordon started mixing with a strange crowd after that."

"Strange in what way?"

"Ah, they probably just appeared strange to us," her mother said with a small laugh. "Your dad was getting started in the construction business and I was in college and we were what you might call normal. Gordon resisted being normal, and his friends, they kind of scared us. We never knew what they were into, but we knew it wasn't anything..."

"*Normal.*"

"Exactly. They scared your dad most of all though."

"Why?"

Stephanie's father walked out of the house, shoes on, and closed the front door after him.

"I think he was more like Gordon than he liked to let on," her mother said quietly, and then her dad got into the car.

"OK," he said proudly. "I'm ready."

They looked at him as he nodded, chuffed with himself. He strapped on his seatbelt and turned the key. The engine purred to life. Stephanie waved to Jasper, an eight-year-old boy with unfortunate ears, as her dad backed out on to the road, put the car in gear and they were off, narrowly missing their wheelie bin as they went.

The drive to the solicitor's office in the city took a little under an hour and they arrived twenty minutes late. They were led up a flight of creaky stairs to a small office, too warm to be comfortable, with a large window that offered a wonderful view of the brick wall across the street. Fergus and Beryl were there, and they showed their displeasure at having been kept waiting by looking at their watches and scowling. Stephanie's parents took the remaining chairs and Stephanie stood behind them as the solicitor peered at them through cracked spectacles.

"Now can we get started?" Beryl snapped.

The solicitor, a short man named Mr Fedgewick, with the girth and appearance of a sweaty bowling ball, tried smiling. "We still have one more person to wait on," he said and Fergus's eyes bulged.

"Who?" he demanded. "There can't be anyone else, we are the only siblings Gordon had. Who is it? It's not some charity, is it? I've never trusted charities. They always want something from you."

"It's, it's not a charity," Mr Fedgewick said. "He did say, however, that he might be a little late."

"Who said?" Stephanie's father asked, and the solicitor looked down at the file open before him.

"A most unusual name, this," he said. "It seems we are waiting on one Mr Skulduggery Pleasant."

"Well who on earth is that?" asked Beryl, irritated. "He sounds like a, he sounds like a... Fergus, what does he sound like?"

"He sounds like a weirdo," Fergus said, glaring at Fedgewick. "He's not a weirdo, is he?"

"I really couldn't say," Fedgewick answered, his paltry excuse for a smile failing miserably under the glares he was getting from Fergus and Beryl. "But I'm sure he'll be along soon."

Fergus frowned, narrowing his beady eyes as much as was possible. "How are you sure?"

Fedgewick faltered, unable to offer a reason, and then the door opened and the man in the tan overcoat entered the room.

"Sorry I'm late," he said, closing the door behind him. "It was unavoidable I'm afraid."

Everyone in the room stared at him, stared at the scarf and the gloves and the sunglasses.and the wild fuzzy hair. It was a glorious day outside, certainly not the kind of weather to be wrapped up like this. Stephanie looked closer at the hair. From this distance, it didn't even seem real.

The solicitor cleared his throat. "Um, you are Skulduggery Pleasant?"

"At your service," the man said. Stephanie could listen to that voice all day. Her mother, uncertain as she was, had smiled her greetings, but her father was looking at him with an expression of wariness she had never seen on his face before. After a moment the expression left him and he nodded politely and looked back to Mr Fedgewick. Fergus and Beryl were still staring.

"Do you have something wrong with your face?" Beryl asked.

Fedgewick cleared his throat again. "OK then, let's get down to business, now that we're all here. Excellent. Good. This, of course, being the last will and testament of Gordon Edgley, revised last almost one year ago. Gordon has been a client of mine for the past twenty years, and in that time, I got to know him well, so let me pass on to you, his family and, and friend, my deepest, deepest—"

"Yes yes yes," Fergus interrupted, waving his hand in the air. "Can we just skip this part? We're already running behind schedule. Let's go to the part where we get stuff. Who gets the house? And who gets the villa?"

"Who gets the fortune?" Beryl asked, leaning forward in her seat.

"The royalties," Fergus said. "Who gets the royalties from the books?"

Stephanie glanced at Skulduggery Pleasant from the corner of her eye. He was standing back against the wall, hands in his pockets, looking at the solicitor. Well, he *seemed* to be looking at the solicitor; with those sunglasses he could have been looking anywhere. She returned her gaze to Fedgewick as he picked up a page from his desk and read from it.

"'To my brother Fergus and his beautiful wife Beryl,'" he read, and Stephanie did her best to hide a grin, "'I leave my car, and my boat, and a gift.'"

Fergus and Beryl blinked. "His car?" Fergus said. "His boat? Why would he leave me his boat?"

"You hate the water," Beryl said, anger rising in her voice. "You get seasick."

"I *do* get seasick," Fergus snapped, "and he knew that!"

"And we already have a car," Beryl said.

"And we already have a car!" Fergus repeated.

Beryl was sitting so far up on her chair that she was almost on the desk. "This gift," she said, her voice low and threatening, "is it the fortune?"

Mr Fedgewick coughed nervously, and took a small box from his desk drawer and slid it towards them. They looked at this box. They looked some more. They both reached for it at the same time, and Stephanie watched them slap at each other's hands until Beryl snatched it off the desk and tore the lid open.

"What is it?" Fergus asked in a small voice. "Is it a key to a safety deposit box? Is it, is it an account number? Is it, what is it? Wife, what is it?"

All colour had drained from Beryl's face and her hands were shaking. She blinked hard to keep the tears away, then she turned the box for everyone to see, and everyone saw the brooch, about the size of a drinks coaster, nestled in the plush cushion. Fergus stared at it.

"It doesn't even have any jewels on it," Beryl said, her voice strangled. Fergus opened his mouth wide like a startled fish and turned to Fedgewick.

"What else do we get?" he asked, panicking.

Mr Fedgewick tried another smile. "Your, uh, your brother's love?"

Stephanie heard a high-pitched whine, and it took her a moment to realise it was coming from Beryl. Fedgewick returned his attention to the will, trying to ignore the horrified looks he was getting from Fergus and his wife.

"'To my good friend and guide Skulduggery Pleasant I leave the following advice. Your path is your own, and I have no wish to sway you, but sometimes the greatest enemy we can face is ourselves, and the greatest battle is against the darkness within. There is a storm coming, and sometimes the key to safe harbour is hidden from us, and sometimes it is right before our eyes.'"

Stephanie joined in with everyone else as they stared at Mr Pleasant. She had known there was something different about him, she had known it the first moment she saw him – there was something exotic, something mysterious, something *dangerous*. For his part, his head dipped lower and that was the only reaction he gave. He offered no explanations as to what Gordon's message had meant.

Fergus patted his wife's knee. "See, Beryl? A car, a boat, a brooch, it's not that bad. He could have given us some stupid advice."

"Oh, shut up, would you?" Beryl snarled and Fergus recoiled in his chair.

Mr Fedgewick read on. "'To my other brother, Desmond, the lucky one of the family, I leave to you your wife. I think you might like her.'" Stephanie saw her parents clasp each other's hands and smile sadly. "'So now that you've successfully stolen my girlfriend, maybe you'd like to take her to my villa in France, which I am also leaving to you.'"

"They get the villa?" Beryl cried, jumping to her feet.

"Beryl," Fergus said, "please..."

"Do you know how much that villa is worth?" Beryl continued, looking like she might lunge at Stephanie's parents. "We get a brooch – they get a villa? There are only three of them! We've got Carol and Crystal! We have more! We could do with the extra space! Why do *they* deserve the villa?" She thrust the box towards them. "Swap!"

"Mrs Edgley, please retake your seat or we shall be unable to continue," Mr Fedgewick said, and eventually, after much bug-eyed glaring, Beryl sat down.

"Thank you," Fedgewick said, looking like he had had quite enough excitement for one day. He licked his lips, adjusted his glasses, and peered again at the will. "'If there is one regret that I have had in my life, it is that I have never fathered any children. There are times when I look at what Fergus and Beryl have produced and I consider myself fortunate, but there are also times when it breaks my heart. And so, finally, to my niece Stephanie.'"

Stephanie's eyes widened. What? *She* was getting something? Leaving the villa to her parents wasn't enough for Gordon?

Fedgewick continued reading. "'The world is bigger than you know and scarier than you might imagine. The only currency worth anything is being true to yourself, and the only goal worth seeking is finding out who you truly are.'"

She could feel Fergus and Beryl glaring at her and she did her best to ignore them.

"'Make your parents proud, and make them glad to have you living under their roof, because I leave to you my property and possessions, my assets and my royalties, to be inherited on the day you turn eighteen. I'd just like to take this opportunity to say that, in my own way, I love you all, even those I don't particularly like. That's you, Beryl.'"

Fedgewick took off his spectacles and looked up.

Stephanie became aware that everyone was staring at her and she hadn't a clue what she was supposed to say. Fergus was again doing his startled fish impression and Beryl was pointing one long bony finger at her, trying to speak but failing. Her parents were looking at her in stunned surprise. Only Skulduggery Pleasant moved, walking behind her and gently touching her arm.

"Congratulations," he said and moved on towards the door. As soon as it clicked shut behind him, Beryl found her voice.

"HER?" she screamed. "HER?"

3

LITTLE GIRL, ALL ALONE

That afternoon Stephanie and her mother took the fifteen-minute drive from Haggard to Gordon's estate. Her mum opened the front door and stepped back.

"Owner of the house goes first," she said with a little smile and a bow, and Stephanie stepped inside. She wasn't thinking of this house as her property – the idea was too big, too silly. Even if her parents were, technically, the custodians until she turned eighteen, how could she own a house? How many other twelve-year-old kids owned houses?

No, it was too silly an idea. Too far-fetched. Too crazy. Exactly the kind of thing that Gordon would have thought made perfect sense.

The house was big and quiet and empty as they walked through it. Everything seemed new to her now, and Stephanie found herself reacting differently to the furniture and carpets and paintings. Did she like it? Did she agree with this colour or that fabric? One thing that had to be said for Gordon, he had a good eye. Stephanie's mother said there was very little she would change if she had to. Some of the paintings were a little too unnerving for her taste maybe, but on the whole the furnishings were elegant and understated, exuding an air of distinction that befitted a house of this stature.

They hadn't decided what they were going to do with the house. Any decision was left up to Stephanie, but her parents still had the villa to consider. Owning three houses between them seemed a bit much. Her father had suggested selling the villa but her mother hated the thought of letting go of a place so idyllic.

They had also talked about Stephanie's education, and she knew *that* conversation was far from over. The moment they had left Mr Fedgewick's office they warned her not to let all this go to her head. Recent events, they had said, should not mean she could stop studying, stop planning for college. She needed to be independent, they said, she needed to make it on her own.

Stephanie had let them talk, and nodded occasionally and muttered an agreement where an agreement was appropriate. She didn't bother to explain that she needed college, she needed to find her own way in the world because she knew that if she didn't, she'd never escape Haggard. She wasn't about to throw her future away simply because she had come into some money.

She and her mother spent so long looking around the ground floor that by the time they got to the bottom of the stairs, it was already five o'clock. With their exploring done for the day, they locked up and walked to the car. The first few drops of rain splattered against the windscreen as they got in. Stephanie clicked her seatbelt closed and her mother turned the key in the ignition.

The car spluttered a bit, groaned a little and then shut up altogether. Stephanie's mother looked at her.

"Uh oh." They both got out and opened the bonnet.

"Well," her mother said, looking at the engine, "at least that's still there."

"Do you know *anything* about engines?" Stephanie asked.

"That's why I have a husband, so I don't have to. Engines and shelves, that's why man was invented." Stephanie made a mental note to learn about engines before she turned eighteen.

She wasn't too fussed about the shelves.

Her mum dug her mobile phone out of her bag and called Stephanie's dad, but he was busy on site and there was no way he could get to them before nightfall. They went back inside the house and her mother called a mechanic, and they spent three quarters of an hour waiting for him to arrive.

The sky was grey and angry and the rain was falling hard by the time the truck appeared around the corner. It splashed through puddles on its way up the long drive, and Stephanie's mum pulled her jacket over her head and ran out to meet it. Stephanie could see a great big dog in the cab of the truck, looking on as the mechanic got out to examine their car. After a few minutes, her mother ran back inside, thoroughly drenched.

"He can't fix it here," she said, wringing out her jacket on the porch, "so he's going to tow it to the garage. It shouldn't take too long to fix."

"Will there be room for both of us in the truck?"

"You can sit on my knee."

"Mum!"

"Or I can sit on your knee, whatever works."

"Can I stay here?"

Her mother looked at her. "On your own?"

"Please? You just said it won't take long, and I'd like to have another look around, just on my own."

"I don't know, Steph..."

"Please? I've stayed on my own before. I won't break anything, I swear."

Her mother laughed. "OK fine. I shouldn't be any more than an hour, all right? An hour and a half at the most." Her mother gave her a quick kiss on the cheek. "Call me if you need anything."

She ran back outside and jumped in the cab next to the dog, who proceeded to slobber all over her face. Stephanie watched their car being towed off into the distance and then it vanished from sight.

She did a little more exploring, now that she was on her own. She climbed the stairs and went straight to Gordon's study.

His publisher, Seamus T. Steepe of Arc Light Books, had phoned them earlier that day, passing on his condolences and enquiring about the state of Gordon's last book. Her mother had told him that they'd find out if Gordon had completed it, and if he had, they'd send it on. Mr Steepe was very keen to get the book on the shelves, certain that it would crash on to the bestseller list and stay there for a long time. "Dead writers sell," he had said, like he approved of Gordon's clever marketing ploy.

Stephanie opened the desk drawer and found the

manuscript in a neat stack. She pulled it out carefully and laid it on the desktop, careful not to smudge the paper. The first page held the title, nothing more, in bold lettering:

And The Darkness Rained Upon Them.

The manuscript was thick and heavy, like all of Gordon's books. She'd read most of them, and the odd splash of pretension aside, had quite enjoyed his work. His stories tended to be about people who could do astonishing and wonderful things, and the strange and terrible events that invariably led up to their bizarre and horrible deaths. She noticed the way he would set up a strong and noble hero, and over the course of the book systematically subject this hero to brutal punishment in a bid to strip away all his arrogance and certainty so that by the end he was humbled and had learned a great lesson. And then Gordon killed him off, usually in the most undignified way possible. Stephanie could almost hear Gordon laughing with mischievous glee as she'd read.

She lifted the title page and carefully laid it face down on the desk beside the manuscript. She started reading. She didn't mean to spend long at it, but soon she was devouring every word, oblivious to the creaking old house and the rain outside.

Her mobile phone rang, making her jump. She had been reading for two hours. She pressed the answer button and held it to her ear.

"Hi, sweetie," came her mother's voice, "everything OK?"

"Yes," Stephanie answered. "Just reading."

"You're not reading one of Gordon's books, are you? Steph, he writes about horrible monsters and scary stuff and bad people doing worse things. It'll give you nightmares."

"No, Mum, I'm... I'm reading the dictionary."

Even the brief silence from the other end of the phone was sceptical. "The dictionary?" her mother said. "Really?"

"Yeah," Stephanie said. "Did you know that *popple* is a word?"

"You are stranger than your father, you know that?"

"I suspected as much... So is the car fixed yet?"

"No, and that's why I'm calling. They can't get it going and the road up to you is flooded. I'm going to get a taxi up as far as it'll go and then I'll see if I can find some way around on foot. It's going to be another two hours at least."

Stephanie sensed an opportunity. Ever since she was a child she had much preferred her own company to the company of others, and it occurred to her that she had never spent a whole night without her parents nearby. A small taste of freedom and it almost tingled on her tongue.

"Mum, it's fine, you don't have to. I'm OK here."

"There's no way I'm leaving you in a strange house by yourself."

"It's not a strange house; it's Gordon's and it's fine. There's no point in you trying to get here tonight – it's lashing rain."

"Sweetie, it won't take me long."

"It'll take you ages. Where's it flooded?"

Her mother paused. "At the bridge."

"The bridge? And you want to walk from the bridge to here?"

"If I speed-walk—"

"Mum, don't be silly. Get Dad to pick you up."

"Sweetheart, are you sure?"

"I like it here, really. OK?"

"Well, OK," her mother said reluctantly. "I'll be over first thing in the morning to pick you up, all right? And I saw some food in the cupboards, so if you're hungry you can make yourself something."

"OK. I'll see you tomorrow then."

"Call us if you need anything or if you just want some company."

"I will. Night Mum."

"I love you."

"I know."

Stephanie hung up and grinned. She slipped the phone back into her jacket and put her feet up on the desk, relaxing back into the chair, and went back to reading.

When she looked up again she was surprised to find that it was almost midnight and the rain had stopped. If she were home right now, she'd be in bed. She blinked, her eyes sore, stood up from the desk and went downstairs to the kitchen. For all his wealth and success and extravagant tastes, she was thankful that when it came to food, Gordon was a pretty standard guy. The bread was stale and the fruit was a bit too ripe, but there were biscuits and there was cereal, and the milk in the fridge was still good for one more day. Stephanie made herself a snack and wandered to the living room, where she flicked on the TV. She sat on the couch and was just getting comfy when the house phone rang.

She looked at it, resting there on the table at her elbow. Who would be calling? Anyone who knew Gordon had died wouldn't be calling because they'd know he had died, and she didn't really want to be the one to tell anyone who didn't know. It could be her parents, but then why didn't they just call her mobile?

Figuring that as the new owner of the house, it was her

responsibility to answer her own phone, Stephanie picked it up and held it to her ear. "Hello?"

Silence.

"Hello?" Stephanie repeated.

"Who is this?" came a man's voice.

"I'm sorry," Stephanie said, "who do you want to speak to?"

"Who is this?" responded the voice, more irritably this time.

"If you're looking for Gordon Edgley," Stephanie said, "I'm afraid that he's—"

"I know Edgley's dead," snapped the man. "Who are you? Your name?"

Stephanie hesitated. "Why do you want to know?" she asked.

"What are you doing in that house? Why are you in his house?"

"If you want to call back tomorrow—"

"I *don't* want to, all right? Listen to me, girlie, if you mess up my master's plans, he will be *very* displeased and he is *not* a man you want to displease, you got that? Now tell me who you are!"

Stephanie realised her hands were shaking. She forced herself to calm down and quickly found anger replacing her nervousness. "My name is none of your business," she said. "If you want to talk to someone, call back tomorrow at a reasonable hour."

"You don't talk to me like that," the man hissed.

"Goodnight," Stephanie said firmly.

"You do *not* talk to me like—"

But Stephanie was already putting the phone down. Suddenly the idea of spending the whole night here wasn't as appealing as it had first sounded. She considered calling her parents, then scolded herself for being so childish. *No need to worry them*, she thought to herself. *No need to worry them about something so—*

Someone pounded on the front door.

"Open up!" came the man's voice between the pounding. Stephanie got to her feet, staring through to the hall beyond the living room. She could see a dark shape behind the frosted glass around the front door. "Open the damn door!"

Stephanie backed up to the fireplace, her heart pounding in her chest. He knew she was in here, there was no use pretending that she wasn't, but maybe if she stayed really quiet he'd give up and go away. She heard him cursing, and the pounding grew so heavy that the front door rattled under the blows.

"Leave me alone!" Stephanie shouted.

"Open the door!"

"No!" she shouted back. She liked shouting – it disguised her fear. "I'm calling the police! I'm calling the police right now!"

The pounding stopped immediately and Stephanie saw the shape move away from the door. Was that it? Had she scared him away? She thought of the back door – was it locked? Of course it was locked… It had to be locked. But she wasn't sure, she wasn't certain. She grabbed a poker from the fireplace and was reaching for the phone when she heard a knock on the window beside her.

She cried out and jumped back. The curtains were open, and outside the window was pitch-black. She couldn't see a thing.

"Are you alone in there?" came the voice. It was teasing now, playing with her.

"Go away," she said loudly, holding up the poker so he could see it. She heard the man laugh.

"What are you going to do with that?" he asked.

"I'll break your head open with it!" Stephanie screamed at him, fear and fury bubbling inside her. She heard him laugh again.

"I just want to come in," he said. "Open the door for me, girlie. Let me come in."

"The police are on their way," she said.

"You're a liar."

Still she could see nothing beyond the glass and he could see everything. She moved to the phone, snatching it from its cradle.

"Don't do that," came the voice.

"I'm calling the police."

"The road's closed, girlie. You call them, I'll break down that door and kill you hours before they get here."

Fear became terror and Stephanie froze. She was going to cry. She could feel it, the tears welling up inside her. She hadn't cried in years. "What do you want?" she said to the darkness. "Why do you want to come in?"

"It's got nothing to do with *me*, girlie. I've just been sent to pick something up. Let me in. I'll look around, get what I came here for and leave. I won't harm a pretty little hair on your pretty little head, I *promise*. Now you just open that door right this second."

Stephanie gripped the poker in both hands and shook her head. She was crying now, tears rolling down her cheeks. "No," she said.

She screamed as a fist smashed through the window, showering the carpet with glass. She stumbled back as the man started climbing in, glaring at her with blazing eyes, unmindful of the glass that cut into him. The moment one foot touched the floor inside the house Stephanie was bolting out of the room, over to the front door, fumbling at the lock.

Strong hands grabbed her from behind. She screamed again as she was lifted off her feet and carried back. She kicked out, slamming a heel into his shin. The man grunted and let go and Stephanie twisted, trying to swing the poker into his face but he caught it and pulled it from her grasp. One hand went to her throat and Stephanie gagged, unable to breathe as the man forced her back into the living room.

He pushed her into an armchair and leaned over her and no matter how hard she tried she could not break his grip.

"Now then," the man said, his mouth contorting into a sneer, "why don't you just give me the key, little girlie?"

And that's when the front door was flung off its hinges and Skulduggery Pleasant burst into the house.

The man cursed and released Stephanie and swung the poker, but Skulduggery moved straight to him and hit him so hard Stephanie thought the man's head might come off. He hit the ground and tumbled backwards, but rolled to his feet as Skulduggery moved in again.

The man launched himself forward. They both collided and went backwards over the couch and Skulduggery lost his hat. Stephanie saw a flash of white above the scarf.

They got to their feet, grappling, and the man swung a punch that knocked Skulduggery's sunglasses to the other side of the room. Skulduggery responded by moving in low, grabbing the man around the waist and twisting his hip into him. The man was flipped to the floor, hard.

He cursed a little more, then remembered Stephanie and made for her. Stephanie leaped out of the chair, but before he could reach her, Skulduggery was there, kicking the man's legs out from under him. The man hit a small coffee table with his chin and howled in pain.

"*You think you can stop me*?" he screamed as he tried to stand. His knees seemed shaky. "*Do you know who I am*?"

"Haven't the foggiest," Skulduggery said.

The man spat blood and grinned defiantly. "Well, I know about *you*," he said. "My master told me all about *you*, detective, and you're going to have to do a lot more than that to stop me."

Skulduggery shrugged and Stephanie watched in amazement as a ball of fire flared up in his hand and he hurled it and the man was suddenly covered in flame. But instead of screaming, the man tilted his head back and roared with laughter. The fire may have engulfed him, but it wasn't burning him.

"More!" he laughed. "Give me more!"

"If you insist."

And then Skulduggery took an old-fashioned revolver from his jacket and fired, the gun bucking slightly with the recoil. The bullet hit the man in the shoulder and he screamed, then tried to run and tripped. He scrambled for the doorway, ducking and dodging lest he get shot again, the flames obstructing his vision so much that he hit a wall on his way out.

And then he was gone.

Stephanie stared at the door, trying to make sense of the impossible.

"Well," Skulduggery said, "that's something you don't see every day."

She turned. When his hat came off, his hair had come off too. In the confusion all she had seen was a chalk-white scalp, so she turned expecting to see a bald albino maybe. But no. With his sunglasses gone and his scarf hanging down, there was no denying the fact that he had no flesh, he had no skin, he had no eyes and he had no face.

All he had was a skull for a head.

4

THE SECRET WAR

Skulduggery put his gun away and walked out to the hall. He peered out into the night. Satisfied that there were no human fireballs lurking anywhere nearby, he came back inside and picked the door off the ground, grunting with the effort. He manoeuvred it back to where it belonged, leaving it leaning in the doorway, then he shrugged and came back into the living room, where Stephanie was still standing and staring at him.

"Sorry about the door," he said.

Stephanie stared.

"I'll pay to get it fixed."

Stephanie stared.

"It's still a good door, you know. Sturdy."

When he realised that Stephanie was in no condition to do anything but stare, he shrugged again and took off his coat, folded it neatly and draped it over the back of a chair. He went to the broken window and started picking up the shards of glass.

Now that he didn't have his coat on, Stephanie could truly appreciate how thin he really was. His suit, well-tailored though it was, hung off him, giving it a shapeless quality. She watched him collect the broken glass, and saw a flash of bone between his shirtsleeve and glove. He stood, looking back at her.

"Where should I put all this glass?"

"I don't know," Stephanie said in a quiet voice. "You're a skeleton."

"I am indeed," he said. "Gordon used to keep a wheelie bin out at the back door. Shall I put it in that?"

Stephanie nodded. "Yes OK," she said simply and watched Skulduggery carry the armful of glass shards out of the room. All her life she had longed for something else, for something to take her out of the humdrum world she knew – and now that it looked like it might actually happen, she didn't have one clue what to do. Questions were tripping over themselves in her head, each one vying to be the one that was asked first. So many of them.

Skulduggery came back in and she asked the first question. "Did you find it all right?"

"I did, yes. It was where he always kept it."

"OK then." If questions were people she felt that they'd all be staring at her now in disbelief. She struggled to form coherent thoughts.

"Did you tell him your name?" Skulduggery was asking.

"What?"

"Your name. Did you tell him?"

"Uh, no..."

"Good. You know something's true name, you have power over it. But even a given name, even Stephanie, that would have been enough to do it."

"To do what?"

"To give him some influence over you, to get you to do what he asked. If he had your name and he knew what to do with it, sometimes that's all it takes. That's a scary thought now, isn't it?"

"What's going on?" Stephanie asked. "Who was he? What did he want? Just who are you?"

"I'm me," Skulduggery said, picking up his hat and wig and placing them on a nearby table. "As for him, I don't know who he is, never seen him before in my life."

"You shot him."

"That's right."

"And you threw fire at him."

"Yes, I did."

Stephanie's legs felt weak and her head felt light.

"Mr Pleasant, you're a skeleton."

"Ah, yes, back to the crux of the matter. Yes. I am, as you say, a skeleton. I have been one for a few years now."

"Am I going mad?"

"I hope not."

"So you're real? You actually exist?"

"Presumably."

"You mean you're not sure if you exist or not?"

"I'm fairly certain. I mean, I could be wrong. I could be some ghastly hallucination, a figment of my imagination."

"You might be a figment of your own imagination?"

"Stranger things have happened. And do, with alarming regularity."

"This is too weird."

Skulduggery put his gloved hands in his pockets and cocked his head. He had no eyeballs so it was hard to tell if he was looking at her or not. "You know, I met your uncle under similar circumstances. Well, kind of similar. But he was drunk. And we were in a bar. And he had vomited on my shoes. So I suppose the actual circumstances aren't *overly* similar, but both events include a meeting, so... My point is, he was having some trouble and I was there to lend a hand, and we became good friends after that. Good, good friends." His head tilted. "You look like you might faint."

Stephanie nodded slowly. "I've never fainted before, but I think you might be right."

"Do you want me to catch you if you fall, or...?"

"If you wouldn't mind."

"No problem at all."

"Thank you."

Stephanie gave him a weak smile and then darkness clouded her vision and she felt herself falling and the last thing she saw was Skulduggery Pleasant darting across the room towards her.

Stephanie awoke on the couch with a blanket over her. The room was dark, lit only by two lamps in opposite corners. She looked over at the broken window, saw that it was now boarded up. She heard a hammering from the hall, and when she felt strong enough to stand, she slowly rose and walked out of the living room.

Skulduggery Pleasant was trying to hang the door back on its hinges. He had his shirtsleeve rolled up on his left forearm. *Ulna*, Stephanie corrected herself, proving that her first year of Biology class had not gone to waste. Or was it *radius*? Or both? She heard him mutter, then he noticed her and nodded brightly.

"Ah, you're up."

"You fixed the window."

"Well, covered it up. Gordon had a few pieces of timber out back, so I did what I could. Not having the same luck with the door though. I find it much easier to blast them off then put them back. How are you feeling?"

"I'm OK," Stephanie said.

"A cup of hot tea, that's what you need. Lots of sugar."

He abandoned the door and guided her to the kitchen. She sat at the table while he boiled the water.

"Hungry?" he asked when it had boiled, but she shook her head. "Milk?" She nodded. He added milk and spoonfuls of sugar, gave the tea a quick stir and put the cup on the table in front of her. She took a sip – it was hot, but nice.

"Thank you," Stephanie said, and he gave a little shrug. It was hard discerning some of his gestures without a face to go by, but she took the shrug to mean "think nothing of it".

"Was that magic? With the fire, and blasting the door?"

"Yes, it was."

She peered closer. "How can you talk?"

"Sorry?"

"How can you talk? You move your mouth when you speak, but you've got no tongue, you've got no lips, you've got no vocal cords. I mean, I know what skeletons look like, I've seen diagrams and models and stuff, and the only things that hold them together are flesh and skin and ligaments, so why don't you just fall apart?"

He gave another shrug, both shoulders this time. "Well, that's magic too."

She looked at him. "Magic's pretty handy."

"Yes, magic is."

"And what about, you know, nerve endings? Can you feel pain?"

"I can, but that's not a bad thing. Pain lets you know when you're alive, after all."

"And *are* you alive?"

"Well, *technically*, no, but..."

She peered into his empty eye sockets. "Do you have a brain?"

He laughed. "I don't have a brain, I don't have any organs, but I have a consciousness." He started clearing away the sugar and the milk. "To be honest with you, it's not even *my* head."

"What?"

"It's not. They ran away with my skull. I won this one in a poker game."

"That's not even yours? How does it feel?"

"It'll do. It'll do until I finally get around to getting my own head back. You look faintly disgusted."

"I just... Doesn't it feel weird? It'd be like wearing someone else's socks."

"You get used to it."

"What happened to you?" she asked. "Were you born like this?"

"No, I was born perfectly normal. Skin, organs, the whole shebang. Even had a face that wasn't too bad to look at, if I do say so myself."

"So what happened?"

Skulduggery leaned against the worktop, arms folded across his chest. "I got into magic. Back then – back when I was, for want of a better term, alive – there were some pretty nasty people around. The world was seeing a darkness it might never have recovered from. It was war, you see. A secret war, but war nonetheless. There was a sorcerer, Mevolent, worse then any of the others, and he had himself an army, and those of us who refused to fall in behind him found ourselves standing up against him.

"And we were winning. Eventually, after years of fighting this little war of ours, we were actually winning. His support was crumbling, his influence was fading, and he was staring defeat in the face. So he ordered one last, desperate strike against all the leaders on our side."

Stephanie stared at him, lost in his voice.

"I went up against his right-hand man who had laid out a wickedly exquisite trap. I didn't suspect a thing until it was too late.

"So I died. He killed me. The twenty-third of October it was, when my heart stopped beating. Once I was dead, they stuck my body up on a pike and burned it for all to see. They used me as a warning – they used the bodies of all the leaders they had killed as warnings – and, to my utter horror, it worked."

"What do you mean?"

"The tide turned. Our side starting losing ground. Mevolent got stronger. It was more than I could stand, so I came back."

"You just... *came back*?"

"It's... complicated. When I died, I never moved on. Something was holding me here, making me watch. I've never heard of it happening before that and I haven't heard of it happening since, but it happened to me. So when it got too much, I woke up, a bag of bones. Literally. They had gathered up my bones and put them in a bag and thrown the bag into a river. So that was a marvellous new experience right there."

"Then what happened?"

"I put myself back together, which was rather painful, then climbed out of the river and rejoined the fight, and in the end, we won. We finally won. So, with Mevolent defeated, I quit that whole scene and struck out on my own for the first time in a few hundred years."

Stephanie blinked. "Few *hundred*?"

"It was a long war."

"That man, he called you detective."

"He obviously knows me by reputation," Skulduggery said, standing a little straighter. "I solve mysteries now."

"Really?"

"Quite good at it too."

"So, what, you're tracking down your head?"

Skulduggery looked at her. If he'd had eyelids, he might well be blinking. "It'd be nice to have it back, sure, but..."

"So you don't need it, like, so you can rest in peace?"

"No. No, not really."

"Why did they take it? Was that another warning?"

"Oh, no," Skulduggery said with a little laugh. "No, *they* didn't take it. I was sleeping, about ten or fifteen years ago, and these little goblin things ran up and nicked it right off my spinal column. Didn't notice it was gone till the next morning."

Stephanie frowned. "And you didn't feel that?"

"Well, like I said, I was asleep. Meditating, I suppose you'd call it. I can't see, hear or feel anything when I'm meditating. Have you tried it?"

"No."

"It's very relaxing. I think you'd like it."

"I'm sorry, I'm still stuck on you losing your head."

"I didn't *lose* it," he said defensively. "It was stolen."

Stephanie was feeling stronger now. She couldn't believe that she'd fainted. *Fainted.* It was such an old woman thing to do. She glanced up at Skulduggery. "You've had a very unusual life, haven't you?"

"I suppose I have. Not over yet though. Well, *technically* it is, but..."

"Isn't there anything you miss?"

"About what?"

"About living."

"Compared to how long I've been like this, I was only technically alive for a blink of an eye. I can't really remember enough about having a beating heart in my chest to miss it."

"So there's nothing you miss?"

"I... I suppose I miss hair. I miss how it... was. And how it was there, on top of my head. I suppose I miss my hair." He took out his pocket watch and his head jerked back. "Wow, look at the time. I've got to go, Stephanie."

"Go? Go where?"

"Things to do, I'm afraid. Number one is finding out why that nice gentleman was sent here, and number two is finding out who sent him."

"You can't leave me alone," she said, following him into the living room.

"Yes," he corrected, "I can. You'll be perfectly safe."

"The front door's off!"

"Well, yes. You'll be perfectly safe as long as they don't come through the front door."

He pulled on his coat but she snatched his hat away.

"Are you taking my hat hostage?" he asked doubtfully.

"You're either staying here to make sure no one else attacks me or you're taking me with you."

Skulduggery froze. "That," he said eventually, "wouldn't be too safe for you."

"Neither would being left here on my own."

"But you can hide," he said, gesturing around the room. "There's so many places to hide. I'm sure there are plenty of good solid wardrobes your size. Even under a bed. You'd be surprised how many people don't check under beds these days."

"Mr Pleasant—"

"Skulduggery, please."

"Skulduggery, you saved my life tonight. Are you going to undo all that effort by leaving me here so someone else can come along and just kill me?"

"That's a very defeatist attitude you've got there. I once knew a fellow, a little older than you. He wanted to join me in my adventures, wanted to solve mysteries that beggared belief. He kept asking, kept on at me about it. He finally proved himself, after a long time, and we became partners."

"And did you go on to have lots of exciting adventures?"

"I did. He didn't. He died on our very first case together. Horrible death. Messy too. Lots of flailing around."

"Well, I don't plan on dying any time soon and I've got something he didn't."

"And that is...?"

"Your hat. Take me with you or I'll stand on it."

Skulduggery looked at her with his big hollow eye sockets, then held out his hand for his hat. "Don't say I didn't warn you."

5

MEETING CHINA SORROWS

Skulduggery Pleasant's car was a 1954 Bentley R-Type Continental, one of only 208 ever made, a car that housed a six-cylinder, 4.5-litre engine, and was retro-fitted with central locking, climate control, satellite navigation and a host of other modern conveniences. Skulduggery told Stephanie all of this when she asked. She'd have been happy with, "It's a Bentley."

They left Gordon's land via a back road at the rear of the estate to avoid the flooding, a road that Stephanie hadn't even noticed until they were on it. Skulduggery told her he was a regular visitor here, and knew all the little nooks and crannies. They passed a sign for Haggard and she thought about asking him to drop her home, but quickly banished that idea from her head. If she went home now she'd be turning her back on everything she'd just seen. She needed to know more. She needed to *see* more.

"Where are we going?" she asked as they drove on.

"Into the city. I've got a meeting with an old friend. She might be able to shed some light on recent events."

"Why were you at the house?"

"Sorry?"

"Tonight. Not that I'm not grateful, but how come you happened to be nearby?"

"Ah," he said, nodding. "Yes, I can see how that question would arise."

"So are you going to answer it?"

"That's unlikely."

"Well, why not?"

He glanced at her, or at least he turned his head a fraction. "The less you know about all this, the better. You're a perfectly normal young lady, and after tonight, you're going to return to your perfectly normal life. It wouldn't do for you to get too involved in this."

"But I am involved."

"But we can limit that involvement."

"But I don't want to limit that involvement."

"But it's what's best for you."

"But I don't want that!"

"But it might—"

"Don't start another sentence with 'but'."

"Right. Sorry."

"You can't expect me to forget about all of this. I've seen magic and fire and *you*, and I've learned about wars they don't tell us about in school. I've seen a world I never even knew *existed*."

"Don't you want to get back to that world? It's safer there."

"That's not where I belong."

Skulduggery turned his whole head to her and cocked it at an angle. "Funny. When I first met your uncle, that's what he said too."

"The things he wrote about," Stephanie said, the idea just dawning on her, "are they true?"

"His books? No, not a one."

"Oh."

"They're more *inspired* by true stories, really. He just changed them enough so he wouldn't insult anyone and get hunted down and killed. Your uncle was a good man, he really was. We solved many mysteries together."

"Really?"

"Oh, yes, you should be proud to have had an uncle like him. Of course, he got me into a hundred fights because I'd bring him somewhere, and he wouldn't stop pestering people, but... Fun times. Fun times."

They drove on until they saw the lights of the city looming ahead. Soon the darkness that surrounded the car was replaced with an orange haze that reflected off the wet roads. The city was quiet and still, the streets almost empty. They pulled into a small outdoor car park and Skulduggery switched off the engine and looked at Stephanie.

"OK then, you wait here."

"Right."

He got out. Two seconds passed, but Stephanie hadn't tagged along just to wait on the sidelines – she needed to see what other surprises the world had in store for her. She got out and Skulduggery looked at her.

"Stephanie, I'm not altogether sure you're respecting my authority."

"No, I'm not."

"I see. OK then." He put on his hat and wrapped his scarf

around his jaw, but did without the wig and the sunglasses. He clicked his keyring and the car beeped and the doors locked.

"That's it?"

He looked up. "Sorry?"

"Aren't you afraid it might get stolen? We're not exactly in a good part of town."

"It's got a car alarm."

"Don't you, like, cast a spell or something? To keep it safe?"

"No. It's a pretty good car alarm."

He started walking. She hurried to keep up.

"*Do* you cast spells then?"

"Sometimes. I try not to depend on magic these days, I try to get by on what's up here." He tapped his head.

"There's empty space up there."

"Well, yes," Skulduggery said irritably, "but you know what I mean."

"What else can you do?"

"Sorry?"

"With magic. Show me something."

If Skulduggery had had eyebrows, they would most likely be arched. "What, a living skeleton isn't enough for you? You want more?"

"Yes," Stephanie said. "Give me a tutorial."

He shrugged. “Well, I suppose it couldn’t hurt. There are two types of mages, or sorcerers – Adepts practise one branch of magic, Elementals practise another. Adepts are more aggressive; their techniques are more immediately powerful. In contrast, an Elemental, such as myself, chooses the quieter course and works on mastering their command of the elements.”

“Command of the elements?”

“Maybe that’s a bit of an exaggeration. We don’t command them as such, we manipulate them. We influence them.”

“Like what? Like earth, wind—”

“Water and fire, yes.”

“So show me.”

Skulduggery tilted his head a little to the right and she could hear the good humour in his voice. “Very well,” he said and held up his open hand in front of her. She frowned, feeling a little chilly, and then she became aware of a droplet of water running down her face. In an instant her hair was drenched, like she had just surfaced from a dive.

“How did you do that?” she asked, shaking her head, flinging drops of water away from her.

“You tell me,” Skulduggery answered.

“I don’t know. You did something to the moisture in the air?”

He looked down at her. "Very good," he said, impressed. "The first element, water. We can't part the Red Sea or anything, but we have a little influence with it."

"Show me fire again," Stephanie said eagerly.

Skulduggery snapped his gloved fingers and sparks flew, and he curled his hand and the sparks grew to flame, and he held that ball of flame in his palm as they walked. The flame intensified and Stephanie could feel her hair drying.

"Wow," she said.

"Wow indeed," Skulduggery responded and thrust his hand out, sending the ball of fire shooting through the air. It burned out as it arced in the night sky and faded to nothing.

"What about earth?" Stephanie asked, but Skulduggery shook his head.

"You don't want to see that, and hopefully you'll never have to. The earth power is purely defensive and purely for use as a last resort."

"So what's the most powerful? Is it fire?"

"That's the flashiest, that gets all the 'wows', but you'd be surprised what a little air can do if you displace it properly. Displaced air doesn't just disappear – it needs somewhere to be displaced *to*."

"Can I see?"

They reached the edge of the car park and passed the low wall that encircled it. Skulduggery flexed his fingers and suddenly splayed his hand, snapping his palm towards the wall. The air rippled and the bricks exploded outwards. Stephanie stared at the brand-new hole in the wall.

"*That*," she said, "is so cool."

They walked on, Stephanie glancing back at the wall every so often. "What about the Adepts then? What can they do?"

"I knew a fellow, a few years ago, who could read minds. I met this woman once who could change her shape, become anyone, right in front of your eyes."

"So who's stronger?" Stephanie asked. "An Elemental or an Adept?"

"Depends on the mage. An Adept could have so many tricks up his sleeve, so many different abilities, that he could prove himself stronger than even the most powerful Elemental. That's been known to happen."

"The sorcerer, the worst one of all, was he an Adept?"

"Actually, no. Mevolent was an Elemental. It's rare that you get an Elemental straying so far down the dark paths, but it happens."

There was a question Stephanie had been dying to ask, but

she didn't want to appear too eager. As casually as she could, thumbs hooked into the belt loops of her jeans, she said, as if she had just plucked this thought out of thin air, "So how do you know if you can do magic? Can anyone do it?"

"Not anyone. Relatively few actually. Those who can usually congregate in the same areas, so there are small pockets of communities, all over the world. In Ireland and the United Kingdom alone, there are eighteen different neighbourhoods populated solely by sorcerers."

"Can you be a sorcerer without realising it?"

"Oh, yes. Some people walk around every day, bored with their lives, having no idea that there's a world of wonder at their fingertips. And they'll live out their days, completely oblivious, and they'll die without knowing how great they could have been."

"That's really sad."

"Actually it's quite amusing."

"No, it's not, it's sad. How would you like it if you never discovered what you could do?"

"I wouldn't know any better," Skulduggery answered, stopping beside her. "We're here."

Stephanie looked up. They had arrived outside a crumbling old tenement building, its wall defaced with graffiti and its windows cracked and dirty. She followed him up the concrete steps and into the foyer, and together they ascended the sagging staircase.

The first floor was quiet and smelled of damp. On the second floor, splintered shards of light escaped through the cracks between door and doorway into the otherwise dark corridor. They could hear the sound of a TV from one of the apartments.

When they got to the third floor, Stephanie knew they had arrived. The third floor was clean, it didn't smell and it was well-lit. It was like an entirely different building. She followed Skulduggery to the middle of the corridor and noticed that none of the doors were numbered. She looked at the door Skulduggery knocked on, the door that had a plaque fastened to it: 'Library'.

While they waited there, Skulduggery said, "One more thing. No matter how much you might want to, do not tell her your name."

The door opened before she could ask any more questions and a thin man with large round spectacles peered out. His nose was hooked and his wiry hair was receding. He wore a checked suit with a bow tie. He glanced at Stephanie then nodded to Skulduggery and opened the door wide for them to come through.

Stephanie realised why none of the doors were numbered – it was because they all led into the same room. The walls between apartments had been taken away in order to accommodate the vast number of books on the shelves. Stacks and stacks of books, a labyrinth of bookshelves that stretched from one side of the building to the other. As they followed the bespectacled man through the maze she saw more people, their attention focused on their reading, people half-hidden in shadow, people who didn't look exactly *right*...

In the middle of the library was an open space, like a clearing in a forest, and in this open space stood the most beautiful woman Stephanie had ever seen. Her hair was black as raven wings, and her eyes were the palest blue. Her features were so delicate Stephanie feared they might break if she smiled, and then the lady smiled and Stephanie felt such warmth that for an instant she never wanted to be anywhere else but at this lady's side.

"Stop that," said Skulduggery.

The lady let her eyes move to him and her smile turned playful. Stephanie stared, enraptured. Her body felt so heavy, so clumsy; all she wanted to do with her life was just stand here, in this spot, and gaze at pure and true beauty.

"Stop that," Skulduggery said again, and the lady laughed and shrugged and looked back at Stephanie.

"Sorry about that," she said, and Stephanie felt a fog lift from her mind. She felt dizzy and staggered, but Skulduggery was there, a hand on the small of her back, supporting her.

"My apologies," the lady said, giving her a small bow. "I do forget the effect I have on people. First impressions and all that."

"Seems like every time you meet someone new, you forget that little fact," Skulduggery said.

"I'm a scatterbrain, what can I say?"

Skulduggery grunted and turned to Stephanie. "Don't feel self-conscious. The first time anyone sets eyes on China, they fall in love. Believe me, the effect lessens the more you get to know her."

"Lessens," the woman named China said, "but never entirely goes away, does it, Skulduggery?"

The detective took off his hat and looked at China, but ignored her question. China smiled at Stephanie and handed her a business card. It was eggshell white and bore a single telephone number, etched with delicate elegance.

"Feel free to call me if you ever stumble across a book or an item you think I might be interested in. Skulduggery used to. He doesn't any more. Too much water has flowed under that proverbial bridge, I'm afraid. Oh, where are my manners? My name is China Sorrows, my dear. And you are...?"

Stephanie was about to tell China her name when Skulduggery turned his head to her sharply, and she remembered what he had said. She frowned. The urge to tell this woman everything was almost overwhelming.

"You don't need to know her name," Skulduggery said. "All you need to know is that she witnessed someone breaking into Gordon Edgley's house. He was looking for something. What would Gordon have that someone might want?"

"You don't know who he was?"

"He wasn't anyone. His master, that's who I'm after."

"So who do you think his master is?"

Skulduggery didn't answer and China laughed. "Serpine *again*? My darling, you think Serpine is the culprit behind practically every crime."

"That's because he is."

"So why come to me?"

"You hear things."

"Do I?"

"People talk to you."

"I *am* very approachable."

"I was wondering if you'd heard anything: rumours, whispers, anything."

"Nothing that would help you."

"But you have heard *something*?"

"I've heard nonsense. I've heard something that doesn't even deserve to be *called* a rumour. Apparently Serpine has been making inquiries about the Sceptre of the Ancients."

"What about it?"

"He's looking for it."

"What do you mean? The Sceptre's a fairy tale."

"Like I said, it's nonsense."

Skulduggery fell silent for a moment, as if he was storing that piece of information away for further study. When he spoke again, it was with a new line of questioning. "So what would Gordon have that he – or anyone else – might want?"

"Probably quite a lot," China answered. "Dear Gordon was like me: he was a collector. But I don't think that's the question you should be asking."

Skulduggery thought for a moment. "Ah."

Stephanie looked at the two of them. "What? *What*?"

"The question," Skulduggery said, "is not what did Gordon have that someone might want to steal, but rather what did

Gordon have that someone had to wait until he was dead in order to steal it?"

Stephanie looked at him. "There's a difference?"

China answered her. "There are items that cannot be taken, possessions that cannot be stolen. In such a case, the owner must be dead before anyone else can take advantage of its powers."

"If you hear anything that might be of use," Skulduggery said, "will you let me know?"

"And what do I get in return?" China responded, that smile playing on her lips again.

"My appreciation?"

"Tempting. That is tempting."

"Then how about this?" Skulduggery said. "Do it as a favour, for a friend."

"A friend?" China said. "After all these years, after everything that's happened, are you saying that you're my friend again?"

"I was talking about Gordon."

China laughed and Stephanie followed Skulduggery as he walked back through the stacks. They left the library and travelled back the way they'd come.

When they were out on the street, Stephanie spoke up at last.

"So that was China Sorrows," she said.

"Yes, that was," Skulduggery responded. "A woman not to be trusted."

"Beautiful name, though."

"Like I said, names are power. There are three names for everyone. The name you're born with, the name you're given and the name you take. Everyone, no matter who they are, is born with a name. You were born with a name. Do you know what it is?"

"Is this a trick question?"

"Do you know what your name is?"

"Yes. Stephanie Edgley."

"No."

"No?"

"That's your given name. That's the name other people handed you. If a mage with any kind of knowledge wanted to, he could use that name to influence you, to attain some small degree of control – to make you stand, sit, speak, things like that."

"Like a dog."

"I suppose so."

"You're likening me to a dog?"

"No," he said, and then paused. "Well, yes."

"Oh, cheers."

"But you have another name, a real name, a true name. A name unique to you and you alone."

"What is it?"

"I don't know. You don't know it either, at least not consciously. This name gives you power, but it would also give other people absolute power over you. If someone knew it, they could command your loyalty, your love, everything about you. Your free will could be totally eradicated. Which is why we keep our true names hidden."

"So what's the third name?"

"The name you take. It can't be used against you, it can't be used to influence you and it's your first defence against a sorcerer's attack. Your taken name seals your given name, protects it, and that's why it's so important to get it right."

"So Skulduggery is the name you took?"

"It is."

"What about me? Should I have a third name?"

He hesitated for only a moment. "If you're going to be accompanying me on this, then yes, you probably should."

"And *am* I going to be accompanying you?"

"That depends. Do you need your parents' permission?"

Stephanie's parents wanted her to find her own way in life.

That's what they'd said countless times in the past. Of course, they'd been referring to school subjects and college applications and job prospects. Presumably, at no stage did they factor living skeletons and magic underworlds into their considerations. If they had, their advice would probably have been very different.

Stephanie shrugged. "No, not really."

"Well, that's good enough for me."

They reached the car and got in, and as they pulled out on to the road, she looked at him.

"So who's this Serpine you were talking about?"

"Nefarian Serpine is one of the bad guys. I suppose, now that Mevolent is gone, he'd be considered *the* bad guy."

"What's so bad about him?"

The purr of the engine was all that filled the car for a few moments. "Serpine is an Adept," Skulduggery said at last. "He was Mevolent's most trusted lieutenant. You heard what China was saying, about how she is a collector, how Gordon was a collector? Serpine is a collector too. He collects magic. He has tortured, maimed and killed in order to learn other people's secrets. He has committed untold atrocities in order to uncover obscure rituals, searching for the one ritual that he, and religious fanatics like him, have been seeking for generations. Back when the war broke out, he had this... weapon. These days he's full of surprises, but he still uses it because, quite frankly, there is no defence against it."

"What's the weapon?"

"To put it simply, agonising death."

"Agonising death... on its own? Not, like, fired from a gun or anything?"

"He just has to point his red right hand at you and... well, like I said, agonising death. It's a necromancy technique."

"Necromancy?"

"Death magic, a particularly dangerous Adept discipline. I don't know how he learned it, but learn it he did."

"And what does the Sceptre thing have to do with all this?"

"Nothing. It has nothing to do with anything."

"Well, what is it?"

"It's a weapon of unstoppable destructive power. Or it would be, if it actually existed. It's a rod, about the length of your thigh bone... Actually, I think I might have a picture of it..."

He pulled the car over and got out to open the Bentley's boot. Stephanie had never been to this part of town before. The streets were quiet and empty. She could see the bridge over the canal in the distance. Moments later Skulduggery was back behind the wheel, they were driving again and Stephanie had a leather bound book on her lap.

"What's this?" she asked, opening the clasp and flicking through the pages.

"Our most popular myths and legends," said Skulduggery. "You just passed the Sceptre."

She flicked back and came to a reproduction of a painting of a wide-eyed man reaching for a golden staff with a black crystal embedded in its hilt. The Sceptre was glowing and he was shielding his eyes. On the opposite page was another picture, this time of a man holding the Sceptre, surrounded by cowering figures, their heads turned away. "Who's this guy?"

"He's an Ancient. In the legends, they were the very first sorcerers, the first to wield the power of the elements, the first to use magic. They lived apart from the mortal world, had no interest in it. They had their own ways, their own customs and their own gods. Eventually, they decided that they wanted to have their own destinies too, so they rose up against their gods, rather nasty beings called the Faceless Ones, and battled them on the land, in the skies and in the oceans. The Faceless Ones, being immortal, won every battle, until the Ancients constructed a weapon powerful enough to drive them back – the Sceptre."

"You sound like you know the story well."

"Tales around the campfire might seem quaint now, but it's all we had before movies. The Faceless Ones were banished, forced back to wherever they came from."

"So what's happening here? He's killing his gods?"

"Yep. The Sceptre was fuelled by the Ancients' desire to be free. That was the most powerful force they had at their disposal."

"So it's a force for freedom?"

"Originally. However, once the Ancients no longer had the Faceless Ones to tell them what to do, they started fighting among themselves, and they turned the Sceptre on each other and fuelled it with hate."

The streetlights played on his skull as they passed in and out of darkness, flashing bone-white in a hypnotic rhythm.

"The last Ancient," he continued, "having driven his gods away, having killed all his friends and all his family, realised what he had done and hurled the Sceptre deep into the earth, where the ground swallowed it."

"What did he do then?"

"Probably went for a snooze. I don't know, it's a legend. It's an allegory. It didn't really happen."

"So why does Serpine think it's real?"

"Now that *is* puzzling. Like his master before him, he believes some of our darker myths, our more disturbing legends. He believes the world was a better place when the Faceless Ones were in charge. They didn't exactly approve of humanity, you see, and they demanded worship."

"The ritual that he's been looking for – is it to bring them back?"

"It is indeed."

"So he might think that the Sceptre, which drove them away, could somehow call them home, right?"

"People believe all kinds of things when it comes to their religion."

"Do you believe in any of it? The Ancients, Faceless Ones, any of it?"

"I believe in me, Stephanie, and that's enough for now."

"So could the Sceptre be real?"

"Highly unlikely."

"So what does any of this have to do with my uncle?"

"I don't know," Skulduggery admitted. "That's why they call it a mystery."

Light filled the car and suddenly the world was bucking, the only sounds a terrifying crash and the shriek of metal on metal. Stephanie lurched against her seatbelt and slammed her head against the window. The street outside tilted wildly and she realised the Bentley was flipping over. She heard Skulduggery curse beside her and for an instant she was weightless, and then the Bentley hit the ground again and jarred her against the dashboard.

It rocked back on to its tyres. Stephanie looked at her knees, her eyes wide but her brain too stunned to think. *Look up*, said a faint voice in her head. *Look up to see what's happening*. The Bentley was still, its engine cut out, but there was another engine. A car door opening and closing. *Look up*. Footsteps, running footsteps. *Look up now*. Skulduggery beside her, not moving. *Look up, there's someone coming for you. Look up NOW.*

A window exploded beside her for the second time that night, and the man from the house was grabbing her and hauling her out of the car.

6

A MAN APART

His clothes were ragged and charred but his skin had been untouched by the fireball that had enveloped him at Gordon's house. She glimpsed his face as she was dragged through the yellow light of the Bentley's headlamps, a face that was twisted in anger and hatred, and then she was lifted and slammed on to the bonnet of the car that had hit them. His hands had her collar bunched, his knuckles digging into her throat.

"You will die," he hissed, "right here and now if you do not give me that damned key."

Her hands were on his, trying to break his grip. Her head felt light, blood pounding in her temples. "Please," she whispered, trying to breathe.

"You're going to make me look bad," the man growled. "My master is going to think I'm a fool if I can't get one stupid little key off one stupid little girl!"

The street was empty around them. Shopfronts and businesses, closed for the night. No one was going to hear her. No one was coming to help her. Where was Skulduggery?

The man lifted her off the bonnet and slammed her down again… Stephanie cried out in pain and the man leaned in, his right forearm pressed beneath her chin. "I'll snap your scrawny neck," he hissed.

"I don't know anything about a key!" Stephanie gasped.

"If you don't know anything you're of no use to me and I'll kill you here."

She looked up at that horribly twisted face and stopped trying to pull his hands away. Instead she dug her thumb into the bullet hole in his shoulder. He screamed and let her go and staggered back, cursing, and Stephanie rolled off the car and ran to the Bentley. Skulduggery was pounding at the door but it had buckled under the impact, trapping his leg.

"Go!" he shouted at her through the broken window. "Get away!"

Stephanie glanced back, saw a figure loom up, and pushed herself away from the car. She slipped on the wet road but scrambled to her feet and ran, the man right behind her, clutching his injured shoulder.

He lunged and she ducked, caught a streetlight and swung herself from her course, and the man shot by her and sprawled on to the pavement. She took off the opposite way, passing the two cars and running on. The street was too long, too wide, and there was nowhere she could lose him. She turned off into a narrow lane and sprinted into the shadows.

She heard him behind her, heard the footsteps that seemed to be moving much more quickly then her own. She didn't dare look back – she didn't want the fear that was lending her speed to suddenly sabotage her escape. It was too dark to make out anything ahead of her: she couldn't see one arm's length ahead. She could be about to run smack into a wall and she wouldn't—

Wall.

Stephanie twisted at the last moment and got her hands up and hit the wall then pushed away, kicking off without losing too much momentum, continuing around the corner. The man couldn't see in the dark any better than she could and she heard him hit the wall and yell out a curse.

Up ahead was a break in the darkness. She saw a taxi pass. The man slipped and stumbled behind her – she was getting away. All she had to do was run up to the nearest person she could find and the man wouldn't dare follow her.

Stephanie plunged out of the shadows and screamed for help, but the taxi was gone and the street was empty. She screamed again, this time in desperation. The streetlights tinted everything orange and stretched her shadow out before her. Then there was another shadow moving up behind and she threw herself to one side as the man barrelled past, narrowly missing her.

The canal was ahead, the canal that flowed through the city. She ran for it, aware that the man was once again behind her and gaining fast.

She felt his fingers on her shoulder. The first touch was fleeting, but the second was a grip. His hand curled around her shoulder and tightened just as she reached the edge of the canal, and she managed to throw herself forward before he could drag her back. She heard a panicked shriek from behind and realised she had pulled him after her.

Then the freezing water enveloped them both.

The cold stunned her for a moment but Stephanie fought it and kicked out. She clutched at water and dragged it down to her sides, just like she had done countless times off the Haggard beach. Now she was moving up, up to where the lights were.

She broke the surface with a gasp and turned her head, saw the man struggling, flailing his arms in terror. For a moment she thought he couldn't swim, but it was more than that. The water was hurting him, working through him like acid, stripping pieces of him away. His cries became mere guttural sounds and Stephanie watched as he came apart and was silent and most dead.

She turned from the bits of him that floated to her and ploughed through the water. Her hands and feet were already numb with the cold, but she kept going until the bridge was far behind.

Shivering, Stephanie reached the edge of the canal and managed to haul herself out. Arms crossed over her chest, trainers squelching with every step and her hair plastered to her scalp, she hurried back to the Bentley.

When she got there, the Bentley was empty. Stephanie hung back, out of the light. A truck passed, slowing when it approached the crash. When the driver didn't see anyone, he drove on. Stephanie didn't move from her spot.

A few minutes later, Skulduggery emerged from the narrow lane she'd been chased down. He was walking quickly, looking up and down the street as he returned to his car. Stephanie stepped out of the shadows.

"Hey," she said.

"Stephanie!" Skulduggery exclaimed, rushing over to her. "You're all right!"

"I went for a swim," she said, trying to stop her teeth from chattering.

"What happened?" he asked. "Where is he?"

"Here and there." The light breeze was passing through her soaking garments. "The water kind of... took him apart."

Skulduggery nodded. "It happens."

He held out his hand and she felt herself drying and saw the water drifting off her, collecting as mist in the air over her head. "You're not surprised?" she asked.

He moved the cloud away and released it. A faint shower fell to the street. "Certain types of Adept magic don't come cheap. As we saw at Gordon's house, your attacker had made himself impervious to fire, and was probably very proud of himself for doing so. Unfortunately for him, the cost of that little spell was that a large amount of water would be lethal. Every big spell has a hidden snag."

He clicked his fingers and conjured fire, and Stephanie started to feel warm again.

"Neat trick," she said. "You'll have to teach me it some time."

With quite a bit of effort, Stephanie pulled open the car door. She wiped the broken glass from the seat and got in, buckling the seatbelt. Skulduggery went around the other side to his own broken window and climbed in behind the wheel. He twisted the key and the engine turned, complained and then came to life.

Her body was tired. Her mind was tired. Her limbs felt heavy and her eyes wanted to close. She dug her mobile phone out of her pocket – miraculously, the canal water hadn't ruined it. She pressed a button and the time flashed up and she groaned then looked outside as the first light of the morning started to seep into the sky.

"What's wrong?" Skulduggery asked. "Are you hurt?"

"No," she said, "but I will be if I don't get back to Gordon's house. Mum will be picking me up soon."

"You don't look too happy."

"Well, I don't want to go back to that world – a boring old

town with nosy neighbours and nasty aunts."

"You'd rather stay in a world where you get attacked twice in one night?"

"I know it sounds crazy, but yes. Things *happen* here."

"I'm going to see a friend later today, someone who might be able to help us out. You can come along if you want."

"Really?"

"I think you might have a real feel for this line of work."

Stephanie nodded and gave a little shrug, and when she spoke she fought hard to keep the sheer joy out of her voice. "And what about magic?"

"What about it?"

"Will you teach me?"

"You don't even know if you're *capable* of doing magic."

"How do I find out? Is there a test or something?"

"Yes, we cut off your head. If it grows back, you can do magic."

"You're being funny again, aren't you?"

"So glad you noticed."

"So will you teach me?"

"I'm not a teacher. I'm a detective. I already have a career."

"Oh, right. It's just, I'd really like to learn, and you know it all."

"Your flattery is subtle."

"But it's OK, if you don't want to teach me, that's OK. I suppose I could always ask China."

Skulduggery looked at her. "China won't teach you. She won't teach you because there is nothing that she does that is not for her own gain. You mightn't see it at first, you might think she's actually being nice to you, but you can never trust her."

"OK then."

"OK. So we're agreed?"

"We're agreed. No trusting China."

"Good. Glad we've got that sorted."

"So will you teach me magic?"

He sighed. "Dealing with you is going to be a trial, isn't it?"

"That's what my teachers at school say."

"This is going to be fun," Skulduggery said dryly. "I just know it."

Skulduggery dropped Stephanie off at Gordon's house, and half an hour later her mother's car splashed through huge puddles and Stephanie went outside to meet her. She managed to keep her mother's attention off the house, lest she notice that the front door was merely leaning against the doorframe.

"Good morning," her mother said as Stephanie got in the car. "Everything OK?"

Stephanie nodded. "Yeah, everything's fine."

"You're looking a little bedraggled."

"Oh, thanks Mum."

Her mother laughed as they drove back towards the gate. "Sorry. So tell me, how was your night?"

Stephanie hesitated, then shrugged. "Uneventful."

7

SERPINE

Nefarian Serpine had a visitor.

The Hollow Men bowed deeply as he strode through the corridors of his castle. They looked real from a distance, but up close they were nothing more than cheap imitations of life. Their papery skin was a mere expressionless shell, inflated from within by the foulest of gases. It was only their hands and feet that were solid and heavy – their feet clumped when they walked and their hands weighed down their arms, so they stood with a perpetual stoop.

Their number increased the closer he got to the main hall. They were simple creatures, but they did what they were told, and they hadn't known what to make of the visitor. Serpine entered the main hall, the crowd of Hollow Men parted and a man in a dark suit turned to him.

"Mr Bliss," Serpine said politely. "I thought you were dead."

"I heard that too," Bliss responded. He was an elegant man of muscle and mass, as tall as Serpine, but whereas Serpine had black hair and glittering emerald green eyes, Bliss was bald, with eyes of the palest blue. "In fact, it was a rumour I started. I thought it might make people leave me alone in my retirement."

"And has it?"

"Unfortunately, no."

Serpine motioned for the Hollow Men to leave them and then led his guest into the drawing room.

"Can I get you a drink?" Serpine asked, heading to the liquor cabinet. "Or is it too early in the day?"

"I'm here on business," Bliss said. "Elder business."

Serpine turned, gave him a smile. "And how are the Elders?"

"Worried."

"When are they not?"

Serpine went to the armchair by the window, watched the sun as it struggled to rise then settled into the chair, crossed his legs and waited for Bliss to continue. The last time they had been in the same room together they had been trying to kill each other while a hurricane tore the place down around them. The very fact that Bliss remained standing right now told Serpine that he was thinking the same thing. Bliss was wary of him.

"The Elders called me in because, five days ago, two of their people went missing – Clement Gale and Alexander Slake."

"How very unfortunate, but I don't believe I've ever had the pleasure of meeting either of them."

"They were assigned to... observe you, from time to time."

"Spies?"

"Not at all. Merely observers. The Elders thought it prudent to keep tabs on a few of Mevolent's followers, to make sure no one strayed from the terms of the Truce. You were always at the top of that list."

Serpine smiled. "And you think I had something to do with their disappearance? I'm a man of peace these days, not war. I seek only knowledge."

"You seek secrets."

"You make that sound so sinister, Mr Bliss. As for the missing 'observers', maybe they'll turn up safe and well, and the Elders can apologise for dragging you out of your retirement."

"They turned up yesterday."

"Oh?"

"Dead."

"How terrible for them."

"Not a mark on their bodies. No indication at all as to how they died. Sound familiar?"

Serpine thought for a moment then arched an eyebrow and held up his gloved right hand. "You think this *did it? You think* I *killed those men? I haven't used this power in years. When I first learned it, I thought it was a wonderful thing, but now I look on it as a curse, and a reminder to me of my many mistakes and transgressions in my servitude to Mevolent. I don't mind telling you, Mr Bliss, that I am deeply ashamed of what I have done with my life."*

Bliss stood there and Serpine almost spoiled it all by laughing, but he managed to retain his look of mocking innocence.

"Thank you for your co-operation," Bliss said, turning to leave. "I shall be in touch if I need to ask you more questions."

Serpine waited until Bliss was at the door before speaking again. "They must be scared."

Bliss stopped. "What makes you say that?"

"They sent you, didn't they? Why didn't they send the detective, I wonder?"

"Skulduggery Pleasant is busy with another investigation."

"Is that so? Or maybe they thought I would be intimidated by you."

"They thought you'd listen to me. This Truce will hold only for as long as both sides want it to. The Elders want it to hold."

"That must be nice for them."

Mr Bliss looked at him like he was trying to read his thoughts. "Be careful, Nefarian. You might not like what's at the end of this road you're on."

Serpine smiled. "You're sure you won't join me for a drink?"

"I have a plane to catch."

"Going somewhere nice?"

"I have a meeting in London."

"I hope that goes well for you. We'll have a drink some other time then."

"Perhaps."

Mr Bliss inclined his head in a small bow, and left.

8

GHASTLY

Stephanie went to bed as soon as she got home and woke at a few minutes past two in the afternoon. She padded to the bathroom and showered, her body aching as she stood under the spray. Her knees were scraped and cut from when she'd been dragged along the road. Her skin was mottled with deep bruises. Her neck was stiff.

She turned off the water and stepped out of the shower, dried herself off and pulled on fresh jeans and a T-shirt. Barefoot, she took her old clothes downstairs and threw them in the washing machine, added the powder and turned it on. It was only after she'd had something to eat that she allowed herself to think about the previous night.

Well, she said to herself, *so that happened.*

She pulled on her shoes and went out, the sunshine warm on her face. At the end of her road, she passed the old pier and started towards Main Street. Normality. Kids playing football, riding bikes and laughing, dogs running about, tails wagging, neighbours talking to neighbours and the world being as she'd always thought it was. No living skeletons. No magic. No men trying to kill her.

A crazy laugh escaped her lips when she reflected on how much her life had changed in the space of a day. She had gone from being a perfectly ordinary girl in a perfectly ordinary world to becoming a target for water-soluble weirdos and a partner for a skeleton detective out to solve her uncle's murder.

Stephanie faltered. Her uncle's *murder*? Where had she got that from? Gordon had died of natural causes: the doctors had said so. She frowned. But these were doctors who lived in a world without walking, talking skeletons. But still, why assume he'd been murdered? What on earth had made her think that?

"There are items that cannot be taken," China had said, "possessions that cannot be stolen. In such a case, the owner must be dead before anyone else can take advantage of its powers."

Her attacker, and whoever had sent him, wanted something. They wanted something badly enough to kill her to get it. And if they wanted it that badly, would they really have waited for her uncle to die of natural causes before they went looking for it?

Stephanie felt cold. Gordon had been murdered. Someone had killed him and no one was doing anything about it. No one was asking the questions, no one was trying to figure out who did it.

Except for Skulduggery.

She narrowed her eyes. He must have known Gordon was murdered. If he hadn't already suspected it when they first met, he must have worked it out in the library. China probably knew as well, but neither of them had told her. They didn't think she could handle it, maybe. Or maybe they didn't think it was any of her business. It had to do with their world after all, not hers. But Gordon was still her uncle.

A car pulled up behind her. People stared. She looked back and saw the Bentley.

The driver's side was still badly buckled from where the car had rammed it, and the windscreen was cracked. Three of the windows were without glass and the bonnet had a series of ugly dents running up its left side. The usual purr of the engine was replaced by a worrying rattle that cut out abruptly when the engine turned off. Skulduggery – in hat, scarf and sunglasses – went to get out, but the door wouldn't open.

"Oh, boy," Stephanie muttered.

She watched him lean away from the door and raise his knee, and then he kicked it open and got out, adjusting his coat as he walked over.

"Good afternoon," he said brightly. "Wonderful weather we're having, isn't it?"

"People are staring," Stephanie whispered as he neared.

"Are they really? Oh, so they are. Good for them. So, are we ready to go?"

"That depends," she answered, speaking softly and keeping a smile on her face. "When were you going to tell me that my uncle was murdered?"

There was a slight hesitation. "Ah. You worked that out, then?"

Stephanie turned down a narrow lane between two buildings, moving away from the prying eyes of Haggard's gossip mongers. Skulduggery hesitated a moment, then caught up to her, walking fast.

"I had a very good reason for not telling you."

"I don't care." Now that no one could see her, she dropped the smile. "Gordon was *murdered*, Skulduggery. How could you not have told me?"

"This is a dangerous business. It's a dangerous world that I'm part of."

She stopped suddenly. Skulduggery kept walking, realised she wasn't beside him any more and turned on his heel. She crossed her arms. "If you don't think I can handle it—"

"No, you've certainly proved yourself capable." She heard the tone of his voice change slightly. "I knew from the moment I met you that you're just the type of person who would *never* walk away from danger, simply out of stubbornness. I wanted to keep you out of it as much as I could. You've got to understand – Gordon was my friend. I thought I owed it to him to try and keep his favourite niece out of harm's way."

"Well, I'm *in* harm's way, so it's not your decision any more."

"No, apparently it isn't."

"So you won't keep anything from me again?"

He put his hand to his chest. "Cross my heart and hope to die."

"OK."

He nodded and led the way back to the Bentley.

"Though you don't actually have a heart," she said.

"I know."

"And technically, you've already died."

"I know that too."

"Just so we're clear."

"What's he like?" Stephanie asked as they drove.

"What's who like?"

"This guy we're going to see. What's his name?"

"Ghastly Bespoke."

She looked at Skulduggery to make sure he wasn't joking, then realised there was no way she could tell. "Why would anyone call themselves Ghastly?"

"All manner of names suit all manner of people. Ghastly is my tailor and also happens to be one of my closest friends. He first taught me how to box."

"So what's he like?"

"Decent. Honourable. Honest. But more fun than I'm making him sound, I swear. Also, he's not magic's biggest fan..."

"He doesn't like magic? How could he not like magic?"

"He just doesn't find it interesting. He prefers the world he reads about in books and sees on TV, the world with cops and robbers and dramas and sports. If he had to choose, I expect he'd live in the world without magic. That way, he could have gone to school and got a job and been... normal. Of course, he's never been given the choice. I suppose, for him, there could never really *be* a choice. Not really."

"Why not?"

Skulduggery hesitated for only a moment, as if he was choosing how best to say it, then told her that Ghastly was born ugly.

"Not just unattractive," he said, "not merely unappealing, but really, honestly ugly. His mother was jinxed when she was pregnant with him and now his face is ridged with scars. They tried everything to fix it – spells, potions, charms, glamours, various and sundry creams, but nothing worked."

He explained that, as a child, Ghastly had always told his friends that he got his love of boxing from his father and his love of sewing from his mother. The truth was, his father was the one who was constantly making alterations to hemlines and such, and his mother was a bare-knuckle boxing champ, who boasted twenty-two consecutive wins. Skulduggery had seen her fight once. She had a right hook that could take a head clean off. And according to legend, it *had* once too.

Regardless, Ghastly was brought up in these two separate disciplines and, figuring he was ugly enough already, decided to try a career as a tailor, rather then a boxer.

"And I for one am glad he did," Skulduggery said. "He makes extraordinary suits."

"So we're going to see him because you need a new suit?"

"Not quite. You see, his family has amassed a unique collection of artwork, paintings and literature about the Ancients, from all over the world. Included are a couple of rare volumes that could be very useful indeed. All anyone knows about the Sceptre is based on half-forgotten myths. Those books, and whatever else is in Ghastly's collection, will hold a far more detailed description of the legends, about what the Sceptre does and, in theory, how one would go about defending oneself against it."

They parked and got out. The neighbourhood was dirty and run down, and people hurried by without even glancing at the battered car in their midst. A little old lady shuffled past, nodding to Skulduggery as she went.

"Is this one of those secret communities you were telling me about?" Stephanie asked.

"Indeed it is. We try to keep the streets as uninviting as possible so no casual passer-by will stop and have a look around."

"Well, you've succeeded."

"You should be realising by now that looks are, more often than not, deceiving. A neighbourhood like this, with its graffiti and litter and squalor, is the safest neighbourhood you could possibly visit. Open the door to any one of these houses around us and you walk into a veritable palace. Surface is nothing, Stephanie."

"I'll try to remember that," she said as she followed him to a little shop perched on the corner. She looked around for a sign. "Is this the tailor's?"

"Bespoke tailor's, yes."

"But there's no sign. There aren't any clothes in the window. How would anyone know it's even open?"

"Ghastly doesn't need to advertise. He has a very specific clientele, and he can't really afford to let ordinary people wander in when he's measuring out a new suit for an eight-armed octopus-man."

"Are you serious? There's an eight-armed octopus-man?"

"There's a whole colony of octopus people," Skulduggery said as they approached the door.

"Really?"

"Good God, Stephanie, of course not. That would be far too silly."

He walked on before she could even *try* to hit him. The shop door was unlocked and he led the way in. Stephanie was surprised by how clean and bright and ordinary-looking it was. She didn't know what she was expecting – mannequins that came alive and tried to eat you, perhaps. There was a nice smell in here too. Comforting.

Ghastly Bespoke walked out from the backroom and when he saw them he smiled. He shook Skulduggery's hand warmly. He was broad-shouldered and his scars covered his whole head. When Skulduggery turned to introduce Stephanie, and he saw the way she was staring at Ghastly, he shrugged.

"Don't mind her," he said. "She stares. That's what she does when she meets new people."

"I'm quite used to it," Ghastly said, still smiling. "Do you want to shake hands, Miss, or start off with something easy, like waving?"

Stephanie felt herself blush and she stuck out her hand quickly. His hand was normal, no scars, but tough and strong.

"Do you have a name?" he asked.

"Not yet," she admitted.

"Better make sure that you really want one before you think any more about it. This life isn't for everyone."

She nodded slowly, not sure what he was getting at. He took a moment, looking her up and down.

"There's been some trouble?"

"Some," answered Skulduggery.

"Then the proper attire is probably called for." Ghastly took out a small pad, started jotting down notes. "Do you have a favourite colour?" he asked her.

"I'm sorry?"

"To wear. Any preference?"

"I'm not sure I understand..."

"Not all of the clothes I make are merely examples of exquisite tailoring. Sometimes, if the situation arises, special requirements are catered for."

"Such as keeping you safe until this whole thing is over," Skulduggery said. "Ghastly can make you a suit, nothing too formal, which could very possibly save your life."

"Fashion," said Ghastly with a shrug. "It's life or death." His pen was at the ready. "So, once more, do you have a favourite colour to wear?"

"I... I'm not sure I could afford it..."

Ghastly shrugged. "I'll put it on Skulduggery's tab. Go nuts."

Stephanie blinked. To go from her mother buying most of her clothes to *this* was a step she hadn't been expecting. "I don't know, I'm not sure... Black?"

Ghastly nodded and scribbled in his notebook. "Can't go wrong with black." He looked up at Skulduggery. "Just let me lock up," he said, "then we can talk properly."

While they waited for him to do so, Skulduggery and Stephanie wandered into the back of the shop. Material and fabrics of all types and textures were arranged very neatly in massive shelves that lined the walls. There was a single workplace in the centre of the room and another doorway leading further back.

"He's going to make me clothes?" Stephanie whispered.

"Yes, he is."

"Doesn't he need to take measurements or something?"

"One glance, that's all he needs."

They passed through into a small living room, and moments later Ghastly joined them. Stephanie and Skulduggery sat on the narrow sofa and Ghastly sat in the armchair opposite, both feet flat on the ground and fingers steepled.

"So what's all this about?" he asked.

"We're investigating Gordon Edgley's murder," Skulduggery said.

"Murder?" Ghastly said after a short pause.

"Indeed."

"Who would want to kill Gordon?"

"We think Serpine did it. We think he was looking for something."

"Skul," Ghastly said, frowning, "usually when you want my help you just call and we go off and you get me into a fight. You've never explained what's going on before, so why are you doing it now?"

"This is a different type of help I need."

"So you don't need me to hit anyone?"

"We'd just like your help in finding out what Serpine is after."

"I see," Ghastly said, nodding his head.

"You don't see, do you?"

"No," Ghastly said immediately. "I really don't know what you want me to do."

"We think Serpine is after the Sceptre of the Ancients," Stephanie said and she felt Skulduggery sink lower into the cushion beside her.

"The what?" Ghastly said, his smile reappearing. "You're not serious, are you? Listen, I don't know what my dear friend here has been saying, but the Sceptre isn't real."

"Serpine thinks it's real. We think that has something to do with my uncle's death."

"I'm sorry for your loss," Ghastly said, "I really am. I

respected Gordon. He knew there was magic in the world and he wasn't seduced by it. He just wanted to observe and to write about it. That takes a strength that I hope has been passed on to you."

Stephanie didn't answer. Skulduggery didn't look at her.

"But," Ghastly continued, "to say that his death has something to do with a legend that has been passed down from generation to generation, and that has changed with each telling, is just nonsense. He had a heart attack. He was mortal. He died. That's what mortals do. Let him have his death."

"I think my uncle knew where the Sceptre is, or he had it and Serpine killed him, and now Serpine knows where it is and that's why he wants the key."

"What key?"

"The key to get the Sceptre maybe. We're not sure. What we do know is that he tried to kill me twice to get it."

Ghastly shook his head. "This isn't your world."

"I'm a part of it now."

"You've just stepped into it. You've seen magic and sorcerers and a living skeleton and I bet you're having great fun – but you haven't the slightest idea what's at stake."

Skulduggery didn't say anything. Stephanie got to her feet.

"You know what?" she said. "For me, this *is* an adventure.

That's what you're saying, isn't it? Well, you're right. I do look at all this as a big adventure, and I'm fascinated and excited and thrilled by it all. I've seen amazing people do amazing things, and I've been amazed." Her eyes hardened. "But don't you dare, for one second, think that this is just a game to me. My uncle left me a fortune: he left me everything I could ever want. He did all that for me, but he's dead now. So now I'm going to do something for *him*. I'm going to find out who killed him, and I'm going to do what I can to make sure they don't just walk away from it. He's got to have *someone* on his side."

"This is insane!" Ghastly said, leaning forward in his chair. "The Sceptre's a fairy tale!"

"I believe it exists."

"Of course *you* believe it exists! You've been dragged into a world where you think anything can happen, but that's not how it works. Your uncle involved himself in this and if what you say is true, he got killed for it. Are you so eager to do the same? You're playing with fire."

"Everyone plays with fire around here."

"This hasn't gone the way I was expecting," Skulduggery said.

"There are rules for things like this," Ghastly said, ignoring her and speaking to Skulduggery. "There's a reason we don't tell everyone we're out there. She is a prime example of *why*."

Stephanie's anger flared and she knew she couldn't talk now without her voice cracking and betraying her, so she dashed past Ghastly. She walked through the shop, unlocked the door and walked out on to the street. She could feel the anger twisting in her insides, making her fingers curl. She hated not being treated as an equal, she hated being talked down to and she hated the feeling of being protected. She didn't much like to be ignored either.

Skulduggery emerged from the shop a few minutes later, hat back on. He walked up to her as she leaned against the Bentley, arms crossed and staring at a crack in the pavement.

"So that went well," he said eventually. When she didn't answer, he nodded and said, "Did I tell you how I first met Ghastly?"

"I don't want to know."

"Ah. All right then." Silence drifted down like smog. "It's not very interesting anyway. But it has pirates in it."

"I couldn't care less," Stephanie said. "Is he going to help us or not?"

"Well, he doesn't think it's a great idea to have, you know, to have you with me on this one."

"Oh, really?" Stephanie responded bitterly.

"He seems to think I'm being irresponsible."

"And what do you think?"

"I have been known to be irresponsible in the past. It's entirely plausible that it's happening again."

"Do you think I'm in danger?"

"Oh, yes. Serpine still believes you are in possession of whatever key he's looking for. The moment he learns who you are or where you are, he'll send someone else. You're in – and I don't think I'm exaggerating here – especially *grave* danger."

"Then let's be absolutely clear on this, OK? I can't leave this. I can't go back to my dull, boring, ordinary life, even if I wanted to. I've seen too much. I'm involved here. It's *my* uncle who was murdered, it's *my* life that was in danger and I am not about to just walk away. That's all there is to it."

"Well, I'm convinced."

"So why are we standing around?"

"My question exactly," Skulduggery said, unlocking the Bentley. They got in and the Bentley rattled to life at the turn of the key. Skulduggery checked the rear-view, then the wing mirrors, then remembered that he didn't have any wing mirrors any more, and pulled out on to the road.

"So we don't get to look at his family's collection?"

Stephanie asked as they drove.

"Ghastly is a good man, and a good friend, and precisely the kind of person you want on your side, but he is also one of the most stubborn people I know. In four days, once he has had time to think, he will change his mind, and he will quite happily let us see what we need to see, but until then we don't have a hope."

"Wouldn't the books be in China's library too?"

Skulduggery made a noise halfway between a laugh and a grunt. "China has been after those books for years, but they're locked away where even she can't reach them."

"You know where they are?"

"In the Vault."

"In a vault? So what?"

"Not *a* vault, *the* Vault. It's a series of chambers housed beneath the Dublin Municipal Art Gallery, very well protected, where they don't take kindly to trespassers."

Stephanie took a moment then spoke. "Ghastly will change his mind in four days?"

"That's how long it usually takes, yes."

"But we don't have four days, do we?"

"No, we don't."

"So you know what we have to do, right?"

"Unfortunately, yes."

"We *need* to look at that collection."

Skulduggery looked at her. "I knew you'd be good at this. The moment I saw you, I knew you had an instinct for this job."

"So we break into the Vault?"

He nodded reluctantly. "We break into the Vault."

The Dublin Municipal Art Gallery was situated in one of the more affluent parts of the city. A gleaming triumph of steel and glass, it stood alone and proud, its lush gardens keeping the other buildings at a respectable distance.

Stephanie and Skulduggery parked across the road as part of what Skulduggery was calling a *preliminary stake-out*. They weren't going to break into the Vault *yet*, he assured her; they were just here to get some idea of what they were up against. They had just seen the gallery staff and a half-dozen security guards leave the building, their shift over for the day. Two people, a man and a woman, dressed in blue overalls, passed them on the steps and entered the gallery, locking the doors behind them.

"Ah," Skulduggery said from beneath his scarf. "We may have a problem."

"What problem?" Stephanie asked. "Them? Who are they?"

"The night shift."

"Two people? That's all?"

"They're not exactly people."

"So who are they?"

"It's not so much *who* as *what.*"

"I swear, Skulduggery, you either give me a straight answer or I'm finding the biggest dog you've ever seen and I'm going to make him dig a hole and bury you in it."

"Oh that's charming, that is," Skulduggery said, then made a sound like he was clearing his throat, though there was nothing to clear and no actual throat to clear it from. "Did you notice the way they moved?"

"Very, I don't know... gracefully. What about it? Are they dancers? The Vault has ballerina security guards?"

"They're vampires," Skulduggery said. "The Vault has *vampire* security guards."

Stephanie made a show of poking her head out of the window and looking up at the sky. "The sun's still out, Skulduggery. It's still bright."

"Doesn't matter to them."

She frowned. "Doesn't sunlight kill them? Doesn't it turn

them to dust, or make them burst into flames or something?"

"Nope. Vampires tan, just like you and me. Well, just like you. I tend to bleach."

"So sunlight has no effect on them?"

"It binds them. It dampens their powers. During the day, they are for all intents and purposes mortal, but when the sun goes down, their powers flare up."

"I didn't know that."

"And the Vault employs two of them as their nightshift. The ultimate guard dogs."

"If sunlight doesn't hurt them, I don't suppose crosses will scare them off?"

"The best way to stop a vampire is with a whole lot of bullets, and since we don't want to hurt anyone, this is that problem I was telling you about."

"There must be a way to get by them. We could disguise ourselves as cleaning staff or something."

"No one works when vampires are around – vampires don't make a distinction between allies and prey. They can't resist the bloodlust any more than a moth can resist a big bright light. They're killers: the most efficient, deadly killers on the face of the planet."

"Scary."

"Yes, well, vampires aren't known for being cute."

"Well then, we're going to have to come up with something really really clever."

Skulduggery paused then shrugged. "I suppose I *am* good at that."

9

THE TROLL BENEATH WESTMINSTER BRIDGE

Skulduggery took Stephanie home, and as she was lying in bed that night, finally drifting off to sleep, a young woman in London was hunkering down and peering into the darkness.

"Hello?" she said. "Anyone down there?"

The Thames was dark and rushing beneath her, but no one answered. She glanced at her watch then looked around. It was seven minutes to midnight and Westminster Bridge was empty except for her. Perfect.

"Hello?" she said again. "I need to talk to you."

A voice answered: "There's no one down here."

"I think there is," she said.

"No," came the voice. "No one."

"I think there's a troll down there," the young woman said. "And I need to talk to him."

A face rose up out of the shadows, small and wrinkled, with large ears and a shock of spiky black hair. Huge eyes blinked at her.

"What do you want?" the troll asked.

"I want to talk to you," the young woman answered. "I'm Tanith Low. What's your name?"

The troll shook his head. "No no, not telling. Not telling that."

"Oh yes," Tanith said, "trolls only have one name, isn't that right?"

"Yes yes, one name. No telling."

"But I can guess, isn't that how it goes? If I guess your name correctly, what happens then?"

The troll grinned, showing lots of sharp yellow teeth. "You get to live," he said.

"And if I get it wrong?"

The troll giggled. "You get eaten!"

"That sounds like a fun game," Tanith said with a smile.

"What time do you usually play?"

"Midnight, stroke of midnight, yes yes yes. When I'm *strong*."

"And you pop out from under there at whoever's passing, don't you?"

"Three chances," the troll said, nodding. "Three chances is what they get. Guess the name, don't get eaten; get it wrong, come along."

"Do you want to play it with me?"

The grin faded on the troll's face. "Not strong yet. Need to wait, yes yes. Stroke of midnight."

"*We* don't have to wait, do we?" Tanith said with a pout. "I want to play *now*. I bet I can guess your name."

"No, you can't."

"Bet I can."

"No, you can't!" the troll said, giggling again.

"Come on up out of there, we'll see."

"Yes yes, play the game."

Tanith glanced at her watch and stepped back as the troll scampered up. Two minutes to midnight. He was small, up to her waist, with thin arms and legs and a bloated belly. His fingernails were hardened and pointed and he was grinning in anticipation, though keeping his distance.

She let her coat fall open a little and smiled at him. "You're a handsome little fellow, aren't you? Are you the only troll in London?"

"Only one," he said proudly. "Now we play! Guess the name, don't get eaten; get it wrong, come along. Guess guess guess."

"Let's see," she said, taking a step closer. The troll narrowed its eyes and stepped back, towards the edge of the bridge. She stopped moving. "Is your name Bollohollow?"

The troll roared with laughter. "No no, not Bollohollow! Two guesses left, only two!"

"This is harder than I thought," said Tanith. "You're really good at this, aren't you?"

"Best! Very best!"

"Not many people have guessed your name, huh?"

"*No one,*" the troll cackled. "Guess guess!"

"Is it... Ferninabop Caprookie?"

The troll whooped and hollered and danced, and Tanith moved a little closer.

"Not Ferninabop!" he laughed. "Not Caprookie!"

"Wow," Tanith said, looking worried. "I'm not doing too well here, am I?"

"Gonna get eaten!"

"You eat a lot of passers-by?"

"Yes yes, yum yum."

"You gobble them all up, don't you? They scream and cry and run away—"

"But I catch them!" the troll giggled. "Stroke of midnight, I'm big and strong and fast, gobble them up, gobble them all up! They struggle and wriggle and tickle inside me!"

"I'd better get my last guess right then, eh?" said Tanith. "Is it... Rumplestilskin?"

The troll laughed so hard he fell on to his back. "No no!" he managed to say between gales of laughter. "They always say that! Always get it wrong!"

Tanith took one more step, and dropped her smile. The sword flashed from her coat but the troll saw it just in time and squealed and rolled.

Tanith cursed and swiped again, but the troll dodged beneath her and she spun and kicked out, sending him sprawling. He scrambled to his feet, hissing and spitting at her as she advanced, and then, in the warm London night, the sound of Big Ben. Midnight.

Tanith lunged but it was too late. The troll skipped back as his shoulders hunched and he snarled and started to grow.

"Nuts," Tanith whispered to herself.

Muscles bulged in his arms and legs, stretching the skin so

tight it looked like it might split. She moved forward again but he flipped back through the air, and when he landed he was as tall as she was. His chest broadened and his neck thickened and still he grew, and still he snarled. His bones popped and he finished growing. He was now almost twice her size.

Facing down a fully-grown troll was not what she had planned. She held the sword down by her leg and circled the creature.

"You cheated," the troll said, his voice deep and guttural now.

"You've been a very naughty boy," she said.

"Gobble you up. Gobble you all up, yes yes."

Tanith shot him a smile. "Come and have a go if you think you're hard enough..."

The troll roared and lunged, moving fast despite his size, but Tanith was ready. She slipped to the side and then past him, her sword opening up his thigh. He hissed in pain and swung a massive fist that slammed into her back. She hit the ground hard. He went to stamp on her but she rolled, coming up on one knee and bringing the sword from her side to her shoulder and the blade found his arm.

The troll stumbled back and she got to her feet.

"Gonna bite you," the troll growled, "gonna bite you into little pieces, yes yes."

"The game's not so much fun when you're playing with someone who can fight back, is it?"

"*My* bridge," he snarled. "*My* game."

She smiled at him. "My rules."

Another roar and he dived straight at her and she stood her ground. One swipe of the sword took the fingers on his left hand and he howled in pain and staggered back and she jumped. She planted her feet on his chest and swung, the blade flashing in the bridge's lights as it took his head. The troll's body stumbled back and she jumped off. The body hit the barrier and tipped backwards into the river.

Tanith stooped to pick up the head and moved to the barrier. She turned as a man walked up. She had never met him before but she knew who he was. He was tall and bald, and his face was lined and his eyes were a startling blue, the palest eyes she had ever seen. His name was Mr Bliss.

Mr Bliss nodded to the head in her hand. "Risky."

"I've fought trolls before," she said respectfully.

"I meant the risk you took with being seen."

"It had to be done. This troll has killed many innocent people."

"But that's what trolls do. You can't blame him for doing what nature intended." She didn't know how to respond. Mr Bliss smiled.

"I'm not berating you," he said. "You've done a noble and selfless thing. That is to be admired."

"Thank you."

"You puzzle me, however. I have been keeping an eye on your progress over the last few years. It is unusual to find a mage, even an Adept like you, focusing as heavily on physical conflict as you have done. Yet you don't seek power."

"I just want to help people."

"And that is what puzzles me."

"My mother used to tell me stories about the war," she said. "I think you may be forgetting some selfless acts of your own."

Mr Bliss smiled softly. "There is no heroism in war – there are simply things that need to be done. The heroes come later. But I am not here to discuss philosophies."

He looked at her with his startling blue eyes. "A storm is brewing, Miss Low. Coming events will threaten to turn the tide of power in this world, and so I have left my place of solitude and come here, searching for you. I have a need for someone of your ability and your outlook."

"I'm not sure I understand."

"The sorcerer Serpine is about to break the Truce. If I fail in my endeavours, we will once again slip into war. I need you on our side."

"It would be an honour," Tanith said.

"We have much to learn from each other," Mr Bliss responded, bowing. "Make your way to Ireland," he said, "and I will be in touch with you soon."

She nodded and he walked away. Tanith threw the troll's head into the Thames and, hiding her sword under her coat, walked off in the other direction.

10

THE GAL IN BLACK

Stephanie was woken the next morning by the stereo playing very loudly indeed. Her dad had been trying to tune into a news station and the volume knob had snapped off, so instead of a quiet little traffic report they were treated to Wagner's *The Ride of the Valkyries* at full blast. He had lost the remote control down the back of the sofa and hadn't the first clue how to turn the stereo off. The music reverberated through the floor and in the walls. There was no escaping its sheer power. By the time her mother had yanked the plug out of the socket, Stephanie was wide awake.

Her mother poked her head in to say goodbye, and as her parents went off to work Stephanie threw on a pair of jeans and a T-shirt. While she waited for Skulduggery to arrive, she thought about what would be a good name for her to take. Skulduggery had explained how the actual taking of a new name casts a seal around the old one – so if Stephanie took the name Crystal Hammer (she didn't plan on it) then the name Stephanie Edgley would be instantly immune to any controlling spells. But while she only went by her given name, she was vulnerable.

If she were to have a new name, it would have to be a name she wouldn't be embarrassed about in years to come. It would have to be something classy and also something she felt comfortable with. Skulduggery had told her about people who'd taken names like Razor and Phoenix, and how he wouldn't advise anyone to take a name that seemed cool. He'd once been introduced to a woman who had put on a little weight over the years, and her hair had been a bit windswept and she had spinach in her teeth, and he was told her name was Jet. Jet did not suit this woman, the same way Razor did not suit the short fat man who took that as a name.

Stephanie looked up from her desk as Skulduggery

knocked on the window. She opened it.

"I thought girls were supposed to be tidy," he said as he peered in.

Stephanie kicked some underwear under her bed and ignored the comment. "You OK out there?"

"I've been perched on worse roofs, believe me."

"My parents have gone to work, you know. You could have used the door."

"Doors are for people with no imagination."

"Are you sure no one saw you? The last thing I need is for a neighbour to be passing and see you climbing up the side of the house."

"I was careful, don't you worry. And I have something for you." He gave her a short piece of chalk.

"Uh, thank you," she said slowly.

"Go to your mirror."

"I'm sorry?"

"Go to your mirror and draw this symbol on it." He handed her a small card that showed an eye in a circle with a wavy line through it.

"What's this for?"

"It's to help you. Go on."

She frowned, then went to the mirror.

"No," Skulduggery said, "a full length mirror. Do you have one?"

"Yeah," Stephanie said. Still with no clue why she was doing this, she opened her wardrobe and used the chalk to copy the symbol on to the mirror on the other side of the door. When she was done, she handed the card and the chalk back to Skulduggery. He thanked her, put them away and then looked at the mirror.

"Surface speak, surface feel, surface think, surface real." He looked at her again. "Could you wipe the symbol off now, please?"

"What is going on? What are you doing? Did you just cast a spell on my mirror?"

"Yes. Could you wipe the symbol off?"

"Well what does the spell *do*?" she asked as she used her sleeve to erase the chalk.

"You'll see," he answered. "Are you wearing a watch?"

"My watch broke. I wore it swimming. I thought it was waterproof."

"Was it?"

"As it turned out, no. Why do you need to know the time?"

"Oh, I don't. Touch the mirror."

She narrowed her eyes. "Why?"

"Touch it."

Stephanie hesitated, then did as he said and reached out, touching her fingers lightly against the mirror. But when she pulled back, her reflection did not. She watched in amazement as her reflection blinked, as if awakening from a trance, then dropped its arm to its side and looked around. Then, very slowly, it stepped out through the mirror.

"Oh my God..." Stephanie said, moving back as the reflection joined her in the room. "Oh my God," she said again, because she couldn't think of anything else to say.

Skulduggery looked on from the window. "It will carry on with your life while you're away, so you won't be missed."

Stephanie stared. "She's me."

"Not she, *it*. And it isn't you, it's a surface copy. It walks like you, talks like you, behaves like you, and it should be enough to fool your parents and anyone else it comes into contact with. When you return, it goes back into the mirror and the experiences and the memories it has made transfer to you."

"So... so I can be in two places at once?"

"Precisely. It can't spend too long in other people's company or they'll start to notice that things aren't quite right, and it would never fool a mage, but it is ideal for your needs."

"Wow." Stephanie peered closer at the reflection. "Say something."

The reflection looked back at her. "What do you want me to say?"

Stephanie laughed suddenly, then clapped a hand over her mouth. "You sound just like me," she said through her fingers.

"I know."

"Do you have a name?"

"My name is Stephanie."

"No, a name of your own."

Skulduggery shook his head. "Remember, it's not a real person. It has no thoughts or feelings of its own: they're all imitations of yours. It's your reflection – that's all it is. Operating instructions are as follows: it cannot change out of the clothes you're wearing when you cast it, so make sure you're not wearing anything with a logo or insignia. They'll come out backwards. Make sure you're not wearing a watch or a ring – they'll appear on the opposite hand. Apart from that, it's pretty simple."

"Wow."

"We should go."

She turned to him, frowning. "Are you sure they won't realise it's not me?"

"It'll stay out of other people's way for most of the time and try to avoid any long conversations. Even if your parents corner it and bombard it with questions, they'll just think you're acting strange."

Stephanie chewed her lip then shrugged. "I suppose jumping to the conclusion that it's my reflection come to life is a *bit* unlikely."

"You'd be surprised by how many things we get away with that fall into the category of 'unlikely'. You ready to go?"

"I suppose I am."

"Do you want to leave by door or window?"

"Doors are for people with no imagination," Stephanie grinned and joined Skulduggery on the window sill. She took one look back. The reflection was standing in the middle of the room, perfectly still.

"Bye," Stephanie said.

"Bye," the reflection responded and tried a smile for the first time. It looked kind of eerie.

Stephanie climbed out and hung on to Skulduggery as he jumped, displacing the air beneath them to act as a cushion. They landed gently and made it to the end of the road without any neighbours seeing them, but when they reached the pier, Stephanie's face fell. She stared in horror as Skulduggery marched onwards.

"What the hell is *that*?" she demanded.

"It's my car," Skulduggery answered, leaning against it with his arms folded. The sea breeze ruffled his wig beneath his hat.

She stared at him, at the car, and then at him again.

"What happened to the Bentley?" she asked.

His head tilted. "I don't know if you noticed, but it was ever-so-slightly dinged."

"And where is it now?"

"It's getting fixed."

"Right. That's a good answer. Fixed is a good answer. But I don't know, I'm kind of drawn back to my original question. What the *hell* is *that*?"

Skulduggery was leaning against a canary yellow hatchback with lime-green seat covers.

"It's my replacement car," he said proudly.

"It's hideous!"

"I don't mind it actually."

"Well, you're wearing a disguise, so no one will recognise you anyway!"

"That may have something to do with it..."

"When will the Bentley be fixed?"

"That's the nice thing about living in a world of magic and

wonder, even our most extreme car repairs happen in less than a week."

Stephanie glared at him. "*A week*?"

"Not a week," he said quickly. "Six days. Sometimes five. Definitely four. I'll call him, tell him I'll pay the extra..." She was still glaring.

"Day after tomorrow," he said quietly.

Her shoulders sagged. "Do we really have to ride around in this?"

"Think of it as an adventure," he said brightly.

"Why should I do that?"

"Because if you don't you'll just become really really depressed. Trust me. Now hop in!"

Skulduggery hopped in. Stephanie dragged her feet around to the other side and more kind of *fell* in. She squirmed down in the lime-green seat as much as she could as they drove through Haggard. There was a parcel in the back seat, wrapped in brown paper and tied with string. Beside that was a black bag.

"Is that the gear for breaking into the Vault?" she asked. "Is that where we're going?"

"Well, to answer your first question first, yes. That bag contains all the equipment needed for a beautifully executed break-in. To answer your second question, no, that is not where we're going. Before I get to introduce you to a life of crime, I get to introduce you to the Elder Mages."

"Crime sounds more fun."

"As indeed it is, though I would never condone crime in any of its forms. Except when *I* do it, naturally."

"Naturally. So why are we delaying the fun? What do these Elder Mages want?"

"They've heard that I've been dragging a perfectly nice young lady into all manner of trouble and they want to admonish me for it."

"Tell them it's none of their business."

"Well, while I do admire your moxie..."

"What's moxie?"

"...I'm afraid that won't work too well with these fellows. One thing you have to remember about the Elder Mages is that they're—"

"Really old sorcerers?"

"Well, yes."

"Worked that out all by myself."

"You must be so proud."

"Why do you have to report to them? Do you work for them?"

"In a way. The Elders pass the laws, and they have people

who enforce the laws, but there are only a few of us who actually investigate the *breaking* of those laws – murders, robberies, a couple of kidnappings, the usual. And while I may be freelance, most of my work, and my money, comes from the Elders."

"So if they want to wag their fingers at you..."

"I have to stand there and be wagged at."

"So why do they want me to be there? Aren't I the innocent young girl being led astray?"

"See, I don't really want them to view you as the innocent young girl. I want them to view you as the rebellious, insubordinate, troublesome tearaway who has made herself my partner. Then maybe they'll take pity on me."

"Wait, do they even know I'm coming with you?"

"No. But they like surprises. Almost always."

"Maybe I should wait in the car."

"In *this* car?"

"Ah, good point."

"Stephanie, we both know something serious is going on, but as yet the Elders have refused to consider that their precious Truce might be in jeopardy."

"And why would they believe me and not you?"

"Because I go to them loaded with baggage. I have a history and, some might say, an agenda. Besides, tales of horror are always more effective coming from a lady."

"I'm no lady."

He shrugged. "You're the closest I've got."

Skulduggery had another surprise for her as they drove. He pulled into a fast-food place and nodded to the parcel in the back seat.

"What's that?" she asked.

"What do you think it is?"

"It looks like a parcel."

"Then that's what it is."

"But what's inside it?"

"If I tell you, I deprive the parcel of its whole reason to be."

She sighed. "And what *is* its reason to be?"

"To be opened, of course, and to reveal what it's holding."

"You are so annoying," Stephanie muttered, reaching back and taking the parcel. It was soft to the touch. She looked at Skulduggery. "The clothes?"

"I'm saying nothing."

"Ghastly made the clothes already? I didn't think he was going to make them *at all*, not after, you know... the argument."

Skulduggery shrugged and started humming. Stephanie sighed, then took the parcel. She got out of the yellow car and walked into the fast food restaurant, making her way to the toilets at the back. Once secured inside a cubicle, she pulled open the string and the parcel unfolded before her. It was the clothes. They were the deepest black, made of a material she had never seen before.

She got changed quickly, noting how perfectly everything fitted, and stepped out of the cubicle to admire herself in the mirror. The trousers and the tunic, a sleeveless garment with silver clasps, were pretty good by themselves, and the boots fitted as though she'd been wearing them for years. But it was the coat that completed the picture. Three-quarter length, shaped especially for her, made of a material so black it nearly shimmered. She resisted the temptation to leave her other clothes in the toilet, and instead wrapped them in the brown paper and left the restaurant.

"Surprise!" Skulduggery said when she was back in the Canary Car. "It's the clothes!"

She looked at him. "You are so weird."

Twenty minutes later they were walking into the Waxworks Museum. The building was old, in dire need of repair, and the street wasn't much better. Stephanie didn't say a word as they paid and went wandering through the dark corridors, surrounded on both sides by imitation celebrities and fictional characters. She had been here two or three times as part of school trips when she was younger, but couldn't see the point of visiting *now*. They hung back from a small group of tourists until they were certain they were alone, and only then did Stephanie say anything.

"What are we doing here?"

"We're here to visit the Elders' Sanctuary," Skulduggery replied.

"And are the Elders made of wax?"

"I like coming here," he said, taking off his sunglasses and ignoring her question. "It's very liberating."

He took off his hat and wig and pulled the scarf from his neck. Stephanie looked around nervously.

"Aren't you afraid someone might see?"

"Not in the slightest."

"Well, maybe we should go and talk to the Elders then."

"Good idea."

Skulduggery moved to one side of the corridor and traced his hand over the wall. "Where is it?" he muttered. "Bloody idiots keep changing it..."

The tourists came back around the corner and Stephanie went to drag Skulduggery out of sight but it was too late – they had already seen him. A small American boy left his parents' side and walked right up to him. Skulduggery was frozen to the spot.

"Who's that meant to be?" the boy asked, frowning slightly.

Stephanie hesitated. Now the entire tour was looking at her, including the tour guide. "This is," Stephanie said, racking her brains for a likely-sounding explanation, "this is Sammy Skeleton, the world's worst detective."

"Never heard of him," the boy said, giving Skulduggery's arm a poke. He shrugged and lost interest, and Stephanie watched the tourists carry on. When they were out of sight, Skulduggery swivelled his head to her.

"'World's worst detective'?" he asked.

She shrugged and hid her grin, and Skulduggery *harumphed* good-naturedly and went back to running his hand along the wall. He found what he was looking for and pressed inwards. A section of the wall slid open to reveal a hidden passage.

"Wow," Stephanie said. "The Sanctuary is *here*? I used to come here when I was little..."

"Never knowing that beneath your feet was a world of magic and wonder?"

"Exactly."

He tilted his head slightly. "Better get used to that feeling."

She followed him in and the wall sealed shut behind them.

The stairway downwards was lit by torches that flickered in their brackets, but the closer they got to wherever it was they were going, the brighter it became.

They emerged into the gleaming foyer of the Sanctuary. It would have reminded Stephanie of the lobby to a high tech company building – all marble and varnished wood panelling – were it not for the lack of windows. Two men stood guard against the far wall, hands clasped behind them. Dressed entirely in grey, with long coats and some sort of helmet with a visor that covered their entire faces, they each had a scythe, a wicked-looking blade on a one-and-a-half-metre staff, strapped to their backs. A slight man in a suit came out to greet them.

"Detective," he said, "you are early. The Council is not ready to convene. I could show you to the waiting area, if you wish."

"Actually, I might take the opportunity to show our guest around, if that's all right."

The man blinked. "I'm afraid access is strictly limited, as well you know."

"I was just going to show my friend the Repository," Skulduggery said. "The Book, in fact."

"I see. Well, as Administrator of the Sanctuary, I would have to accompany you, naturally."

"Wouldn't have it any other way."

The Administrator bowed and spun on his heel, and led them down an adjoining corridor. They passed more people in grey uniforms as they walked. Stephanie was getting used to dealing with people with no eyes and no expressions, but there was something about them that unnerved her. Skulduggery, living skeleton though he was, was still fundamentally human, and yet these people, who merely wore helmets to hide their faces, seemed to her much more sinister.

"Who are they?" Stephanie whispered as they walked.

"Cleavers," Skulduggery replied in a low voice. "Security guards, enforcers and army, rolled into one. Dangerous individuals. Be glad they're on our side."

She did her best not to look at them as they passed. "Where are we going?" she asked, trying to change the subject.

"I'm taking you to see the Book of Names," Skulduggery said. "Some say it was created by the Ancients, but the truth is no one knows who really made it or how it was made. It lists the names of every person living on this earth: the given name, the taken name – when and if a name is taken – and the true name. Every time a baby is born, a new name appears in its pages. Every time someone dies, their name fades away."

Stephanie looked at him. "So my true name is in that Book?"

"As is mine. As is everyone's."

"Isn't that dangerous? If someone got their hands on that, they'd be able to rule the world." She let a few moments pass. "And I felt ridiculous even saying that."

The Administrator glanced over his shoulder as he walked. "Not even the Elders open the Book. It is too powerful – it can corrupt too easily. But they can't find a way to destroy it – it can't be torn; it can't be burnt; it can't be damaged by any means we have at our disposal. If the legends are true and the Book *was* created by the Ancients, then it stands to reason that only the Ancients could destroy it. The Elders, for their part, see it as their responsibility to protect it, to keep it away from prying eyes."

They reached a set of double doors. The Administrator waved his hand and the heavy doors swung slowly open. They walked into the Repository – a large room with marble pillars – which, as Skulduggery explained, housed some of the rarest and most unusual magical artefacts in existence. They passed row upon row of shelves and tables, on which lay items so bizarre they defied description. The Administrator pointed out one of the strangest of these – a two-dimensional box that held wonders to sate the most jaded of appetites, but which only existed if approached from a right angle. In contrast to this clutter, however, was the centre of the room, which was empty save for a pedestal, and on that pedestal, a book.

"That's the Book of Names?" Stephanie asked.

"Yes, it is," the Administrator answered.

"I thought it'd be bigger."

"It's as big as it needs to be, no more, no less."

"And it's OK to leave it out in the open like that?"

"It's not as vulnerable as you might think. When it was placed here, the security arrangements did cause the Elders some concern. How would it be protected? Guards can be overcome. A locked door can be unlocked. A wall can be broken. A shield can be pierced."

"So, what? They decided not to bother?"

"Actually, they came up with a most ingenious defence. Willpower."

"Sorry?"

"The Book is protected by the Will of the Elders." Stephanie wasn't sure if he was joking or not.

"See for yourself," the Administrator said. "Take the Book."

"Me?"

"You. You won't be harmed."

Stephanie glanced at Skulduggery, but he gave no indication as to what she should do. Finally, she just turned and started walking towards it.

Her eyes darted from one side of the room to the next. She thought about trapdoors and immediately started examining the floor she walked on. What form did willpower take? She hoped it wasn't bullets or anything painful like that. She was mildly annoyed that she was even doing this, walking right into whatever trap the Elders had set up, and doing so willingly. For what? To prove a point that wasn't even hers? She didn't even *want* to take the Book. This whole thing was ridiculous.

She glanced back, saw the Administrator standing there with a placid expression on his face, obviously anticipating whatever was about to happen, whatever was going to pop out in front of her to stop her from taking their precious Book. She stopped walking. If he wanted the Book, he could get it himself. She turned and walked right back again. The Administrator peered at her.

"You didn't take it," he said.

Stephanie forced herself to remain polite. "No, I didn't. But I'll take your word for it that it's well protected."

"When you started walking, you wanted to take the Book, yes?"

"I suppose so."

"And why didn't you?"

"Because I changed my mind."

"Because you didn't want to take it any more."

"Well, yes. So?"

"That is the Will of the Elders. No matter how badly you want that Book in your hands, the closer you get, the less you want it. It doesn't matter if you want it for yourself, if you want it because you were ordered to take it or because your very life depends on it. With every step you take, your indifference towards the Book increases, no matter who you may be or what power you may have. Even Meritorious himself couldn't get close to it."

Stephanie looked at him, taking it all in. Finally, she had to say it, there was no way she couldn't: "That's very impressive."

"It is, isn't it?" The Administrator turned his head a little, as if hearing something. "The Council is ready for you now. Please come this way."

They walked into an oval-shaped room and stood facing a large door. There was only one light source, from somewhere overhead, and the edges of the room remained in relative darkness.

"The Elders will be but a moment," the Administrator said and walked quietly away.

"They always do this," Skulduggery said. "Keep people waiting."

"My headmaster does the same thing whenever someone's called to his office. He thinks it makes him look important."

"Does it work?"

"It makes him look late."

The door ahead opened and an old man entered. He had short white hair and a tightly cropped beard, and he was tall, taller than Skulduggery. He wore a suit the colour of granite, and as he walked, Stephanie became aware of the shadows to his right. They seemed to shift and stretch alongside him, and she watched as more of them reached over from the corners of the room to join the mass. The shadows suddenly rose up from the floor and melted into an elderly woman in black. She fell into step beside the tall man and their footsteps slowed as they neared. A third person faded up from nothing, materialised right out of thin air on the other side of the tall man. He looked a little younger than the others and he wore a sky-blue suit, the jacket of which was struggling to contain his hefty paunch.

Stephanie looked at the Elder Mages and the Elder Mages looked at Stephanie.

"Skulduggery," the tall man said eventually, his voice deep and resonant, "trouble follows in your wake, doesn't it?"

"I wouldn't say follows," Skulduggery answered. "It more kind of sits around and waits for me to get there."

The man shook his head. "This is your new partner then?"

"Indeed it is," Skulduggery answered.

"No taken name?"

"No."

"That's something, at least." The man shifted his focus to Stephanie. "I am Eachan Meritorious, Grand Mage of this Council. Beside me are Morwenna Crow and Sagacious Tome. Can I assume, because you have not yet picked a name, that you do not intend to involve yourself in our affairs for very much longer?"

Stephanie's throat was dry. "I'm not sure."

"See?" Skulduggery said. "Insubordinate."

"You have been placed in dangerous situations," Meritorious continued. "Surely you would prefer to go back to the safety of your normal life?"

"What's so safe about it?"

"Ah," Skulduggery chimed in. "Rebellious."

"I mean," Stephanie continued, "I could get knocked down crossing the road tomorrow. I could get mugged tonight. I could get sick next week. It's not safe anywhere."

Meritorious raised an eyebrow. "While this is true, in your normal life you never had to deal with sorcerers and murder attempts."

The Elders were gazing at her with interest. "Maybe," she admitted. "But I don't think I can just forget about all this."

Skulduggery shook his head sadly. "Troublesome."

The woman, Morwenna Crow, took over. "Detective, you have petitioned the Council on numerous occasions concerning a supposed threat to the Truce."

"I have."

"And as yet you have failed to produce evidence."

"This girl standing beside me is my evidence," Skulduggery said. "Twice she has been attacked and twice her attacker has been after a key."

"What key?" asked Sagacious Tome. Skulduggery hesitated.

"Mr Pleasant?"

"I believe the attacker's master to be Serpine."

"What key, detective?"

"If Serpine is ordering attacks on civilians, this is a clear breach of the Truce and the Council has no choice but to—"

"The key, Mr Pleasant, what does it open?"

Stephanie glanced at Skulduggery's inscrutable visage and

thought she could detect hints of frustration in the small movements he was making.

"I believe the key will lead Serpine to the recovery of the Sceptre of the Ancients."

"I never know when you're joking, Skulduggery," Meritorious said, starting to smile.

"I hear that a lot."

"You are aware that the Sceptre is a fable?"

"I am aware that it is *thought* to be, yes. But I am also aware that Serpine has been working on tracking it down, and I believe Gordon Edgley may have had it."

"Nefarian Serpine is now an ally," said Sagacious Tome. "We live in a time of peace."

"We live in a time of fear," Skulduggery said, "where we're too scared of upsetting the status quo to ask the questions we need to be asking."

"Skulduggery," Meritorious said, "we all know what Serpine did; we all know the atrocities he has committed in the name of his master Mevolent, and for his own gains. But for as long as the Truce holds, we cannot act against him without good cause."

"He has ordered the attacks on my companion."

"You have no proof."

"He murdered Gordon Edgley!"

"But you have no proof."

"He is after the Sceptre!"

"Which doesn't even *exist.*" Meritorious shook his head sadly. "I am sorry, Skulduggery. There is nothing we can do."

"As for the girl," said Morwenna, "we had hoped her involvement in all this would be minimal."

"She's not going to tell anyone," Skulduggery said quietly.

"Maybe so, but if she takes one more step deeper into our world, it may be impossible for her to step out again. We want you to consider this carefully, detective. Consider what it would mean."

Skulduggery gave a slight nod of acknowledgement but said nothing.

"Thank you for agreeing to meet us," Meritorious said. "You may leave." Skulduggery turned and walked out, Stephanie right behind him. The Administrator hurried over.

"I know the way out," Skulduggery growled and the Administrator backed off. They passed the Cleavers, standing as still as the wax models above them, and climbed the staircase out of the Sanctuary. Skulduggery donned his disguise and they walked back to the Canary Car in silence. They had almost reached it when he stopped and turned his head.

"What's wrong?" Stephanie asked.

He didn't answer. She couldn't see anything beneath his disguise. Stephanie looked around, paranoid. It appeared to be a normal street, populated by normal people doing normal things. Granted, the street had potholes and the people were scruffy, but there was nothing out of the ordinary. And then she saw him, a tall man, broad and bald, his age impossible to gauge. He walked towards them like he had all the time in the world, and Stephanie stood by Skulduggery and waited.

"Mr Pleasant," the man said when he had reached them.

"Mr Bliss," Skulduggery responded.

Stephanie looked at this man. He radiated power. His pale blue eyes settled on her.

"And you must be the girl who attracts all sorts of attention."

Stephanie couldn't speak. She didn't know what she would have said, but she did know that her voice would have been thin and reedy if she tried. There was something about Mr Bliss that made her want to curl up and cry.

"I haven't seen you in a while," Skulduggery said. "I heard you'd retired."

There was something peaceful about Mr Bliss's eyes, but it wasn't the calming kind of peaceful. It wasn't a peaceful that comforted you and made you feel safe. It was another kind of peaceful, the kind that promised you no more pain, no more joy, no more anything. Looking at him was like looking into a void with no beginning and no ending. Oblivion.

"The Elders asked me to return," Mr Bliss said. "These are troubling times, after all."

"Is that so?"

"The two men who had Serpine under surveillance were found dead a few days ago. He is up to something, something he doesn't want the Elders to know about."

Skulduggery paused. "Why didn't Meritorious tell me this?"

"The Truce is a house of cards, Mr Pleasant. If it is disturbed, it will all come down. And you are known for your disturbances. The Elders hoped my involvement would be enough of a deterrent, but I fear they have underestimated Serpine's ambition. They refuse to believe that anyone would benefit from war. And, of course, they still think the Sceptre of the Ancients is a fairy tale."

Skulduggery's voice changed, but only slightly. "You think the Sceptre's real?"

"Oh, I know it is. Whether it can do everything the legends claim, that I do not know, but as an object, the Sceptre is quite real. It was uncovered during a recent archaeological dig. As I understand it, Gordon Edgley had been searching for the Sceptre for some time, as part of his research for a book about the Faceless Ones, and he paid a substantial amount of money to gain possession of it. I imagine he worked to verify its authenticity, and once he had done so, he realised he couldn't keep it. Nor could he pass it on. Gordon Edgley, for all his faults, was a good man, and if there was a chance that it did have the destructive capabilities we've all heard about, he would have felt that the Sceptre was too powerful for anyone to possess."

"Do you know what he did with it?" Stephanie asked, finding her voice at last.

"I don't."

"But you think Serpine's willing to risk war?" Skulduggery asked.

Mr Bliss nodded. "I think he views the Truce as having outlived its usefulness, yes. I imagine he has been waiting for this moment for quite some time, when he can seize all the power and plunder every secret, and invite the Faceless Ones back into the world."

"*You* believe in the Faceless Ones?" Stephanie asked.

"I do. I grew up with those teachings and I have carried my faith through to this day. Some dismiss them; some view them as morality tales; some view them as stories to tell children at night. But I believe. I believe that once we were ruled by beings so evil, even their own shadows shied away from them. And I believe they have been waiting to come back, to punish us for our transgressions."

Skulduggery cocked his head. "The Elders would listen to you."

"They are bound by their rules. I have learned what I can, and I have passed it on to the only person who would know what to do with it. What you do next is up to you."

"With you on our side," Skulduggery said, "things would be a lot easier."

A small smile appeared on Mr Bliss's face. "If I have to act, I will."

Without even a "Good day", Mr Bliss turned and walked away. They stayed where they were for a few moments then got in the Canary Car and Skulduggery pulled away from the curb. They drove for a bit before Stephanie spoke.

"He's kind of scary."

"That happens when you rarely smile. Mr Bliss is, physically, the most powerful individual on the face of the planet. His strength is beyond legendary."

"So he *is* scary?"

"Oh, yes, very much so."

He drove on, and settled into silence. Stephanie let a few moments drift by.

"What are you thinking?"

Skulduggery gave a small shrug. "Lots of clever little things."

"So do you believe that the Sceptre is real?"

"It certainly looks that way."

"I suppose this is a big deal for you, huh? Finding out that your gods really existed?"

"Ah, but we don't know that. If the Sceptre *is* real, its true history could have been mixed up with the legends. Its existence does not prove that it was used to drive away the Faceless Ones."

"Funny. I wouldn't have thought that a living skeleton would be such a sceptic. So what's our next move?"

Skulduggery was silent for a bit. "Right, well, we've got to work out what we need. We've got to work out what we need, how we get it and what we need to get to get what we need."

"I think I actually understood that," Stephanie said slowly. The car went over a bump. "No, it's gone again."

"We need the Elders to take action, so we need proof that Serpine has broken the Truce. We need to find the Sceptre and we also need to find out how to destroy the Sceptre."

"OK, so how do we do the first one?"

"We'll get the proof once we find the Sceptre."

"And how do we find the Sceptre?"

"We find the key."

"And how do we destroy the Sceptre?"

"Ah," he said. "That'll be the little bit of crime that we'll have to embark on."

"Crime," Stephanie said with a smile. "Finally."

11

THE LITTLE BIT OF CRIME

From their vantage point, parked across the road, they watched the vampires, once again in their blue overalls, walk up the steps and enter the gleaming art gallery. They were chatting and didn't look intimidating at all. A few minutes later the staff and day shift security started to trickle out of the building. When every one of them was accounted for, Skulduggery reached into the back seat and pulled the black bag into his lap.

"We're going now?" Stephanie asked, looking up into the evening sky. "But it's still bright."

"And that's precisely why we're going now," he said. "Twenty minutes from now, there'll be two fully-fledged vampires prowling around in there. I want to get in, find out how to destroy the Sceptre and get out before that happens."

"Ah. Probably wise."

"Very probably."

They got out of the horrible Canary Car and crossed the street, left the pavement and moved through the garden area to a tall tree behind the gallery. Making sure they wouldn't be seen, Skulduggery put the bag over his shoulder and started to climb. Stephanie jumped for the lowest branch, grabbed it and started climbing up after him. She hadn't done anything like this in years, but climbing a tree was like falling out of one – easy. The tree's limbs were long and strong, and they quickly came adjacent to the gallery's roof, which was ridged with a dozen skylights. Stephanie hoisted herself up on a branch and sat there, regarding the large gap between building and tree with curiosity. It looked too far to jump.

"You sure I can't come with you?" Stephanie asked.

"I need you out here in case something goes terribly, terribly wrong."

"Like what?"

"Oh, any one of a number of things."

"Fills me with confidence, that," she muttered.

Skulduggery manoeuvred himself on to the longest branch and then walked along it, bent-legged and stooped over. His balance was unnatural. But there was still that gap. Without pausing he sprang forward, off the branch. He brought his arms up by his sides and out in front, and a tremendous gust of wind buffeted him over to the rooftop.

Stephanie promised herself that, one day, she'd get him to teach her how to do that.

Skulduggery looked back. "The gallery is outfitted with the most elaborate security systems," he said as he opened the bag. "But because of the vampires, the alarms on the outer corridors are never set, so once I get by the main hall, it should be plain sailing, as they say."

"As who say?"

"I don't know. People who sail presumably." He opened the bag and took out a harness that he started to strap himself into. He looked up at her. "Where was I?"

"I have no idea."

"Oh, yes, my cunning plan. I need to access a control panel on the east wall. From there, I can disable everything. The floor is pressure sensitive, so I'm going to have to stay off it, but that shouldn't be a problem for someone of my natural grace and agility."

"You're very impressed with yourself, aren't you?"

"Exceedingly so." He secured a thin wire on to a ventilation duct, looped it through his harness and led it back to one of the skylights.

Stephanie frowned. "You're going to lower yourself down from here?"

"Yes. That's the fun bit."

"Right. But you're going to have to *open* the skylight, yes? Won't *that* set off an alarm?"

"Only a small one," Skulduggery said with confidence.

She stared at him. "And wouldn't that be enough?"

"It's a silent little thing, hooked up to the nearby police station. Or it *was* hooked up. I passed by their transformer box before I collected you this morning. Oddly enough, it happened to short out at the exact same time. Something to do with a large amount of water mysteriously manifesting inside. I think they're baffled. They certainly *looked* baffled..."

"And your entire plan hinges on the hope that they haven't restored electricity yet?"

"Well, yes," he said, after a slight hesitation. "But anyway." He looked over at the setting sun then back at Stephanie.

"If you hear any screaming," he said, "that'll be me."

He passed his hand over the lock and it broke apart, then opened up one of the halves of the skylight and climbed over the side. She watched him disappear into it, and then heard a slight whirring as he used the hand-held control to lower himself down in the harness.

Stephanie sat back against the tree trunk, keeping an eye out for... whatever she was supposed to be keeping an eye out for. Anything unusual. She frowned to herself, not entirely certain of what constituted "unusual" any more, and then she heard an unsettling scraping noise. She looked up.

The wire Skulduggery had attached to the ventilation duct was slipping.

She watched in horror as it slipped again, getting closer to the edge, closer to slipping off entirely. She thought of the pressure-sensitive floor, thought about Skulduggery crashing down and setting off every alarm in the place and the vampires running in and catching him. Although he didn't have any blood for them to drink, she was sure they'd be able to find some other ways to punish the trespass.

The wire slipped again and Stephanie knew she didn't have a choice. She crawled along the same branch Skulduggery had jumped from and it groaned beneath her weight. Skulduggery was nothing but bones, she reminded herself, in an effort not to feel fat.

The gap was gaping. It was a gaping gap.

Stephanie shook her head – she couldn't make it. There was no way she could jump that. With a decent run at it, she might have had a chance, but from crouching on the end of an unsteady branch? She closed her eyes, forcing the doubts from her mind. It wasn't a choice, she reminded herself. It wasn't a question of whether she *could* jump, or *would* jump. Skulduggery needed her help, and he needed it now, so it was a question of when she *did* jump, what would happen then?

So she jumped.

She stretched out and the ground moved far beneath her and the edge of the building rushed at her and then she started to dip. Her right hand thudded against the edge and her fingers gripped. The rest of her body slammed into the side of the building and she almost fell, but she shot her left hand up to join her right and held on. She pulled herself up, little by little, until she could get an arm over the edge and soon she was safe. She had made it.

The wire slipped again. It was about to snap from the duct and then it'd all be over. Stephanie ran to it, got her fingers around the wire and tried to tug it down again but it was no use. She stood, put the sole of her boot against the wire and used all her weight to try and push it down, but she didn't make the slightest bit of difference. She looked around for something to use, saw the bag and snatched it up. Nothing inside but more wire.

She grabbed the wire and dropped to her knees, tying a new piece to the wire already attached to the harness. Her father had taught her all about knots when she was little, and although she couldn't remember the names of most of them, she knew which knot suited this occasion.

With the new length of wire added, she looked around for something to secure it to. There was another skylight right in front of her. She ran to it, wrapping the wire around the entire concrete base and getting it tied off just as the first piece of wire shot off the duct. There was a sudden snap as the wire went taut again, but it stayed secure.

Stephanie hurried over to the open skylight and looked down. Skulduggery was hovering right above the floor, trying to stay horizontal after the sudden drop. The motion control for the harness was still in his hand, but both arms were outstretched for maximum balance and he couldn't move himself back up.

There was a second control on the roof beside Stephanie, attached to the harness with a lead that twisted down through the skylight around the wire. Stephanie grabbed the control, jammed her finger against the UP button and Skulduggery started whirring upwards.

When he was safe he raised his head, saw her and gave her the thumbs up. He took over the controls, positioning himself next to the wall, by the panel that he had already opened. Stephanie watched him flick a few switches, and then he spun himself gently. His feet touched the floor. No alarms went off.

He undid the clasp on the harness and stepped out of it, then looked up. A moment passed and he motioned for her to come down. Grinning, Stephanie recalled the harness, strapped herself in, climbed over the edge, and lowered herself down. Skulduggery helped her unclip it.

"I suppose I *could* do with some back-up," he whispered and she smiled.

The gallery was big and spacious and white. There were huge glass sections in the walls. The main hall was full of paintings and sculptures, artfully arranged so it was neither cluttered nor sparse.

They moved to the double doors and listened intently. Skulduggery opened one of the doors, checked outside, nodded to Stephanie. They crept out, closing the door behind them. She followed him through the white corridors, around turns and through archways. She caught him glancing out of the windows as they passed. Night was coming.

They got to a small alcove, away from the main hub of the gallery. Within this alcove was a heavy wooden door, criss-crossed by a grid of bolted steel. Skulduggery whispered for her to keep watch and then hurried to the door, taking something from his pocket.

Stephanie crouched where she was, peering into the ever-increasing gloom. She glanced back at Skulduggery as he worked at picking the lock. There was a window next to her. The sun had gone down.

She heard footsteps and shrank back. The man in the blue overalls had appeared around the corner on the far side of the corridor opposite. He was walking slowly, like any security guard she'd seen in a mall. Casual, disinterested, bored. She felt Skulduggery sneak up behind her, but he didn't say anything.

The man's hand went to his belly and then he doubled over in pain. Stephanie wished she was closer. If he sprouted fangs she'd hardly be able to see them from here. The man straightened up and arched his spine, and the sounds of his bones cracking echoed through the corridor. Then he reached up and grabbed his hair and pulled his skin off.

Stephanie stifled a gasp. In one fluid movement he had pulled it all off – hair, skin, clothes – and he was pale underneath, and bald, and his eyes were big and black. He moved like a cat, kicking off the remnants of his human form. She didn't have to be closer to see his fangs, they were big and jagged and hideous, and now she was quite content to be viewing them from a distance. These weren't the vampires she'd seen on TV; these weren't sexy people in long coats and sunglasses. These were animals.

She felt Skulduggery's hand on her shoulder and he pulled her back a fraction, very gently, just before the vampire looked over. It moved away from them, down the corridor, in search of prey.

Stephanie followed Skulduggery to the door, and they passed through and closed it behind them. Skulduggery wasn't creeping any more, but Stephanie didn't dare make a sound. He led the way down beneath the gallery, a flame in his hand lighting the steps. It was cold down here. They were in an old corridor now with heavy doors on either side, and they walked until they came to a door with a crest etched into it – a shield and a bear. Skulduggery raised both hands and lowered his head and didn't move for almost a minute. Then the door clicked and they stepped in.

12

VAMPIRES

Skulduggery clicked his fingers and candles flared up all around the chamber. There were books piled on books, and artefacts and statues, and paintings and wood carvings, and there was even a suit of armour to one side.

"This is all to do with the Sceptre?" Stephanie asked in a whisper.

"It's all to do with the Ancients," Skulduggery answered, "so I'm sure there must be something about the Sceptre in all this. I honestly didn't expect there to be this much. You don't have to whisper by the way."

"There are vampires above us."

"These chambers are sealed. I broke the locking seal, but the sound seal is still in place. Did you know locking seals have to be dismantled every single time you want to go through, and then crafted again once you leave? I don't see what's wrong with a good old-fashioned key. That would certainly keep someone like me out. Well, until I knocked the door down."

"What's a sound seal?" Stephanie whispered.

"Hmm? Oh. Even if they were standing outside the door and you were shouting at the top of your voice, they wouldn't hear you."

"Ah," she said, "OK then." But she still kept her voice low.

They started searching. Some of the books were about the legends of the Ancients, some took a more practical and analytical viewpoint and some were written in a language Stephanie didn't recognise. A few of the books held nothing but blank pages, yet Skulduggery seemed able to read them, although he said they contained nothing of immediate interest.

She started rooting through a collection of paintings, stacked in frames against the wall. A lot of them showed people holding the Sceptre aloft and looking heroic. The paintings toppled over and she stooped to push them back up. She looked at the painting in front of her, recognising it from the book she had seen in Skulduggery's car – a man shielding his eyes from a glowing Sceptre as he reached for it. This was the full painting, not the truncated little rectangle on a page. Skulduggery glanced over as Stephanie put the pictures back as she had found them. She approached the suit of armour, noting the shield and bear etched into the breastplate.

"Family crest?" she asked.

"Sorry?" Skulduggery said, looking up. "Oh, yes. We don't have family names that we can keep, so crests serve as our only link to our ancestors."

"Do you have a crest?"

He hesitated. "I used to. I don't any more."

She turned. "Why not?"

"I abandoned it actually."

"Why?"

"You ask an awful lot of questions."

"When I grow up I want to be a detective just like you."

He looked over and saw her grinning. He laughed. "I suppose you do share my penchant for raising Cain."

"Raising what now?"

"It's an old expression. It means to make trouble."

"Well why can't you say 'make trouble'? Why do you always have to use these words that I don't know?"

"You should read more."

"I read enough. I should get out more."

Skulduggery held a small box up to the light, turning it over in his hands and examining it from every angle.

"What's that?" she asked.

"It's a puzzle box."

"Can't you play with it some other time?"

"The purpose of a puzzle box, its whole *raison d'être*, is to be solved."

"What kind of raisin?"

"*Raison d'être*. It's French for *reason to be*."

"There you go again. Why didn't you just say *reason to be*? Why do you have to complicate things?"

"My point is, leaving a puzzle box unsolved is like leaving a song unsung. It may as well cease to exist."

"There's a crossword in the paper my dad gets every single day. He starts it, ends up making up nonsensical words to fill in the blanks, and abandons it. I'll give you every paper we have lying about the house if you put that down and get back to searching."

"I've given up searching."

She stared at him. "And they say my generation has a short attention span."

"That painting you were looking at, notice anything strange about it?"

"There were a lot of paintings."

"The man reaching for the Sceptre."

"What about it?"

"Did you notice anything unusual about it?"

Stephanie went over to the wall again, moved the frames one by one till she came to the painting he was talking about.

"OK, unusual like how?"

"Describe it to me."

She moved the others out of the way so she could take a better look. "There's this man, he's reaching for the Sceptre, it's glowing... and that's it."

"Nothing strange about him?"

"No, not really..." She frowned. "Well..."

"Yes?"

"The Sceptre's really bright and he's got one hand shielding his eyes, but both eyes are wide open."

"So?"

"So if it's really that bright, you'd kind of expect him to be squinting at least. Even if it *is* just a picture."

"Anything else strike you as a little off?"

She scanned the painting. "The shadows."

"What about them?"

"He's got two of them."

"So? The Sceptre *is* magical, remember. It could be casting two shadows as easy as one, for whatever bizarre magical reason."

"But the Sceptre isn't casting these shadows. The angles are wrong."

"So what would cause that?"

"Two different light sources."

"And what is the primary source of light?"

"The sun?"

"If it *is* the sun, what time of day would it be?"

"Well, the shadow at his feet would make it noon, when the sun is directly overhead, but the shadow behind him would make it either morning or evening."

"Which one?"

"How should I know? It's behind him, so it might be morning."

"So what you're looking at is a painting of a man reaching for the Sceptre, seeing everything, at a time when it is both the past and the present?"

"I suppose so. What does this have to do with the puzzle box?"

"Who painted it?"

Stephanie peered at the bottom corner. "There's no name, only a crest. A leopard and crossed swords."

Skulduggery raised the puzzle box for her to see what was carved into its base – a leopard and crossed swords.

"Right," she said, standing, "guessing games are over."

"That painting tells us that the painter, or the painter's family, can offer us a glimpse into the past, and that is what we in the profession call a *clue*. A clue is part of a mystery, a mystery is a puzzle. I hold in my hands a puzzle box."

Skulduggery's fingers played over the surface of the box and Stephanie saw his head tilt. He pressed his hands against opposite sides, making subtle rotations until something clicked. There was a noise, like the whirring of a motorised part, and the top of the box opened to reveal a blue gemstone.

"Ah," Skulduggery said.

Stephanie peered closer. The gem was a little bigger than a golf ball. "What? What is it?"

"It's an Echo Stone," he said. "Very rare. Generally, it's used by people who are dying. They sleep with the stone close by for three nights, and in doing so they imprint it with their memories and personality. It's given to loved ones to help comfort them through their grief, or to answer any lingering questions they might have, things like that."

"How does it work?"

"I'm not entirely sure," he said. "I've never seen one up close." He pressed a fingertip to the Stone and it immediately started to glow. His head tilted again and he sounded very pleased with himself. "Would you look at that? I'm such a genius."

"You just *touched* it."

"Still a genius, Stephanie." She sighed.

A moment slipped by and then an old man faded up from nothing before them. Stephanie stepped back.

"Don't be alarmed," the old man said, smiling. He was wearing a robe and he had kind eyes. "I'm not going to hurt you, young lady. I am here to answer questions and provide whatever information I can to assist you in your..." His voice trailed off. He was looking at Skulduggery. "My, oh my. You're a skeleton."

"I am."

"As I live and breathe... figuratively speaking, of course, as I neither live nor breathe. But a *skeleton*, and a *talking* skeleton at that!"

"I *am* very impressive," Skulduggery said. "Who are you?"

"My name is Oisin and I am here to answer whatever questions you may have."

"Well that's good news, because we're looking for a few answers."

"How did you manage that then?" Oisin asked.

"I'm sorry?"

"Becoming a skeleton. That's a new one on me."

"Well, it's a long story."

Oisin waved his hand. "Better not tell me. This Stone will only work for a short while before it needs to be charged. I don't have a lot of time to give you the answers you seek."

"Then we'd better start."

"Yes, we had better. Was it painful, though? Losing your flesh?"

"I, uh, I don't mean to be rude, Oisin, but aren't you the one supposed to be *answering* questions? Not asking them?"

Oisin laughed. "I admit, I'm a little too curious for my own good. On the other hand, I do have an in-depth knowledge of the Stories of the Ancients, so in many ways, I'm the ideal candidate. Better suited to this than my colleagues, believe me. Before we get started, could I ask what century this is?"

"The twenty-first," Stephanie said.

"Twenty-first?" he repeated, laughing with delight. "Oh, my! So this is what the future looks like, eh? Kind of... gloomy and cluttered. I always thought it'd be *brighter*, you know? So what's been happening in the world?"

"You... you want us to tell you everything you missed?"

"Well, not *everything*. Just the high points. What language am I speaking, by the way?"

Stephanie frowned. "English."

"English, eh? Marvellous. I've never spoken English before. How does it sound?"

"Uh, fine, I suppose. Does the stone translate what you're saying?"

"Yes, it does. I could have used something like this on my travels, I'll tell you that much. It would have really impressed the ladies!" He started to chuckle, then stopped. "Not that I travelled far. Or at all. I don't trust boats, you see. If nature had intended us to travel across water, we would have been provided with fins."

"Can we ask you a question?" Skulduggery asked. "Again, I don't want to be rude, but if the Stone runs out of power before we learn what we need..."

The old man clapped his hands and rubbed them together. "Of course, my boy! Say no more! Ask me your first question!"

"You're an expert on the Ancients?"

"Yes, I am. I'm the one charged with the task of documenting their existence. It's a great honour, even if it does leave me with precious little time to travel. Not that I would, even if I could. But it'd be nice to have options, you know?"

"Yes... Anyway, we need to know about the Sceptre. We need to know its power."

Oisin nodded. "The Sceptre of the Ancients was created to destroy and destroy it does. There is nothing that will not crumble to dust under its glare."

"Is there any kind of defence against it?"

Oisin shook his head. "No shield, no spell, no barrier. It can't be stopped and it can't be destroyed."

"What about its power source?" Stephanie asked.

"A single crystal, a black crystal, embedded in its hilt, capable of channelling the energy that's poured into it."

"And can the *crystal* be destroyed?"

Oisin gave a little frown. "I've thought about this, actually. I know more about the Sceptre than anyone else since the time of the Ancients, certainly more than any of my colleagues, and while there is no record of a weakness, we have translations of texts that suggest the crystal can be destroyed from within."

"How?" Stephanie asked.

"I, um... I don't really know."

"Who created the Sceptre?" Skulduggery asked.

Oisin puffed out his chest. "'The Sceptre was created by the

Ancients as a weapon to be used against their gods. For one year they toiled, out of sight and in darkness, so that the gods could not see what they were creating.'"

His chest deflated and he smiled. "That's a direct quote from one of the first texts we found. I found it, actually. The others were so jealous. That's probably why they didn't want me to be the one to answer your questions."

Stephanie frowned. "You're not supposed to be here?"

"We had a vote. I voted for me. No one else did. They're just jealous. They said I'd waste time, talk too much. So I stole the stone and went away for a few days to imprint it with my consciousness. They can't imprint anything over it, you see. And now here I am." He beamed, then his whole body faded, became suddenly transparent, and his beaming smile vanished. "Ah. Time seems to be running out. If you have any more questions..."

"Who created the crystal?" Skulduggery asked quickly.

"Well, if you'll allow me to quote from the text that I discovered: 'The Faceless Ones created the crystal and the crystal sang to the Faceless Ones when an enemy neared. But when the Ancients approached the crystal was silent, and it did not sing to the Faceless Ones, and the Faceless Ones did not know it was taken.'"

"So their security system had a blind spot," Stephanie said.

"It looks that way," Oisin said, nodding. His image grew even fainter, and he held up a hand and gazed through it. "This is sort of unnerving."

"The Sceptre has returned," Skulduggery said.

Oisin looked up. "What?"

"It was uncovered recently, then hidden again. We need to know how to find it."

"Oh my," Oisin said. "If the wrong sort of person takes possession of the Sceptre..."

"It'll be bad, we know. Oisin, how do we find it?"

The old man vanished for a moment, then flickered back into sight. "I don't know, dear boy. Who hid it?"

"My uncle," Stephanie said. "He realised it was too powerful for anyone to own."

"A wise man, it seems. Of course, a truly wise man would return it to the place he found it. Failing that, somewhere similar."

Skulduggery straightened. "Of course."

A smile popped up on Oisin's face. "Have I helped you?"

"You have. I know where it is. Thank you, Oisin."

Oisin nodded proudly. "I knew I could do this. I knew I could answer questions and not talk too much. That's what I told them, right before they called for a vote, I said, listen, I can—"

And he vanished and the Echo Stone stopped glowing.

Stephanie looked at Skulduggery. "Well?"

"Gordon followed the example of the Last of the Ancients, and buried the Sceptre deep within the earth. It's in the caves."

"What caves?"

"Beneath Gordon's land is a network of caves and tunnels, stretching for miles in each direction. It's a death trap, even for the most powerful sorcerer."

"Why?"

"There are creatures in those caves who feed off magic. It would be the safest place to hide the Sceptre. I should have thought of it sooner."

Beneath Gordon's house, a world of magic and wonder Stephanie never knew was there. Bit by bit, she was seeing how close magic had been to her when she was growing up, if only she had known where to look. It was such a strange sensation – but what had Skulduggery told her when they were about to enter the Sanctuary? *Better get used to that feeling.*

Skulduggery closed his hand over the puzzle box and the top slid over, hiding the Echo Stone once again.

"Maybe Oisin has more information," Stephanie said. "How long does it take to recharge the stone?"

"About a year."

She blinked. "Ah. Well... OK then, that's probably a little too long. Still, who knows what else he could help people with? I'm sure it'll be invaluable to, you know, folks who are interested in history. Historians, like."

"Actually, we can't tell anyone we were here."

"You could tell Ghastly. I'm sure he'd forgive the little trespass if you told him what we'd found."

"Not really. See, this is his family's chamber. It's a sacred thing. Us being here is inexcusable."

"What? You said this was just like a storage shed. You didn't say anything about it being *sacred*."

"Now you know why I have difficulty keeping friends."

Skulduggery put the box back where he had found it. Stephanie was still staring at him.

"Is this disrespectful?" she asked. "Is this like dancing on someone's grave?"

"A little worse then that," he admitted. "It's like digging up that grave, taking out the body, rifling through its pockets and *then* dancing on the whole thing. It's a little more than disrespectful."

"Then yes," she said as he walked over, "I can see why you have difficulty keeping friends."

Skulduggery waved his hand and every candle in the chamber flickered out. They were plunged into darkness. Stephanie opened the door and peeked out. The corridor was long and silent and empty. She stepped out and Skulduggery followed, closing the door behind them.

They crept along the corridor, up the stone steps and out of the wood and iron door. They moved quickly through the gallery. The corners were the worst, as they were always expecting a vampire to round them just as they approached. They were nearing the main hall when Skulduggery held up his hand.

Ahead of them, crouching in the middle of the corridor, was a vampire.

Stephanie stopped breathing. Its back was to them, so they moved backwards, careful not to make a sound. They were just turning when Stephanie saw something out of the corner of her eye. She clutched Skulduggery's arm.

The other vampire was approaching from the opposite direction.

They sank behind a marble pillar, trapped. Across from them was an archway leading into another section of the gallery, but Stephanie was pretty sure that even if they made it through without being seen, they'd be cut off. Their only way out was back in the main hall, with the harness, but their chances of making it without being torn to pieces were getting slimmer with every moment. Skulduggery had his powers, and he had his gun, but she knew he didn't hold out much hope that he'd be able to fend off *one* of those creatures, let alone two.

He turned to her, hand raised. One finger, pointing at her, then pointing at the ground. *Stay.* That finger, pointing at himself, then pointing at the arch. *Go.*

Stephanie's eyes widened and she shook her head but now that finger was pressed to his mouth. If he'd had lips, she knew his finger would be on them. She didn't want to, she didn't want to agree to this, but she knew she had no choice.

Skulduggery took his gun from his jacket and passed it to her, and gave her a nod, and then immediately sprang up and lunged for the arch.

The vampire approaching from behind saw him and broke into a run. The vampire up ahead turned and sprang off its haunches, and Stephanie shrank back as it passed the pillar and took off through the archway, joining the hunt for the intruder.

The gun was surprisingly heavy in her hand as Stephanie crept out and started running for the main hall. Her footsteps echoed loudly in the dark corridors but she didn't care – the only thing going through her mind was the fact that she needed to get out. She took each corner quickly, knowing the threat was behind her, and every time she took a corner she let herself glance back.

Empty corridor. Nothing coming for her. Not yet.

She was approaching the Main Hall. Just a few more turns and she'd be there. She tucked the gun into her coat – she'd need both hands to strap herself into the harness. She turned the next corner and skidded to a stop.

No. No, this couldn't be right.

She looked up at the blank wall, her eyes wide. This couldn't be right. This wall should not have been here.

She'd taken a wrong turn. She'd taken a wrong turn in this stupid gallery and now she didn't know where she was. She was lost.

She turned away from the dead end, wanting to scream at herself in frustration. She hurried back the way she had come, glancing through every arch and doorway she passed, looking for something she recognised. Everything looked the same in the gloom. Why weren't there any signs? Where were the signs?

There was an intersecting corridor up ahead. Could that be it? Stephanie tried remembering their trail from the hall to the iron door and mentally reversing it. Had they turned at an intersecting corridor? She cursed herself for not paying attention, cursed herself for relying on Skulduggery to lead the way. They must have come from there. Every turn behind her seemed to lead to the dead end, so they *must* have come from there.

She was ten paces from the intersecting corridor when the vampire emerged from a small hall up ahead. It saw her instantly. She didn't even have time to duck down.

The corridor was ten paces away. The vampire was about thirty paces beyond that. She couldn't go back. If she went back she'd be cut off. She had to go forward. She didn't have a choice.

Stephanie bolted. The vampire kicked off and bounded towards her. It was going to cover the thirty paces faster than she would cover the ten. They ran straight at each other and the vampire leaped. Stephanie dropped and slid beneath it and she felt the rushing air as it passed overhead. She came out of the slide on her feet and twisted her body, then sprinted down the intersecting corridor. This was it.

She recognised the statue. Only a few more turns.

She heard the vampire behind her. Every corner she turned cost her precious moments, but the vampire just leaped to the outer wall and sprang diagonally to the wall beyond the corner.

It was closing the distance between them.

Stephanie burst through the doors to the main hall and Skulduggery was there, launching himself at the vampire as it reached for her. They crashed backwards and tumbled.

"Get out of here!" Skulduggery shouted, kicking the vampire away and scrambling to his feet.

Stephanie grabbed the harness and hit the button. Her arms were almost jerked out of their sockets as the harness withdrew. She rose to the skylight too fast, and when the harness hit the top she lost her grip. She managed to get one hand around the edge of the skylight as her body swung wildly.

Her other hand clawed on and she gritted her teeth and pulled herself up. Her head and shoulders emerged into the night air, and she hauled herself up the rest of the way to tumble out on to the roof. Fighting to catch her breath, she immediately went back to the skylight and looked down, just in time to see the vampire leap.

She cried out and fell backwards as the vampire burst through the closed section of the skylight, showering her with glass. It hit the roof in a crouch. Stephanie didn't even have time to get to her feet before it dived at her.

She turned away and its claws raked across her coat but didn't penetrate the material, although the impact slammed her to the roof again. The vampire overshot but spun as soon as it landed, snarling. Its fangs dripped with saliva and its eyes locked on to hers.

For a moment neither of them made a move, then Stephanie slowly got to her hands and knees. The vampire hissed, but she didn't break eye contact. She tucked her feet beneath her and squatted. The vampire was waiting for her to make a sudden move. The gun was in her pocket but she didn't go for it.

Stephanie moved slowly. She kept her eyes open, didn't blink, didn't do anything that might give it an excuse to resume its attack. Her knees straightened, though she stayed bent over. She took her first step, to her left. The vampire moved with her.

Its eyes blazed with sheer animal ferocity. All it wanted to do was rip her apart. All it wanted was her complete and utter annihilation. She forced herself to keep calm.

"Easy, boy," she said softly and the vampire snapped at the air. Its claws clicked against themselves. Even though they hadn't pierced her coat, her back was throbbing in pain. She knew that if it hadn't been for whatever material this coat was made from, that single swipe would have killed her.

The vampire began moving towards her. Stephanie started to back away but the moment she tried moving her foot behind her, the vampire's hackles rose. She froze. If it leaped from that distance it would be on her before she knew what was happening. It kept coming, moving slowly, stalking its prey.

The second skylight exploded and then everything was happening too fast.

The vampire broke its eye-lock and lunged but Stephanie was already moving, twisting to the side as the claws lacerated the space where she had just been. The other vampire was on the roof and closing in, and Stephanie sprinted for the edge of the building and she jumped.

Her legs hit branches and she flipped over and was crashing headlong into the tree and falling. She smacked from one branch to the next, each impact spinning her and making her cry out. She hit a branch with her ribs and the breath rushed out of her and still she fell, then there were no more branches and for a moment it was just her and the sound of rushing air, and then the ground slammed into her from behind.

Stephanie lay on the grass, trying to breathe. She could see the tree; she could see the gallery; she could see the sky. Something was falling towards her. Two things, two figures, dropping from the edge of the building. The vampires hit the ground and came at her.

The window to her left shattered and the security alarm pierced the night. Skulduggery landed in front of her. He thrust his hand out and the air shimmered and he caught one of the vampires, sending it hurtling back. The second one kept coming and Skulduggery threw fire at it but it leaped, cleared the flame and landed with both feet on Skulduggery's chest. They went down and Stephanie's body started obeying her again. She got up, still struggling to breathe. The vampire swiped and Skulduggery's shirt parted and he cried out in pain.

Stephanie wrapped both arms around the vampire's neck and pulled back. It hissed and flailed and Stephanie stumbled back to avoid its claws. Skulduggery sat up and he pressed his hand against the vampire. The vampire shot backwards like it had been fired from a cannon. It hit the wall of the building with a sickening thwack and fell to the ground and didn't get up. Stephanie grabbed Skulduggery's arm and dragged him to his feet, and they ran for the car.

13

THE RED RIGHT HAND

"How are you?"

Stephanie shrugged and managed not to wince. Her entire body ached. "I'm good," she lied.

Skulduggery glanced at her as he drove. "Are you hurt? Are you injured?"

"No, just a bruise or two. I'm fine, really. You don't have to worry about me."

"Stephanie, you jumped off a building."

"Yes, but the branches broke my fall. Every one of them."

"And how *were* the branches?"

"A lot unlike pillows."

"You could have been killed."

"But I wasn't."

"But you could have been."

"But I wasn't."

"I'm not denying that you make a good point, but the fact is you could have been. I've already lost a dear friend to all this and I don't want that to happen again."

She looked at him. "Are you saying you'd be very upset if I died?"

"'Very' is such a strong word..."

"Well, if you teach me some magic, maybe I won't get hurt as bad next time."

"You said you weren't hurt."

"Are you kidding? I jumped off a building, of course I'm hurt."

"Stephanie—"

"Yes, Skulduggery?"

"You can be really annoying at times."

"I know. So where are we going?"

"We're going to at least *find* the doorway to the caves. Then we'll concentrate on finding the key to open it."

Half an hour later they were driving into Gordon's estate.

Stephanie climbed stiffly out of the Canary Car and followed Skulduggery inside.

The cellar was chilly and dark, and the single bulb hanging amid cobwebs wasn't doing its job very well. Countless years' worth of junk was collecting dust down here, and from somewhere in the dark corners came the occasional scuffle of rats. Stephanie wasn't scared of rats as a rule, but she wasn't too keen on them either, so she stayed away from the corners.

Skulduggery had no such qualms. He examined the walls, scanning their surface as he moved sideways along them. Now and then he'd tap the wall, mutter to himself and move on.

"Is this the same as the way into the Sanctuary?" Stephanie asked. "Are you looking for a secret passageway?"

"You watch too many haunted-house movies," he said.

"But *are* you looking for a secret passageway?"

"Yes," he admitted. "But that's just a coincidence."

She pulled up the sleeve of her coat, revealing an ugly bruise on her arm, and covered it up again before Skulduggery glanced over.

"Did Gordon build the passage?" she asked.

"No, it was included in the original designs. A few hundred years ago, this was a sorcerer's house."

"And he built a secret passageway to the caves? I thought you said the caves were a death trap for sorcerers."

"I did say that, yes."

"So why did he build himself a short cut? Was he a stupid sorcerer?"

"No, he just wasn't a very nice one. He used to drag his enemies down there and leave them to whatever creatures were hungriest."

"What a charming history. I can see why my uncle bought the place."

"*Aha.*"

Stephanie moved closer. Skulduggery's hand was flat against the wall. He moved it and she could see a slight indentation, almost invisible to the naked eye.

"That's the lock?"

"Yes, this is one of those good old-fashioned key-required locks – the kind a spell won't open. Damn it."

"Can you break it?"

"I *could* break it, but then it wouldn't work and we couldn't get the door open."

"I meant break *through* it."

"That would work if the door was in the same place as the lock, but things are rarely that straightforward."

"So we need the key."

"We need the key."

"I don't suppose we'll find it on one of Gordon's keyrings."

"Indeed. This is not a regular key we're looking for."

"We don't have to solve a puzzle to get to it, do we?"

"We may."

Stephanie groaned. "How come nothing's ever simple?"

"Every solution to every problem is simple. It's the distance between the two wherein the mystery lies."

They turned off the light and climbed the stairs out of the dank mustiness of the cellar. They walked into the living room and a man in a suit, a suit that looked almost Victorian in design, turned to them.

He had black hair and thin lips and his right hand, which was skinless, glistened with blood and wet muscle, and before Stephanie could even register surprise Skulduggery was pulling the gun from his jacket. The man moved as gunshots filled the room, stepping to one side and waving his right hand.

She didn't know what he did but it worked, and no bullets hit him.

"Run!" Skulduggery said, pushing her out of the room.

She stumbled and something moved beside her and she turned as another man came at her. There was something wrong with him – something wrong with his skin, with his features – they didn't look real: they looked almost papery. She tried to hit it, but it was like hitting a bag of air. A fist swung at her, but unlike its body the fist was heavy and solid, and it snapped her head back. She staggered and it reached for her, but then Skulduggery was there, hurling it away.

Three more of them came through the front door. Stephanie ran to the stairs, Skulduggery covering her escape. Halfway up she looked back as the man in the suit strolled into the hall. She shouted a warning and Skulduggery turned to face him but it was too late. Purple vapour gathered in the man's left palm and he released it in a stream that flowed into Skulduggery and arced out behind him and above, flowing back into the man's other hand, forming a circle. Skulduggery dropped to his knees, tried to raise the gun but couldn't hold it, and it fell to the floor.

"Take him," the man said, cutting off the purple stream. Skulduggery sagged and three of the paper men grabbed him, started dragging him out of the house. The man motioned to the fourth. "You, kill the girl."

And he walked out.

Stephanie sprinted to the landing, the papery thing clumping up the stairs behind her. She ran to Gordon's dark study, slammed the door and pushed over one of the bookcases. It toppled and crashed and books spilled across the floor.

The door opened a fraction and hit the bookcase. Heavy fists started to pound on it from the other side.

She went to the window, opened it and looked down. Even if she made the drop without breaking her legs, she'd land right in front of the man with the red hand. She backed off, looked around for a weapon.

The bookcase slowly scraped across the floor. The door opened wider. Stephanie turned, moved behind the desk and hid. The pounding continued. She peered out. She could see a papery arm now, reaching around. Then a shoulder, and a head. She ducked back into hiding.

One last heave and the door was open wide enough for the thing to step over the fallen bookcase. Stephanie stopped breathing. She peeked out. It crossed to the window and leaned out, hands on the sill.

Stephanie rose and launched herself forward. It heard her and tried to turn but she slammed into it. Its heavy hands slipped off the window sill and dragged it through, and Stephanie reached down, grabbed its lower leg and hauled. The thing tried to reach back through the window but it was too late, and out it went with a faint rustle of paper.

It landed in a heap and she saw the man in the suit glare up at her. He waved his arm and she threw herself away from the window as the air turned purple and the window exploded. Glass shards rained down on her back, but they didn't tear through the coat.

She lay where she was, hands over her head, until she heard a car start up. Then she got up, glass and splinters of wood falling from her, and reached the window just in time to see the silver car leave the estate. They'd left her, obviously deciding it wasn't worth the effort to make sure she was dead.

Stephanie pulled the crumpled business card from her pocket, got out her phone and dialled the number. The call was picked up almost immediately. She spoke urgently.

"I need help. They've taken Skulduggery."

"Tell me where you are," China Sorrows said. "I'll send someone to pick you up."

14

ELEMENTAL MAGIC

China Sorrows was very still. She sat with her legs crossed, hands flat on the arms of the chair. The sounds of the city at night did not seep into her apartment – they were alone in here, the only two people left on the face of the earth. Stephanie watched her and waited.

The apartment was vast, occupying the space across the hall from her library. Stephanie had leaped out of the car China had sent, run up the stairs and had been directed in here by the man in the bow tie. No time had been lost.

Skulduggery was in danger and they needed to get him back *now*.

China spoke at last. "How can you be sure it was Serpine?"

"What?" Stephanie said, exasperated. "Of course it was Serpine! Who else could it have been?"

A delicate shrug of delicate shoulders. "We have to be sure, that's all."

"I *am* sure, OK?"

China looked at her, and Stephanie felt ashamed of her impatience. She lowered her eyes and closed her mouth. She was so sore, her body was so sore, but it was all right now because she was safe, and China would know what to do. Everything would be OK. Stephanie would wait for her to make a decision, no matter how long she deliberated, and she felt sure that Skulduggery would be safe and well. Even if he wasn't, what did it matter? China knew what was best, and if she wanted to wait, then Stephanie would be happy to wait with her.

No, she said to herself, *that's the spell, that's China's spell working on me*. She dragged her eyes up, met China's gaze and thought she saw a flicker of surprise.

"What are you going to do?" Stephanie asked.

China rose from the chair in one graceful movement. "I will see to it," she said. "You should go home, dear: you look dreadful."

Stephanie felt herself blush. "I'd rather stay," she said.

"It could take some time before plans are in place. Wouldn't you be more comfortable in familiar surroundings?"

Stephanie didn't like disagreeing with China but she couldn't go home, not while Skulduggery was in trouble. "I'd rather stay," she repeated softly.

"Very well," China said with a small smile. "I must leave, but I'll return when I have news."

"Can I come with you?"

"I'm afraid not, child." Stephanie nodded, hiding her disappointment.

China left the building, accompanied by the man in the bow tie. Stephanie stayed in the apartment for a while, but despite the fact that it was almost three in the morning, she couldn't relax. There was no TV and the only book in a language she could understand was a leather-bound address book on a small table.

She crossed the hall and stepped into the library. She passed a man in a porcelain mask, too engrossed in his reading to notice her. She walked slowly, reading the titles on the spines of the books, trying to keep her mind occupied. If she could find something here, a book that had what she needed, then maybe she wouldn't be so helpless next time she went up against

Serpine, or anyone else. If she'd had even the slightest bit of power, she might have been able to help Skulduggery.

Stephanie followed one shelf to its end then chose another one, wandering deeper into the labyrinth. She couldn't work out the system – the books weren't arranged alphabetically, or by author, or even by topic. It all seemed completely random.

"You look lost."

She turned. The young woman who had addressed her slipped a book back into its place. She had tousled blonde hair and she was pretty, but her eyes were hard and she wore a sleeveless tunic that showed her strong arms. She spoke with an English accent.

"I'm looking for a book," Stephanie said, unsure.

"This would seem to be the place for that."

"Are there any books here on magic?"

"They're *all* books on magic," the young woman replied.

"I mean learning magic. I just need something. *Anything*."

"You have no one to teach you?"

"Not yet. I don't know how to find anything in here."

For a moment, Stephanie felt like she was being studied. Finally the young woman spoke again. "My name is Tanith Low."

"Oh, hi. I'm afraid I can't tell you my name. No offence."

"None taken. The books are arranged in terms of experience. These are far too advanced for someone without instruction. Two rows over, you might find what you need."

Stephanie thanked her and Tanith walked away, disappearing in the maze of shelves. Stephanie found the section she was referring to and started scanning the titles. *An Introductory Guide to Monster Hunting, The Sorcery Doctrines, A History So Far, Three Names...*

Stephanie took the *Three Names* book from the shelf, and flicked through it. She came to the part on Taken Names, a chunk of the book that went on for roughly 200 pages, and scanned the headings in bold print. She turned pages, skimmed paragraphs, looking for anything that stood out. The best advice it had for taking a name was this: "*The name you take should fit you, define you, and already be known to you.*"

She put the book back, unimpressed, and scanned a few more titles before she found it: *Elemental Magic*. She took it down, opened it and started reading. This was it. This was what she was looking for. She found an old chair in one corner and sat, bringing her legs up under her.

Her mobile phone was perched on the arm of the chair.

Stephanie held one hand closed, trying to think of the space between her hand and the phone as a series of interlocking objects. Moving one would move another, which would move another, which would move the phone. She focused, opened her hand slowly and then snapped open her palm, like she had seen Skulduggery do.

Nothing happened.

She made a fist, then tried again. The phone stayed where it was. Just like it had done the previous fifty times she'd tried.

"How's it going?" She looked up as Tanith Low approached.

"You're starting off too big," Tanith said. "A phone's too heavy. A paper clip would be enough."

"I don't have a paper clip," Stephanie said.

Tanith took the book from her, opened it and balanced it on the arm of the chair. "Use that," she said.

Stephanie frowned. "But that's even heavier than the phone."

"Not the book. Just the page."

"Oh," Stephanie said. She concentrated again, flexed her fingers and splayed her hand. The page didn't turn. It didn't even lift.

"It takes time," Tanith said. "And patience."

"I don't have time," Stephanie said bitterly. "And I've never had patience."

Tanith shrugged. "There's always the possibility that you just can't do magic. It's one thing to know it exists – it's quite another to be able to do it yourself."

"I suppose," Stephanie said.

"That's some bruise you've got there."

Stephanie glanced at her arm, to where her sleeve was pulled back. "I had a bit of trouble," she said.

"So I see. Did you give as good as you got?"

"Not really," Stephanie admitted. "But most of the bruising was done by a tree anyway, so..."

"I've fought just about every type of opponent you could name," Tanith said, "but I've never been attacked by a tree. Well done."

"Thank you."

Tanith dug into her pocket and brought out a piece of yellow porous rock. "Run a bath, let this dissolve. A few minutes in there, the bruises will be gone."

Stephanie took the rock. "Thank you," she said, and Tanith shrugged.

"I don't want to scare you, but this mightn't be the best time for someone to start learning magic. Bad things are happening."

Stephanie didn't say anything. She didn't know anything about Tanith, and she didn't know how many sides there were in the coming conflict. She wasn't about to start trusting perfect strangers.

"Thanks for the rock," she said.

"Not a problem," Tanith responded. "Us warriors have to look out for one another."

Stephanie saw movement through the stacks – the man in the bow tie was back. Which meant China had returned.

"I have to go," she said at once, getting up off the chair.

She found China in the apartment, her back to Stephanie as she approached.

"Have you told the Elders?" Stephanie asked.

"Word has been sent," China said without turning.

"You sent *word*? That's it?"

"Do not presume to question me, child."

Stephanie glared at her. "I really wish you wouldn't call me child."

China turned. "And I really wish you would pick a name, so I wouldn't have to."

"Why aren't we going to the rescue?"

"Going to the rescue?" China said with a laugh. "On our horses, is that right? With bugles sounding and flags flying? You think that's how it works?"

"Skulduggery has come to my rescue."

"Well, they don't make them like him any more, do they?"

"Sending word isn't good enough. Meritorious has to be told. Tell him that we need Skulduggery to get the Sceptre; tell him that without Skulduggery, Serpine will destroy everything. Tell him whatever you want, but we *have* to make the Elders act!"

"And then what? They call the Cleavers to action, they call their allies together, and then we all go merrily along to war? Child, you know nothing about war. You think it's big and it's loud and it's good versus evil. It's not. War is a delicate thing: it requires precision. It requires timing."

"We don't have time."

"Not so. Time is in short supply, but we still have it."

"So you're *delaying*? Why?"

"I cannot have chaos erupting around me until I am prepared for it. I am a collector. I am an observer. I don't participate. My resources, and my standing, must be secure before I can allow the uncertainty of war to crash down upon us."

"And what about Skulduggery? While you're waiting for the right moment to tell everyone Serpine is the bad guy, Skulduggery might be killed!"

The hesitation that flickered across China's face was barely noticeable. "There are casualties in every conflict."

Stephanie hated her. She turned and stormed back to the open door.

"Where are you going?" China called after her.

"I'm going to do what you're too scared to do yourself!"

"No, you're not."

The door slammed shut before Stephanie reached it and she spun around. China was walking towards her, her exquisite face perfectly calm.

"You have no right," China said softly, "to plunge us all into war. Who are you to decide when we fight? Why should you decide when we die?"

"I just want to help my friend," Stephanie said, taking a step back.

"Skulduggery is not your friend."

She narrowed her eyes. "You don't know what you're talking about."

"And you don't know *him*, child. He has anger in him like you have never seen. He has hatred in him that you would never dream about. There is not one place he would rather be than where he is right now."

"You're crazy."

"He told you how he died then?"

"Yes," Stephanie said. "He was killed by one of Mevolent's men."

"Nefarian Serpine killed him," China said. "He tortured him first, purely for fun. He ridiculed him and he stripped him of his powers. And then he pointed at him. Did you know that's all it takes, with that red right hand of his? For him to *point* and then it's all over?"

Agonising death, Skulduggery had said. Stephanie hadn't realised he had felt it himself. She shook her head defiantly. "That doesn't change anything."

"When he came back, he fought Mevolent's forces with a single-minded determination – not to defeat evil, but to have his revenge on Mevolent's lackey. Mevolent himself fell, but just as Skulduggery was in a position to claim his vengeance..."

"There was the Truce," Stephanie said slowly.

"And suddenly his enemy was now a protected citizen. Skulduggery has been waiting a long time to get his revenge, and he will risk anyone and anything in order to get it."

Stephanie stood up straighter. "Even if you're right, that doesn't change the fact that he has been the only one investigating my uncle's murder, or that he seems to be the only one around here who cares about what is really going on, or that he has saved my life."

"And put it at risk. Every good thing he has done *for* you has been cancelled out by every bad thing he has done *to* you. You don't owe him anything."

"I'm not going to abandon him."

"It is hardly your choice."

"What are you going to do?" Stephanie challenged.

"I am simply going to ask you to do what I say."

"Then the answer's no."

"My dear Stephanie..."

Stephanie froze. China looked at her. "I've known your name since before I met you, child. Your uncle spoke of you often."

Stephanie lunged for the door but it was no use.

"Stephanie," China said softly. Stephanie's hands dropped to her sides and she turned. "Tell no one of this."

Stephanie felt it inside her and knew she would obey, knew no matter how much she raged against it, she would obey. She had no choice. So she nodded as tears stung her eyes and China smiled that beautiful smile of hers.

15

THE TORTURE ROOM

The moon was out and the stars were twinkling and it really was a beautiful night for pain.

Serpine descended into the castle's cold, dank depths and strode through the stone corridors. Already, he was beginning to smile. He came to the heavy wooden door and paused with his hand over the latch, savouring the deliciousness of the moment.

The latch lifted and Serpine stepped in. "Here we are again," he said.

Skulduggery Pleasant raised his head, practically the only part of his body he could move. Serpine had placed a binding spell on the shackles that secured him to the chair and so, unable to use magic, the detective could only watch as Serpine closed the door behind him.

"Life is a cycle, isn't it, Skulduggery? We are all destined to repeat ourselves, over and over. You, at my mercy. Me, merciless."

"You, talking," the detective said. "I thought you'd have grown out of the whole villainy thing by now, Nefarian."

Serpine smiled as he sat in the wooden chair opposite. The room was small, with stone walls and a single light bulb hanging from the ceiling. "Being a respectable citizen wasn't for me, but then you knew that, didn't you? You warned them about me, but they didn't listen. That must have been annoying, for the Elders not to even respect you enough to take you seriously."

"I think it's because I'm always smiling."

"Perhaps you're right. Oh, Skulduggery, what am I going to do with you?"

"Untie me?"

Serpine laughed. "Maybe later. We always seem to be at each other's throats, don't we?"

"Let me ask you a question. Let's pretend, just for a moment, that we live in your world, where things are crazy and the Faceless Ones are real. When you call them, what do you hope to gain? A pat on the head?"

"How my lords and masters will reward me for my servitude is up to them. I would never presume to guess."

"The door is closed, Nefarian. Just us two guys in here, chatting. What's in it for you?"

Serpine leaned in. "I get to be by their side when they raze this world, when they expunge the stain of humanity. And when it's over, I get to bask in their terrible glory."

Skulduggery nodded. "Yeah, I haven't a clue what you just said." Serpine laughed.

"You're going to fall," Skulduggery continued.

"Really?"

"You're going to fall hard and I'm going to be there. I'll be the one pushing you."

"Big talk from the man tied to the chair. Or are you even a man? A thing, perhaps? An oddity?"

"They'll come for you."

"Who will? The Elders? Meritorious and his lot? Please. They're too busy worrying about being rude to me."

"Not after this. They're probably at your doorstep as we speak."

Serpine stood, walked behind his captive. "Somehow I don't think they would be able to marshal their forces so quickly. Or so efficiently. No, my old enemy, I think for the moment anyway, we're all alone. And you have something I want."

"A winning sense of style?"

"The key," Serpine said as he walked back into the detective's line of sight.

"Don't know what you're talking about."

Serpine was moving his left hand slightly, like he was conducting music. "Obviously you're not going to just offer up the information, so I think a spot of torture is required."

"Ah," the detective said. "Old times."

"I remember those dark autumn days that I'd while away, cutting you, making you cry out."

"Fun for the whole family."

"You may think my options would be limited as far as torture is concerned, especially now that you don't have skin to cut. But I've picked up a few new tricks that I think you'll enjoy."

Serpine moved his fingers in a wave motion, directing it at the chair he had just been sitting on. The wood creaked and groaned as it expanded and contracted, like it was breathing. The detective couldn't avoid looking at it.

"If I can do that to the chair," Serpine said, enjoying the moment, "think what I can do to bone." There was a loud crack as the chair splintered.

Serpine hunkered down in front of him. "Well, Skulduggery? Where is that tired old defiance – the taunting, the goading? Where are the endless heroic clichés? Aren't you going to look me in the eye and tell me to do my worst?"

"Actually, I was going to ask that you go easy on me. I'm feeling kind of tender today."

Serpine stood, opened his left hand in front of the detective. "This is your one chance. Tell me where the key is."

"OK."

Serpine raised an eyebrow. "Really?"

"No, only joking. Do your worst."

Serpine laughed and his fingers started moving and the detective started screaming.

16

WHAT'S IN A NAME?

Stephanie soaked her elbow in the sink. She had broken off a piece of the rock Tanith Low had given her and dissolved it in the water, filling the sink with bubbles and the Library's restroom with a pungent odour. Whatever the rock was, it was doing its job. The bruises on her arms were fading.

She dried herself with a spotless white towel, let the water gurgle into the drain and allowed herself to sag against the wall.

Her body may have been tired but her mind was alert and racing, surging with anger. She was still furious at herself for being unable to disobey China's instruction. How could China have done that to her, to Skulduggery? After he had trusted her?

No, she reminded herself. He hadn't trusted her. That had been *Stephanie's* mistake, not his. And because she went to China before the Elders, or even Ghastly, now it could be too late to do anything. And it was all her fault.

What had Tanith Low called Stephanie? A warrior? That was laughable. No matter what Tanith had thought she had seen in her, she was wrong. There was nothing warrior-like about her. She ran straight into trouble without thinking, without one moment of hesitation. Not because she was brave or heroic, but because she was *stupid*. Because she didn't want to be left out, because she didn't want to wait. She didn't have a plan, she didn't have a tactic, all she had was a penchant for raising Cain.

It came to her then. Her eyes widened and she stood up straight, a new strength coursing through her limbs.

And just like that, China's command over her was broken.

She needed Ghastly. She didn't really know where he lived so she needed his address, and there was only one way she could think of to get it. She left the restroom, passing the window, realising that it was morning already. She crossed the hall to China's apartment and knocked. No answer. She knocked again.

China wasn't in. Stephanie looked at the door. Nothing special about it. She hadn't noticed anything unusual about it on the other side either, no chains or bolts or extra locks. There could be a locking spell placed on it, and if there was then she'd be wasting her time, but she didn't think there was. Skulduggery had said a locking spell needed to be dismantled every time a door is opened, then cast again. She doubted China would have the patience to do that on a daily basis.

Stephanie took a step back. An ordinary door. An ordinary, flimsy door. It was possible; she knew it was possible. She was tall and strong. This door was all that stood between her and saving Skulduggery. She had strong legs. Her legs were muscled, a swimmer's legs. They were strong. The door was weak. She could do it. She had to do it. She had to save her friend.

Her boot slammed against the door. She kicked again... and again... and again... Her legs were strong. She couldn't fail. Desperation lent her strength. The door was weak and it burst open.

She hurried in, moving right for where she had seen the address book. It wasn't there. It wasn't on the small table. Where was it?

She looked around. China had moved it. Where? Why? Had she known Stephanie would be looking for it? No, there was no way she could have predicted that. Then she had moved it for some other reason, some other ordinary, average reason. She had put it away; she had put it back. Yes, she had put it back in its usual place.

Where would China keep an address book?

Stephanie went to the desk, opening the drawers and rifling through them. Papers, letters, no address book. She turned, eyes scouring the room, aware that China could walk through that broken door at any time. She went to the shelves: no address book. Where?

She moved into the bedroom. There, on the bedside table, the address book. She snatched it up, finding the B's, her finger moving down the page. Bespoke tailors. She memorised the address, dropped the book on the bed and turned to go.

"Hello, dear," China said. She walked in and Stephanie stepped back, wary.

"I saw your handiwork outside," China said. "What did my poor door ever do to you? Did you break anything else while you were here? A vase? A teacup perhaps?"

"Just the door."

"Ah, well, I suppose I should be thankful for small mercies. Did you find what you were looking for, child?"

Stephanie tightened her fist. "Don't call me that."

China laughed. "That look in your eye is almost scary."

"Have you done anything to help Skulduggery, or are you still too busy helping yourself?" asked Stephanie.

"He inspires loyalty, doesn't he?" China said, an eyebrow raised. "You can't be around our Mr Pleasant without liking him, without wanting to fight alongside him. You should have been there during the war, you know. You should have seen him then."

"I just can't understand how you'd betray him like this."

For the first time since she'd known her, China's eyes turned cold. "I haven't betrayed him, child. I may have failed him, but I haven't betrayed him. To betray is to act *against*. I just haven't acted at all."

"Whatever," Stephanie said.

"Not interested in semantics?" China asked, her smile returning. "But of course not. You're a straightforward kind of girl, aren't you?"

"I'm leaving now," Stephanie said as she headed for the door.

"Straightforward," China continued, "but not too bright. Stephanie, would you be a dear and stop?" Stephanie stopped.

"I admire your courage, child, I really do. But rallying a cavalry to go after Skulduggery is just too risky. Too much could go wrong. Now sit in the corner there, like a good little girl."

Stephanie nodded and walked for the door.

"Stop," China ordered. "I said the corner."

Stephanie reached the door and looked back. China was frowning. "I don't understand. How are you able to do this? Stephanie, answer me!"

"I'm not Stephanie," Stephanie answered. "And if you want to keep me here, then you'd better be ready to kill me."

China's frown disappeared. "I don't want to kill you, my dear," she said and the hint of a smile appeared. "So you've finally chosen a name."

"Yeah. And I'm leaving. Right now."

"Maybe you stand some chance after all. Before you go, will you do me the honour of introducing yourself?"

"Of course," Stephanie said right before she walked out of the apartment. "My name is Valkyrie Cain."

Ghastly opened the door, saw Stephanie and nodded.

"I'm sorry if I upset you yesterday," he said. "I realise I have no right to tell you what you can and cannot do, but please believe that I was acting in your best—"

"They have Skulduggery," Stephanie said, interrupting him.

"What?"

"Serpine has him. Last night, he came in with his paper men and they attacked him and took him away with them. We need to tell the Elders."

Ghastly tried a smile to see if she'd return it, to see if she'd admit her joke. Stephanie didn't smile back.

"You don't know if I should be involved in any of this," she said. "That's fine. That's your opinion and that's fine. But let's forget about opinion. Let's look at facts. Serpine has Skulduggery. He's broken the Truce. He believes the Sceptre is real and he has proved that he's willing to kill to get to it. He has to be stopped and I need your help to stop him."

"You saw this? You actually saw Serpine do this?"

"I was there."

He looked at her and nodded. "Then I suppose it's a very good thing you decided to stick around."

Ghastly brought his car around and Stephanie told him exactly what had happened as they sped through the streets to the Sanctuary. The windows were heavily tinted, but even so he had a scarf wrapped around his face and a hat pulled low over his eyes.

The Waxworks Museum hadn't opened yet so they let themselves in the back and hurried through the darkness. Ghastly searched the darkened wall for the switch, found it and the wall parted. Stephanie was the first to reach the bottom of the stairs, and she strode into the Sanctuary. The Administrator hurried up to her, frowning.

"I'm sorry," he said, "you do not have an appointment."

"We're here to see Meritorious."

"The Elders cannot be disturbed," the Administrator insisted. "I must ask you to leave at once."

"It's an emergency," Ghastly said as he joined her, but the Administrator still shook his head.

"All requests to visit the Elders must go through the proper channels," he said, but Stephanie had heard enough. She barged past him, heading for the corridor. Suddenly there was a flash of grey and a Cleaver was before her, holding the blade of his scythe to her throat.

Stephanie froze. There was movement all around her, sound all around her, and the only still things in her world were herself and the Cleaver. She could hear Ghastly threatening the Administrator, threatening the Cleavers, and the Administrator protesting and insisting they leave. Ghastly's voice was rising, becoming angry, telling the Cleaver to lower the weapon, but the Cleaver was still and silent, a statue. Stephanie could see her burnished reflection in his visor. She didn't dare move.

Before the situation could spiral out of control, before

Stephanie's head became separated from her body, the Administrator gave in and agreed to ask Meritorious if he would receive visitors.

At a nod, the Cleaver stepped back and swung the scythe down by his side and behind him, making the mere sheathing of the weapon into an art form.

Stephanie backed off, moving slowly, but the Cleaver had gone back to his post like nothing had happened.

They stayed in the foyer while the Administrator hurried off, and presently they heard footsteps approaching. Eachan Meritorious entered and looked mildly surprised when he laid eyes on Ghastly.

"Mr Bespoke," he said, coming forward. "Will wonders never cease?"

"Grand Mage," Ghastly said as they shook hands. "You've already met Valkyrie Cain, I think."

"So you chose a name after all," Meritorious said with a slightly disapproving look. "I hope your Mr Pleasant knows what he's doing."

"Skulduggery's been captured," Stephanie blurted out. "Serpine has him."

"Not this again."

"It's true," Ghastly said.

Meritorious peered at him. "You saw it yourself?"

"Well," Ghastly said, hesitating, "no, but—"

Meritorious waved his hand. "Skulduggery Pleasant is an excellent detective, and we value his help and his expertise on many difficult cases. But when it comes to Nefarian Serpine, he does not have his usual detached perspective."

"Serpine has captured him!" Stephanie insisted.

"My dear, I like you. And I can see why Skulduggery likes you. You are a frighteningly upfront person and this is a quality to be admired. However, you are new to our culture and our ways, and you have heard a decidedly skewed version of our history. Serpine is not the villain he once was."

"I was there," Stephanie said, struggling to remain calm. "Serpine came with his paper creatures and they took him."

This made Meritorious pause. "Paper creatures?"

"Well, it *looked* like they were made out of paper."

He nodded slowly. "Hollow Men. Minions of Serpine. Terrible things, bloated by stink and evil."

"Now do you believe me? We need to get him back."

"Grand Mage," Ghastly said, "my friend is in danger. I know you don't want it to be true, but the Truce has been broken. Serpine and the sorcerers allied with him will waste no time in seizing power. The Elders must act *now*."

"On what authority?" Meritorious asked. "On the word of a girl I barely know?"

"I'm not lying," said Stephanie.

"But you may be mistaken."

"I'm not. Serpine wants the Sceptre and he thinks Skulduggery can get it for him."

"The Sceptre is a fairy tale—"

"The Sceptre is real," Stephanie said, cutting him off. "It's real enough that Serpine is after it, and he killed the two men you had spying on him so that you wouldn't find out about it until it was too late."

Meritorious hesitated for a moment. "Miss Cain, if you're wrong, and we move against Serpine now, then we are starting a war we are not ready for."

"I'm sorry," Stephanie said, seeing the trepidation in the Elder's eyes and speaking softly now. "But the war has already started."

The paper clip lay on the tabletop and didn't move. Stephanie focused, flexed her fingers and then thrust her palm towards it, trying to genuinely believe that thin air was nothing more than interlocking objects. The paper clip still didn't move. She nudged it, just to make sure it wasn't stuck or anything. Ghastly entered the room.

"We're ready to go," he said. "You're sure you want to do this?"

"Very sure." She put the paper clip in her pocket and nodded to the door behind him. "Is there an army out there?"

"Uh, not quite."

"How many?"

He hesitated. "Two."

"Two? He has an army of Cleavers and he gives us *two*?"

"Sending any more would arouse suspicion," Ghastly said. "Meritorious needs a little time to contact Morwenna Crow and Sagacious Tome and convince them that action is necessary, and until he does, this rescue mission is strictly unofficial."

"Please tell me they're as good as Skulduggery said they are?"

"Both their uniforms and their scythes can ward off the majority of magical attacks, and there aren't many deadlier in close combat."

"*Close* combat?" Stephanie said with a frown. "What about throwing fireballs and stuff? Are they Elementals or Adepts?"

Ghastly cleared his throat. "Neither, actually. Magic corrupts certain people, and Cleavers need to be seen as completely impartial, so..."

"So they're not magic? At all?"

"They have *some* magic, but it just adds to their combat abilities. They're quite strong and very fast."

"So what are they going to do? Run around Serpine until he gets dizzy and falls over?"

"If it all goes according to plan, Serpine won't even know we're there."

"And what are the chances of that happening?"

Ghastly looked at her and for a moment he held his ground. Then he looked away. "They're not great," he admitted.

"Exactly."

He looked up again. "But Mr Bliss has offered us his help."

"He's coming?" Stephanie asked nervously. She didn't like the idea of going anywhere with Mr Bliss.

"Not him," Ghastly said, "but he's sending someone. Five is a good number; we can sneak in, grab Skulduggery, sneak out. Simple."

The door opened behind them and Meritorious appeared. "I have arranged your transport," he said.

They followed him up out of the Sanctuary and exited the Waxworks from the back, where a large van was parked. As soon as Meritorious emerged into the sunlight, two Cleavers walked forward. They took the scythes from their sheathes before they climbed in. Stephanie hoped the van didn't go over any potholes or she'd be skewered before they even reached Serpine's castle.

Another person walked forward, a person she recognised from the library.

"Tanith Low," Meritorious said, "this is Ghastly Bespoke and Valkyrie Cain."

"We've met," Tanith said, giving Stephanie a polite nod. She carried a sword in a black scabbard, its lacquered surface criss-crossed with nicks and marks.

"Mr Bliss sent you?" Ghastly asked.

"He did. He thought I could be of use."

"That's quite a recommendation."

"He just wants this business to be over with as soon as possible," Tanith said. "I'm at your disposal for the duration."

"Then let's go."

Tanith climbed into the van and Ghastly got behind the wheel.

"Good luck," Meritorious said as Stephanie was about to join them.

"Thank you."

He shrugged. "You'll need it."

17

A FABULOUS RESCUE INDEED

The rescue team stood by the side of the road and looked up at the wall surrounding Serpine's land. It was maybe three times as tall as Stephanie. Beyond it lay woodland, and beyond that, the castle.

It occurred to Stephanie that if they didn't get Skulduggery back, it was all over. Serpine would get the Sceptre and the Faceless Ones would return. The fate of the entire planet rested on the shoulders of a skeleton, and the five people sent to rescue him.

"What if we *do* go up against Serpine?" Stephanie asked, fighting to keep the dread out of her voice. She had to remain strong. She couldn't let them see that she was just an ordinary twelve-year-old. "What if we can't just get in and get out without anyone noticing? Do we have a plan if we have to face him?"

"Oh," Ghastly said, considering it. "No, not really."

"I'm going to try and cut him with my sword," Tanith said helpfully.

"Right," Stephanie said. "Excellent. What about guards? Do you think they'll be expecting us?"

"Serpine is used to the Elders taking forever to make their calm, thought-out decisions," Tanith said. "So he won't be expecting anything as amazingly rash and reckless as this."

Ghastly nodded. "That'll teach him to underestimate stupid people."

"All right then," Stephanie said. "Just wanted to make sure we'd thought of everything. So let's go."

Without a word, the Cleavers ran forward and jumped, legs tucked beneath them, and cleared the top of the wall and disappeared from view.

"Show-offs," Ghastly muttered, sweeping both hands down by his sides. A gust of wind lifted him and swung him up towards the wall. He grabbed on and pulled himself to the top. Tanith turned to Stephanie.

"Want a boost?"

"If you wouldn't mind."

Tanith crouched, interlocked her fingers and Stephanie put one foot in her hands. On the count of three, Stephanie shot upwards. Tanith was strong, stronger than she looked, because Stephanie had no trouble catching the top of the wall. Ghastly helped her up, then dropped down the other side and turned to wait for her. She let herself hang down then released her grip, and her boots crunched on to dried leaves and brittle twigs. A moment later Tanith landed beside her.

The woodland was thick, and as they moved deeper into it, it became darker. The evening sun had difficulty filtering through the tall trees and it was cold enough to make Stephanie grateful for her coat. The Cleavers didn't seem to make a sound as they walked. The woodland was quiet, quieter than it had any right to be. No birds sang. Nothing rustled in the undergrowth. It was an eerie sensation.

They reached the tree line at the rear of the castle and ducked down. A small army of Hollow Men patrolled the grounds.

"Oh, joy," Ghastly said grimly. "How are we going to get by *them*?"

"We need a diversion," Tanith said.

"Any suggestions?" Tanith didn't answer, but after a moment she looked at the Cleavers. Ghastly understood immediately.

"But there are too many," he protested.

Tanith's tone was flat, but firm. "We don't have a choice."

The Cleavers tilted their heads towards her, and after a moment they nodded. They stole back among the trees and were gone. Stephanie waited with Tanith and Ghastly.

"They won't be able to hold them off for long," Ghastly said.

"Long enough for us to sneak in," Tanith said.

"That's not what I meant. You've just sent them to their deaths."

She didn't look at him. "They'll do their jobs. We'll do ours. Do you want your friend back or not?" Ghastly didn't answer.

"Look," Stephanie said.

The Hollow Men were moving fast, moving out of their field of vision.

"Let's go," Tanith said.

They broke from the trees, sprinting across the wide-open space towards the castle. Stephanie glanced to her right as she ran, saw the Cleavers standing back to back in the distance as the Hollow Men closed in.

They reached the castle. Tanith placed her hand flat on the lock and twisted her wrist. Stephanie heard the lock break within the door and Tanith pushed it open slowly. They crept in, closing the door behind them.

They kept to the outer corridors, staying away from the cold heart of the castle. They found a stairway leading down and Tanith went first, sword in her right hand, scabbard in her left. Stephanie followed a few paces behind, and Ghastly came last.

They reached the basement, although Stephanie thought that dungeon would probably be more accurate. Tanith held up her hand and they stopped and watched a Hollow Man clump ahead of them and pass out of sight.

They made their way forward. Tanith approached the first heavy iron door, and put her ear against it. After a moment, she pushed it open. The hinges groaned in protest, but the room was empty.

Ghastly went to the next door, listened, and opened it. Again, it was empty.

Tanith glanced at Ghastly and they shared a look, and Stephanie knew what it was about.

"We should split up," Stephanie whispered.

"No," said Tanith.

"No way," said Ghastly.

"If we waste time, the Hollow Men will be back outside the door and we won't be able to get away."

"Then you come with me," Ghastly whispered.

Stephanie shook her head. "I'll be fine. I'll listen at the doors. If I hear anything, I'll get you. If I meet a bad guy, you can be pretty sure you'll know about it. We don't have a choice."

They looked at her but didn't argue. Tanith went to the next door, Ghastly hurried down the length of the corridor and Stephanie turned back and rounded the corner. She came to another row of iron doors and listened intently at each one. She followed the maze of corridors wherever they took her. She found herself breathing through her mouth and tasted the foulness of the air on the back of her throat. There were puddles here, stagnant pools of water on the uneven stone floor. The doors were no longer made of iron, but of rotting wood. The flickering of the torches in the brackets made shadows dance on the walls.

She saw someone moving ahead and was about to duck back when she recognised Ghastly. He waved to her and she waved back, and started checking the doors closest to her. They were working their way towards each other when Stephanie came to a door and heard a low whistling. She frowned. Could Skulduggery whistle? He could *talk* without lips or breath, so she couldn't see a reason why he wouldn't be able to whistle. She didn't recognise the tune, however. She motioned to Ghastly and he crept forward. After listening for a moment, he nodded.

"That's 'The Girl From Ipanema'," he whispered. "That's him."

He held up three fingers, then two, then one and they burst into the room. Skulduggery looked up and stopped whistling. "Oh, hello," he said. "I know where the key to the caves is."

Stephanie closed the door as Ghastly hurried around behind him, stooping to examine the shackles.

"Quality workmanship," he said.

"I thought you'd appreciate it. There's a binding spell woven into the metal."

"Nice. It'll take me a moment."

"I'm not going anywhere."

"Are you OK?" Stephanie asked.

"I've been treated well," he answered with a nod. "Apart from all the torture. It's given me time to think, actually. I know where the key is."

"So you said."

Ghastly stood and the shackles fell. Skulduggery got to his

feet. "Is Meritorious here?" he asked.

"He's telling the other Elders what's going on," Ghastly said.

"Ah," Skulduggery said. "So you're doing this on your own?"

"Tanith Low is here, but basically, yes."

Skulduggery shrugged. "I must admit, it's going rather fabulously so far."

"The key," Stephanie said. "You didn't tell Serpine where it is, did you?"

"I couldn't have, even if I'd have wanted to. Just worked it out a few minutes ago. Simple really. It was right in front of us."

"We can talk about this later," Ghastly said. "We have to go."

"Will there be fighting?"

"I hope not."

"I'm in the mood for some fighting."

"If there is," Stephanie said, handing him his gun, "here's something you can use."

"Ah, bless. I've missed her. Do you have bullets?"

"Uh, no."

Skulduggery paused. "Excellent," he said, and tucked the gun away.

"Let's go," Ghastly said and stepped out of the door.

Stephanie and Skulduggery followed. They hurried down the corridor and turned a corner. A group of Hollow Men froze in mid-step and regarded them vacantly. Time stood still.

"Yes," Skulduggery said. "This is a fabulous rescue indeed."

The Hollow Men came at them, and Skulduggery and Ghastly went into action. Skulduggery worked with elbows and knees, wristlocks and armlocks. Ghastly deftly wove in and around attacks, firing out punches at whoever got close.

Beyond the silent Hollow Men, Stephanie saw Tanith sprinting forward, and then she ran up the wall and across the ceiling and continued running, upside down. Stephanie stared. She hadn't known Tanith could do that.

From the ceiling, Tanith joined the attack, swinging the sword and slicing through the tops of heads. Within a matter of moments, the Hollow Men were reduced to tatters and a foul smell.

Tanith jumped down, flipping to land on her feet. "There are more coming," she said, then added helpfully; "We should probably leave."

They reached the stairs without encountering any more opposition, but as they were running for the exit, two massive doors were kicked open ahead and the Hollow Men reinforcements arrived.

Skulduggery and Ghastly stepped up, clicking their fingers and hurling fireballs at the ground. Stephanie watched their hands move, manipulating the flames until there was a wall of fire keeping the Hollow Men back.

Tanith turned to Stephanie. "Coat."

"What?"

Without giving an explanation, Tanith gripped Stephanie's collar and pulled the coat off. She then ran for the window, covering her head with the coat, and jumped. She crashed through in an explosion of glass.

"Oh," Stephanie murmured.

She ran over, climbing through the window as Tanith got to her feet.

"Thanks," Tanith said, handing her back the coat.

"Watch out!" Ghastly shouted.

Stephanie dodged to one side as Ghastly and Skulduggery dived through the window – Ghastly lower down, Skulduggery above him – like two lunatic acrobats. They hit the grass and rolled, coming up at the same time.

"Flee," Skulduggery said.

As they ran for the trees, Stephanie saw one of the Cleavers who had accompanied them. Judging by the tattered paper strewn around him, the Cleavers had obviously put up an amazing fight, but the sheer numbers of Hollow Men had proven too much. He lay dead on the grass. She saw no sign of the other one.

And then they were in the trees and not slowing down, and Hollow Men were crashing through the undergrowth after them.

Ghastly reached the wall first, swept his hands beneath him and let the air lift him over the wall.

Tanith just kept running. Right before she was about to smack straight into it she gave a little jump and then she was running up the wall.

Before Stephanie could ask Skulduggery for a boost his arm wrapped around her waist and she found herself rushing upwards, the wind in her ears, and the top of the wall passing beneath her feet. They landed on the other side with such ease and gentleness that Stephanie almost laughed despite herself.

They got in the van and Ghastly turned the key and pulled out on to the road, and they left the castle behind them.

18

ON THE ROOF, AT NIGHT

Laughter drifted in the distance and Skulduggery looked towards it. They were standing on the roof of Ghastly's shop. Dublin City twinkled as it got ready for sleep. Stephanie could see over rooftops, over streets, down lanes. She could see the cars passing, and here and there people walking. When he turned back, he said, "So, Valkyrie Cain, eh?"

"You don't think it sounds silly, do you?"

"On the contrary, I think it sounds perfect. Valkyrie. Warrior women who guide the souls of the dead off the battlefield. A tad morbid, but then, who am I to judge? I'm technically dead."

Stephanie looked at him and took a moment before speaking again. "So was it bad? The torture?"

"It wasn't fun," he said. "I think after the first few hours he knew I had no idea where the key was. After that, he was torturing me purely for the sake of torturing me. Did I thank you for coming to my rescue, by the way?"

"Don't worry about it."

"Nonsense. Thank you."

She smiled. "You're welcome."

"Your friend Tanith seemed a bit quiet on the trip home."

"I think she regrets using the Cleavers as a diversion."

"I would have made the same decision," Skulduggery said. "The Cleavers have a job to do – let them do it."

"That's what she said."

"Ah, but it's one thing to understand that and quite another to accept it. Until that happens, she's going to have one or two nightmares about it. But she's a warrior. She'll make it."

"She's a good fighter."

"Indeed she is."

"If I started training now, would I be able to fight like her when I'm her age?"

"I don't see why not. Sixty years of good solid training is

enough to turn anyone into a tidy little scrapper."

"What?"

"What *what*?"

"Sixty years? How old is she?"

"I'd say seventy if she's a day."

Stephanie stared. "Right," she said firmly, "it's time for you to tell me how you people live so long."

"Diet and exercise."

"Skulduggery—"

"Clean healthy living."

"I swear..."

"Magic then."

She looked at him. "Do all sorcerers live forever?"

"Not forever, no. Not even close to forever. We do age, it's just we do it slower then the rest of humanity. The regular use of a certain amount of magic rejuvenates the body, keeps it young."

"So if I started learning magic now, I'd stay twelve?"

"It would take you a few years to reach the level where ageing slows, but yes, after that, you would stay young for a lot longer than is strictly fair. I know it's impolite to discuss a lady's age, but China is the same age as I am, and even I have to admit that she wears it better!" He laughed, then stopped and peered at her. "Because I'm a skeleton," he explained.

"Yes, I got it."

"You weren't laughing."

"I didn't think it was funny."

"Oh."

"So what are you going to do about her?"

"China? There is nothing *to* do. She behaved exactly as I expected her to behave. The scorpion stings the fox because that is its nature. You can't deny your nature."

"And what's *your* nature?"

His head tilted. "Odd question."

"China said some things about you. And Serpine. She said all you want is revenge."

"And you're wondering how far I'll go to *get* that revenge, is that it? You're wondering how much I'm willing to sacrifice in order to make him pay for killing me all those years ago."

"Yes."

He paused a moment then slipped his hands into his pockets and spoke. "What China didn't tell you, what *I* didn't tell you, is that I was not the only one caught in Serpine's trap." Stephanie didn't say anything. She waited for him to continue.

"The trap was exquisite. A thing of beauty, it really was. You see, Valkyrie, a successful trap needs one important quality, the same quality any trick or illusion needs. Misdirection. When your attention is focused on one thing, something else is happening behind your back.

"I didn't even realise it *was* a trap until it was sprung. Serpine knew me, you see, and he knew how I'd react to certain stimuli. He knew, for instance, that if he murdered my wife and child right in front of me, I'd never even suspect that the handle of the dagger I reached for was dipped in poison."

Stephanie stared at him, but Skulduggery just looked out over the city.

"I didn't use magic, you see, and he knew I wouldn't. He knew I'd be too angry, he knew my rage would fuel a *physical* attack, that I'd need to kill him up close and personal. And the moment my hand closed around that dagger, I realised my mistake. Of course, by then it was too late. I was helpless.

"It took him a few days to finally kill me. I died hating him, and when I came back, the hatred came back with me." He turned his head to her. "You asked me what is my nature? It is a dark and twisted thing."

"I don't know what to say," Stephanie said softly.

"Not much you *can* say to a story like that, is there?"

"Not really."

"Yep, I win on the ol' dramatic story front every time." They stood in silence for a while. Despite the warmth of the night it was chilly up there, but Stephanie didn't mind.

"What happens now?" she asked.

"The Elders go to war. They'll find the castle empty – Serpine wouldn't stay there after this – so they'll be looking for him. They'll also be tracking down his old allies to make sure they don't get the opportunity to organise."

"And what do we do?"

"We get to the Sceptre before Serpine."

"The key," she said, "where is it?"

He turned to her. "Gordon hid it. Clever man, your uncle. He didn't think anyone should have access to that weapon, but he hid the key in a place where if we *truly* needed to find it, if the situation got so dire that we *truly* needed the Sceptre, all it would take was a little detective work."

"So where is it?"

"The piece of advice he gave me, in the solicitor's office, do you remember what it was?"

"He said a storm is coming."

"And he also said that sometimes the key to safe harbour is hidden from us and sometimes it is right before our eyes."

"He was talking about the key, literally? It's right before our eyes?"

"It *was*, when those words were first spoken in the solicitor's office."

"Fedgewick has the key?"

"Not Fedgewick. He gave it away."

Stephanie frowned, remembering the reading of the will then the lock in the cellar, no bigger than Skulduggery's palm. She looked up at him. "Not the brooch?"

"The brooch."

"Gordon gave the key, the key to the most powerful weapon in existence, to Fergus and Beryl?" she asked incredulously. "Why would he do that?"

"Would you ever have thought to look for it with them?"

She let the notion sink in then started to smile. "They were left the most valuable possession Gordon had and they didn't even realise it."

"It's actually quite amusing."

"It actually is."

"So now all we have to do is get it."

Stephanie smiled again and nodded, then her smile dropped and she shook her head vehemently. "I'm not getting it."

"You're going to have to."

"No, I don't."

"Just pay them a visit—"

"Why can't you break in? You broke into the Vault."

"That was different."

"Yes, it had alarms and vampires – this'll be so much easier!"

"There are times when extreme measures are unnecessary."

"Extreme measures are *very* necessary here!"

"Valkyrie—"

"You can't ask me to visit them!"

"We don't have a choice."

"But I *never* visit! They'll suspect something!"

"Being a detective isn't all about torture and murder and monsters. Sometimes it gets truly unpleasant."

"But I don't *like* them!" she whined.

"The fate of the world may depend on whether or not you can bring yourself to visit your relatives."

She turned her head, looking at him out of the corner of her eye. "It *may* depend?"

"Valkyrie—"

"Fine, I'll go."

"Good girl." She crossed her arms and didn't respond.

"Are you sulking now?" he asked.

"Yes," she answered curtly.

"OK."

19

THE EXPERIMENT

The Cleaver lay strapped to the table. Fluids ran through the clear rubber tubes that pierced his skin, flowing into the quiet machine behind him. That which was unnecessary was removed, replaced with liquid darkness, with concoctions that mixed science with sorcery. The Cleaver's face was unremarkable and expressionless. He had stopped struggling over an hour ago. It was beginning to take effect.

Serpine stepped into the light and the Cleaver's eyes flickered to him. They were glassy and dull, without any of the fierceness that had met his gaze when the Hollow Men had brought the Cleaver to him and removed the helmet. Then, even as Skulduggery Pleasant made good his escape, Serpine had been given a new captive and he knew what he would do with him.

It was time. Serpine held up the dagger he was holding, let the Cleaver see it. No reaction. No wariness, no fear, no recognition. This man, this soldier, who had lived his entire life with blind obedience to others, was now about to enter into death, equally as blind. A pathetic existence. Serpine held the dagger in both hands and raised it above his head then brought it down, and the blade plunged into the Cleaver's chest and he died.

Serpine removed the blade, wiped it clean and put it to one side. If this worked some changes would obviously need to be made, some alterations, some improvements. The Cleaver was a test subject after all, no more then an experiment. If it worked, a little refinement would be in order. It wouldn't take long. An hour at most.

Serpine waited by the Cleaver's corpse. The warehouse was quiet. He'd had to abandon the castle, but he had been well prepared for that eventuality. Besides, it wouldn't be for long. In a matter of days, his enemies would be dead, and there would be no one left to fight him, and he would have everything he would need to usher in the Faceless Ones – a feat his old master Mevolent had never managed.

Serpine frowned. Had it been a trick of the light, or had the Cleaver moved? He looked closer, searching for the rise and fall of the chest, searching for a sign of life. But no, no sign of life. The Cleaver's pulse, when he checked it, was absent.

And then the Cleaver opened his eyes.

20

THE FAMILY CURSE

Stephanie climbed through her bedroom window to find her reflection sitting on the bed in the darkness, waiting for her.

"Are you ready to resume your life?" it asked.

Stephanie, who was finding it very disconcerting to hold a conversation with herself, merely nodded. The reflection went to the mirror and stepped through, then turned and waited. Stephanie touched the glass and a day's worth of memory flooded into her mind. She watched the reflection change, the clothes Stephanie was wearing appearing on it.

And then it was nothing more then a reflected image in a mirror.

Stephanie woke the next morning, not happy with what she had to do. Dressed in jeans and T-shirt, she thought about calling on the reflection to imitate her again, then decided against it. The reflection gave her the creeps.

Realising that she could not put it off any longer, Stephanie trudged over to her aunt's house and knocked on the door. The sun was shining and the birds were singing and Stephanie forced a smile on to her face, but it wasn't a smile that was returned when the door opened and Crystal looked out at her.

"What do you want?" her cousin asked suspiciously.

"Just thought I'd call round," Stephanie said brightly. "See how you all are."

"We're fine," Crystal said. "We've got a stupid car and a stupid boat. How's your *house*?"

"Crystal," she said, "I know you're probably angry about the inheritance and everything, but I don't know why I was left all that either."

"It's because you were sucking up to him," Crystal sneered. "If we'd have known that all it took was just to be all smiles and have conversations with him, then we'd have done that stuff too."

"But I didn't know—"

"You cheated."

"I didn't cheat."

"You had an unfair advantage."

"How? How could I have even known he was going to die?"

"You knew," Crystal said. "You knew that sooner or later he was going to die, but you got in so early, the rest of us didn't stand a chance."

"Did you even like him?"

There was that sneer again. "You don't have to like someone to get something from them."

Stephanie resisted the urge to punch Crystal's smirking face long enough for Beryl to pass the doorway. She saw Stephanie and her eyes widened in surprise.

"Stephanie," she said, "what are you doing here?"

"She thought she'd call round," Crystal said, "to see how we are."

"Oh, that's very nice of you, dear."

Crystal took this opportunity to walk away without saying goodbye. Stephanie focused on Beryl.

"You're not wearing the brooch Gordon left you?"

"That horrid thing? No, I am not, and I don't think I ever will. It doesn't even sparkle for heaven's sake. People know something is cheap if it doesn't sparkle."

"That's a shame. It looked pretty, though, from where I was standing; it would have looked nice with one of your cardigans—"

"We saw you yesterday," Beryl interrupted.

"I'm sorry?"

"In a horrid yellow car, with that dreadful Skulduggery Pleasant."

Stephanie felt the instant flutters of panic in her belly, but she made herself frown and give a puzzled laugh. "Um, I think you may be mistaken. I was home all day yesterday."

"Nonsense. You passed right by us. We saw you quite clearly. We saw *him*, too, all covered up like last time."

"Nope, wasn't me."

Beryl smiled piously. "Lying is a sin, did you know that?"

"I'd heard the rumour..."

"Fergus!" Beryl shouted back into the house and a few moments later her husband walked out of the living room. He was at home every day now after suffering a "serious fall" at work. He was in the process of suing his employers, claiming that it was their negligence that resulted in his debilitating injuries. He didn't look too debilitated as he approached the door.

"Fergus, Stephanie here says she wasn't in the car with that awful Mr Pleasant."

Fergus scowled. "She's calling us liars?"

"No," Stephanie said with a half-laugh. "Just that it must have been somebody else."

"Stephanie," Beryl chided, "let's not play games. We know it was you. It's such a tragic thing to see, a dear sweet innocent child like you falling in with the wrong crowd."

"Wrong crowd?"

"Weirdos," Fergus said with a sneer. "I've seen their kind before. Gordon used to surround himself with people like that, people with... secrets."

"And why does he hide his face anyway?" Beryl asked. "Is he *deformed*?"

"I wouldn't know," Stephanie said, fighting to keep her voice even.

"You can't trust people like that," Fergus continued. "I've been around them my whole life, seen them coming and going. Never wanted anything to do with them. You never know who you're dealing with or what sordid little things they get up to."

"He seemed all right to me," Stephanie said as casually as

she could. "He seemed quite nice, actually."

Beryl shook her head sadly. "I don't expect you to understand. You're only a child."

Stephanie bristled. "You've never even spoken to him."

"Adults don't have to speak to other adults to know if they're bad news or not. One look, that's all we need."

"So anyone different from you is bad news?"

"Anyone different from *us*, dear."

"My parents always told me never to judge someone by how they look."

"Yes, well," Beryl said primly. "If they think they can afford to live in ignorance, then that's their mistake."

"My parents aren't ignorant."

"I never said they were, dear. I just said they *lived* in ignorance."

Stephanie couldn't take this any more. "I need to pee," she said suddenly.

Beryl blinked. "I'm sorry?"

"Pee. I need to pee. Can I use your bathroom?"

"I... I suppose..."

"Thanks."

Stephanie stepped in past them both and hurried up the stairs. She went into the bathroom, and when she was sure Beryl wasn't going to follow her up, she crept into the master bedroom and went straight to the jewellery box on the dresser. It was a massive thing, each of its compartments bulging with tacky trinkets that sparkled and twinkled and glittered. She found the brooch in a slide-out compartment at the base of the box, where it nestled with a single hoop earring and a pair of tweezers. She stuck it in her pocket, closed the jewellery box and left the room, then flushed the toilet in the bathroom and bounded down the stairs.

"Thank you," she said brightly, and Beryl opened her mouth to continue their conversation but Stephanie was already halfway down the garden path.

Stephanie sat on one of the boulders that sealed off the north end of the beach, waiting for Skulduggery. The weathermen had been predicting an end to the dry spell, but the morning sky was blue and cloud free. There was a shell on the boulder next to her, a pretty shell, a shell she suddenly found herself loving.

It moved. The air didn't do that cool rippling thing around her hand, but the shell still moved and it wasn't because of the breeze either. Stephanie's heart quickened but she didn't let herself celebrate. Not yet. It could have been a fluke. If she could do it a second time, then she could celebrate.

She concentrated on the shell. She held her hand up, seeing the space between her hand and the shell as a series of interlocking objects, waiting to be moved. Her fingers uncurled slightly and she felt it, she felt the air against her palm, solid somehow. She pushed against it and the shell shot off the boulder.

"Yes!" she exclaimed, sticking both arms up in the air. Magic! She'd done magic! She laughed in delight.

"You look happy."

Stephanie turned so suddenly she almost fell off the boulder, and her dad grinned as he approached. She blushed deeply, and dug her phone out of her pocket without him seeing, then held it up.

"Got a good text message," she said, "that's all."

"Ah," he said as he sat beside her. "Anything I should know about?"

"Probably not." She looked around as casually as she could, praying that she wouldn't see the Canary Car suddenly pull up. "Why aren't you at work?"

Her dad shrugged. "I have a big meeting this afternoon but I left the house without something important, so I thought I'd nip back during lunch."

"What did you forget? Architect's plans or something?"

"Something like that," he said with a nod. "Actually, nothing like that. I forgot my underwear."

She looked at him. "What?"

"When I was getting dressed my mind was on other things. It happens sometimes. Usually it wouldn't bother me but these trousers really *itch*—"

"Dad, ew, don't want to know!"

"Oh, right, sorry. Anyway, I saw you walking down here so I thought I'd say hi. You used to come down here all the time when you were younger, sit here and look out there, and I always wondered what was going through your mind..."

"Lots of clever little things," she responded automatically and he smiled.

"Your mother's worried about you," he said after a while.

She looked up at him, startled. "What? Why?"

He shrugged. "You just, you haven't been yourself lately." So they *had* noticed the difference between her and her reflection.

"I'm fine, Dad. Really. I've just, you know, I've been going through some moods."

"Yes, yep, I understand that, and your mother explained the whole thing to me, about young girls and their moods... But we still worry. Ever since Gordon died..."

Stephanie kept her frown to herself. So this wasn't just about the reflection.

"I know you were close," he continued. "And I know you got on so well, and I know that when he died, you lost a good friend."

"I suppose I did," she said quietly.

"And we don't want to stop you from growing up, even if we could. You're growing into a fine young woman and one that we're really proud of."

She smiled awkwardly and didn't meet his eyes. Gordon's death *had* changed her, but the change was far more drastic than even her parents realised. It had set her on the course she was on now, the course that had led to her becoming Valkyrie Cain, the course that would lead to whatever fate was waiting for her. It had changed her life – given it direction and purpose. It had also put her in more danger than she could have ever imagined.

"We just worry about you, that's all."

"You don't have to."

"It's a parent's job. You could be forty and we'd be stuck in the Old Folks' Home, and we'd still be worrying about you. It's a responsibility that never stops."

"Makes you wonder why anyone has kids."

He laughed softly. "You'd think that, yes. But there is nothing more wonderful then watching your child grow up, nothing more fulfilling. Of course, there's a certain age you wish they wouldn't go beyond, but there's not a whole lot you can do about that."

Not unless you have magic on your side, Stephanie thought to herself.

"Beryl called," her father said. "She said you'd just been to see her."

Stephanie nodded. She couldn't have noticed that the brooch was missing already, could she? "I felt like going around, seeing how everyone was. I think, you know, Gordon's death has made me value the family we have left, or something. I think it's important that we stay close."

He looked at her, a little startled. "Well, that's... that's a really lovely thing to be able to say, Steph, it really is. It's a beautiful sentiment." There was a brief pause. "I don't have to go round, do I?"

"No."

"Oh, thank God."

She didn't like lying to him. She had made it a point, years before, to be as honest as she could where her parents were involved. But things were different now. She had secrets. "So what else did Beryl say?"

"Well... she seems to think she saw you with Skulduggery Pleasant yesterday."

"Yeah," Stephanie said, as casually as she could, "she told me. That's weird."

"She thinks you've fallen in with the wrong crowd."

"You should hear her, Dad, the way she talks about him, and she doesn't even know him. She probably thinks I'm part of a cult or something..."

"And are you?"

She looked at him, appalled. "What?"

Her father sighed. "Beryl has good reason to think that."

"But it's insane!"

"Well, insanity runs in the family." She could see something in his eyes, a reluctance, but also a resignation.

"My grandfather," he said, "your great-grandfather, was a wonderful man – us kids loved him. Me, Fergus, Gordon, we'd sit around and he'd tell us all these fantastic stories. My father, however, didn't have a lot of time for him. All the stories he was telling us, he'd told my father when he was a kid. And when my dad grew up, he realised it was all nonsense, but my granddad refused to see it. My grandfather believed... He believed that we were magic."

Stephanie stared at him. "What?"

"He said it'd been passed down, this magic, generation to generation. He said we were descendants of a great sorcerer called the Last of the Ancients."

The sound of the sea faded to nothing, the sun dimmed and the beach vanished, and the only thing that existed in the world was her father, and the only sounds were the words he was speaking.

"These stories, this belief, has followed the family for centuries. I don't know how it began or when, but it seems like it's always been a part of us. And now and then, there have been members of our family who have chosen to believe it.

"Gordon believed. A rational man, an intelligent man, and yet he believed in magic and sorcery and people who never age. All the stuff he wrote about, he probably believed in most, if not *all*, of it.

"And because of this, he got involved in things that were... unhealthy. The people he mixed with, people who fed into his delusions, who shared his madness. Dangerous people. It's a sickness, Steph. My granddad had it, Gordon had it... and I don't want you to get it."

"I'm not mad."

"And I'm not saying you are. But I know how easy it is to be swept away by stories, by things that you wish were real. When

I was younger, I believed. I believed even more than Gordon did. But I stopped. I made a decision to live in the real world, to stop indulging this, this *curse* that has plagued us. Gordon introduced me to your mother and I fell in love. I put it all behind me."

"So you think Gordon was part of a cult?"

"For want of a better word, yes."

She remembered the look on her father's face the first time he had encountered Skulduggery, in Mr Fedgewick's office. It had been a look she had never seen before – suspicion, mistrust, hostility – and it had passed as quickly as it had appeared. Now she understood why.

"And you think, what, that I'm part of the cult now?"

He gave a gentle laugh. "No, I suppose I don't. Not really. But what Beryl was saying, it got me thinking. In the last few days, sometimes there's a distance in your eyes I haven't seen before. I don't know what it is. I look at you now and you're my little girl. But I've been getting the feeling that... I don't know. Recently, it seems like you're somewhere else."

Stephanie didn't dare respond.

"I just wish you'd talk to someone. You don't have to talk to *me* because you know how much I babble, but your mother... You could tell her, you could tell *us*, anything. And as long as you're honest with us, you know we'd help you in whatever way we can."

"I know, Dad."

He looked at her and for a moment she thought he was going to shed a tear, but then he wrapped an arm around her and kissed her forehead. "You're my little sweetheart, you know that?"

"I know."

"Good girl." He got off the boulder. "I better get back to work."

"See you later." He looked at her, gave her a smile and walked back off the beach.

Stephanie stayed where she was. If it was true, if the family legend was true, then this was, this was... Actually she didn't know what this was. It felt important, though. It felt big. She left the beach and waited by the road, and when Skulduggery arrived in the hideous Canary Car she told him everything her father had said.

Mr Bliss turned the brooch over in his hands. "Are you sure this is it?"

Mr Bliss was in black and Skulduggery was wearing a dark blue pinstriped suit that Ghastly had finished working on that very morning, along with a crisp white shirt and a blue tie. They were standing in the shade of the Martello tower, a centuries-old ruin that stood atop the grassy cliffs along Haggard's coast. Far below them, the sea whipped at the jagged rocks.

"I'm sure," Skulduggery said. "See how the pin folds back, actually becomes a makeshift handle? That's our key."

Stephanie tried her best not to be intimidated by Mr Bliss' presence, but whenever he glanced at her she looked away. She hadn't objected when Skulduggery told her that Mr Bliss would be accompanying them into the caves, but she hadn't exactly jumped for joy either.

"Thank you for calling me," Mr Bliss said, handing the brooch back to Stephanie.

"We need all the help we can get," Skulduggery admitted, "although I was surprised when you made yourself available."

"Serpine has become extremely powerful, much more so than anyone realises."

"You almost sound afraid of him."

Mr Bliss paused for a moment. "I don't feel fear," he said eventually. "When you no longer have hope, the fear evaporates. But I do respect his power. I respect what he can do."

"If he gets to the Sceptre before us, we're all going to *see* what he can do firsthand."

"I still don't get it," Stephanie said. "If he gets the Sceptre, OK, he's unstoppable, but how can he use it to bring back the Faceless Ones?"

"I don't know," Skulduggery replied. "In theory, the ritual could be known to no more than two people in the world – I wouldn't even know who to start threatening."

Mr Bliss shook his head. "He doesn't plan to threaten anyone. From what he has said, I think the Sceptre of the Ancients is merely a stepping stone, a toy that he needs to get what he wants."

"And what is that?" Mr Bliss looked out over the sea, but didn't answer.

"I don't understand," Skulduggery continued. "Were you talking to him?"

"This morning," Mr Bliss said. He had a resigned tone to his voice, and Stephanie narrowed her eyes. Something was wrong. Something was very wrong. She stepped back, but Skulduggery was too caught up in the conversation to notice.

"Did you see him?" Skulduggery said, moving closer to Bliss. "You saw him and you didn't take him down?"

"The reaches of his power were unknown to me and I do not start battles I cannot win. It was too dangerous."

"Where is he? The Elders are looking for him!"

"They don't need to. He will go to them when the time is right."

"Why did you meet him?"

"Serpine had something to say. I listened."

"What are you talking about?"

"He already knows about the caves. The only thing that had delayed him is the search for the key."

Skulduggery looked at Mr Bliss. Mr Bliss looked at Skulduggery. Stephanie realised that he was standing right on the edge of the cliff.

Mr Bliss put a hand on Skulduggery's chest and before Stephanie could even shout he shoved, and Skulduggery shot backward over the edge and disappeared from view. And then Mr Bliss turned to her.

21

THE CAVE

Stephanie ran.

She glanced back but Bliss wasn't there, and then a shadow fell across her and he dropped from the sky. She ran straight into him and stumbled back. His hand moved like an attacking snake, snatching the brooch from her grasp. She landed on the seat of her jeans.

She looked to the edge of the cliff, expecting to see Skulduggery swoop up to save her. He didn't. Mr Bliss slipped the brooch into his jacket.

"You're going to give it to him," Stephanie said.

"I am."

"Why?"

"He's too powerful to fight."

"But you're stronger than anyone! If you *all* go after him—"

"I do not gamble, Miss Cain. If we went after him, we might beat him, or he might elude us and strike at us when we least expect it. It is far too unpredictable for my liking. War should be a delicate thing. It requires precision."

Stephanie frowned. Those words. Those eyes, the palest blue...

"China betrayed us too," she said, understanding. "It must run in the family."

"My sister's affairs, and her motivations, are her own."

"Is she siding with Serpine as well?"

"Not to my knowledge," Mr Bliss answered. "But then, I could be lying. That's the thing about allies and enemies – you're never quite sure which is which until the final move is made."

Stephanie got to her feet as he walked to his car, powerless to get the brooch back.

"We're going to stop him," she called out.

"Do what you must," Mr Bliss said without looking back. He got into his car and, without another glance at her, drove off down the dirt road away from the Martello tower, heading out of town. She watched the dust kick up in his wake then hurried down the narrow path to the bottom of the cliffs.

Please be all right, she repeated in her head. *Please be all right please be all right.*

When she finally reached the bottom of the path she looked over at the rocks, terrified that she might see him there. A fall like that would have smashed his bones to pieces. He wasn't on the rocks, however, so she turned her attention to the sea, just as Skulduggery's head broke the surface of the water.

"Skulduggery?" she called out, relief sweeping through her. "Are you all right?" He didn't answer immediately. Instead, he kept rising, rising straight up out of the sea until he was standing on the waves.

"I'm fine," he said curtly, walking to her. Stephanie had seen such peculiarities over the past few days that she was mildly surprised when anything struck her as odd any more, but Skulduggery walking on water definitely struck her as odd. He bobbed up and down with the waves but kept his balance perfectly, and when he stepped off the water on to the path, the vapour rose from his suit and dropped back into the sea. His clothes, she noticed, were undamaged by the fall.

"So that's why Serpine didn't send anyone after us," he said sourly. "He let us go so that we'd get the key, knowing he had someone on the inside to get the key *from* us. That's just... that's just cheating."

"Do you know anyone who *wouldn't* betray you?" Stephanie asked as they started walking back up the path.

"Hush now."

"And thanks for letting me know that Mr Bliss and China were brother and sister, by the way."

"You're welcome."

"If I'd have known that, I might have been able to warn you not to trust him."

"I must admit, China's treachery didn't come as a surprise, but Mr Bliss... He never does anything without due consideration."

"I suppose he thought Serpine was the winning side."

"Maybe."

"So what do we do now? We can't let Serpine find the Sceptre; he'll be unstoppable."

"What do you suggest?"

"I suggest I go get my work clothes, let my reflection out of the mirror, and we follow him into the caves and get the Sceptre before he does."

"That's a very good plan. We'll do that then."

*

They arrived at Gordon's estate to find a gleaming silver car parked outside and the front door once again lying in the hallway. Skulduggery led the way into the house, revolver in hand. Stephanie followed close behind, clad all in black. They gave the ground floor a cursory examination before moving downstairs into the cellar.

The key was in the lock and the door was revealed. A section of the floor was open, exposing stone steps descending into the earth. They followed these steps, sinking deeper into the gloom. They walked in near darkness for a few minutes until they came to the bottom, then walked through a narrow tunnel carved out of the rock. It was brighter down here, their way lit by dozens of small holes designed to catch the sunlight from above and cast it down into the depths.

They stepped out of the tunnel into a cave that split in two directions.

"Which way?" Stephanie whispered.

Skulduggery extended his arm and opened his hand. After a moment, he nodded. "A group of them, headed north."

"Are you reading the air?" Stephanie asked, frowning.

"Reading *disturbances* in the air, yes."

"So do we go after them?"

Skulduggery thought on this. "They don't know the exact

location of the Sceptre any more then we do. They chose that path as simply the place to start their search."

"So we should go the other way, hope we find it first?"

"If we can get it without Serpine even knowing we're here, we can seal the tunnel behind us, trap him here while we alert the Elders."

"Then why are we standing around looking pretty?"

They took the path to their left, moving quickly but quietly. The cave system soon proved itself to be enormous, but Skulduggery assured her he could find the way back without a problem. Here and there, the pinpricks of sunlight opened up to larger streams, which reflected off the rock walls and stabbed through the darkness. Strange plants and mushrooms grew, but Skulduggery warned her to stay away from them. Even the fungus was dangerous down here.

They had been walking for ten minutes when Stephanie saw something move ahead of them. She touched Skulduggery's arm and pointed, and they stepped back into the shadows to watch.

The thing that lumbered into view was magnificent in its awfulness. Standing well over two metres tall, its chest was broad and its arms were long, the forearms hugely distorted by bulging muscles. Its hands were the size of dinner plates, tipped with claws built for ripping. Its face was dog-like in appearance, like a Dobermann, and it had a dirty brown mane that ran from the back of its skull and joined the long matted hair on its shoulders.

"What is it?" Stephanie whispered.

"That, my dear Valkyrie, is what we call a monster."

She looked at Skulduggery. "You don't know what it is, do you?"

"I told you what it is – it's a horrible monster. Now shut up before it comes over here and eats us." They watched it disappear into an adjoining cave.

"Let's not go that way," Stephanie said.

"Good plan," Skulduggery agreed and they hurried forward.

Their path took them to the scene of a cave-in, so they doubled back and took another route, moving into a long tunnel. Things scuttled in the shadows beside them and fluttered in the shadows above, but as long as those things didn't jump out and bite them, Stephanie was OK with it. Skulduggery crouched, picking something up off the ground. A dusty chocolate-bar wrapper, or as he put it, "A clue."

Stephanie looked at him. "Gordon?"

"We're on the right track."

They set off again, scanning the ground for any further

evidence that Gordon had passed this way. Unfortunately, less then five minutes later Skulduggery stopped again and turned, hand out, reading the air.

"We're being followed," he whispered.

Precisely the words Stephanie did not want to hear. She looked back the way they had come. The tunnel was long and straight, and despite the gloom she could see a fair distance. She saw no one behind them.

"Are you sure?" she asked quietly.

Skulduggery didn't answer. He was holding both arms up – his left hand was reading the air, his right hand holding the gun.

"We should back away now," he said. They started backwards. She could hear something now, something echoing up to them.

"We should back away a little faster," he said.

They picked up their pace. Stephanie had to keep glancing at her feet to make sure she wasn't about to trip over anything, but Skulduggery seemed able to move as confidently backwards as he did forwards.

She realised the sound she could hear was bounding footsteps. She realised this because they belonged to the dog-faced creature that was now galloping towards them at a terrible pace.

"OK," Skulduggery said, "now I think we should run."

They turned and ran. Skulduggery fired six shots in quick succession, each one of them finding their mark, each one of them hitting the creature but not slowing it. Skulduggery reloaded on the run, dropping the empty shells and slipping fresh bullets into the chambers, snapping the gun shut with a flick of the wrist. The tunnel widened, the mouth just ahead.

"Keep going," Skulduggery ordered.

"What are you going to do?"

"I don't know," he answered, glancing behind them. "Probably something really brave."

He pulled up sharply and Stephanie shot past him, reaching the end of the tunnel and finding a vast cavern. Vines cascaded down from the darkness above, hanging over the yawning abyss before her.

She looked back just in time to see the beast collide with Skulduggery. The gun flew from his hand and he hit the ground hard and the creature closed its claws around his ankle. It stepped back and swung, lifting Skulduggery into the air and slamming him against the tunnel wall. He hit the ground with his shoulder but the creature wasn't finished swinging, and Stephanie watched as Skulduggery was thrown against the other wall. The creature roared and yanked and Skulduggery was flung back, deeper into the tunnel, and the creature was left holding one skeletal leg.

It snarled in confusion then snapped its head up, catching Stephanie's scent.

"Run!" Skulduggery yelled from the tunnel as the creature dropped the leg and came straight for her. Stephanie spun on her heel but there was nowhere else to run, so she sprinted for the edge and leaped upwards.

Her hands clutched at the slippery vines, desperately searching for a good grip as she started to drop. Her fingers closed around a thick vine and her whole body snapped up again, her momentum taking her forward. She glanced at the vast darkness below, felt the chilled, stale air that wafted up from the emptiness. She twisted as she swung back, just in time to raise her legs to avoid the beast's claws. It roared its displeasure at having being cheated out of its prey, swiping at her from the edge of the abyss. Her momentum took her away from it again.

Stephanie saw Skulduggery dragging himself along the tunnel floor and grabbing his limb, the shoe and sock still attached. He sat up, feeding the thighbone through his trouser leg until it met his hip, then twisted and tested it, bending it towards him. He snatched his gun from the ground beside him and got up, leaving the tunnel and moving up behind the creature as it continued to snarl and swipe at Stephanie. She was now just hanging there, swaying slightly on the vine, her heart no longer beating in her ears.

She kept eye contact, tried to keep its attention on her, but the closer Skulduggery crept, the harder it became, until one kicked pebble caused the creature to turn.

Skulduggery splayed his hand but nothing happened, and Stephanie remembered Mr Bliss saying that there were creatures in these caves who fed on magic. It looked like they'd just encountered one such creature.

"Damn," was all Skulduggery said and he charged, firing point-blank into the creature's chest and then cannoning into it, driving it back one step.

One more step and the creature would go over.

The beast slammed a huge fist down on to Skulduggery's shoulders and he dropped to one knee but was up again, swinging a punch as high as he could, his fist barely grazing the creature's chin. He ducked under another swipe, moving like a boxer, swinging the butt of the gun against its ribs, with little effect.

Stephanie frowned and glanced at the vine she was holding. Was she moving? She looked back across as Skulduggery grabbed a handful of mane with his left hand and jumped, straight up, bringing the butt of the gun down across the creature's face.

The creature bellowed and took a step back and its foot found nothing but emptiness. Skulduggery pushed away from it as it balanced there for a single moment, but there was nothing it could do to save itself. Skulduggery stumbled backwards as the beast fell into the abyss with a terrified howl.

"Right then," Skulduggery said as he dusted himself off. "That took care of that."

"I think I'm moving," Stephanie said as she felt herself being pulled gently up. Skulduggery stepped to the edge, his head jutting out slightly, curiously, then—

"Stephanie," he said, "that's not a vine."

"What?" Stephanie said, staring at the thing she was holding. "Then what is it?"

"Stephanie, swing towards me," he said, urgency in his voice. "Come on now, swing towards me. Hurry!"

She kicked out, starting the swing, forward and back, each arc bigger than the last, all the time being pulled gently upwards.

"Let go!" Skulduggery said, holding his arms out to catch her. She glanced below her as she swung, remembering the beast's howl as it fell, wondering if it had hit the bottom yet. When she was at the peak of her next swing she released her grip and was in the air, falling forward, falling towards Skulduggery.

But the vine snapped out like a whip, wrapping itself around her wrist and yanking her back painfully. Skulduggery made a grab for her but missed, and Stephanie was speeding upwards.

"Help me!" she screamed, feeling like her arm was about to be yanked from its socket. She heard Skulduggery curse, but she was moving too fast and there was nothing she could do to stop herself being pulled up, and Skulduggery could only watch her vanish into the darkness above.

22

THE SCEPTRE OF THE ANCIENTS

Stephanie was pulled up to a ledge then dragged over it. She tried tearing the tentacle from her wrist, but more slithered from the gloom, wrapping tightly around her arm. She reached back with her free hand and grabbed on to the ledge, but it was no use. Her fingers couldn't take the strain and she had to let go, and she started sliding across the slimy rock.

There was something up ahead, a grey mass of flesh, a growth that had spread unchecked and unchallenged in this dark little corner. The tentacles were pulling her towards its centre, where a large mouth gaped hungrily, razor teeth dripping with viscous saliva.

Her free hand found a large stone and she grabbed it, holding the sharp edge as she would a dagger, and brought it down hard. The stone cut through the tentacles and she pulled her arm free and was up, running, but more tentacles flexed and shot out. They found her legs and Stephanie hit the ground. She tried to kick out but they tightened.

There were tentacles everywhere.

The thing, whatever it was, beat with a sickly pulse as it dragged her closer. She couldn't see any eyes. All it had was its tentacles and that mouth... Which meant it operated by its sense of touch.

Stephanie forced herself to stop struggling. Fighting against every instinct within her, she relaxed her body, and although the speed at which she was moving didn't change, she felt its grip on her loosen slightly. The other tentacles stopped their approach, but they were already too close. They'd be on her in an instant if she tried to pull away.

Stephanie lobbed the stone and it hit a tentacle and bounced away. Sensing another victim nearby, the remaining tentacles slithered after it, searching blindly through the shadows. Stephanie took a deep breath and reached for her ankles, waited until the grip was loosened further, and then grabbed the tentacles and ripped them away.

She got up, but instead of running *away*, she ran *forward*, towards the thing with the mouth. She leaped on to it, over its gaping maw, and her boot almost slipped on its wet, quivering flesh. She jumped, her hands catching the ledge overhead. She hauled herself up as the tentacles snapped and coiled below, their movements becoming more and more frenzied as the thing searched for its missing prey.

Stephanie didn't stop to rest. She got to her feet and hurried from the ledge into the gloom of the passage beyond. She fought off the sudden fear that she'd be lost down in these caves forever. *It won't be forever*, she chided herself. *If one of the monsters doesn't find me and kill me, I'll die of thirst anyway within a few days.*

Stephanie couldn't quite believe she'd just thought that.

Pushing all fears and doubts and pessimistic – though probably realistic – thoughts to the back of her mind, she slowed her pace and concentrated on finding a way back to Skulduggery. And then she saw a light.

She crept forward until she came to a balcony of rock, overlooking a small cavern. She peeked down to see a half-dozen Hollow Men, one of them holding a lantern. Mr Bliss didn't appear to have accompanied this little expedition.

Serpine was there, however, standing in front of a small boulder, its surface flat like a table. On this boulder was a wooden chest with a large lock. Her heart lurched. He'd found it.

She looked down. It wasn't that far to the cavern floor. A couple of metres. She didn't have a choice. She had to try.

The Hollow Men had their backs to her, so Stephanie eased herself over the edge without being noticed and dropped to the cavern floor. The light from the lantern didn't reach this far and the shadows enveloped her so that when one of the Hollow Men turned, its empty gaze passed right over the spot where she crouched. She waited until it had turned back before moving again.

The darkness along the edges of this cavern was so absolute, and her clothes so black, that she could creep up next to her enemies without being seen. She moved achingly slowly, taking only the barest of breaths. She was sure Serpine would hear her heart thundering against her ribcage, but he was preoccupied with the chest.

He tapped the lock with a skinless finger of his red right hand, and the mechanism rusted and snapped in an instant. He smiled as he pulled on his glove, opened the chest and lifted the Sceptre of the Ancients from within.

It was real. The ultimate weapon, the weapon with which the Ancients defeated their gods – it was real. The years hadn't dimmed its golden beauty, and it seemed to hum for a moment, acclimatising itself to its new owner. The ultimate weapon, in the hands of Serpine.

"At last," she heard him whisper.

A strange singing filled the chamber, and Stephanie realised it was coming from the black crystal in the Sceptre. Serpine turned as Skulduggery Pleasant stormed into the cavern.

Skulduggery waved his hand and the Hollow Men flew back off their feet. He crashed into Serpine and the Sceptre clattered to the ground. Serpine threw a punch and Skulduggery ducked under it and moved in close, his hand snaking up to Serpine's shoulder and his hip twisting into him. Serpine pitched over and hit the ground hard.

Stephanie crept through the murk, heading for the Sceptre. The Hollow Men were starting to get up, clumping back to fight at the centre of the cavern.

Skulduggery clicked his fingers and Serpine was too close to dodge the fireball. It hit him square in the chest and enveloped him completely. The Hollow Men froze as their master wheeled about, engulfed in flame. His foot hit the Sceptre and it skidded to the edge of the light…

… and closer to Stephanie.

Skulduggery splayed his hand and Serpine hit the far wall and collapsed to the floor. Skulduggery put out the flames with a casual wave. Serpine lay where he was, his clothes smouldering, his flesh charred and horribly burnt.

"It's over," Skulduggery said. "This is where your past catches up to you. This is where you die."

And then, impossibly, a laugh, and Serpine sat up.

"That," he said, "*hurt.*"

And as Stephanie watched, the burnt flesh started to heal itself and hair regrew along the blistered scalp, leaving not even a scar.

Serpine gathered purple vapour in his palm and threw it at Skulduggery, knocking him back. The vapour became a thin, snaking tendril that darted into the shadows, wrapping around the Sceptre and yanking it into Serpine's hand just as Stephanie reached for it. Skulduggery recovered, but he was too late to do anything. The sorcerer got to his feet, holding the Sceptre, and smiled.

"I'm in two minds," Serpine said as Stephanie moved, unseen, behind him. "Should I use this to destroy you, to reduce your worthless bones to ash, or should I just leave you down here in the darkness? Leaving you here would be more satisfying in the long term, I admit, but what can I say? I crave instant satisfaction. I'm shallow like that."

Stephanie lunged, slamming her shoulder into Serpine's back just as the Sceptre's crystal flashed. Black lightning zigzagged through the air, missing Skulduggery by centimetres and turning the rock behind him to dust. Serpine turned and grabbed her. Stephanie punched him with all of her strength but he just snarled, and then Skulduggery was there and the air rippled. Serpine went sliding across the cavern floor, but he was still clutching the Sceptre.

Skulduggery waved at the Hollow Men and they hurtled backwards, then Stephanie felt a gloved hand close around her wrist and she was dragged out of the cavern. Skulduggery sprinted so fast she just allowed herself to be carried along in his wake.

He knew exactly where he was going, and within minutes they were at the stone steps, hurrying up out of the caves. They reached the cellar and the key flew from the lock into his hand. The floor groaned and rumbled and closed up.

"Will that hold him?" Stephanie asked.

"He's got the Sceptre," Skulduggery said. "Nothing will hold him." As if to prove his point, the floor started to crack.

"Move!" Skulduggery shouted. They bolted up the stairs and Stephanie glanced back just as the floor vanished in a soft *whump* of dust and air.

They plunged out of the house into the bright sunlight, the Hollow Men right behind. Stephanie was three steps from the yellow car when one of the Hollow Men grabbed her.

Stephanie lashed out. Her fingers tore into its face and she ripped downwards and a blast of foul air escaped. The Hollow Man stumbled back, clutching at its head. Its entire body deflated, until it was nothing more than papery skin being trodden on by its brethren.

Another lunged at her and Skulduggery tackled it, rammed an elbow into the side of its neck and flipped it over his shoulder. There was movement to their right and Tanith Low ran towards them, her sword clearing its scabbard. She came in fast, the blade twirling and glinting in the sun, sending pieces of Hollow Men fluttering into the air like confetti.

Black lightning streaked from the doorway and the Canary Car crumbled to nothing. Serpine stalked out of the house. Stephanie felt heat flare beside her face as Skulduggery started hurling fireballs. Serpine waved the first one away and dodged back to avoid the others.

Stephanie was only aware of the other car when it screeched to a stop behind her. The door opened and Tanith sheathed her sword, pushed Stephanie into the car and jumped in after her, and the car was moving again.

Stephanie sat up in time to see Skulduggery hurl one last ball of fire and then turn and dive straight through the open window. He landed on top of her as the car swerved and she felt his elbow against her head. The car swerved again and they separated. Trees zipped past outside and she knew they were out of Serpine's line of fire.

They passed the huge gates that led out of Gordon's estate and Skulduggery righted himself. "Well," he said, "that was bracing."

A familiar voice came from the front seat. "One of these days I won't be around to get you out of trouble, you know."

Stephanie turned her head, saw the man in the bow tie behind the wheel and beside him, in the passenger seat, China Sorrows, poised and perfect.

"I don't know what you'd do without me, Skulduggery," China said. "I really don't."

23

THOUGHTS ON DYING HORRIBLY

The Elders were not happy.

Eachan Meritorious and Sagacious Tome spoke in hushed voices at the other end of the Sanctuary meeting room. Meritorious was calm but solemn. Tome was livid and panicking.

Stephanie sat beside Skulduggery. Across the table, Tanith was cleaning her sword. She had something in her hair.

"Tanith?" Stephanie whispered. Tanith looked up. "You have something..." She pointed to her own head as a hint. "It's a leaf or something."

"Oh, thanks," Tanith said and put her hand to her hair. She felt around until she found it and pulled it out. She examined it and frowned, looked closer, then her face contorted in disgust and she dropped it on the table. "Oh my God."

"What is it?"

"It's a piece of Hollow Man *skin*."

Stephanie blanched. "Oh, that's disgusting."

"It was in my *hair*," Tanith moaned, flicking the skin across the table.

Stephanie recoiled and flicked it back and Tanith started to laugh, but Skulduggery's hand came down, trapping it. He looked at them both.

"Four-year-olds," he said. "We're facing an unimaginable crisis and I'm dealing with four-year-olds."

"Sorry," said Stephanie.

"Sorry," said Tanith.

Morwenna Crow and China Sorrows walked in, followed seconds later by Ghastly Bespoke.

"Did they find anything?" Skulduggery asked, standing.

Morwenna answered. "The Cleavers have stormed every hideout and haunt we know of and they haven't found one trace of Serpine."

"The news about the Sceptre is spreading," China said.

"There are rumours that he is bringing his old allies in from the cold."

Meritorious and Tome joined them.

"If even one of the exiles returns," Meritorious said, "the balance of power will have shifted too much. We'll be overrun."

"We need to get that Sceptre from him," Tanith said, "see how *he* likes it."

"It wouldn't work," China said. "Even if we could get close to it without the crystal warning him that we're near, he owns it now and no one else can use it while he's alive."

"Then we kill him," Tome said.

Meritorious looked to Skulduggery, who nodded and spoke up. "Unfortunately, killing Serpine is not as easy as it may appear. He should be dead right now. I don't mean wounded, I don't mean dying, I mean dead. But he healed himself."

Stephanie frowned. "He can't be killed?"

"*Everyone* can be killed," Skulduggery said, turning his head to her slightly. "That's the one great assurance. I haven't encountered one thing on this planet that I haven't been able to kill, and I'm not going to let *him* be the exception to the rule."

"We need to strike *now*," Morwenna said, "before he can consolidate his power."

"How can we do that if we don't even know where he is?" Sagacious Tome asked impatiently.

"But we might know where he *was*," Skulduggery said. "Last night I received a call from a gentleman who supplies me with information from time to time. A distinctive silver car was seen on Denholm Street, near the docks. I made a call or two, established that almost every building on that street is being leased by a reputable firm. The one exception is a warehouse that has been leased to an individual, Mr Howard L. Craft."

Tome frowned. "So?"

"L. Craft. Lovecraft. Howard Philip Lovecraft wrote a series of stories commonly referred to as the Cthulhu Mythos, about dark gods who wanted to rule the earth. Some historians claim that Mr Lovecraft based his creations, in part, on legends he had heard about the Faceless Ones."

Tome made a face. "That's your only lead? A trick name Serpine *may* have used? We don't have time to waste on such vague half-clues; we've got to act on what we know!"

"Well what exactly do we know?" Morwenna asked. "We know he has a lunatic scheme to bring back the Faceless Ones, but we don't know how he intends to do it."

"Mr Bliss said the Sceptre was nothing more then a stepping stone," Stephanie offered.

"This is a grown-up conversation," Tome said, exasperated. "We don't need input from *you*, child."

Tanith and China spoke as one. "Don't call her child."

Clearly unused to admonitions from anyone who wasn't an Elder, Tome spluttered a bit and his face grew redder. Stephanie did her best to hide her grin behind a mask of serene indifference. Tanith caught her eye and winked.

"If the Sceptre is a stepping stone," Skulduggery said, ignoring Tome's indignation, "then he's going to use it to somehow retrieve the ritual he needs."

"Then it's our job to make sure that doesn't happen," Meritorious said. "Skulduggery, on behalf of the Council of Elders, I apologise for not involving you in this when we found Serpine's surveillance team dead. I also apologise for not listening to your warnings."

"Serpine would have had a back-up plan," Skulduggery said. "That's what makes him so dangerous."

"Maybe so. I'm afraid it's up to you and Miss Cain, and whoever else you might need, to try and find out what his next move is. I'm sorry for saddling you with that responsibility, but my fellow Elders and I are needed to prepare for all-out war."

Skulduggery bowed slightly. "In that case, we'll get right on it."

"Thank you."

Skulduggery wrapped the scarf around his face and put on his hat, then looked at the serious faces around him.

"Cheer up everyone," he said, a new brightness to his voice. "Since we're all going to die horribly anyway, what's there to be worried about?"

Stephanie very much feared she was going ever so slightly insane, because she found herself agreeing wholeheartedly with the living skeleton she was now following out of the room.

The Bentley was waiting for them when they left the Sanctuary. It gleamed like it was glad to be back to its former beauty. Stephanie got in and sank into the seat. The Bentley smelled nice. It smelled how beautiful cars ought to smell. The Canary Car hadn't smelled nice. It had just smelled *yellow*.

"It's good to have it back," Stephanie said when Skulduggery got in. "They worked miracles on it, they really did. Two days and it looks brand new."

Skulduggery nodded. "Cost me a fortune."

"It's worth it."

"Glad you think so. Also glad that I don't have to eat anytime soon. Or at all." She smiled and looked at him. He was looking out of the windscreen. Neither of them spoke for a few seconds.

"What is it?" she asked.

"I'm sorry?"

"You're thinking about something."

"I'm always thinking about something. Thinking is what I do. I'm very good at it."

"But you've just figured something out."

"And how did you know that?"

"You hold your head differently when you've just figured something out. So what is it?"

"It just occurred to me," he said. "In the cave, the Sceptre's crystal warned Serpine that I was close – but it didn't warn him that you were right there beside him."

She shrugged. "Maybe it didn't see me as a threat. It's not like I could have hurt him or anything."

"That's hardly the point," Skulduggery said. "We may have found a weakness in the ultimate weapon."

Stephanie frowned. "What?"

"Remember what Oisin, the nice man in the Echo Stone, said?" Skulduggery asked. "The black crystal sang to the gods whenever an enemy neared, but it was silent when the Ancients took it."

"So, what, it thinks I'm an Ancient?"

"Technically, according to your father at least, you might well be."

"Does that mean you're starting to believe that they were more than just legends and myths?"

"I'm... keeping an open mind about it. The thing I still don't understand, however, is why didn't Gordon tell me about your family history? We were friends for years, we had conversations about the Ancients and the Faceless Ones that went on for days, so why didn't he tell me?"

"Does it mean anything else? Being descended from the Ancients, I mean. What does it, what..."

"What does it signify?"

"Yes."

"It means you're special. It means you're meant to do this – you're meant to be involved in this world, in this life."

"I am?"

"You are."

"Then maybe that's why he didn't tell you. He wanted to write about it, from the outside, not be stuck in the middle of it all."

He cocked his head. "You're wise beyond your years, Valkyrie."

"Yes," she said. "Yes, I am."

24

PLANNING FOR MURDER

Mister Bliss stood in the palm of the Grasping Rock and watched Serpine approach. The Grasping Rock was shaped like a massive upturned hand, jutting from the peak of the mountain, fingers curled, as if reaching for the sun in the blood-red sky.

Serpine climbed into the palm with ease and Bliss bowed slightly. Serpine, for his part, merely smiled.

"Do you have it?" Bliss asked.

"Luckily for you, yes."

"Luckily for me?"

"My dear Mr Bliss, if I had gone down to those caves and emerged without *the Sceptre, where would that have left you? You would be standing in one of those cages in the Sanctuary's Gaol, powerless, awaiting judgement. Instead, you are* here, *standing with* me, *on the verge of a new world. Be thankful."*

"You seem to forget that if you had emerged with nothing, you'd be in the cage next to me..."

Serpine looked at him. A short time ago they would have been equals. But not now.

"...my master," Bliss finished respectfully, inclining his head.

Serpine smiled again and turned his back to him, looking out through the curled fingers of the rock and down at the valley below them.

"Is it as powerful as the scholars have imagined?" Bliss asked.

"What the scholars have imagined pales in comparison to the reality. No one can stop us now."

"The Elders," Bliss said.

Serpine turned his head. "I have a plan to deal with the Elders. They are nothing if not predictable, and they will die because of it. Meritorious himself will crumble to dust. Nothing can stand in our way."

"The Elders may be predictable," Bliss responded, "but that is not a trait Skulduggery Pleasant shares with them. He's cunning, powerful, and very, very *dangerous."*

"Do not concern yourself with the detective. I also have a plan to deal with him."

"Oh?"

"Skulduggery Pleasant has always had one weakness – he forms attachments to people who are very easily killed. In the past, it was his wife and child. Now, it is this girl that is with him, this Valkyrie Cain. He is only a threat to us if he is thinking clearly. You know as well as I do that once he becomes angry, his judgement is clouded."

"So what are you going to do?"

"I have already done it, Bliss. I have sent someone to... cloud his judgement. In less than an hour, Valkyrie Cain will be dead and Skulduggery Pleasant will trouble us no longer."

25

THE WHITE CLEAVER

Day had been beaten back by the time they got to Denholm Street, and the night was soaking through the city. It was a long street, dirty and quiet. The Bentley pulled up outside the warehouse. Ghastly and Tanith were waiting for them when they got out.

"Anyone inside?" Skulduggery asked, checking that his gun was loaded.

"Not as far as we can tell," Ghastly said, "but they could be masking their presence. If Serpine is in there, or Bliss, we're going to need back-up."

"They aren't here," Skulduggery said.

"How do you know?" Stephanie asked.

"Serpine used this place for something, something big and strange enough to raise a few eyebrows. He'd know eyebrows were being raised, he'd know I'd hear about it, so he's already moved on."

"Then why are *we* here?"

"You can only anticipate what someone is going to do if you know exactly what that someone has just done."

They approached the single door, and Tanith put her ear against it and listened. After a moment she put her hand over the lock, but instead of the lock breaking, this time Stephanie heard it click.

"How come you can't do that?" Stephanie whispered to Skulduggery. "It's faster than picking a lock and quieter than blasting the door down."

He shook his head sadly. "A living skeleton isn't enough for you, is it? What does it take to impress young people these days?"

Stephanie grinned. Tanith pushed the door open and they went inside. The door led straight into the warehouse office, a dark, poky room with a desk and an empty corkboard. The place obviously hadn't been used by any reputable company for quite some time. The office had a door that opened out to the warehouse proper, and a grime-covered window that Stephanie peered through.

"Seems quiet enough," she said.

Skulduggery hit a few switches on the wall and lights flickered on. They walked out on to the warehouse floor. There were pigeons in the rafters, high above them, that cooed and hooted and fluttered from one perch to the next, startled by the sudden light. They walked to the middle of the warehouse, where an array of what appeared to be medical equipment was collected around an operating table. Stephanie looked at Skulduggery.

"Any ideas?" she asked.

He hesitated. "Let's get the obvious out of the way. A lot of these machines would suggest that some kind of transfusion took place here."

Tanith held up a tube, examining the residue within. "I'm not a doctor, but I don't think this is the result of medical research."

"Magic then," Ghastly said.

"You can *inject* magic?" Stephanie asked, frowning.

"You can inject fluids with magical properties," Skulduggery told her as he took the tube from Tanith. "Before we had wonderful machines like this, it was a far messier process, but the result was the same."

"And what was the result?"

"The patient came out of the operation a changed man. Or woman. Or... thing. The question here is, what was the object of the game? What changes was Serpine seeking?"

"And who was the patient?"

"Patients, actually."

"Sorry?"

"There are two sets of needles, two IV bags, two of everything – enough to take care of two separate operations. We'll take a sample back to the Sanctuary, break it down and try to find out what it does. But for right now, everyone take a look around."

"What are we looking for?" Stephanie asked.

"Clues."

Stephanie glanced at Tanith, saw her raise an eyebrow sceptically and managed to restrain her grin.

Skulduggery and Ghastly walked slowly, passing their gaze over every surface, examining every centimetre of the machines, the table and the surrounding area. Stephanie and Tanith found themselves side by side, looking straight down at the floor.

"What does a clue look like?" Tanith whispered.

Stephanie fought the giggle down and whispered back. "I'm not sure. I'm looking for a footprint or something."

"Have you found one yet?"

"No. But that's probably because I haven't moved from this spot."

"Maybe we should move, pretend we know what we're doing."

"That's a good idea."

They started to walk, very slowly, still looking straight down.

"How's the magic coming along?" Tanith asked, keeping her voice low.

"I moved a shell."

"Hey, congratulations!"

Stephanie shrugged modestly. "It was only a shell."

"Makes no difference. Well done."

"Thanks. What age were you when you first did magic?"

"I was born into it," Tanith answered. "Folks were sorcerers – my brother was always doing *something*. I grew up doing magic."

"I didn't know you had a brother."

"Oh, yeah, a big brother and all. You have any brothers?"

"I'm an only child."

Tanith shrugged. "I always wanted a little sister. My

brother's great, I love him to death, but I always wanted a little sister to talk to, to share my secrets with, you know?"

"I wouldn't mind a sister either."

"Any chance of that happening?"

"I can't see what would be in it for my parents. I mean, they have the perfect daughter already – what more could they want?"

Tanith laughed, then tried to cover it up with a cough.

"Found something?" Skulduggery asked from behind them.

Tanith turned, looking serious. "No, sorry. I thought I had, but, no, it turned out to be, uh... more floor."

Stephanie hugged herself, trying to stop her shoulders from shaking with laughter.

"OK," Skulduggery said. "Well, keep looking."

Tanith nodded, turned back and nudged Stephanie to get her to shut up. Stephanie clamped a hand over her mouth and had to look away when she saw Tanith's face, straining to hold her composure.

"Cow," Tanith muttered and that was it, the floodgates opened, and Stephanie doubled over with laughter that echoed throughout the warehouse. Tanith pointed at Stephanie and backed away. "Skulduggery, she's not being professional!"

Stephanie's laugh proved infectious and Tanith was soon on

her knees. Skulduggery and Ghastly just looked at them.

"What's going on?" Ghastly asked.

"I'm not entirely sure," Skulduggery answered.

They looked at Stephanie and Tanith and shook their heads. "Women," they said together.

Stephanie wiped the tears from her eyes and looked around at Skulduggery, and then something fell from the ceiling, and landed behind the detective without a sound. Her laughter vanished as she stood. "Behind you!" she yelled.

Skulduggery wheeled, gun in hand, and everyone froze. They looked at the man. His uniform, though identical in design to the Cleavers, was of startling white.

"Stand down," Ghastly said as Stephanie and Tanith ran up to join them. "We are working with the Elder Council. Stand down."

The White Cleaver didn't move.

"What do you want?" Skulduggery asked.

A moment dragged itself by, and then the White Cleaver raised his arm and pointed straight at Stephanie.

"That's all we need to know," Skulduggery said and fired, four shots to the chest and two to the head. The White Cleaver jerked with each impact, but it was clear that the bullets didn't penetrate his coat, and the two to the head ricocheted off the helmet, leaving dark scratches against the white.

"Damn," Skulduggery muttered.

Stephanie stayed back as Skulduggery, Tanith and Ghastly closed in on their new adversary. The helmet denied them any chance of knowing where he was looking, but Stephanie knew he was looking right into her eyes.

Tanith attacked first, feinting with a low kick then snapping it up high. The Cleaver didn't fall for the ruse and slapped the high kick away as Ghastly attacked from behind. The Cleaver spun with a kick of his own that caught Tanith in the gut, and he ducked under the punch that Ghastly sent his way. Ghastly's fists blurred but the Cleaver absorbed the blows and his hand shot out, catching Ghastly in the side of the neck. Ghastly staggered and Skulduggery thrust out his palm and the air rippled.

But instead of being pushed backwards, the Cleaver moved *through* the ripples without being affected. *The uniform*, Stephanie thought. Unfazed, Skulduggery threw a punch that the Cleaver caught.

Skulduggery was flipped over but when he landed he had reversed the grip. His foot sneaked out, striking the Cleaver's knee and now Skulduggery was the one doing the twisting, and the Cleaver was the one who flipped.

While he was in mid-flip, however, the Cleaver got his free hand to the ground to cartwheel back to his feet. A pause followed and Stephanie's three friends reappraised their opponent.

Tanith took her sword from beneath her coat and slid it from its scabbard. Ghastly let his jacket slip off and Skulduggery put away his pistol, freeing his hands.

"You don't have to do this," he said to the Cleaver. "Tell us where Serpine is –tell us what his plans are. We can help you. You are not going to lay one finger on Valkyrie Cain, but we *will* help you."

The Cleaver's answer was to reach behind him and draw his scythe. Skulduggery grunted in dissatisfaction.

The Cleaver darted towards them before anyone could react, using the scythe like a pole-vaulter to swing himself up, kicking both Skulduggery and Ghastly in the chest at the same time.

They went stumbling back and Tanith came in, sword flashing. The Cleaver dodged back, whirling his scythe to parry the blade.

Sparks flew as the metals clashed, sword against scythe, and such was the ferocity of Tanith's assault that the Cleaver didn't notice Ghastly until it was too late. Ghastly's strong arms wrapped around him, pinning his arms to his sides, making him drop the scythe.

Tanith moved in for the kill and the Cleaver's leg blurred in a crescent, his bootheel slamming into her wrist as she neared. She hissed in pain and dropped the sword, clutching her wrist.

The Cleaver rammed his heel into Ghastly's shin and whacked the back of his helmet against his nose. He then kicked both legs into the air and over his head, slipping out from under Ghastly's arms. His hands went to the ground and he continued the movement, sending both boots into Ghastly's face.

Ghastly fell back and the Cleaver held the handstand for a moment, then dropped back to his feet as Skulduggery came at him.

Skulduggery summoned fire and hurled two handfuls into the Cleaver. The flames didn't catch but they did throw him back, and Skulduggery threw a lightning-fast jab that he followed up with a right hook. He didn't seem to mind that he was hitting a helmet, and Stephanie noted with satisfaction the way their opponent was sent stumbling.

The Cleaver recovered quickly, however, and they started trading punches and kicks, elbows and knees, and she watched them block and lock and counter-lock, all the while moving around each other in an elaborate and brutal dance.

"Stephanie!" Skulduggery called out as he fought. "Get out of here!"

"I'm not leaving you!"

"You have to! I don't know how to stop him!"

Tanith snatched her sword off the ground and grabbed Stephanie's arm. "We have to go," she said firmly and Stephanie nodded.

They ran back the way they had come. As they were passing into the office, Stephanie glanced back, saw the Cleaver spin with a kick that sent Skulduggery to the floor. In one fluid movement, he got a toe under the staff of the scythe, flicked it up and caught it, and then he was running after her.

Stephanie burst into the dark alleyway and Tanith pressed her hand against the door as she closed it – Stephanie heard her mutter "Withstand" – and a polished sheen spread across its surface.

"That'll hold him for a minute," she said.

They ran for the Bentley. The Cleaver pounded on the door behind them, but it wouldn't open and it wouldn't break. The pounding stopped.

They reached the Bentley and Tanith looked at Stephanie. "Do you have the key?"

A window exploded, high up near the warehouse's roof, and

the White Cleaver dropped and landed in a crouch in the middle of the alley, shards of glass raining down with him. He straightened up, unfolded his arms and raised his head.

Tanith stood between the Cleaver and Stephanie, holding the sword in her left hand. She cradled her injured right arm by her side. The Cleaver twirled his scythe slowly.

Skulduggery and Ghastly leaped through the broken window. The Cleaver turned and Ghastly crashed into him.

"Start the car!" Ghastly yelled.

Skulduggery pressed the keyring and the locks sprang open with a *beep*, and they all jumped in. The engine roared to life.

"Ghastly!" Skulduggery shouted. "Let's go!"

Ghastly slammed a punch into the Cleaver and rolled to his feet but the Cleaver kicked out and Ghastly stumbled. The scythe flashed, the staff whacking against Ghastly's jaw. He dropped to his knees.

"Ghastly!" Stephanie screamed. Skulduggery opened his door, went to get out, but Ghastly raised his eyes, shook his head.

"We're not leaving you!" Skulduggery shouted.

The Cleaver stepped up to Ghastly, ready to swing the scythe.

"You've got to," Ghastly said, ever so softly.

He lowered his head and clenched his fists, his eyes closed.

As the Cleaver swung, the ground seemed to latch on to Ghastly's knees. It spread instantly, turning his legs to concrete, then his torso, his arms, his head, his entire body in the time it took the scythe to cross the space between them, and when the Cleaver tried to take his head, he could only chip at the neck. Stephanie instinctively knew what he'd done – this was the last Elemental power, earth, the power Skulduggery had described as purely defensive, and purely for use as a last resort.

The White Cleaver looked directly at Stephanie as Skulduggery put the car in gear. They left them there – the White Cleaver and Ghastly – and sped through the city streets.

26

THE LAST STAND OF…

Eachan Meritorious waited in the shadow of Dublin's Christ Church Cathedral, watching the world go about its business. There were times when he felt guilty about hiding magic from the masses, when he felt sure that they would embrace the wonder and the beauty if only they were given the opportunity. But then he'd come to his senses, and realise that humankind had enough things to be worrying about without a subculture that they might see as a threat to their very validity. As an Elder, it was his job to protect the outside world from truths they weren't yet ready to know.

Morwenna Crow walked up, her dark robes flowing over the grass. She was as clean and as elegant as the day he had first met her.

"It's not like Skulduggery Pleasant to be late," she remarked.

"Sagacious said he sounded urgent," Meritorious said. "He may have run into some difficulty."

Morwenna looked around the corner of the cathedral, to the busy street beyond the railing. The bright lights, amber and yellow, framed her face. She seemed almost angelic. "I don't like meeting out in the open like this. We're too exposed. He should know better."

"Skulduggery picked this place for a reason," Meritorious said gently. "I trust his judgement. He's earned that much at least."

They turned as Sagacious Tome appeared beside them, fading up from nothing.

"Sagacious," Morwenna said, "did Skulduggery say why he wanted to meet us here?"

Sagacious looked nervous as the materialisation completed and he became solid. "I'm sorry, Morwenna, he just told me to make sure both of you were outside the cathedral."

"This had better be good," she said. "We don't have a lot of time to spare these days. Serpine could strike anywhere, at any time."

Meritorious watched Sagacious smile sadly. "That's very true," Sagacious said. "And if I may, I just want to take this opportunity to let you both know, in the times when we were friends, they were great times indeed."

Morwenna laughed. "We're not dead yet, Sagacious."

And then he looked at her and the smile turned to something else. "Actually, Morwenna, you *are*."

The Hollow Men converged and Sagacious faded to nothing. Meritorious didn't even have time to register the betrayal before he saw Serpine, striding towards them, holding the Sceptre. He instinctively conjured a protective shield that made the air glimmer, but when the crystal flashed the black lightning came right through the shield like it wasn't even there and then there was—

Nothing.

*

The Administrator charged through a crowd outside the Olympia Theatre, drawing a chorus of angry shouts and curses. He stumbled but managed to stay up, managed to keep running. He glanced behind.

He couldn't see anyone pursuing him. He didn't think he had been seen, but he couldn't be sure. He had been standing by the car when Nefarian Serpine had appeared. He had seen Meritorious explode into dust and ash, saw the black lightning strike Morwenna Crow as she tried to rush her enemies.

He had ducked down, terrified. Tome betrayed them. Tome betrayed them all. The Administrator had abandoned the car and started running.

He had to get back to the Sanctuary. He had to warn the others.

27

NO CALM BEFORE THE STORM

Skulduggery had given her money and Stephanie had gone in to pay while he refilled the Bentley's tank. As she waited for her change she looked at the chocolate bars on display and tried remembering the last time she'd eaten chocolate. She always ate chocolate when something bad happened, but these days chocolate just wasn't enough.

Everything was going wrong. Tanith was injured, Ghastly was nothing more than a statue and now they had the White Cleaver to worry about. It was getting to the point where

Stephanie didn't know why they were bothering to fight any more, although she'd never say that to Skulduggery. He seemed to think she was like him – never give up, never surrender. But she wasn't. The only reason she didn't tell him this was because she liked the way he thought of her, and she didn't want to disappoint him. But the truth was, the Valkyrie Cain he thought he knew was a lot stronger than Stephanie Edgley could ever be.

She walked back outside. Skulduggery was slotting the petrol nozzle back into the pump. Tanith had gone to soak her hand in the same healing mixture she had given Stephanie.

Now that they were alone, Stephanie didn't quite know what to say. Skulduggery screwed the petrol cap shut and stood there, perfectly still. With his hat on and his scarf hiding his jaw, it could have been a mannequin standing there for all the difference it made.

"I'm sorry," Stephanie said. He looked at her.

"If it wasn't for me, Ghastly would be... he'd be with us. It's my fault he had to use the earth power." She fought to keep her voice from trembling. "How long will he stay like that, do you think?"

Skulduggery took a moment. "I sincerely don't know, Valkyrie. It's the most unpredictable power we have. He could be stuck as a statue for a day, a week, or a hundred years. There's no way of knowing."

"I've ruined everything."

"No—"

"That Cleaver was after *me*. Ghastly was forced to—"

"Ghastly wasn't *forced* to do anything," Skulduggery interrupted. "It was his choice. And it wasn't your fault. Serpine sent his assassin after *you* to hurt *me*. It's what he does."

"He sent him after me because he knew I wouldn't be able to defend myself. He knows you're looking after me, he knows I'm your weak spot."

Skulduggery tilted his head. "*Looking after* you? Is that how you see this? You think I'm babysitting you?"

"Well aren't you? I've got no magic; I can't fight; I can't throw fire or run on ceilings. What use am I to you? I'm weak."

Skulduggery shook his head. "No, you're not. You haven't trained in magic or combat, but you're not weak. Serpine underestimates you. Everyone underestimates you. You're stronger than they know. You're stronger than *you* know."

"I wish you were right."

"Of course I'm right. I'm me."

Stephanie heard a phone ring as Tanith walked into the light of the forecourt. She had wrapped a bandage around her wrist.

The magical properties of the healing mixture would already be working to reduce the swelling and mend the damage. Tanith held her phone to her ear. Stephanie didn't like the way her face seemed to slacken as she listened to whatever was being said.

She hung up without replying. "Skulduggery," she said softly. "You have your phone on?"

"Battery's low," he said.

"They've been trying to contact you. The Administrator, the Sanctuary."

"What's wrong?" Stephanie asked.

"The Elders," Tanith said, her voice empty. "Sagacious Tome betrayed them. The Elders are dead."

Stephanie's hand was at her mouth. "Oh, God."

"Tome's been working with Serpine all along. He's a traitor. Like Mr Bliss. They're all traitors. Skulduggery, what are we going to do?"

Stephanie looked to him, praying that he'd come up with a great new plan, a scheme to ensure victory and a happy ending. He didn't answer.

"Did you hear me?" Tanith continued, the emptiness in her voice giving way to sudden anger. "Are you even listening? Do you even *care*? Maybe you don't. Maybe you *want* to die again;

maybe you want to join your wife and child, but hey! *We* don't want to die, OK? I don't. Valkyrie doesn't."

Skulduggery stood there. A mannequin. Silent.

"Do you think we stand a chance against Serpine?" Tanith asked. "Tome? Bliss? That Cleaver? Do you really think we stand a chance against all of them?"

"What do you suggest we do?" Skulduggery said, his voice slow and steady. "Stand back and let Serpine grow stronger? Stand back and let him recruit more allies, let him open the door and let the Faceless Ones come through?"

"He's *winning*, OK? Serpine is winning this war!"

"No such thing."

"What?"

"There's no such thing as winning or losing. There is *won* and there is *lost*; there is *victory* and *defeat*. There are absolutes. Everything in between is still left to fight for. Serpine will have won only when there is no one left to stand against him. Until then, there is only the struggle, because tides do what tides do – they turn."

"This is insane—"

He turned to her so sharply Stephanie thought he might strike her.

"I've just seen a very dear friend turn into a *statue*, Tanith.

Meritorious and Crow, two of the few people in this world I respected, have been murdered. So yes, you're right when you say our allies are dropping like flies, but this was never going to be an easy fight. Casualties are to be expected. And you know what we do? We step over them and we move on because we don't have any other choice. Now I'm going to stop Serpine once and for all. Anyone who wants to come with me, they're welcome. Anyone who doesn't, it won't make a blind bit of difference. Serpine *will* be stopped and that's all there is to it."

He got into the Bentley and started the engine. Stephanie hesitated, then opened the passenger door and slid in. She glanced at Skulduggery as she buckled up but he was staring straight ahead. He waited three seconds, then put the car in gear and was about to drive off when Tanith got in behind them.

"No need to get all dramatic about it," she muttered and Stephanie managed to smile. Skulduggery pulled out on to the road, driving fast.

"Where are we going?" Stephanie asked.

"Weren't you listening?" Skulduggery responded, sounding like he was back to his old self. "We're going to stop Serpine. I just made a whole speech about it. It was very good."

Tanith leaned forward. "You know where he is?"

"Yes, I do. It came to me just there as I was filling the tank."

"What did?"

"The Sceptre. Why did Serpine go after the Sceptre?"

Stephanie frowned. "Because it's the ultimate weapon."

"And why did he want it?"

"To, you know, to retrieve the ritual he needs to bring the Faceless Ones back, to force whoever knows it to tell him."

"No."

"He *isn't* going to use it to retrieve the ritual?"

"The Sceptre's too clumsy, too unwieldy. If he threatens to kill the only person in the world who knows how to work the ritual – what if that person chooses death rather than hand it over? What's he supposed to do then? No. He used the Sceptre to kill the Elders. That's the only reason he wanted it. He knew he wasn't powerful enough to take them on without it."

"And so how does that help him retrieve the ritual?"

"This isn't just about the ritual any more. What do you get if you kill the Elders?"

"This sounds like a joke."

"Valkyrie—"

"I don't know."

"Yes, you do. Now think. What would killing the Elders result in?"

"Panic? Fear? Three empty parking spaces in the Sanctuary?"

Skulduggery looked at her and Stephanie's confusion lifted. "Oh, God," she said.

"He's after the Book," Skulduggery said. "He needed the Sceptre to kill Meritorious and Morwenna Crow in order to dismantle the spell protecting it. He doesn't have to force anyone to do anything; all he'll have to do is *ask*. He's been after the Book of Names all along."

28

CARNAGE

Dublin City was quiet when they reached the Waxworks Museum, as if it was holding its breath. The stars were obscured by a veil of dark clouds, and as they left the Bentley and approached the rear entrance, the rain fell steadily. On the street beyond the gates, cars splashed through puddles and the occasional pedestrian hurried by with his head down. Skulduggery moved quickly but cautiously up to the open door, and Stephanie and Tanith followed.

Stephanie had expected to arrive in the middle of a pitched

battle – she expected to hear the sounds of fighting. But the Waxworks was silent. As they walked through the exhibits to the hidden door, Skulduggery slowed and eventually came to a complete stop.

"What's wrong?" Stephanie whispered.

He turned his head slowly, peering into the darkness. "I don't want to alarm anybody, but we're not alone."

That's when they came, the Hollow Men, detaching themselves from the shadows with only the faintest rasp of warning. In an instant they were surrounded by the mindless, heartless, soulless *things*.

Tanith waded through them, her sword strokes deliberate and devastating, every move claiming another un-life. Skulduggery clicked his fingers and a group of Hollow Men were suddenly alight. Stephanie shrank back as they wheeled around blindly. The flames ate through their skin and ignited the putrid gas trapped inside, and with a burst of fire and heat, the Hollow Men fell.

One of them avoided the flames and lunged at Stephanie and she punched it square in the face, her fist sinking into its head slightly. Its own fist swung at her and she ducked, then moved into it like she'd seen Skulduggery do, jammed her hip into it and twisted, and the Hollow Man hit the ground. It wasn't graceful and it wasn't pretty, but it worked. While it was down there she grabbed its wrist and stomped on its chest, and with a loud tear she pulled its arm off.

As the Hollow Man deflated beneath her, Stephanie realised everything had gone quiet again. She looked up at Skulduggery and Tanith, realised they'd been watching her.

"Not bad," Tanith said, an eyebrow raised.

"That's the last of them," Skulduggery said. "Now for the main event."

The hidden door to the Sanctuary hung open like a gaping wound. A dead Cleaver lay just inside. Stephanie hesitated for a moment, then stepped over the body and they followed the steps down.

The Sanctuary's foyer had witnessed most of the carnage. It was littered with the dead. There were no wounded here, there were no dying – there were only corpses. Some had been cut to ribbons, some were unmarked and there were places, spread across the floor, where there was only the dust of those who had fallen before the Sceptre. Stephanie tried to step without touching the remains, but they were piled so deep that this was impossible.

She passed the Administrator. His body was curled, his fingers hooked and frozen in death. His face was a mask of agony. A victim of Serpine's red right hand.

Skulduggery went to the doorway on their left and peered around, making sure the corridor was empty. Tanith passed, pressing herself against the wall and nodding to him. He moved forward, stopped, nodded back to her, and they continued like this as they stalked deeper into the Sanctuary.

No more walking straight into danger, Stephanie thought to herself. This was the only sign they gave that they might actually be afraid.

She followed along behind. Her palms were slick with sweat and her mouth was dry. She felt as if her legs weren't going to support her for very much longer. Her thoughts went to her parents, her loving parents. If she died here, if she died tonight, would they even notice? Her reflection would carry on with its empty masquerade and they'd gradually begin to realise that this thing, this thing they thought was their daughter, its affections weren't even real. They'd realise it was all an act, but they'd still think it was *her*. And they'd live out the rest of their days thinking that their own daughter didn't love them.

Stephanie didn't want to put them through that. She *was* going to die, she knew she was. She should turn now, and run, run away. This wasn't her business. This wasn't her world. It was like Ghastly said, the first time she met him – Gordon had already lost his life because of this nonsense. Was she so keen to join him?

She didn't hear him. She didn't hear his footsteps, not even when he was so close he could have reached out and stroked her hair. She didn't catch a glimpse out of the corner of her eye, and she didn't notice his shadow or see a reflection, because if he didn't want to be seen, he wouldn't be seen. But as he was moving behind her she felt his presence, she felt the air shift slightly and brush against the skin of her hands and she didn't even have to turn her head – she just *knew*.

She launched herself forward and Skulduggery and Tanith looked back as she rolled and came up.

The White Cleaver stood there, silent as a ghost, deadly as a plague.

Tanith turned to see Valkyrie coming up out of her roll and saw the White Cleaver standing behind her.

"Valkyrie," Tanith said, keeping her voice low and steady, "get behind me."

Stephanie moved backwards and the Cleaver attempted to stop her.

"I'll hold him off," Tanith said, not taking her eyes off her adversary. "You stop Serpine."

Tanith drew her sword, and she heard Skulduggery and

Stephanie hurry away. The White Cleaver reached over his shoulder and pulled out his scythe.

Tanith stepped towards him.

"I ordered you to distract the Hollow Men, didn't I?" she said. "You were one of the Cleavers assigned to us."

He didn't answer. He didn't even move.

"For whats it's worth," Tanith said, "I'm sorry about what happened to you. But it was necessary. And for what it's worth, I'm sorry for what is *going* to happen to you. But that's necessary too." He started twirling his scythe and she raised an eyebrow. "Come and have a go if you think you're hard enough."

He lunged and she blocked and sprang at him, her sword slicing through the air. He ducked back and blocked, spinning as the scythe whistled over Tanith's head. Her sword clashed with his blade and then the handle of the scythe, and his blade clashed with her sword and then the lacquered scabbard she still held in her left hand.

She ducked under his guard, staying in close, where she had the advantage, where he couldn't manoeuvre the scythe.

His blocks were lightning fast but he was on the defensive and one of her strikes would get through eventually. Her sword sliced through his side and he stumbled back, out of range. Tanith looked at the blood on his white coat and gave him a smile. Then the blood started to darken and a black stain moved over the red.

Her smile dropped and the bleeding stopped altogether.

She backed away. There was a door behind her and she waved it open as the Cleaver advanced.

The room she backed into was filled with cages, and in these cages, men and women stood and sat. She realised instantly where she was – the Sanctuary's Gaol. The people in these cages were the worst of the worst, criminals of such a sickening and grotesque order that they had to be held here, in the Sanctuary itself. The cages bound their powers while at the same time sustaining their bodies, keeping them healthy and nourished. It meant neither the Elders nor the Cleavers had to bring them food and water – these criminals only had themselves for company. And when the person in the cage next to each of them was as maniacal and as egotistical as they were, that was hell itself.

The Cleaver pursued her steadily down the steps, sparks flying as their blades clashed.

The prisoners watched, and for the first few moments, they were confused. The Cleavers were their jailers, yet this Cleaver wore white, and they recognised something within him, something that identified him as one of them. They started to shout and cheer as Tanith was forced back, enemies all around her.

She blocked a strike and her bruised wrist gave way. The Cleaver took full advantage, his blade passing along her belly, drawing blood. She grimaced in pain and retreated under the Cleaver's impossibly fast onslaught, barely managing to keep up her defence.

The prisoners laughed and jeered, reaching through the cage bars at her, pulling at her hair, trying to scratch her. One of them snagged her coat and she spun out of it, throwing her sword and scabbard into the air as she freed her arms from the sleeves and catching them again before the Cleaver could close the gap.

He swung and she blocked with the scabbard and flicked up with the sword but he was twisting the scythe, deflecting the strike and coming back with one of his own.

Tanith dodged back, lost her footing and went into a backwards roll as he brought the scythe down, the point of the blade striking the ground where she had just been.

The prisoners howled with laughter as she turned and ran to the wall, the Cleaver right behind her. She jumped to the wall and kept going till she was upside-down, and she crossed the ceiling, trading strikes with the Cleaver below her. He was forced to walk backwards, to defend and attack over his own head.

The Cleaver slashed and missed and she saw her chance and took it. She struck his left hand with her scabbard and his fingers opened. She dropped and flipped, landing before he could recover, and snatched the scythe from his grasp. She kicked out and he stumbled back and she drove her sword into him.

The prisoners stopped jeering. The Cleaver took a step back.

Tanith swung the scythe, burying the blade in his chest. He fell to his knees, black blood dripping on to the floor.

She looked down at him, felt his eyes through his visor, looking back at her. Then his weight fell back onto his haunches, his shoulders sagged and his head lolled forward.

The prisoners were muttering now, cheated out of seeing her die. Tanith gripped her sword and pulled it from the Cleaver's body, snatched up the scabbard and ran for the steps.

She heard a crash from elsewhere in the Sanctuary – the Repository – and urgency lent her speed. Just as she neared the top step, however, one of the prisoners laughed.

She turned and, to her horror, saw the White Cleaver standing, pulling the scythe from his chest. *He can't be stopped*, she said to herself. *Just like Serpine, he can't be stopped.* She ran the last few steps to the door and just as she reached it the breath went out of her.

She stopped, frowning, willing her body to move, but it wouldn't listen. She looked down, at the tip of the scythe that protruded through her chest.

She turned, cursing herself, saw the Cleaver walking up the steps toward her. That was some throw. She almost laughed. Her right arm was numb and her sword fell from her grip. He stepped up beside her and took hold of the scythe. He circled, moving her around, looking at her like he was observing her pain, remembering what it was like.

A twist of his hands and she was forced to her knees. She gasped when he removed the weapon, saw her own blood, deep red, mix with the black blood already on the blade. Her body was shutting down. She wasn't going to be able to defend herself.

He raised the scythe. Tanith looked up, ready to die, then realised that when he had circled her he had passed through the doorway, and was now standing out in the corridor.

She lunged, slamming the door in his visored face. She pressed her hand against it and whispered "Withstand." The sheen spread over the door just as the Cleaver began to pound on it from the other side.

She had failed. She had slowed him down but she hadn't stopped him, and now Serpine had his attack dog back.

Tanith tried standing but her body couldn't take any more. She slumped to the ground. The prisoners watched from their cages with delighted eyes, and as her blood seeped through her tunic, they started whispering.

29

DEEP IN DUBLIN, DEATH

The White Cleaver stood there, silent as a ghost, deadly as a plague.

"Valkyrie," Tanith said. "Get behind me." Stephanie backed up until she was beside Skulduggery.

"I'll hold him off," Tanith said. "You stop Serpine." She drew her sword. The Cleaver drew his scythe.

Stephanie felt Skulduggery touch her arm and they moved off. "You're going to have to go after the Sceptre," Skulduggery whispered as they jogged through the corridor. "You can get close to it, I can't. It's not much of a plan, but sometimes simplicity is the way to go."

The Repository was just ahead. They slowed, and Skulduggery gripped both her arms and turned to her. "But you listen to me. If it goes wrong, if we lose the element of surprise, I want you to get out of here. No matter what happens to me, I want you to run, do you understand?"

Stephanie swallowed. "Yes."

He hesitated. "Serpine used my wife and child as a weapon against me. In order to do so, he had to kill them. He took my family's death and he made it about me. Valkyrie, when you die, it will be *your* death and yours alone. Let it come to you on your own terms." She nodded.

"Valkyrie Cain," he said, "it has been an absolute pleasure knowing you."

She looked back at him. "You too." If he'd had lips, she knew he'd be smiling.

They sneaked up to the doors. They were already open and Stephanie could see Serpine, the Sceptre in his hand and his back to them, taking slow, deliberate steps towards the Book of Names. Sagacious Tome was watching, but he too had his back to the doors.

"I can't see Mr Bliss," Stephanie whispered and Skulduggery shook his head – neither could he.

Stephanie hesitated, then passed into the Repository and crept to her left. She reached a heavy table laden with artefacts and peered around. Serpine had stopped walking, and for a moment she thought he knew she was there, but as she watched he turned and walked back, shaking his head.

"It's still too strong," he said.

"It's as weak as it's going to get," Sagacious Tome said. "I thought with Meritorious and Morwenna dead, the barrier wouldn't pose a problem. But I can't withdraw my contribution to the spell, not without the others joining me in the ceremony."

Serpine rejoined Tome, arching an eyebrow. "Then perhaps we shouldn't have killed them."

"*I* didn't kill them!" Tome said defensively. "You did!"

Stephanie stayed low as she crept from behind the table. Serpine laughed. "I may have been the one to turn them to dust, but you set them up, Sagacious, you drew them in. You betrayed them."

Tome spun on Serpine, jabbing at the space between them with his finger. "No, I didn't! It was their weakness that led to their downfall, their own shortcomings. They had all this power and they were satisfied to just, to just *sit* there and let it all go to waste."

"Until recently, I had never thought of you as ambitious..."

"No one had. *Sagacious Tome*, they said, *he's a non-entity. He's not the strongest, he's not the wisest... he's nothing.* That's what they said. I know it. For years, people have been underestimating me. It's time people recognised my power."

Stephanie got to her hands and knees and started crawling. She was in shadow and they weren't looking her way, but if either turned there was a chance they would see her. Stephanie wasn't in the mood to take any chances.

"I'm going to make them pay," Tome was saying. "Everyone who ever questioned me. The streets will run red with their blood."

"How dramatic," Serpine said and raised his hand. Stephanie saw the Book lift off its pedestal and hover there for a moment, then he grunted impatiently and let it drop again.

"I told you, that's not going to work!" Tome said. "It's how close you are to *getting* it. It doesn't have to be *physically* close; it isn't a *physical* barrier. It's a *mental* barrier!"

Stephanie held her breath. She was behind the pillar next to them. Serpine's voice was so close he could have been speaking right into her ear. "So with you, the final Elder, remaining, the barrier isn't sufficiently weakened to let me through, is that right?"

"Yes, but that's not my fault! I did what I could!"

"Yes, you did, yes, you did. And now there's one more thing you can do to help solve this little problem."

"What are you talking about?" Tome asked and then his tone changed suddenly, became afraid. "What are you doing? Point that thing somewhere else, Serpine. *I'm warning you, point that—*"

There was a black flash, and silence.

After a moment, she heard Serpine's footsteps move off again, and Stephanie took a peek. He was walking slowly, concentrating on the Book, his back to her. This was the only chance she was going to get.

She crept out from behind the pillar, ignoring the fresh pile of dust at her feet. There was no way she could close the distance without giving herself away. He'd hear her, sense her, whatever. But he was holding the Sceptre in his hand so *loosely*...

Stephanie narrowed her eyes and stepped forward.

He had heard her and was turning, but she didn't care. The Sceptre was coming up, the black crystal starting to glow. She flexed her fingers and splayed her hand, snapping open her palm and pushing at the air, and the space around her hand rippled and the Sceptre flew from Serpine's grasp, flew away from them both and hit the far wall.

Serpine hissed in anger and turned. They heard the Sceptre

start to sing as Skulduggery sprinted in. He dived into the air and the space around him shimmered as he shot forward. He covered the distance in the blink of an eye. He crashed into Serpine, taking him off his feet.

They hit the pedestal and it toppled, the Book falling as they sprawled on to the ground. Skulduggery was the first to stand and he hauled Serpine up, shoved him against a pillar and fired off a punch that jerked his head back.

Serpine lunged but Skulduggery snagged his wrist and stepped in and then *under* the arm. He turned and wrenched and Serpine yelled in pain as a loud *crack* echoed through the chamber.

Serpine tried gathering purple vapour in his hand but Skulduggery batted the hand away, chopped into the side of his neck. Serpine gagged and dropped back, and Skulduggery kicked his legs out from under him.

"You never could fight worth a damn," Skulduggery said, standing over him. "But then you didn't need to, did you? Not when you had lackeys to do the fighting for you. Where are your lackeys now, Nefarian?"

"I don't need them," Serpine muttered. "I don't need anyone. I'll crush you myself. Grind your bones to *dust*."

Skulduggery tilted his head. "Unless you've got an army

tucked away in that fancy coat of yours, I sincerely doubt it."

Serpine scrambled up and rushed at him, but Skulduggery drove in a kick and brought his closed fist down on to his shoulder, and Serpine fell to his knees.

Stephanie had to get to the Sceptre before Serpine recovered. She was pushing herself off the ground when she realised that the Book of Names was lying open right beside her. She glanced at the pages and the columns of names started to rearrange themselves before her eyes. She saw her own name written there, but she looked up when she heard Skulduggery grunt.

Serpine was on his knees but his lips were moving, and the wall behind Skulduggery came alive with hands that reached out and grabbed him. Skulduggery was pulled back and Serpine stood. There were a series of dull cracks and pops as Serpine's broken bones mended and realigned.

"Where are your oh-so-clever taunts *now*, detective?"

Skulduggery struggled against the grip of a dozen hands. "You've got big ears," he managed to say, before he was pulled even further back, *into the wall*, and then he was gone.

Serpine looked over, saw Stephanie, saw how close she was to the Sceptre.

He snapped out his hand and a thin purple tendril whipped towards the Sceptre. He pulled his arm back and the Sceptre flew off the ground but Stephanie lunged and managed to grab it.

She was jerked off her feet but her grip was strong and the tendril broke, becoming vapour, and she hit the floor. She heard a crash and looked around as a table hurtled straight at her. She tried to dive out of the way but she wasn't quick enough.

It hit her and she screamed, dropped the Sceptre and clutched at her broken leg. She shut her eyes against the tears of pain, and when she opened them again, Mr Bliss was walking into the room.

"Where have you been?" Serpine snapped.

"I was delayed," Mr Bliss answered. "But you seem to have done fine without me."

Serpine narrowed his eyes. "Indeed. Still, there's one more adversary to deal with."

Mr Bliss looked at Stephanie. "You're going to kill her?"

"Me? No. You are."

"I'm sorry?"

"If you want to reap the rewards of this night, you have to get your hands a little bloody."

"You want *me* to kill an unarmed child?" Mr Bliss asked doubtfully.

"Look on it as a test of your commitment to our lords and

masters. You don't have a problem with that, do you?"

Mr Bliss looked at him coolly. "Do you have a weapon for me, or do you just want me to beat her to death with a large stick?"

Serpine took a dagger from his coat and lobbed it over to him. Mr Bliss snatched it out of the air and held it, testing its weight. Stephanie felt her throat go dry.

Mr Bliss looked at her but didn't say anything. He just sighed and hurled the dagger, and Stephanie made a face and turned her head...

...and heard Serpine laugh.

She looked back. The dagger hadn't touched her. It hadn't even come close. It was in Serpine's hand. He had caught it before it had sliced into his glittering left eye.

"I thought as much," Serpine said.

Mr Bliss flung himself at Serpine, but Serpine ripped his glove off and raised his red right hand and Mr Bliss collapsed. Serpine listened to him scream for a few moments before dropping his hand, and Mr Bliss gasped.

"No doubt you want to kill me," Serpine said as he approached him. "No doubt you want to rip me limb from limb, and with your legendary strength, I know you could do it and not even exert yourself. But answer me this, Mr Bliss – what good is legendary strength when you can't get close enough to use it?"

Mr Bliss tried to stand, but his knees gave out and he hit the ground again.

"I'm curious," Serpine continued. "Why the pretence? Why go to all this trouble; why put yourself in this position? Why didn't you just stick with the detective?"

Mr Bliss managed to shake his head. "We mightn't have been able to stop you," he said. "I know you, Serpine... you always have plans to fall back on. You were too... dangerous... too unpredictable. I needed you to get the Sceptre."

Serpine smiled. "And why was that?"

Mr Bliss echoed that smile with one of his own, albeit a drained and sickly version. "Because once you had the Sceptre, I could predict your actions."

"So you predicted my invulnerability?" Serpine laughed. "Oh, well done."

"No one's invulnerable," Mr Bliss whispered.

"Yes, well," Serpine said with a shrug. "*You're* certainly not."

Stephanie watched in horror as Serpine again pointed his right hand and Mr Bliss contorted in agony. His screams reached new heights, and just when it seemed like he could take no more, Serpine picked him up and, with his hands pressed against him, gathered the purple vapour in his fists. Mr Bliss was blasted backwards through the air, into a group of shelves at the far side of the room. He didn't get up.

Serpine turned back to Stephanie.

"Sorry for the interruption," he said as he picked her up. His hands gripped the lapels of her coat and he lifted her off her feet, looking up at her as he spoke. Her right leg dangled uselessly, and that pain was all she felt. "How did you do it? How did you get so close without the Sceptre alerting me? Some magic I don't know about?" Stephanie didn't answer.

"Miss Cain, I know you're trying to hide it, but I can see the fear in your eyes. You don't want to die today, do you? Of course you don't. You have your whole life ahead of you. If only you'd kept out of all this, if only you'd left the death of your uncle alone, you wouldn't be here right now.

"Your uncle was a very stubborn man. If he had just given me the key when I asked, you wouldn't be in this predicament. He delayed my plans, you see, caused a lot of unnecessary stress and bother. A lot of people are dead now because of him."

Stephanie's face twisted. "Don't you *dare* blame my uncle for the people you've killed!"

"I didn't want this. I didn't want conflict. I just wanted to eliminate the Elders and take the Book. Do you see how simple that would have been? Instead, I had to wade through a river of corpses. Those deaths are on your uncle's head." Stephanie's hatred became a cold thing in her centre.

"But you don't have to join them, Miss Cain. You can survive this. You can *live.* I see something in you. I think you'd like the new world that's coming."

"I wouldn't bet on it," Stephanie said quietly.

Serpine smiled patiently and leaned his face in close to her. "You can survive... if you tell me how you got so close without the Sceptre alerting me."

With no weapons left, Stephanie spat on him. He sighed and threw her against a pillar. She smacked into it and her body twisted and she dropped on to her back.

Her eyes wouldn't focus. The pain was far away. She heard his voice like there was a wall separating them.

"No matter. I am about to make slaves of the entire population of this planet, and then there will be no more secrets. There will be no magic hidden from me. And when the Faceless Ones return, this world will be remade as a place of splendid darkness."

He passed her, a vague shape in the corner of her eye. She had to get up. She had to snap out of this. The pain. The pain from her broken leg, she had to let it in. It was nothing more than a sensation now – she had to allow it to flood her.

She focused on her leg. It was throbbing, the pain spiking, and with each new height it reached her mind sharpened a little more. Then the pain came at her, cascaded over her with its full force, and she had to bite her lip to stop from crying out.

She looked up. Serpine was approaching the Book. Stephanie gripped the edge of a table-top and pulled herself up on to her good leg. She grabbed the first thing she saw – a glass vial filled with green liquid – and threw it. It hit Serpine in the back and shattered, and the liquid turned to vapour and dissipated into the air. He spun round, angry.

"You, my dear, have proven yourself to be far too troublesome for your own good." He raised his red hand.

He raised his red hand, and from somewhere behind her she heard the Sceptre singing again. And then Skulduggery dropped through the ceiling, landing in a heap next to Serpine. The detective looked around.

"Ah," he said. "I'm back."

"You are," Serpine said, and Skulduggery looked up and saw him.

Serpine lashed a kick into Skulduggery's side and Skulduggery grunted. He tried to get up, but Serpine batted his hands away and grabbed his skull. He drove his knee into the side of Skulduggery's head and Skulduggery sprawled on to his back.

Serpine looked over to Stephanie and then to the ground behind her and she turned, saw the Sceptre. She lunged for it but a purple tendril wrapped itself around her waist and she was yanked back on to her broken leg. She cried out as the pain shot through her.

Serpine whipped the tendril to the Sceptre, yanked it into his left hand and whirled, the crystal flashing with a black light that streaked towards Skulduggery. The detective dived as a whole section of the wall behind him turned to dust. Skulduggery drew his gun and fired, hitting Serpine in the chest.

"Still with that little toy of yours," Serpine said, amused and unharmed. "How quaint."

Skulduggery circled him. Serpine held the Sceptre down by his side. "You'll be stopped," Skulduggery said. "You've always been stopped."

"Oh, my old foe, but this is different. Those days are gone. Who is there to rise up against me? Who is left? Remember when you were a man? A real man, I mean, not this mockery I see before me. Do you remember what it was like? You had an army on your side, you had people willing to fight and die for your cause. We wanted to bring the Faceless Ones back, to worship them as the gods that they are. You wanted to keep them out, so that this infestation of humanity, this celebration of the mundane, might be allowed to live and thrive. Well, they've lived, and they've thrived, and now their time is up."

Skulduggery's finger tightened on the trigger. Black blood sprayed from Serpine's chest, and the wound instantly healed. Serpine laughed.

"You have caused me so much trouble over the years, detective, it's almost a shame that I have to end it."

Skulduggery cocked his head. "You're surrendering?"

"I'm going to miss this," Serpine said. "If it makes it any easier, you can think of your imminent demise as a good thing. I don't think you'll much like the world once my lords and masters remake it."

"So how are you going to kill me?" Skulduggery asked, dropping his gun and holding his arms out. "With your toy? Or one of these new tricks you've learned?"

Serpine smiled. "I *have* been expanding my repertoire. So good of you to notice."

"And I see you've been playing around with necromancy again."

"Indeed. My very own pet Cleaver. Every home should have one."

"He's a tricky fellow to put down," Skulduggery said. "I tried everything I know – he just kept getting back up."

Serpine laughed. "There's an old Necromancer saying – you can't kill what's already dead."

Skulduggery cocked his head. "He's a zombie?"

"Oh, no, I wouldn't associate myself with those wretched things. He can repair, replenish, heal. A difficult process to master, but I am nothing if not accomplished."

"Of *course*," Skulduggery said, something new in his voice. "The medical equipment in the warehouse. The Cleaver was a test-run, to see if the process worked. Then you did it to yourself."

"Ah, the great detective finally figures something out."

"Bells and whistles aside, Nefarian, he's nothing but a zombie. And so are you."

Serpine shook his head. "Your last words are pathetic insults? I was hoping for more. Something profound, perhaps. Maybe a poem." He raised the Sceptre. "It will be a slightly less strange world without you, I just want you to know that."

Stephanie screamed his name as Skulduggery dived. Serpine laughed and the Sceptre sent out its bolt of black lightning but Skulduggery had seized the Book of Names and held it as a shield.

The black lightning hit the Book and it disappeared in a cloud of dust.

"NO!" Serpine screamed. "*NO*!"

Stephanie stared as the Book that the Elders couldn't destroy sifted through Skulduggery's fingers. He charged through the cloud, slamming into Serpine. The Sceptre fell and rolled away. Serpine's hands closed around Skulduggery's neck, forcing his head back.

"You ruined it!" he hissed. "You ruined it *all*, you pathetic creature!"

Skulduggery slammed a fist into Serpine's face and batted the hands away. He stepped in with a jab that rocked the sorcerer's head. Serpine blasted Skulduggery with purple vapour and Skulduggery was flung off his feet.

He landed on his side and rolled, coming up to his knees as Serpine whipped a tendril out for the Sceptre. It sped towards him but Skulduggery pushed outwards at the air, breaking the tendril and knocking the Sceptre off course.

Skulduggery gathered flame in his fist and threw it at Serpine, who barely managed to deflect it. It exploded on the wall behind him and Serpine hissed again, stumbling away before being launched backwards as the air rippled around him. He hit the wall and stayed there, high off the ground, held up by Skulduggery's outstretched hand from across the room.

"I'll destroy you," he snarled, his emerald eyes blazing with hatred. "I destroyed you once. I will do it again!"

He struggled to raise his right arm. Skulduggery pressed against him harder, drawing on his last reserves. But Serpine refused to be beaten. The fingers of his red hand pointed at Skulduggery.

"Die," Serpine whispered.

Skulduggery inclined his head a little to the right and didn't fall. Serpine's face contorted with rage.

"Die!" he screamed.

Skulduggery remained standing. "Looks like there's something that hand of yours can't kill after all."

A figure moved in the doorway. Serpine's laugh was one of spittle and gritted teeth as the White Cleaver appeared.

"So you have an immunity to my power... No matter. That scythe of his will shear through your bones. You'll be nothing but rubble when he's through with you. Cleaver, *attack*!"

But the Cleaver stayed where he was and Serpine's confidence started to ebb. "What are you doing? Kill him!"

The White Cleaver took another moment, and then walked away.

Serpine screamed his rage.

"You've lost, Nefarian," Skulduggery said. "Even your

henchman is abandoning you. Even he recognises your defeat. I'm placing you under arrest for murder, attempted murder, conspiracy to commit murder and, I don't know, possibly littering."

Serpine spat. "You will never beat me. I will *always* find a way to make you suffer." And then his green eyes flickered towards Stephanie, still lying on the ground.

"Don't," Skulduggery said, but Serpine was already moving his hand across his body. "Serpine, don't!"

Stephanie cried out as a pain more intense then anything she had ever felt scourged her body. Serpine twisted his fingers and the pain intensified, turning her cry into a scream, turning the scream to silent agony. She curled up, feeling something cold spread from her belly, a welcome numbness that cancelled the pain, that moved into her arms and legs, that wrapped itself around her heart and seeped into her mind. And now there was nothing, now there were just vague images, of Serpine and Skulduggery, a distant voice, Skulduggery calling out to her, but that too was fading. No pain now. No sound. Her eyelids fluttered. Serpine, with that grin. Skulduggery, holding his free hand out, and something moving through the air, everything moving so, so slowly.

The Sceptre, it was the Sceptre, and then it was in Skulduggery's gloved hand and his fingers were tightening around it. He was raising his arm and pointing, pointing the Sceptre at Serpine, and the little crystal started to glow. It glowed dark, a pretty little darkness, and then the air cracked.

The coldness had overtaken her now, the numbness was everywhere, and the last bits that made her who she was were gradually drifting away. She didn't care. She didn't mind at all. Let them go. She didn't have a care in the world.

Serpine's grinning face. His eyes. His smile. All those teeth. His skin, creased in savage pleasure. And now that skin was changing, and it was drying, and it was cracking, and the smile was fading, and the emerald green eyes were losing their gleam, clouding over, and Serpine turned to dust that fell to the floor.

And there was a ringing, a ringing in her ears, and her fingertips were tingling, and warmth was rushing back to her and her heart was beating again and her lungs sucked in air and Stephanie gasped.

Skulduggery ran over and kneeled beside her. "Are you all right?" he asked, but all she could do was shiver. Her leg twisted and she hissed in pain, but it was a bearable pain, it was a good pain.

"Come on," Skulduggery said, taking her arm gently. "Let's get you out of here."

She put her weight on him and he half carried her, half lifted her out of the chamber and into the corridor. They passed the gaol as the door opened and Tanith toppled out. She hit the ground and groaned. Stephanie looked down at her friend, at all that blood.

"Tanith?"

Tanith raised her head. "Oh, good," she muttered. "You're alive."

Skulduggery reached for her, pulled her carefully to her feet and, with an arm around each, he guided them both to the foyer. They climbed the stairs slowly and moved through the Waxworks. The rain had stopped and the ground was wet as they emerged into the night.

China Sorrows was standing beside her car, waiting for them. When they were close enough so Stephanie could see the delicate earrings China was wearing, she spoke. "You've all seen better days."

"Could have used your help," Skulduggery said as they came to a stop.

China shrugged her slender shoulders. "I knew you could do it without me. I had faith. Serpine?"

"Dust," Skulduggery said. "Too many plans, too many schemes. Sooner or later they'd cancel each other out. That was always his trouble."

"How did you manage it?"

"He wanted immortality, so he chose death on his own terms – a living death."

China smiled. "Aha. And because the Sceptre can only be wielded when its previous owner is dead, or in this case, when its owner is the *living* dead..."

"I took it and used it on *him*." He held up the Sceptre. "Something happened though. There's no power in it any more."

China took it from him, turning it over in her hands. "It was fuelled by his hate. Obviously, using it against him made it feed on itself. Congratulations, Skulduggery, you've managed to break the ultimate weapon. It's nothing but an ornament now."

"An ornament I'd like back," he said, holding out his hand. She smiled, turning her head slightly to look at him out of the corner of her eye.

"I'll buy it from you," she said.

"Why would you want it?" he asked. "It's worthless."

"Sentimental reasons. Besides, you know what an avid collector I am."

He sighed. "Fine, take it."

There it was, that smile again. “Thank you. Oh, and the Book?”

“Destroyed.”

“How very like you to destroy the indestructible. You have quite an appetite for destruction, don’t you?”

“China, these bones are weary...”

“Then I shall leave you.”

“Bliss is still in there,” Stephanie said. “I think he was working against Serpine the whole time. I don’t know if he’s alive though.”

“That brother of mine is quite resilient. I’ve tried to kill him three times already and he just won’t stay down.” China got into her car, looked at them through the open window. “Oh, by the way, all three of you – congratulations on saving the world.”

She gave them a beautiful smile and they watched her drive off. They stood there for a while. The sky was beginning to brighten, the first rays of the morning sun seeping into the black.

“You know,” Tanith said weakly, “I still have a gigantic hole in my back.”

“Sorry,” Skulduggery said and helped them both towards the Bentley.

30

AN END, A BEGINNING

Somewhere in Haggard, a dog was barking. Somewhere a driver beeped his horn and somewhere else people were laughing. It was a Friday night and music drifted to Stephanie's open window from the bars and pubs on Main Street, snatches of songs, piggybacking on the warm breeze.

Stephanie sat in her swivel chair, her foot resting on the bed. Skulduggery had taken her to a friend of his, a cantankerous old man who had mended her broken leg within an hour. It was still stiff and she couldn't walk on it, but the bruising had gone down and in another few days it would be like it had never been broken at all.

She didn't mind the recuperation period she had been advised to take. After the week she'd just had, a week in which she'd seen wonder and magic and death and destruction, she could do with a little holiday.

Skulduggery Pleasant sat on the windowsill and told her what was happening in the world outside her bedroom. The White Cleaver had vanished, and they still didn't know why, or even *how*, he had ignored his master's final command. Skulduggery had a suspicion that he was under orders from somebody else, but just who this mystery master was, he didn't yet know. Serpine's allies had resurfaced and struck, and then vanished again when the news of the sorcerer's demise had reached them. Serpine's grand scheme may have failed, but because of it, the Cleavers' numbers had been decimated, and their duties now stretched them thin.

"How's Tanith?" Stephanie asked. "Will she be OK?"

"She's lucky to be alive. The injury she took was severe, but she's strong. She'll pull through. I'll take you to see her when you're rested."

"And Ghastly? Any change?"

"I'm afraid not. They're keeping him safe, but... we don't

know how long he'll stay like that. Fortunately for him, the time will pass in the blink of an eye. The rest of us will have to wait. On the bright side, the Sanctuary has a new and interesting addition to their Hall of Statues."

"Do they *have* a Hall of Statues?"

"Well, no. But now that they've got a statue, maybe they'll start."

"What are they going to do about the Elder Council?"

"Meritorious was a good man and the most powerful Grand Mage we had seen in a long time. The other Councils in Europe are worried about who will fill the vacuum now that he's gone. The Americans are offering their support, the Japanese are sending delegates to help us wrest back some control, but..."

"It sounds like a lot of people are panicking."

"And they have a right to. Our systems of power, our systems of self-government, are delicate. If we topple, others will follow. We need a strong leader."

"Why don't you do it?"

He laughed. "Because I'm not well liked, and I'm not well trusted, and I already have a job. I'm a detective, remember?"

She gave her own little shrug. "Vaguely."

Another snippet of pub music drifted by the window, and Stephanie thought about the world she'd grown up in, and how different it was from the world she'd been introduced to, and yet how similar. There was joy and happiness in both, just as there was heartbreak and horror. There was good and evil and everything in between, and these qualities seemed to be shared equally in the worlds of the magical and the mundane. It was her life now. She couldn't imagine living without either one.

"How are you?" Skulduggery asked, his voice gentle.

"Me? I'm fine."

"Really? No nightmares?"

"Maybe one or two," she admitted.

"They'll always be there, reminding us of where we went wrong. If you pay attention to your bad dreams, they can help you."

"I'll be sure to keep that in mind next time I'm asleep."

"Good," said Skulduggery. "In any event, get well soon. We have mysteries to solve, and adventures to undertake, and I need my partner and student with me."

"Student?"

He shrugged. "Things are going to get a lot rougher from here on in, and I need someone to fight by my side. There's something about you, Valkyrie. I'm not quite sure what it is. I look at you and..."

"And you're reminded of yourself when you were my age?"

"Hmm? Oh, no, what I was going to say is there's something about you that is really annoying, and you never do what you're told, and sometimes I question your intelligence, but even so I'm going to train you, because I like having someone follow me around like a little puppy. It makes me feel good about myself."

She rolled her eyes. "You are such a moron."

"Don't be jealous of my genius."

"Can you get over yourself for just a moment?"

"If only that were possible."

"For a guy with no internal organs, you've got quite the ego."

"And for a girl who can't stand up without falling over, you're quite the critic."

"My leg will be fine."

"And my ego will flourish. What a pair we are."

She had to laugh. "Go on, get out. Mum'll be up soon to check on me."

"Before I go..."

"Yes?"

"Aren't you going to show me what you've been practising? You've been dying to show off from the moment I knocked on this window."

Stephanie looked at him and arched an eyebrow, but he

was right and he knew it. The other good thing about this recuperation period was that she had all the time she wanted to develop her powers, and she hadn't wasted the few days that had passed already.

She clicked her fingers, summoning a small flame into the palm of her hand. She watched it flicker and dance, then looked up at Skulduggery and grinned.

"Magic," he said.

Skulduggery
Pleasant
PLAYING WITH FIRE

This book is dedicated to my family – because otherwise I'd never hear the end of it...

Nadine: warm, kind and considerate. I am all of these things.

Audrey: the greatest thrill of your life is probably the fact that I'm your brother.

Ivan: meaningless words such as "brilliant", "amazing" and "inspirational" have been used to describe me, but not nearly enough.

If any of you thought that there'd be anything sincere or heartfelt in your dedications, allow me a moment to quietly laugh at you...

Because the heartfelt sincerity is reserved for my nana.

Chic, this book is also dedicated to you, for all the love and support you've shown me over the years. I love you much more than any of your other grandchildren do, I swear.

1

HANGING AROUND

Valkyrie Cain hit the parapet and tumbled, unable to stop herself, and with a panicked gasp she disappeared off the edge.

The church tower stood high and proud, looking out over Dublin City. The night breeze was brisk and carried snatches of laughter from the street below. It was a long way down.

A man in a tattered coat walked up to the edge and peered over. He smirked.

"This is insulting," he said. "Don't they know how dangerous I am? I am very, very dangerous. I'm a killer. I'm a trained killing *machine*. And still, they send *you*. A *child*."

Valkyrie felt her grip on the ledge loosen. She ignored the goading of the man standing above her, and looked around for something else to grab on to. She looked everywhere but down. Down was where the street was, where the long drop and the sudden stop was. She didn't want to look down. She didn't want anything to do with *down* right now.

"What age are you?" the man continued. "Thirteen? What kind of responsible adult sends a thirteen-year-old child to stop me? What kind of thinking is that?"

Valkyrie swung herself gently towards the tower, planting her feet against a small buttress. The fear started to work through her and she felt herself freeze up. She closed her eyes against the oncoming wave of paralysis.

The man was Vaurien Scapegrace, currently wanted in five countries for various counts of attempted murder. He hunkered down at the edge and smiled happily.

"I am turning murder into an art form. When I – when I *kill*, I'm actually painting a big, big picture, using blood and, and... messiness. You know?"

Below Valkyrie, the city twinkled.

"I'm an artist," Scapegrace continued. "Some people don't appreciate that. Some people don't recognise true talent when they see it. And that's fine. I'm not bitter. My time will come."

"Serpine tried to bring the Faceless Ones back," Valkyrie managed to say. Her fingers were burning and the muscles in her legs were screaming at her. "We stopped him. We'll stop you, too."

He laughed. "What, you think I want the old gods to walk the earth once again? Is that it? You think Nefarian Serpine was my leader? I'm not one of those nutbag disciples, all right? I'm my own man."

Valkyrie had one chance, but she needed to be calm to take advantage of it. Her powers, limited though they were, were Elemental – the manipulation of earth, air, fire and water. But at this stage of her training they didn't work when she was panicking.

"So if you don't want the Faceless Ones to return," she said, "what *do* you want? Why are you doing this?"

He shook his head. "You wouldn't understand. It's grown-up stuff. I just want a little appreciation for who I am, that's all. That's not much to ask, is it? But of course, you wouldn't know. You're just a kid." He shrugged. "Oh, well. Time to die." He reached down to shove her.

"Have you killed anyone?" she asked quickly.

"What? Did you miss what I said, about turning murder into an art form?"

"But you haven't actually *killed* anyone yet, have you? I read your file."

He glowered. "Technically, yeah, all right, maybe I haven't, but tonight's the night. You're going to be my first."

She readied herself, controlled her breathing. "Find the space where everything connects," she murmured.

Scapegrace frowned. "What?"

Valkyrie kicked upwards, taking her right hand from the outcrop and feeling the air against her palm. She pushed at it like she'd been taught, and it shimmered and hit Scapegrace, throwing him off his feet. Valkyrie clutched at the edge of the parapet, her legs swinging in open air. She grunted and pulled herself up, then flung her left arm across the edge and hauled herself the rest of the way. She got to her feet, her arms and legs trembling with the strain, and moved away from the edge. The wind whipped her dark hair across her face.

Scapegrace was already getting up and Valkyrie saw anger mottle his face. She clicked her fingers, generating a spark that she caught in her hand. She tried to focus, tried to build it into a flame, but Scapegrace was coming at her like a freight train.

Valkyrie jumped and thrust out both feet. Her boots

slammed into his chest and he hit the ground again and went sprawling. He turned to her just as she lashed a kick into his jaw. His body twisted and he tumbled back, came up to his feet then lost his balance, fell again. He spat blood and glared.

"You little brat," he snarled. "You uppity, sneaky little *brat.* You don't know who you're messing with, do you? I am going to be the greatest killer the world has ever known." He stood up slowly, wiping his sleeve across his burst lip. "When I'm finished with you I'm going to deliver your mutilated, bloody corpse to your masters, as a warning. They sent you up against me, alone. Next time they're going to have to send a battalion."

Valkyrie smiled, and Scapegrace's anger flared. "*What the hell is so funny*?"

"First of all," she said, her confidence growing, "they're not my *masters*. I don't have a *master*. Second, they don't need a battalion to take you down. And third – and this really is the most important point – whoever said I came alone?"

Scapegrace frowned, turned, saw someone walking up behind him, a skeleton in a black suit, and he tried to attack, but a gloved fist hit his face, a foot hit his shin and an elbow slammed into his chest. He fell in an awkward heap.

Skulduggery Pleasant turned to Valkyrie. "You all right?"

"I'll kill you both!" Scapegrace howled.

"Hush," Skulduggery said.

Scapegrace launched himself forward and Skulduggery moved into him, grabbed his outstretched arm and spun him around, then abruptly cut him off by slamming a forearm into his throat. Scapegrace flipped in midair, landed painfully. Skulduggery turned to Valkyrie again.

"I'm OK," she said. "Really."

Scapegrace had his hands to his face. "I think you broke my nose!" They ignored him.

"He talks a lot," Valkyrie said, "but I don't think he knows what all the words mean."

Scapegrace leaped up. "I am the Killer Supreme! I make murder into an art form!"

Skulduggery hit him again and Scapegrace did a little twirl before falling.

"Vaurien Scapegrace," he said, "by the power endowed unto me under the Sanctuary Rule of Justice, I am placing you under arrest for the attempted murder of Alexander Remit and Sofia Toil in Oregon, Cothurnus Ode and Armiger Fop in Sydney, Gregory Castallan and Bartholomew—"

Scapegrace tried one last desperate attack that Skulduggery cut short by punching him very hard on the nose. The Killer Supreme wobbled, collapsed and started crying.

2

KILLER ON THE LOOSE

The car was a 1954 Bentley R-Type Continental. It sliced through the quiet Dublin night like a black shark, gleaming and powerful. It was a beautiful car. Valkyrie had grown to love it almost as much as Skulduggery did.

They turned on to O'Connell Street, passed the Spire and the Parnell Monument. Scapegrace sat in the back and complained that the shackles were too tight. It was four in the morning. Valkyrie fought a yawn.

This time last year she would have been in bed, snuggled up

and dreaming about... well, whatever it was she dreamed about back then. Things were a lot different now, and she was lucky if she could get a few hours sleep a night. If she wasn't going up against crazies like Scapegrace, she was practising magic, and if she wasn't practising magic, she was training to fight with either Skulduggery or Tanith Low. These days, her life was a lot more exciting, a lot more fun, and a lot more dangerous. In fact, one of the major downsides to her new life was that she rarely had sweet dreams any more. When she slept, it was the nightmares that came to her. They waited patiently, and they were always eager to play.

But that was the cost, she reasoned. The cost of living a life of adventure and excitement.

The owners of the Waxworks Museum had closed it down after the events of the previous year, and set up a new and improved version in another part of the city. So now the new building stood quietly beside its neighbours, humble and drab, its front doors closed and locked and sealed. But Valkyrie and Skulduggery had never used the front doors anyway.

They parked in the loading area at the back and took Scapegrace in through the rear door. The corridors were dimly lit, and they walked past the lonely historical figures and cinematic icons that had been left to collect dust. Valkyrie traced her hand along the wall to find the switch, and the door slid open beside her. She led the way through and down the steps, her mind flashing back to the summer of the previous year, when she had stepped into the Sanctuary's foyer to find it littered with dead bodies...

Today, however, there were no corpses in sight. Two Cleavers stood guard against the far wall, dressed all in grey, their scythes strapped to their backs, visored helmets pointing straight ahead. The Cleavers acted as the Sanctuary's law enforcers and its army. Silent and lethal, they still gave Valkyrie the creeps.

The double doors to their left opened and the new Grand Mage, Thurid Guild, came out to them. He looked to be in his sixties, with thinning grey hair, a lined face and cold eyes.

"You found him then," Guild said. "Before or after he managed to kill someone?"

"Before," Skulduggery said. Guild grunted and gestured to the Cleavers. They stepped forward and Scapegrace shrank away from them. They took him firmly by the arms and he didn't resist. He even stopped whining about his broken nose as they led him away.

Valkyrie looked back at Guild. He wasn't a friendly man by any means, but he seemed especially uncomfortable around her, like he wasn't yet sure if he should take her seriously. He tended to speak directly to Skulduggery, and only glanced at Valkyrie when she asked a question.

"A situation has arisen which requires your attention," said Guild. "This way."

Skulduggery fell into step beside the Grand Mage, but Valkyrie stayed two paces behind. Guild had taken over as head of the Council of Elders, but he still had to select the two sorcerers who would rule with him. It was a long and arduous process apparently, but Valkyrie suspected she knew who would be Guild's first choice. He was a man who respected power, after all, and there were few more powerful in this world than Mr Bliss.

They walked into a room with a long table, and Mr Bliss rose – bald, tall and broad shouldered, his eyes a piercing blue.

"I have received some disturbing news," Bliss said, getting straight to the point as usual. "It seems that Baron Vengeous has been freed from the confinement facility in Russia."

Skulduggery was silent for a moment. When he spoke, he spoke slowly. "How did he get out?"

"Violently, from the reports we've been getting," Guild said. "Nine Cleavers were killed, along with approximately one third of the prisoners. His cell, like all the cells, was securely bound. Nobody should have been able to use magic in any of them."

Valkyrie raised an eyebrow and Skulduggery answered her unspoken question. "Baron Vengeous was one of Mevolent's infamous Three Generals. Dangerously fanatical, extremely intelligent, and very, very powerful. I saw him *look* at a colleague of mine and my colleague... ruptured."

"Ruptured?"

Skulduggery nodded. "All over the place." He turned to Guild. "Do we know who freed him?"

The Grand Mage shook his head. "According to the Russians, one wall of his cell was cracked. Still solid, but cracked, like something had hit it. That's the only clue we have at the moment."

"The prison's location is a closely guarded secret," Bliss said. "It is well hidden and well protected. Whoever is behind this had inside knowledge."

Guild made a face. "That's the Russians' problem, not ours. The only thing we have to concern ourselves with is stopping Vengeous."

"You think he'll come here then?" Valkyrie asked.

Guild looked at her and she saw his fist clench. He probably didn't even realise he was doing it, but it signalled to Valkyrie loud and clear that he still didn't like her.

"Vengeous will come home, yes. He has a history here." He looked at Skulduggery. "We have already sent our people to airports and docks around the country, in the hope of preventing him from entering. But you know better than anyone how difficult the Baron is to... contain."

"Indeed," Skulduggery murmured.

"I think we can assume," Guild continued, "that if Baron Vengeous is not already here, then he will be arriving shortly. You arrested him eighty years ago. I'm relying on you to do it again."

"I'll do my best."

"Do better, Detective."

Skulduggery observed Guild for a moment before answering. "Of course, Grand Mage."

Guild dismissed them with a curt nod, and as they were walking back through the corridors, Valkyrie spoke.

"Guild doesn't like me."

"That's true."

"He doesn't like you either."

"That *is* mystifying."

"So what about Vengeous? Is he bad news?"

"The worst. I don't think he's ever forgotten the time I threw a bundle of dynamite at him. It didn't kill him obviously, but it definitely ruined his day."

"Is he all scarred now?"

"Magic gets rid of most *physical* scars, but I like to think that I scarred him emotionally."

"How about on the Evil Villain Scale? Ten being Serpine, one being Scapegrace?"

"The Baron, unfortunately, turns it all the way up to eleven."

"Seriously? Because, you know, that's one more evil."

"It is indeed."

"So we're in trouble then."

"Oh, yes," said Skulduggery darkly.

3

VENGEOUS

The first thing Baron Vengeous did when he set foot on Irish soil was murder someone. He would have preferred to arrive without incident, to have stepped off the boat and disappeared into the city, but his hand had been forced. He had been recognised.

The sorcerer had seen him, picked him out in the crowd as he disembarked. Vengeous led the sorcerer somewhere quiet, out of the way. It was an easy kill. He had taken the sorcerer by surprise. A brief struggle and Vengeous' arm had wrapped around the man's throat. He hadn't even needed to use his magic.

Once he had disposed of the body, Vengeous walked deeper into Dublin City, relishing the freedom that was his again after so long.

He was tall and his chest was broad, his tightly-cropped beard the same gun-metal grey as his hair. His clothes were dark, the jacket buttons polished to a gleam, and his boots clacked on the streetlit pavements. Dublin had changed dramatically since he'd been here last. The world *had changed dramatically.*

He heard the quiet footsteps behind him. He stopped but he didn't turn. The man in black had to walk around him, into his line of sight.

"Baron," the man said in greeting.

"You're late."

"I'm here, which is the main thing."

Vengeous looked into the man's eyes. "I do not tolerate insubordination, Mr Dusk. Perhaps you have forgotten."

"Times have changed," Dusk responded evenly. "The war is over."

"Not for us."

A taxi passed, and the sweeping headlights illuminated Dusk's pale face and black hair. "Sanguine isn't with you," he noted.

Vengeous resumed walking, Dusk by his side. "He will join us soon, have no fear."

"Are you sure you can trust him? I appreciate that he freed you from prison, but it took him eighty years to do it."

Were Dusk any other man, this remark would have been the height of hypocrisy, as he himself had not lifted one finger to help Vengeous either. But Dusk was not any other man. Dusk was scarcely a man*, and as such, loyalty was not in his nature. A certain level of obedience perhaps, but not loyalty. Because of this, Vengeous harboured no resentment towards him.*

The resentment he harboured towards Sanguine *on the other hand...*

Dusk's breathing suddenly became strained. He reached into his coat and fumbled with a syringe, then jabbed the needle into his forearm. He depressed the plunger, forcing the colourless liquid into his bloodstream, and moments later he was breathing regularly again.

"I'm glad to see you're still in control," Vengeous said.

Dusk put the syringe away. "I wouldn't be much good to you if I wasn't, would I? What do you need me to do?"

"There will be some obstacles to our work, some enemies we will no doubt face. The Skeleton Detective for example. Apparently he has an apprentice now – a dark-haired girl. You will wait for them outside the Sanctuary, tonight, and you will follow them, and when she is alone, you will fetch her for me."

"Of course."

"Alive, *Dusk."*

There was a hesitation. "Of course," Dusk repeated.

4

THE BEAUTY, THE BEAST

They left the Sanctuary and drove across town, until they came to a street lined with ugly tenement buildings. Skulduggery parked the Bentley, wrapped his scarf around his jaw and pulled his hat down low, and got out.

"I notice you haven't mentioned how I was thrown off a tower tonight," Valkyrie said as they crossed the road.

"Does it need mentioning?" Skulduggery queried.

"Scapegrace threw me off a tower. If *that* doesn't require mentioning then what does?"

"I knew you could handle it."

"It was a *tower*." Valkyrie led the way into one of the tenement buildings.

"You've been thrown off higher," Skulduggery said.

"Yes, but you were always there to catch me."

"So you've learned a valuable lesson – there will be times when I'm not there to catch you."

"See, that sounds to me like a lesson I could have been *told*."

"Nonsense. This way, you'll never forget."

Skulduggery removed his disguise as they climbed the stairs. Just as they reached the second floor, Valkyrie stopped and turned to him.

"Was it a test?" she asked. "I mean, I know I'm still new at this, I'm still the rookie. Did you hang back to test me, to see if I'd be able to handle it alone?"

"Well, kind of," he said. "Actually, no, nothing like that. My shoelace was untied. That's why I was late. That's why you were alone."

"I could have been killed because you were tying your *shoelace*?"

"An untied shoelace can be dangerous," Skulduggery said. "I could have tripped."

She stared at him. A moment dragged by.

"I'm joking," he said at last.

She relaxed. "Really?"

"Absolutely. I would never have tripped. I'm far too graceful."

He moved past her and she glowered then followed him to the third floor. They walked to the middle door and a slight man with large round spectacles and a bow tie opened it and let them in.

The library was a vast labyrinth of tall bookcases, one that Valkyrie had managed to get herself lost in no fewer than eleven times. It seemed to amuse Skulduggery greatly whenever she found herself at a dead end, or even better, back where she had started, so she let him lead the way.

China Sorrows passed in front of them, wearing a dark trouser suit with her black hair tied off her face. She stopped and smiled when she saw them. The most exquisitely beautiful woman Valkyrie had ever seen, China had a habit of making people fall in love with her at first glance.

"Skulduggery," she said. "Valkyrie. So good to see you both. What brings the Sanctuary's esteemed investigators back to my door? I'm assuming it *is* Sanctuary business?"

"You assume correctly," Skulduggery said. "And I'm sure you already know why we're here."

Her smile turned coy. "Let me think... a certain recently-liberated Baron? You want to know if I've heard any particularly juicy rumours?"

"Have you?" Valkyrie asked.

China hesitated, looked around and gave them another smile. "Let us talk privately," she said, leading them out of the library and across the hall, into her luxurious apartment. Once Skulduggery had closed the door she took a seat.

"Tell me, Valkyrie," she said, "how much do you know about Baron Vengeous?"

Valkyrie sat on the couch, but Skulduggery remained standing. "Not a whole lot," she said. "He's dangerous. I know that much."

"Oh yes," China agreed, her blue eyes twinkling in the lamplight. "Very dangerous. He is a fanatical follower of the Faceless Ones, and there is nothing more dangerous than a zealot. Along with Nefarian Serpine and Lord Vile, Vengeous was one of Mevolent's most trusted generals. He was assigned to their most secret operations. Have you ever heard of the Grotesquery, my dear?" Valkyrie shook her head.

"Before he was caught, Baron Vengeous was given the task of resurrecting a Faceless One from the remains found in a long-forgotten tomb."

Valkyrie frowned. "Is that even possible? Bringing one of them back to life after all this time?"

It was Skulduggery who answered her. "Bringing a Faceless One back *whole* proved to be beyond his abilities, so Vengeous combined the remains with parts and organs from other creatures, forming a hybrid, what he called a Grotesquery. But even then an ingredient was missing."

China took over. "Two ingredients actually. First, he needed a Necromancer's power to revive it and then, once it was alive, he needed something to keep it that way.

"When Lord Vile died, Vengeous thought he could harness Vile's power. Vile was a Necromancer, a practitioner of death magic – shadow magic. It is the Necromancer way to place most of their power in an object, or a weapon or, in this case, his armour."

"So if Vengeous wore that armour," Valkyrie said, "he'd have all Vile's power..."

"But he couldn't find the armour," Skulduggery said. "Lord Vile died alone, and his armour was lost."

"What about the other missing ingredient? Did he find out what that was?"

China answered. "From what I have heard, yes. He did."

"So what is it?"

"He knows. We don't."

"Ah."

"Fortunately for us, and the world at large, Skulduggery was around to foil this plot before Vengeous could find the armour and retrieve this mysterious missing ingredient. He tracked the Baron to a known enemy hideaway and brought him to justice, in what became one of the most talked-about battles of the entire war. Skulduggery was badly injured in that fight, if I remember correctly."

Valkyrie looked at Skulduggery and he folded his arms.

"This is a history lesson," he said. "Why are we going over this?"

"Because," China said with a smile, "I have heard that this final missing ingredient – whatever it is – has at last been recovered, or at least located, by the Baron's associates."

Skulduggery's head tilted. "Who *are* these associates?"

"I'm afraid not even I know that."

"So if Vengeous now has the missing ingredient," Valkyrie said uneasily, "can he revive the, uh, the Grow Thing?"

"Grotesquery," China corrected.

"And no," Skulduggery said, "it's impossible. He'd need Vile's armour, which he doesn't have."

"But if he *did*, and he revived this thing, what would it do? Would we be able to stop it?"

Skulduggery hesitated for a split second. "The threat the Grotesquery would pose is a little bigger than that. Theoretically, it would be able to summon the Faceless Ones back to this world by opening a portal through realities."

"A portal?" Valkyrie said, a little doubtfully.

"Yes, but the Grotesquery would have to be at full strength to do it and that's not going to happen."

"Why not?"

"A heart had to be provided for it, but the only one suitable was the heart of a Cu Gealach."

"I'm sorry?"

"Cú na Gealaí Duibhe," China said, "to give it its full Irish title. They *do* still teach you Gaelige in school, yes?"

"Yes, it means... it's Black Hound of something, right?"

"Almost. Hound of the Black Moon. Terrible creatures. They're virtually extinct now, but they were ruthless, savage things."

"Ruthless, savage things," Skulduggery said, "that were only ruthlessly savage for one night every few years, at a lunar eclipse. So no matter how much power Vengeous pumps into that thing, the Grotesquery will not be strong enough to open a portal until the Earth, moon and sun line up, which won't be for another—"

"Two nights," China said.

Skulduggery sagged and his head drooped. "Well, that's just *dandy*," he muttered.

Later, on the motorway back to Haggard, Valkyrie turned to Skulduggery. "So," she said, "a legendary battle, eh?"

Skulduggery turned his head to her. "I'm sorry?"

"The battle between you and Vengeous, the legendary one. What happened?"

"We had a fight."

"But why is it one of the most talked-about battles of the war?"

"I don't know," he said. "Maybe people had nothing else to talk about."

"China said you were badly injured. Is that why you don't like him? Because you were injured?"

"I don't like him because he's evil."

"So it's got nothing to do with him injuring you?"

"It's because he's evil," Skulduggery said grumpily.

They stayed on the motorway for another five minutes, then took the slip road. The roads became narrower and curved between darkened fields and lone houses, and then orange streetlights appeared on either side and they were driving into

Haggard. They reached the pier, and the Bentley stopped.

"Tomorrow's going to be a big day," Valkyrie said.

Skulduggery shrugged. "Maybe. Maybe not. If we can keep Vengeous out of the country, we've got nothing to worry about."

"And if we can't?"

"Then we have a whole lot to worry about, and I'm going to need you rested and alert."

"Sir, yes sir," she said, raising a mocking eyebrow. She opened the door and got out, and moments later the Bentley's tail lights disappeared into the darkness.

Valkyrie stood beside the pier for a moment, watching the dark sea churn at the rocks and play with the small boats moored nearby. She liked watching the sea. Its power made her feel safe.

Back when Valkyrie Cain's name had been Stephanie Edgley, she didn't know much about life outside of Haggard. It was a small town, tucked into the east coast of Ireland, and things there were always so quiet and peaceful and so, so *dull.*

That all changed when Nefarian Serpine murdered her uncle. Gordon was a bestselling novelist, a writer of horror and fantasy, but he was also a man who knew the Big Secret. He knew about the subculture of sorcerers and mages, about the quiet little wars they had fought. He knew about the Faceless

Ones – the terrible dark gods, exiled from this world – and the people who wanted them to return.

In the days that followed, she had met the Skeleton Detective and learned that she had a bloodline that could be traced back to the world's first sorcerers, the Ancients. She was also faced with taking a new name. Everyone, Skulduggery had told her, has three names – the name they are born with, the name they are given, and the name they take. The name they are born with, their true name, lies buried deep in their subconscious. The name they are given, usually by their parents, is the only name most people will ever know. But this is a name that can be used against them, so sorcerers must take a third name to protect themselves.

And so Stephanie Edgley became Valkyrie Cain, and she started on the road to becoming an Elemental – she started to learn magic.

Valkyrie sneaked behind her house, stood directly beneath her window and concentrated. Until a few weeks ago, she had needed a ladder to climb up to her room, but every lesson with Skulduggery gave her more control over her powers.

She took her time, felt the calmness flow through her. She flexed her fingers, feeling the air touch her skin, feeling the fault lines between the spaces. She felt how they connected, and recognised how each would affect the other once the right amount of pressure was applied...

She splayed her hands beneath her and the air rippled and she shot upwards, just managing to grab the windowsill. She still missed it occasionally, but she was getting better. She opened the window and, grunting with exertion, pulled herself through. Moving as quietly as she could, she closed the window behind her and turned on the light.

She ignored the girl who sat up in her bed, the girl who was an exact replica of herself. She went to the door, put her ear to it and listened. Satisfied that her parents were sound asleep, Valkyrie shrugged off her coat as her replica stood up.

"Your arm," it said. "It's bruised."

"Had a little run-in with a bad guy," Valkyrie answered, keeping her voice low. "How was your day?"

"School was OK. I did all the homework, except the last maths question. I didn't know how to do that. Your mum made lasagne for dinner."

Valkyrie kicked off her boots. "Nothing strange happened?"

"No. A very normal day."

"Good."

"Are you ready to resume your life?"

"I am."

The reflection nodded, went to the full-length mirror and stepped through, then turned and waited. Valkyrie touched the glass and a day's worth of memory flooded into her mind as the reflection changed, the clothes Valkyrie was wearing appearing on it, and then it was nothing more then a reflected image in a mirror.

She sifted through the new memories, arranging them beside the memories she'd formed on her own. There had been a careers class in school. The teacher had tried to get them to declare what they wanted to be when they left school, or at least what they'd like to study in college. Nobody had any idea of course. The reflection had stayed quiet too.

Valkyrie thought about this. She didn't really *need* a regular career after all. She was set to inherit Gordon's estate and all his royalties when she turned eighteen anyway, so she'd never be short of money. Besides, what kind of career would interest her outside of magic? If she'd been in that class, she knew what she would have answered. *Detective.* That would have garnered a few sniggers around the room, but she wouldn't have minded.

The main difference between her and her friends was not the magic, she knew, and nor was it the adventure. It was the fact that she knew what she wanted to do with her life, and she was already doing it.

Valkyrie undressed, pulled on her Dublin football jersey and climbed into bed. Twenty seconds later she was asleep.

5

THE TERROR OF LONDON

A dark shape flitted high above the streets of London, moving from rooftop to rooftop, spinning and twisting and cavorting in the air. He wore no shoes and his footsteps were light, his tread no more than a whisper, snatched away by the night breeze. He sang to himself as he moved, and giggled, a high-pitched giggle. He was dressed in black, with a battered top hat that stayed perched on his misshapen head no matter what acrobatic feat he performed. His suit was torn, old and musty, and his long-fingered hands were tipped with long, hardened nails.

He landed on one leg on the edge of a rooftop and stayed there, his lanky body curled. He looked down on to Charing Cross Road, at the people passing below him, at the cars zipping by. His cracked lips pursed, his small eyes moving, he browsed the selection on offer, making a choice.

"Jack."

He turned quickly to see the young woman walking towards him. Her long coat was closed and the breeze played with her tousled blonde hair, teasing it across her face. And such a pretty face. Jack hadn't seen as pretty a face in many a year. His lips parted, showed small yellow teeth, and he gave her his best smile.

"Tanith," he said in a voice that was high and strained, in an accent that was a cross between East London and... something else, something unknowable. "You're lookin' ravishin'."

"And you're looking revolting."

"You are too kind, I'm sure. What brings you to my neck of the woods?"

Tanith Low shook her head. "It's not your neck of the woods any longer, Jack. Things have changed. You shouldn't have come back."

"Where was I gonna go? Old Folks' Home? Retirement Village? I'm a creature of the night, love. I'm Springheeled Jack, ain't I? I belong out here."

"You belong in a cell."

He laughed. "Me? In captivity? For what possible crime?"

"You mean, apart from murder?"

He turned his head so he was looking at her out of the corner of one eye. "That still illegal then?"

"Yes, it is."

She opened her coat, revealing the sword against her leg. "You're under arrest."

He laughed, did a flip in the air, landed on his right foot and grinned at her. "Now *this* is new. You were always pokin' your nose where it wasn't wanted, always dealin' out what you thought was justice, but you never *arrested* anyone. You a proper copper now, that it? You one of the constabulary?"

"Give up, Jack."

"Bloody hell, you are. Consider me impressed."

He dipped his head, looked at her with those small eyes of his. "What was it you used to say, before things got all rough and tumble? 'Come and have a go—"

"If you think you're hard enough."

He grinned. "Do you?"

She withdrew her sword from its scabbard. It caught a beam of moonlight and held it, and she looked back at him without expression. "I'll let you decide that."

And Springheeled Jack *sprang*.

He flipped over her and she turned, ducking the swipe of hard nails, moving again as he landed, narrowly avoiding the return swipe and twisting to face him as he came at her.

He batted the sword to one side and his right foot went to her thigh, his toenails digging in, and he clambered up, kneeling on her shoulder. She grabbed his wrist to avoid the nails. She stumbled, unable to support his weight, but he jumped before she hit the rooftop, landed gracefully as she rolled to a crouch and then he dived at her again.

They went tumbling. He heard the sword clatter from her grip, and felt her foot on his belly as she kicked. He did a flip and landed, but her fist was right there, smacked him square in the face. He took a few steps back, bright lights dancing before his eyes. She kicked his knee, and he howled in pain, then there was a grip on his wrist and a sudden wrenching. He pushed her away, his vision clearing.

"You should be leavin' me alone!" he spat. "I'm unique, me! They don't even have a name for what I am! I should be on the Endangered Species list! You should be protectin' me!"

"You know how they protect Endangered Species, Jack? They put them in a special enclosure, where no one can harm them."

His face twisted. "*Enclosure*'s a fancy word for a cell, innit? And you're not takin' me anywhere *near* a bloody cell."

And then it drifted up to them, the sound of a baby crying. Jack's expression softened and he smiled again.

"Don't even think about that," Tanith warned.

His smile turned to a grin then a leer.

"Race you," he said.

Jack ran to the edge of the building and then there was nothing beneath his feet but air, and the next rooftop swooped to meet him. He landed and ran on without missing a step. He glanced over his shoulder, saw Tanith Low trying to keep up. She was good, that girl, but this was something Jack was made for. He was the prince of London City. It let him go where it let no one else. He knew it like he knew his own face.

The baby's cry came again and he changed direction, heading away from the busier areas, tracking it over the streets and the alleyways. His powerful legs propelled him through the darkness and he spun and dug his feet into brick. He ran sideways, the length of the building. He saw Tanith moving on a parallel course, jumping from rooftop to rooftop, trying to intercept him before he reached his goal.

One last cry from the baby and Jack zeroed in on an open window, high above street level. He made a series of small jumps, building his momentum. He saw Tanith out of the corner of his eye, sprinting to catch up. *Too slow*, he thought to himself. He leaped from one side of the street to the other and dived straight in, clearing the window and going for the crib.

But the crib held only blankets, and the room was dark and unfurnished, not like a baby's room at all, and why had the window been open? It wasn't warm enough to have the window open—

The baby's cry, much louder, was coming from a small device that sat near the window.

It was a trap. She had tricked him.

He moved to the window, but she had walked up the side of the building and was climbing through.

"Out there," she said, "in the open air, I didn't have a hope of catching you. But in here, in a confined space? You're all mine, ugly."

Jack panicked, went to the door, but it wouldn't budge; there was a sheen to it he could see, even in the darkness, and he knew it would withstand whatever he had to throw at it. He whirled. The only way out was the window- the window that Tanith Low now guarded. She laid her sword on the ground, and took off her coat. Her tunic was sleeveless and her arms were strong. She rolled her neck, loosening up her shoulders, and nodded to him.

"Now," she said, "finally. Come and have a go if you think you're hard enough."

Jack roared and went for her and she kicked him. He swiped and she ducked, and smacked him across the jaw. He tried to flip over her, but the ceiling was too low and he bellyflopped into it, felt his breath leave him and crashed to the floor. After that, all that registered was a whole lot of fists and elbows and knees, and a wall that kept running into his face.

Jack collapsed. He breathed hard and groaned in pain. He stared up at the ceiling. He could see the cracks, even in the dark. Tanith stepped into view, looking down at him.

"You ready for your nice warm cell now?"

Jack whimpered.

6

FIREBALLS IN THE PARK

Valkyrie woke early. She took a pebble from her bedside table and sat on the floor, cross-legged. The pebble was flat and smooth in her hand. She focused on it like Skulduggery had taught her. She focused until she could feel the air on her skin, and she focused on how it all connected. Slowly, the pebble began to rise off her palm, held aloft by the air itself. A part of her still thrilled to see this, but she kept that part of her subdued. To use magic, she couldn't afford to let anything ruin her calm.

And then that voice, drifting up the stairs like the whine of a dentist's drill, and the pebble fell back into her hand. Muttering to herself, Valkyrie stood up and walked into the bathroom, her practice done for the day. She took a shower then pulled on her school uniform before heading down to the kitchen.

Her mother was there, and sitting beside her was Valkyrie's shrill, sharp-featured aunt, Beryl.

"Morning," Valkyrie said as she passed them, going straight for the cupboard.

"Hi, love," her mother said.

"Good morning, Stephanie," Beryl said primly.

"Beryl," Valkyrie said in greeting.

"How is school going for you?"

Valkyrie poured some cereal into her bowl and added milk. She didn't bother sitting. "It's OK."

"Are you studying hard? My girls are always studying. They get it from my side of the family, I have to say. It's a valuable work ethic I've instilled in them."

Valkyrie murmured and scooped a spoonful of cereal into her mouth, doubting the validity of just about everything Beryl had just said. Her aunt didn't like her and Valkyrie didn't like her aunt. Her aunt didn't like her because Valkyrie had inherited her late uncle's estate, and Valkyrie didn't like her aunt, or her aunt's husband Fergus, because they were dislikeable people.

Her father came in, dressed in smart trousers, vest and a tie around his bare neck. He winked at Valkyrie then noticed his sister-in-law.

"Beryl," he said, utterly failing to hide his dismay.

"Desmond, good morning."

"Beryl, what are you doing here? It's not even 8 o'clock. You know I don't like seeing you before I've had my first cup of coffee."

Beryl laughed that hideous fake laugh of hers. "Oh Desmond, you're such a messer! I'm just here to talk to Melissa, that's all. We've got a lot to organise for tomorrow night."

"Oh, dear God, the family reunion thing."

"It'll be wonderful!"

"But you'll be there," her dad said, puzzled, and Valkyrie nearly choked on her cereal.

Her mum looked up at him. "You forgot your shirt."

"Oh, yes, the reason I'm here. I don't have a clean one."

"Behind the door."

He turned, saw the crisp white shirt hanging on the coat hook and rubbed his hands together. He took it off the hook and put it on, sliding the collar up beneath the tie as he buttoned it.

He didn't like wearing ties – he owned a construction company so he'd always thought he'd be in workboots and jeans. But every now and then he had to dress up and pretend – as he put it – to be civilised.

"So Steph," he said, "looking forward to a great day in school?"

"Oh yes," she said with mock enthusiasm.

"What do you think you'll learn today?"

"I can't begin to guess. Maybe how to subtract."

He waved his hand dismissively. "Subtraction's overrated. It's like adding, only backwards. You're not ever going to need it."

"Desmond!" Beryl said sternly. "You shouldn't take that attitude. Stephanie is at an easily-influenced age, and she needs to be taught that everything she learns in school is valuable. Joking around is all well and good, but some things just have to be taken seriously. How can you ever expect Stephanie to be responsible when all you ever do is set a bad example?"

"I don't know," he answered. "Luck, I suppose."

Beryl sighed in exasperation and looked like she was about to give them a lecture. Valkyrie and her father both pounced on the same opportunity before Beryl could utter another word.

"I'm going to school," Valkyrie said quickly, shovelling

the last spoonful of cereal into her mouth.

"I'm going to work," her dad said, only a millisecond behind.

Valkyrie slipped her bowl into the dishwasher and made for the door.

"But Desmond, you haven't had any breakfast," Valkyrie's mother said with a frown.

"I'll get something on the way," her father said, following her out. They got to the hallway and Valkyrie turned for the stairs as her dad picked his keys up off the small table. They looked at each other and nodded their silent goodbyes. Then they both smiled, and he walked out and she went to her room.

Not for the first time, she wondered how her father would react if he knew that the family legends were true, that they *were* descended from the Ancients, that his grandfather and his late brother had been right. But she didn't tell him. If he knew the truth, he'd try and stop her from going out every day, try to protect her from people like Serpine, and Vengeous, and whoever else wanted to kill her. Or worse, maybe he'd want to get involved. She didn't think she'd be able to cope with her father putting himself in danger. She wanted her family to be normal. Normal was good. Normal was safe.

She closed the door then took off her school jumper and

dropped it on the bed. She touched her mirror and a moment later her reflection stepped out. She had forgotten about the logo rule *once* and the reflection had gone to school with the school crest on the wrong side and the school motto written backwards. Valkyrie hadn't made that mistake again. She waited until her reflection had pulled on the jumper then handed it her schoolbag.

"Have fun," she said, and the reflection nodded and hurried out of the room.

Not for the first time, Valkyrie grinned to herself. She'd hardly been to school since Skulduggery had worked his magic on that mirror, yet she was up to date on all the classes, all the gossip, all the day-to-day workings of an ordinary, everyday, run-of-the-mill thirteen year old. Without having to actually set foot through a classroom door.

Sure, there were times when she wished she'd been there to experience something firsthand instead of reliving it through the reflection's eyes. It wasn't the same merely having the memories of, say, a joke being told, instead of actually having been around for the real thing. Just another price to pay, she reckoned.

Moving quietly, Valkyrie took off the rest of her uniform, hid it under her bed and dressed in the black clothes that had been made especially for her. She'd grown a bit since Ghastly

Bespoke had designed them, but they still fitted, and for that she was thankful. They had saved her life on more then one occasion, and it wasn't as if she could ask Ghastly to make her any more. In a fight with the White Cleaver he had used the earth power as a last-ditch defence and turned himself to stone. She hadn't known him that well, but she missed him and she knew that Skulduggery did too.

She slipped into her coat and opened the window. She breathed deep and slow. Checking to make sure she wasn't being watched, she climbed out on to the sill and paused there for a moment, focusing her mind. Then she slipped off the edge, displacing the air beneath her to slow her descent. It wasn't graceful, and her landing was still a little too hard, but it was a lot better than it had been.

She hurried down the road to the pier. When she was younger she used to join her friends there. They used to sprint for the edge and leap as far as they could over the rocks right below them, splashing down into the sparkling water. Yes, it was dangerous, and yes, poor J. J. Pearl once shattered his knee on those rocks, but the danger gave the exercise a certain extra kick. These days, J. J. walked with a slight limp and she'd long since drifted apart from her childhood friends. She missed swimming though. She didn't get to do a whole lot of that now.

The Bentley was waiting for her, parked beside a rusty old Fiat. It stood out by a mile – but then it stood out by a mile wherever it went.

"Good morning," Skulduggery said when she got in. "Well rested, are you?"

"I had two hours' sleep," she said.

"Well, no one said being a great detective leading an action-packed life was easy."

"*You* said it was easy."

"I said it was easy for *me*," he corrected. "Was that your lovely aunt's car I saw outside your house?"

"Yeah, it was," said Valkyrie, and told him about her brief run-in with Beryl.

"Family reunion?" Skulduggery said when she had finished. "Are you going?"

"And, what, leave you to stop the bad guys without me? No way. I'll send the reflection in my place, thank you very much."

"A reunion might be fun."

"Right. Fun. Because I have so much fun with that side of the family. I wouldn't mind so much if it was Mum's side – I have a laugh with them. Dad's side is just... weird, you know?"

"I do. Gordon spoke of them often. Never forget, however, that you're weird too."

She glared at him. "I'm not weird like that. I'm good weird. I'm cool weird."

"Yes," he said doubtfully. "Yes, you are."

"Shut up. But anyway, all of Dad's cousins will be there, with their families, people I hardly know and, of course, Beryl and Fergus and the Toxic Twins, and it's pretty much going to be horrible, so there's no way in hell that I'm going."

"Well, that's good enough for me."

Skulduggery started the engine and Valkyrie sat low in her seat as he pulled out on to the road and started driving.

"So have you found out anything about Vengeous?"

"One of our people at the docks hasn't reported in yet," Skulduggery said. He was wearing his usual disguise – wide-brimmed hat, overlarge sunglasses, fuzzy wig and a scarf wrapped around the lower half of his face. "It might be nothing, but..."

"But Vengeous might already be here?"

"Well, yes."

"That's bad."

"It's not good."

They were driving down Main Street and Valkyrie glanced out as they passed the bus stop. Five bored-looking teens stood in school uniform.

"My reflection's not there," she said with a frown.

"Maybe it got delayed."

She shook her head. "It left before me."

The Bentley slowed. "What do you want to do?"

"It's probably nothing. It could have cut across the Green... although it should still have made it here by now. But no, it's probably nothing."

Skulduggery pulled over to the side of the road and tilted his head at her. "You use that reflection a lot more than is recommended," he said. "You ought to expect some unusual behaviour every now and then."

"I know..."

"But you want to go and look for it, don't you?"

"I just want to check that everything's all right. I'll get out here, go through the Green."

"I'll turn around, head back to the pier, meet up with you there."

Valkyrie nodded, made sure no one was looking and then got out of the car and ran between two buildings. She climbed the fence and dropped to the grass on the other side. The green was actually a small park, an oasis of trees and flowerbeds and a fountain, tucked behind Main Street. It was the site of many a game of football when Valkyrie was younger.

She could have been overreacting. Her reflection had probably met some people Valkyrie knew. In fact, Valkyrie herself could be the one to ruin things, by running straight into a situation that the reflection was handling with its usual efficiency. And then she heard her own scream.

Valkyrie left the main path, running towards the small clump of trees. Beyond the trees, near the fountain, there were two figures struggling. It was her reflection, trying to break free from a man in black.

"Hey!" Valkyrie shouted.

The man in black looked up. He was pale and oddly beautiful, and way too calm. "There you are," he said. "I was almost fooled. Almost. But this one doesn't feel fear. And I can *smell* fear." He thrust the reflection from him, and it stumbled to its knees.

"Get to school," Valkyrie told it. The reflection nodded, picked up the fallen schoolbag and ran past her through the trees, not even glancing back at the attacker.

Valkyrie glared. "Who are you? How did you find out where I live?"

"I followed you," he said. "I lost you when you came into town, so I decided to wait around until you showed up again. I even made some new friends."

Now she saw them, a young couple, walking towards her.

She knew them. She didn't know their names, but she'd seen them around, holding hands, laughing. They weren't laughing now. They were pale, as pale as the man in black. They looked sick and there were bloodstains on their clothes. They watched her with dark, dead eyes. Valkyrie looked at the man in black, remembered the graceful way he had moved. "You're a vampire," she breathed.

"And you are Valkyrie Cain and you're coming with us."

She couldn't fight them. There was no way she was even close to being ready.

So she ran.

The young couple were after her, sprinting, feet thudding on the grass. She kept ahead of them. She didn't even have to look back, she could hear how close they were. But she couldn't hear *him.* The man in black was running at her side, moving without effort. She tried to duck away, but he reached out a lazy hand, his fingers closing around her arm, and stopped suddenly. She jerked to a painful halt.

She swung a punch but he moved slightly and her fist connected with nothing but air. She tried to kick and he took a step, the expression on his face never going beyond bored, and he grabbed Valkyrie's arm and twisted it behind her back and her knees hit the ground.

"The Baron wants you alive," he said. "Bear in mind, he did not specify *unharmed.* Do not try to hit me again."

"How about me?" Skulduggery said as he ran up behind him. "Can *I* hit you?"

The man in black released Valkyrie and turned, too late to stop Skulduggery's fist from smacking into his jaw. He staggered and Skulduggery splayed his hand. The air rushed into the vampire and sent him backwards, head over heels. Instead of sprawling on to the grass, however, his body moved with an inhuman agility and he twisted sideways and landed on his feet.

"Detective," he murmured.

"Dusk," Skulduggery said. "It's been a while. Still evil?"

The man called Dusk smiled. "When the mood takes me." He gestured to the young couple. "Allow me to introduce you to my friends. I like to call them Minion One and Minion Two. You can decide among yourselves which one is which."

The young couple attacked. Skulduggery dodged their clumsy grabs and threw them into each other's way. Dusk blurred and in an eye-blink he was beside Valkyrie, pulling her to her feet.

Skulduggery lunged at Dusk and they went down, and Skulduggery lost his hat and scarf. Valkyrie stumbled back. Minion One, the male, snarled and came at her. He looked even worse close up. His eyes were dull and red-rimmed, and she could see the bite on his neck beneath his shirt collar. It wasn't the dainty twin pin-pricks she'd seen in the movies- his neck had been savagely torn open. She could smell the dried blood on his skin. It smelled of copper.

For a moment she panicked. His hands were gripping her collar, forcing her back, and he was strong. His girlfriend, Minion Two, was right behind him, eager to inflict some damage of her own. Valkyrie made herself relax, remembering the drills she'd run with Skulduggery and Tanith, conditioning her body to relax when every part of her wanted to scream.

She allowed herself to be pushed back. Her left hand gripped Minion One's wrist and her right hand came up between his arms to his face. She planted her left foot and dug in and twisted her hips into him, and Minion One collided with her and went over.

Minion Two snarled and punched and Valkyrie's world rocked. She deflected the grab that followed, tried a lock that didn't work then stomped on Minion Two's knee and shoved her away.

She saw Skulduggery and Dusk. Now that he could no longer be taken by surprise, Dusk's supernatural grace and athleticism were keeping him away from Skulduggery's strikes.

He swept out of range of the punches and kicks, and every hold Skulduggery tried, Dusk eased out of before it was even completed.

He kicked Skulduggery and moved backwards, and as he did so something fell from his pocket. He glanced at it and moved to retrieve it, but Skulduggery held out his hand and it flew into his grip.It was a syringe, filled with a colourless liquid.

Dusk shrugged. "You can keep it," he said. "I've got plenty more."

The Minions were regrouping. Valkyrie clicked her fingers, but failed to ignite a spark. She tried again, and this time she felt the heat of the friction. She focused, curled her hand, and let the energy pour from the centre of her body into her arm, into her palm. Then she took the spark and made it into a flame.

"Stay back," she warned. The Minions didn't answer. She didn't even know if they were *capable* of answering.

The flame expanded into a ball of fire in her hand and she hurled it right at them. And then Skulduggery was shouting something and running forwards, his arms sweeping up, and a rush of wind hit the fireball and knocked it off course even as the flames extinguished. Then he was at Valkyrie's side, holding her arm, walking backwards with her as the Minions stalked them.

"They've been infected," he said, "but they're not lost. Not yet. We don't want to kill them."

Dusk strolled after them. "It's not their fault I chose them after all."

Skulduggery glanced at her. "It takes two nights for an Infected to become a vampire. Until then, they're innocent victims."

"But in two nights," Dusk added, "this will all be over."

Skulduggery took out his gun, aimed it straight at Dusk. The Minions stopped and snarled. Dusk's smile never left his face. "This is your chance to leave," Skulduggery said.

"Why would we do that? *You're* the ones backing away. *You* can't kill my friends. *You* are losing this little altercation."

Skulduggery thumbed back the revolver's hammer. "I said we don't *want* to kill them. I didn't say we *won't*."

"If you fire that gun," Dusk said, "you will have the whole town running to see what's going on and you've dropped your disguise."

"That's the only reason I'm not putting you out of our misery right here and now."

Dusk considered his options then shrugged. "Minions," he said, "we're leaving." The infected couple snarled their displeasure, but did as they were told. They joined Dusk as he backed away.

Skulduggery didn't lower the gun. "Tell Vengeous I expected more from him. Going after my colleague to get to me is the sort of thing Serpine tried. Tell him if he wants me then be a man and come and get me."

"The Baron is an honourable man."

"The Baron is a coward."

Dusk smiled, but didn't respond. Valkyrie stood by Skulduggery's side, and they watched Dusk and his Minions fade into the cover of the trees.

7

UNWELCOME VISITORS

The Hibernian Cinema stood like an old man, stoop-shouldered and grey-faced, squeezed in on either side by taller, broader and healthier buildings. Its façade was a decaying remnant of a forgotten time, and most of the vowels were missing from its name. Fifty years ago, this cinema had thrived, its Dublin audiences flocking to it every weekend. Skulduggery himself had first visited the Hibernian to see *High Society*, and he'd had a crush on Grace Kelly ever since.

He parked the Bentley in the lane at the back, and Valkyrie

followed him in. The carpeted surroundings absorbed their footfalls. They passed framed posters for obscure movies starring dead actors. No paying customer had been in this building for decades.

The cinema was quiet, as usual, and empty. They walked down the steps between the rows of seats. The screen had a heavy red curtain in front of it, musty with age. As they approached, the curtain parted and the screen lit up, showing an old black-and-white film. The film showed a brick wall and an open door. The soundtrack was of a city at night. Valkyrie followed Skulduggery up on to the small stage and they walked to the door, their shadows falling on to the image. Then they walked through the screen.

They took the stairs that lay on the other side and gradually the artificial light swept the gloom away. They reached the top floor, where all signs of the old cinema had been replaced by gleaming corridors and laboratories. The owner of the Hibernian had spent a lot of time renovating the building, developing it into the magic-science facility he'd always dreamed about. Because of the delicate nature of the work done in all the various sections – the medical bay, the brand-new Morgue, the Theoretical Magic (R&D) Department – there were no windows, and the temperature was carefully controlled.

Although he had the run of the entire building, shared only with his two assistants, the owner still chose to work in the smallest, darkest laboratory, and that was where they found him.

Professor Kenspeckle Grouse looked around when Skulduggery said his name. "You again," he said in a voice that was not overflowing with warmth and hospitality. "What do you want?" Kenspeckle was a small, elderly man with a mass of white hair and very little patience.

"We have something for you, Professor," Skulduggery said, showing him the syringe that had fallen from Dusk's pocket. "We were wondering if you'd have time to analyse it."

"Oh, as if I'm not kept busy enough as it is," Kenspeckle said gruffly. "Valkyrie, I haven't seen you in weeks. Staying out of trouble?"

"Not really," Valkyrie admitted.

"Nor did I expect you to," he said with an exasperated sigh. For all his crotchety behaviour and ill manners, the elderly scientist seemed to have a soft spot for Valkyrie. "So what has he dragged you into this time?"

"I haven't dragged her into anything," Skulduggery said defensively.

Valkyrie smiled. "Fights, kidnap attempts, more fights. Business as usual, you know how it is." Skulduggery's phone rang and he stepped away to answer it.

Now that Skulduggery was out of earshot, Kenspeckle let his voice soften in tone. "How is the shoulder from last month?"

"Much better," she answered. "I was barely left with a bruise."

Kenspeckle nodded. "I used a new mixture. The ingredients are a little harder to find, but for my favourite patients I like to make sure the healing process is as painless as possible."

"I'm on that list?" Valkyrie asked, her smile growing wider.

Kenspeckle snorted. "You *are* the list." Valkyrie laughed.

"Your partner certainly isn't," Kenspeckle continued, returning his attention to Skulduggery as his phone call ended. "Let me see that syringe." Skulduggery handed it over.

"Where did you get it?"

"It fell out of a vampire's pocket."

Kenspeckle held the syringe up to the light, examining the liquid within. "Fascinating creatures, vampires. Two completely separate layers of epidermis, the upper layer of which regenerates when the sun comes up. Human by day, gifted with slightly enhanced speed and strength, but essentially mortal. But at night..."

Valkyrie nodded. "I know what they're like at night."

"Hmm? Oh, that's right. You have firsthand knowledge,

don't you? How did you get that, I wonder? Oh, yes." He glared at Skulduggery. "Someone with absolutely no sense of responsibility dragged you in front of a *vampire* and almost got you killed."

Skulduggery tilted his head. "Are you talking about me?" he asked innocently.

Kenspeckle scowled and went back to examining the syringe. "I've seen this before," he said, "but only once. It's a rare concoction of hemlock and wolfsbane. It would be used by a vampire to suppress his bestial nature at night."

"Makes sense," Skulduggery murmured. "Dusk is of no use to Vengeous if he loses control every time the sun goes down."

Kenspeckle loosened his tie and undid his top shirt button. "I had a run-in with a vampire in my youth, and I barely escaped with my life. That's why I carry this with me everywhere I go." He showed them a glass vial that hung around his neck.

"Is that holy water?" Valkyrie asked, a little doubtfully.

"Holy water? No, no, *no*, Valkyrie. It's *sea water*."

"Right," she said slowly.

"Holy water doesn't work," Kenspeckle explained, "and stakes through the heart won't kill them. Decapitation *is* effective, but then decapitation is effective against most things.

The one vampire legend that *does* have merit, however, is running water."

Valkyrie frowned. "OK, and that seems to be the one legend I've never heard of."

Skulduggery spoke up. "There's an old myth that vampires can't pass over running water, so they couldn't cross a bridge that spans a river, for instance. Now, while crossing bridges doesn't phase them in the slightest, the truth of the myth stems from salt water."

"Vampires have an extreme allergic reaction to the stuff," Kenspeckle said. "If ingested, it would swell a vampire's throat, blocking its air passage. Which is why I carry some with me at all times."

"But wouldn't they have to swallow it?" Valkyrie asked.

"Well, yes..."

"And how would you get a vampire to swallow the water before it killed you?" Kenspeckle blinked and didn't say anything.

"Never mind," Valkyrie said quickly. "I'm sure, you know, you'd find a way. Like, you could throw the water into its mouth when it's, uh, about to bite you."

Kenspeckle's shoulders slumped, and Valkyrie felt incredibly guilty that she had poked a hole in his plan. "Leave me," he said a little mournfully.

"I'm sorry..." Valkyrie began, but he held up his hand.

"No need to apologise. I am a *medical* genius, a *scientific* genius, but obviously not a *tactical* genius. And to think, for the last 180 years I was unafraid of vampires because I had a vial of salt water tied around my neck. What an idiot."

Kenspeckle shuffled off and Skulduggery patted Valkyrie on the shoulder. "Congratulations," he said. "You've just reinstated a 300-year old neurosis. Our work here is done."

Feeling absolutely terrible, Valkyrie followed him back the way they had come. They passed the two assistants in white labcoats, Stentor and Civet, wrestling in an empty room. Valkyrie had been here more times than she could count, and sights like this were not uncommon. The assistants waved, then got back to wrestling.

Valkyrie was the first one down the stairs, and she walked to the back of the screen and stepped through. She jumped from the stage, turned and waited for Skulduggery. She watched him pass through the image of the door, and a moment later the film flickered, the screen went blank and the gloom closed in. He left the stage and the curtains began to drift together behind him.

"Who was that on the phone?" she asked, trying to forget about what she had done to Kenspeckle.

"The Grand Mage," Skulduggery said, "checking in on us

once again. His eagerness to recover the Baron is making him quite... irritable."

"He's always irritable."

"Obviously he's decided to take it to new heights."

"I wish Meritorious was still alive. He was a good Grand Mage. Guild is... He's like a politician, like he's got people to please."

They left the cinema and walked into the bright sunshine, and Skulduggery didn't say anything until they got to the Bentley.

"We're supposed to meet Tanith at the library, so I'm going to drop you off there and meet up with you later, if that is OK with you."

"Where are you going?"

"Nowhere special. I just have some... things to do."

"Why did you pause?"

"I'm sorry?"

"You paused. You have some... things to do. Why did you pause?"

"No reason, I just—"

"You're up to something."

"No—"

"Then why'd you pause?"

"Get in the car." She got in. He got in.

"Seatbelt," he said.

"Why'd you pause?"

His head drooped. "Because I'm up to something."

"And why can't I come with you?"

"Because it's something sneaky."

"Do you promise to tell me later?"

"I do."

"Well, all right then." She clicked her seatbelt into place. "Let's go."

Valkyrie went into the tenement building and climbed the stairs, passing a man who didn't have a shadow. She got to the third floor just as China Sorrows crossed from the library to her apartment.

"Valkyrie," China said. "How nice to see you again so soon." The skirt she wore was a light green, and the jacket was of a green deeper than a thousand crushed emeralds. Her necklace was exquisite.

"That's beautiful," Valkyrie said, looking at it.

"Isn't it? This necklace has cost two very fine men their lives. At times, I wear it in tribute to their sacrifice. Other times, I wear it because it goes with this skirt. Would you like to come in?"

"Sure," Valkyrie said and followed China inside. She closed the door after her. She would never have admitted this, but Valkyrie adored China's apartment. The carpet was lush and intricate, the décor was elegant and restrained, and it looked out over Dublin in such a way that the city seemed prettier and more romantic than it had ever been.

"Any new developments?" China asked, picking up a stack of letters and rifling through them.

"Not especially. I was attacked earlier though."

"Oh?"

"By a vampire and his minions."

"Can't stand those things," China said. "Once they bite, the infected person has two nights of mindless slavery to endure, and if they're not treated, they become full vampires. Such a horrible condition. Did you happen to catch his name?"

"Dusk."

"Yes, I know Dusk. He has a habit of holding grudges. I had an associate who crossed him. It took years, but Dusk finally managed to track him down and the death he provided was not a quick one. There was a lot of blood and screaming and..."

She caught herself, and smiled. "I apologise. I must confess to being in a very bad mood of late. Because of this Grotesquery business, everything I've worked so hard for – my library, my collections, my influence – all of it could be wiped out in the blink of an indifferent eye."

"Along with the rest of the world," Valkyrie reminded her.

"Yes. That would be unfortunate also." China put the letters down. "Have you seen him yet? The Baron?"

"No. Not yet."

China sat on the luxurious yet tasteful sofa. "An unusual man. He likes to think of himself as straightforward. He is anything but. He shares the same elitist attitude as Nefarian Serpine, but where Serpine was independent and self-serving, the Baron carried out his duties with a selflessness, and a blind and unwavering faith. What Serpine began, Vengeous seeks to finish. To him, the return of the Faceless Ones is the only thing that has ever truly mattered."

"Sounds like you know him well."

"Oh, I do. Didn't Skulduggery tell you? I too used to worship the Faceless Ones."

Valkyrie felt her face drain. "What?"

China smiled. "Obviously he didn't tell you. Bliss and I were raised in a family that worshipped the dark gods. My brother rejected our family's teachings at an early age, but it took me some time to do the same. While I worshipped, however, I joined a small group of like-minded individuals, of which the

Baron was one. Remember when I told you that there is nothing more dangerous than a zealot? We were dangerous even by a zealot's standards."

"I... I didn't know that."

China shrugged. "I was young and foolish and arrogant. I've changed. I'm not foolish any more." She laughed. Valkyrie forced a smile.

"And now," China continued, "you're wondering, once again, if I can be trusted. After all, when Skulduggery first told you about me, what did he say?"

"He... he said not to trust you."

"Because I am not worthy of it, Valkyrie. I will endanger those close to me for my own advantage. I am not a nice person, my dear. I am not... one of the good guys."

"Then why does he still rely on you?"

"Because he himself has gone through change and he is no hypocrite. He will not condemn me for my past actions, so long as I don't revert to the person I once was. The war with Mevolent changed everyone who fought in it. We each saw things in ourselves that we would rather not admit to."

"What did Skulduggery see?"

"Rage. His family was murdered in front of him, and when he returned from death, his rage came with him. For most, anger that fierce can burn only for so long. Skulduggery, being Skulduggery, is the natural exception. His rage stayed."

"So what happened?"

"He disappeared. If you want my opinion, I think he saw what he was capable of and he knew he had a choice – to let that rage consume him, or to fight it. So he left. He was gone for five years. When he came back, the anger was still there, but there was something else – a realisation I think. A new purpose. He was able to joke again, which was a welcome return, for he is one of the very few men able to make me laugh. Soon after, we received word that Lord Vile had fallen, and then Skulduggery himself brought down the Baron, and Mevolent's plans began to unravel."

"Where did he go? For the five years?"

"I don't know. We all thought he was dead. Dead *again*, you know. But he came back just when we needed him. That's one thing you can count on him for – the nick-of-time rescue. He's quite good at it."

There was a knock on the door. They both stood, and from out in the corridor they heard a muffled voice and then a loud thump.

China looked at Valkyrie. "Go into the bedroom," she said quickly. "Do not argue with me. Go into the bedroom and close the door." Valkyrie did as she was told, but left the door open a crack – just enough to see through. She saw China pick up the telephone, and then the door to the apartment burst open and the slender man in the bow tie came flying through. He landed in a heap and didn't move.

A figure stepped in. He looked to be in his fifties, with grey hair and a tightly cropped beard. His clothes were dark and vaguely militaristic, and his boots were polished to a gleam. He had a cutlass in his belt.

"Hello China," he said. "It's good to see you again."

"Baron Vengeous," China said slowly and put the telephone down. "I dearly wish I could say the same. Why are you here?"

"You mean you don't know?"

"If you wish to return an overdue book, the library is across the hall. I think you will find the fine to be stern, yet reasonable."

"I'm here for you, China. Within a few hours I will have Lord Vile's armour and the final missing ingredient will be within my grasp. It's time to take off this mask you wear, to end this charade. You need to take your place."

"My place is right here."

"We both know that's not true. You could no more turn your back on the Faceless Ones than *I* could. I have seen your devotion."

"My devotion, as you call it, has waned."

Vengeous shook his head. "You have sworn your allegiance to the dark gods. You cannot simply change your mind."

"I'm afraid I can, and I have."

Through the crack in the door, Valkyrie could see the anger seeping into the Baron's face. "You are their servant," he said, his voice low and threatening. "If *you* will not uphold the vow you made on your own then *I* will do it for you. You *will* be there when the Faceless Ones return, even if it is just so you can be the first traitor they kill."

He reached for her, and China put her left hand flat on her belly and flicked her right, and every piece of furniture in the room flew at Vengeous.

Valkyrie stared, open-mouthed, as tables and chairs and bookcases crashed into Vengeous at a terrible speed. They clattered to the floor and he staggered and fell, blood running down his face. China tapped her belly twice and gestured with her right hand, sending everything – the furniture and Vengeous – skidding across the floor and slamming into the wall. Then another tap of her belly and another whip of her hand and the furniture moved away, clearing a space around the Baron.

"You do not threaten me in my own home," China said and sent the furniture hurtling back to him.

But Vengeous was quick and he lunged forward, eyes flashing yellow. The table that was coming directly for him suddenly exploded into a hundred thousand splinters and he dived through them, escaping the rest of the furniture that impacted on the wall behind him. He sent his hand into her chest and she pitched backwards. She hit the wall and fell to one knee.

Valkyrie gripped the door, about to fling it open, but China looked up at Vengeous and her eyes narrowed.

"As my words draw closed, the circle binds, secures you to your fate."

Vengeous reached for her, but hit something, an invisible wall. He tried to back off but he only got a couple of steps before he hit another barrier. He looked down, looked at the elaborate carpet and saw the circle hidden in the design.

"Clever girl..."

"You didn't think I would install some security measures?" China said.

"Very, very clever." His eyes flashed yellow.

"That's not going to work, my dear Baron. Symbols are my power. *Your* powers can't break that shield. You can't hurt me. But I can hurt you." Vengeous looked down at the carpet again, at the hidden intricacies, symbols woven into the very fabric around the circle, symbols that were now pulsing with blue energy. Blood started to run from his nose.

"China," he said, struggling to keep his voice even, "you don't want to do this."

"Who are you allied with?" she asked. "Who ordered you set free? Who is behind all this?"

He barked out a desperate laugh that was cut short by the pain. "You've chosen the wrong... side here, woman. I wish I could... I wish I could let you live to regret it..."

Vengeous dropped to the floor. "I wish I had the time... to make you beg... to make you plead with me. I would have... I would have made you *scream*..."

"Fine," China said, crossing to the phone. "I suppose I'll have to call in the professionals."

"China..." Vengeous gasped.

She turned. "Yes, dear Baron?"

"You didn't... you didn't really think it would be that easy, did you?"

Dusk walked through the door. A man followed. The stranger had blond hair and wore a brown suit, a white shirt and dark sunglasses. His cowboy boots were old and scuffed, and he was grinning. The carpet at his feet frayed and split, and he sank downwards, disappearing into the floor. China dived for the phone, but Dusk darted in and shoved her back.

Valkyrie stared as the stranger's hand burst up through the floor at Vengeous' feet, grabbed him and pulled him down. The floor sealed up behind him and the symbols pulsed one last time, then returned to normal.

A moment later Vengeous and the stranger stepped through the wall beside China.

"Your hospitality used to be so much better," Vengeous said. His eyes flashed and China stumbled. Dusk picked her up.

"Don't let her touch anything," Vengeous told him. "She has symbols everywhere. Some are invisible. Some are even etched on to her body. Don't let her touch *anything*." Dusk grabbed both her wrists and wrenched her arms behind her.

Vengeous took out a handkerchief, used it to wipe away the rest of the blood. "I expected more from you, China. When you left us, I thought you'd be back. No one could do the things you'd done and then walk away. I didn't think it was possible."

She looked up at him, grimacing against the pain that was locking her arms straight behind her. "I found other interests. You can too. Stamp collecting, maybe." Dusk twisted her arms and she gasped. The man in the sunglasses laughed.

Vengeous put the handkerchief away. "I can still be merciful, even if my gods are *not*. The girl, China. Valkyrie Cain. Tell me where she is, and I will let you live."

"Skulduggery doesn't care about her," China said through gritted teeth. "She's a hobby, nothing more. You won't be able to get at him through her."

"My mercy is on a timetable. Tell me where I can find her or I shall torture you until you *beg* to tell me."

"OK," China said, "OK, I'll tell you." She nodded to the bedroom. "She's in there." Valkyrie went cold, but Vengeous just shook his head sadly.

"China, I don't like this side of you, these *jokes*."

"I've been spending too much time around Skulduggery. You remember *his* jokes, don't you, Baron? What else do you remember? You remember him arresting you?"

"I remember almost killing him."

"Almost wasn't enough," China said and actually managed a laugh. "He's coming for you, you know. I hope I'm there when he gets you." Dusk twisted and China cried out in pain.

"Tell me where the girl is," Vengeous said, "or I will have your arms broken."

"Here I am," Valkyrie said, kicking the door open as the fire flared in her hands.

8

BILLY-RAY SANGUINE

Her aim was off on the first fireball she threw and it missed Dusk. The second fireball, however, was on target, and it would have hit Baron Vengeous if he hadn't moved out of the way at the last moment. He was fast. Maybe even faster than Skulduggery.

"Cain," he snarled.

"Run!" China shouted and Valkyrie obeyed. She was out in the corridor before she glanced back, just in time to see China wave her hand. The door slammed shut, sealing the men in the apartment.

Valkyrie got to the stairs, heading down, when something grabbed her ankle and she nearly fell. She kept going, looking back in time to see a hand disappear back into the steps. She reached the second floor, banged off the wall and kept going down. The wall below her cracked and crumbled, and the man in the sunglasses lunged out. Valkyrie gripped the banister and jumped, using her momentum to lend force to the kick. Her boot slammed into his chest and he hit the wall hard and bounced off.

At the first floor she almost tripped over herself, the man right behind her. She jumped the last few steps and ran out on to the street. Cars were passing and people were walking. Too many innocent people that could be caught up in a battle they weren't ready for. She sprinted into the alley beside the tenement building. It was narrow and cut off from the sun. The other side led out on to a quieter road.

The man in the sunglasses was behind her, closing the gap between them to an arm's length. She barely kept out of reach.

Valkyrie dropped and the man's legs crashed into her and he went flying over, losing his sunglasses in the process. He hit the ground and sprawled, and when he snapped his head to her, she saw that he had two small black holes where his eyes should have been. She spun, ran back the way she had come, and glanced over her shoulder in time to see the man sink into the ground, straight down, like he was in an invisible elevator. With five paces left to the street, the ground in front of her exploded and the man surged upwards. She fell back, trying to wipe her eyes clear of gravel and dirt.

"I don't see what all the fuss is about," the man said. He was American and spoke with a strong Deep South drawl. "You're just a little girl."

Valkyrie clicked her fingers, but he smacked her hand down before she could conjure a flame, then grabbed her. She felt something cold and sharp on her throat.

"Don't try that again," the man said. He held a straight razor with a wooden handle, and as her vision cleared she saw the initials B-R. S. engraved on it. She raised her eyes. Up ahead, parked at the side of the quiet street, was a black motorbike. Tanith's black motorbike.

An old woman with a lined face and bad teeth stepped into the alley. She stared at them, then turned and hurried away.

The man shook his head. "See, that's the problem with ordinary, regular folk. They see somethin' freaky, somethin' scary, they run the other way. Y'know what that means, don't you? It means no one's comin' to help you. It means you're all alone."

And then someone coughed right behind them. The man looked around and Tanith Low kicked him in the face. He stumbled and Valkyrie tore herself free, spinning around to keep him in sight as she backed off to the wall. He would have been handsome were it not for those awful black holes.

The man smiled. "And who might you be?"

"You first," Tanith said.

The man chuckled. "Very well. Billy-Ray Sanguine, master of all manner of unpleasant deaths and purveyor of cruel and unusual punishments, at your service."

"You're a hitman?"

"Not merely a hitman, darlin'. I am a hitman *deluxe*. I also do muscle-for-hire and a nice little sideline in mercenary activities. I'm very, very expensive and I'm very, very good. And you are?"

"The end of you," Tanith said.

Sanguine laughed. "Oh, I see. I often wondered what the end of me would look like. Never imagined it'd be somethin' quite so pretty."

Tanith reached into her coat and revealed her sword, still in its sheath. "Are you going to come along quietly, Mr Sanguine, or do I have to hurt you?"

Sanguine's face fell. "Oh come on! Look at the size of yours and look at the size of mine! I just got this little razor here! That's hardly fair!"

"But your blade against an unarmed girl, *that's* fair?"

He hesitated, stepping back as she neared. "Seemed fair to me," he said, "at the time. At this juncture, lookin' back, perhaps it *was* a bit one-sided. Twenty-twenty hindsight and all that."

She took off her coat and let it fall. The muscles moved beneath the skin of her arms. She slid the sword from its scabbard as she walked towards him.

"Ooh," he said. "Gettin' interestin' *now*."

Tanith lunged and Sanguine ducked, the sword whistling over his head. Tanith flicked her wrist and the blade zipped back towards him, but he jumped back out of range, giving a laugh.

"Now this is fun! Two grown people gettin' to know each other the old-fashioned way. Romance is in the air."

"You're not my type."

"You don't know what your type is, darlin'."

"I know you're not it. Mr Sanguine, I've got some shackles with your name on them."

"Shackles can't hold me, pretty lady. I'm immune to just about every binding spell I reckon you ever heard of, and a few more you haven't. That's what makes me special."

"That and your psychopathic tendencies."

"Oh, those don't make me special. They just make me *fun*."

This time it was Sanguine who moved first, feinting right to draw the sword away then skipping in, the razor slicing up through the air. Tanith lifted her elbow, hitting his forearm and making him miss, then she kicked out at his knee and slashed back with the sword. Sanguine had to dive out of the way. He rolled awkwardly and came up, rubbing his knee.

"That hurt," he said with a smile.

"I can make this easy on you."

"You gonna give me that sword of yours?"

"No, but if you tell me what Baron Vengeous is planning, I'll let you walk away from this."

He frowned. "But I drove here."

"This is a one-time offer, Mr Sanguine."

"And very considerate it is too. Unfortunately I am a professional, I got paid to do a job and I intend to do it – I have a reputation to protect after all. So how about this: you stand very still and allow me to kill you, and then I take the girl here and we go about our merry business. That sound good?"

"Afraid not."

"Darn. Ah, well, back to basics, I guess."

He smiled again and stood with his feet together. Valkyrie watched the surface beneath him start to crack and break, and when it was loose enough he sank straight into the ground and disappeared from view.

Tanith held the sword ready. The ground had closed up behind him, leaving only hundreds of little cracks to mark what had happened. Valkyrie kept very still. The seconds ticked by. Tanith was frowning, probably wondering if her opponent had simply run off. She glanced at Valkyrie, about to speak, then the wall behind her crumbled and Billy-Ray Sanguine dived at her.

Tanith, for her part, seemed incapable of being taken by surprise and simply stepped away, her sword casually slicing Sanguine's forearm. Covered in dirt, he howled in pain and the razor fell to the ground. He danced back, trying to stem the flow of blood. Valkyrie looked at the ground beside her feet.

"Don't you dare," Sanguine warned, glaring at her with those black holes, but she paid no heed. She stooped and picked up the straight razor and this infuriated him even further.

"What is it with you women?" he yelled, kicking at the air. "You come into our lives, you take everythin'! Throughout the years you got little pieces of me, of my very *soul*, and *now*? Now you got my damn straight razor! How am I supposed to kill people? How am I supposed to even *shave*?"

Behind Sanguine, Baron Vengeous strode in off the street and stood in the mouth of the alley. Valkyrie tensed.

"Get it done," Vengeous called out angrily.

"Yes sir," Sanguine responded then lowered his voice. "See that? You're getting' me in trouble with the boss. You better hand over the girl right this second." A side door opened, a door Valkyrie had never noticed before.

"Sorry," China said as she stepped out, "that's not about to happen." She had a fresh cut along her forehead, but was otherwise unharmed. A black jeep pulled up beside Vengeous and Dusk got out.

Valkyrie saw something, high above, a figure on the rooftop. For a moment she thought it was another of Vengeous' bad guys, and then the figure stepped off and dropped, and Mr Bliss landed beside them. He straightened up. Valkyrie saw the Baron scowl.

"Sanguine," he called out, "there are too many of them. We're leaving."

"Be right with you, Baron."

But Vengeous wasn't waiting. He got in the jeep and Dusk got back behind the wheel, and they drove off. Suddenly alone, Sanguine stopped glowering. He looked at his adversaries and licked his lips. He was still holding his injured arm, blood trickling between his fingers.

"What is Baron Vengeous planning?" asked Mr Bliss, his voice terrible and quiet.

"I don't know," Sanguine said. "No wait, I'm lyin'. I do know, I'm just not tellin'."

Valkyrie watched him draw his feet together and the ground beneath him started to crumble. "Stop him!" she cried.

Tanith lunged, but it was too late, and he sank down into the earth again.

"Damn," Tanith said, scowling. "Some 'hitman deluxe' *he* turned out to be. Nothing more than a sneaky little coward."

"I heard that!" They tensed, ready to fight, looking down at the piece of broken ground – and at Sanguine, who was poking his head up through the surface. They relaxed their stances.

"I am not a coward," Sanguine said hotly, looking up at them. "I have just been momentarily outclassed. It takes a man to admit when he is beaten."

"You must be very manly then," Valkyrie said, which drew a glare from the American.

"No one likes sarcasm, Miss Cain. I've merely delayed my exit to promise you something. You took my straight razor, li'l darlin'. That I view as an unforgivable offence. So when the time comes, when you have served your purpose, I swear to you I'm gonna kill you for *free*." And with that, Billy-Ray Sanguine disappeared into the ground. Then he popped his head back up.

"Or at least half price." And he was gone again.

9

THE HIDDEN ROOM

After Valkyrie hung up the phone, she used the library bathroom to clean the dirt from her face. She dried her hands and watched them shake. Her hands always shook after a fight, as the leftover adrenaline took the opportunity to charge randomly through her.

Tanith was waiting for her outside, and together they walked down the stairs. They were headed over to Gordon's house, to see if her late uncle's office held any books on the Grotesquery, and they were leaving Bliss to help China restore some order to her apartment. Valkyrie had never seen a brother and sister regard each other with as much wariness as they did.

"How did Skulduggery sound?" Tanith asked.

"Angry," Valkyrie replied, "and worried. He's only OK when I'm attacked by people he knows. He'd never even *heard* of this Sanguine guy."

"Still, at least we know how Vengeous got out of his cell."

Valkyrie nodded. "That little tunnelling trick *is* useful, all right. I just wish he wasn't using it to get *me*. I don't much like the idea of being a hostage. Doesn't sound like fun."

They emerged into the open air, and approached Tanith's motorbike.

"So how's training?" Tanith asked.

"Good. Well, mostly good. There are a few moves I've kind of... mislaid."

"Mislaid?"

"Forgotten."

Tanith smiled. "When this is over we'll run through it again. You'll get it, don't worry. How're the parents?"

Valkyrie shrugged. "Parents are fine."

"Have you been going to school much?"

"Ah, Skulduggery makes me go whenever we're not in the middle of a crisis. But that's the great thing about having the reflection – I don't have to deal with all that."

Tanith pulled on her helmet then flipped up the visor to give Valkyrie a strange look. "I wouldn't get too dependent on that reflection if I were you. You may absorb all its memories so it *feels* like you're going to school, but you're not. You're on the outside, looking in at an important part of your own life. You're thirteen, Val. You should be spending time with people your own age." She swung her leg over the bike.

Valkyrie raised an eyebrow as she pulled the spare helmet over her head. "People my own age don't fight monsters, Tanith. If they did, I'd be hanging out with them a lot more."

Valkyrie got on the motorbike behind Tanith.

The first time Valkyrie had ridden on Tanith's bike she had started off holding the sides of Tanith's coat, but as they picked up speed, her hands had got closer and closer together, until finally her arms were wrapped tightly around Tanith's waist. Once she'd got over her initial fear – that they were roaring along open roads and one bad turn would flip them to a painful and skin-shredding demise – she'd started to enjoy the sensation. Now she loved travelling by bike. It was *fun*.

Tanith swerved through traffic and took bends at an alarming speed, and Valkyrie started to laugh beneath her helmet.

They turned off the road and took a trail, the ride getting decidedly bouncier. It was only Tanith's superior reflexes that saved them from hitting one of the trees that blurred past. They burst from the treeline and shot up a small hill, leaving the ground for a few seconds and landing smoothly on a narrow road, then zipped over a humpbacked bridge. Moments later they were passing through the massive gate that led to Gordon Edgley's house. Valkyrie *still* thought of it as her uncle's house. The fact that she had inherited it changed absolutely nothing.

Tanith braked and let the back wheel skid sideways a little, throwing up a small shower of pebbles. She cut off the engine and leaned the bike on to its kickstand. They got off and removed their helmets.

"Enjoy that?" Tanith said with a little grin.

Valkyrie grinned back, her eyes bright. "I keep telling Skulduggery he should get a bike."

"What does he say?"

"He says people who wear leathers, like you, should ride motorbikes. People who wear exquisite suits, like him, should drive Bentleys."

"He has a point." Tanith looked up at the house. "So are we going to go in?"

Valkyrie laughed, took the key from her pocket and opened

the front door. "I still find it hard to believe you're a fan."

They walked in. The hall was grand, with Gothic paintings on the walls. They passed through into the living room.

"Your uncle was the best writer *ever*," Tanith said. "Why *wouldn't* I be a fan?"

"You just, I don't know, you don't really strike me as being the type. It's like when your friend thinks that your dad is the coolest guy in the world, y'know? It just seems a little silly."

"Well, there was nothing silly about your uncle's writing. Did I tell you that one of his short stories was based on something that happened to *me*?"

"You told me. Many times."

"I never met him, but he must have heard about it somehow. Maybe Skulduggery heard it and he told Gordon."

Tanith stood in the centre of the living room, gazing around with a slightly wistful look on her face. "And this is where Gordon lived. This is where he wrote his masterpiece. You're a lucky girl, Val. What was it like, having an uncle like Gordon Edgley?"

"We're not getting into this conversation," Valkyrie said. "Not again." She went to the bookshelf, took down a book bound in black and handed it to Tanith. Tanith bit her lip.

And The Darkness Rained Upon Them was the last thing Gordon

Edgley had written. It was set to be published in a few months, but Valkyrie had let Tanith read the advance copy. Every time Tanith was at the house, she devoured another few chapters until it was time to go. She loved coming here, and seized every chance she had to drop by.

Without another word spoken, Tanith took the book to the sofa, curled up and resumed reading. Valkyrie tried not to laugh. She left the living room and climbed the stairs, crossing the landing to Gordon's study and closing the door after her.

Unlike the rest of the house, Gordon's study was a chaotic affair, a mass of straining shelves and piles of stacked manuscripts. She went to the bookshelf that covered the far wall, scanning the titles. This was where he had kept his research material. Very occasionally, Valkyrie would find books on magic in this room that she hadn't even been able to find in the library of China Sorrows.

Valkyrie traced her finger along the spines. If anyone had collected information on a being as bizarre and unique as the Grotesquery, it would have been Gordon. That was his kind of thing.

Her fingertip stopped on a thick, leather-bound book with no title on its spine. She'd seen it before but had never paid it much attention. She tried slipping it from the shelf but it wouldn't budge. Frowning, she gripped it and pulled. It came out halfway and stuck, and then the wall started to move.

"No way," Valkyrie breathed, as the bookshelf swung open before her, revealing a room as black as night.

A secret room. An actual real, secret room.

Not bothering to subdue the excited grin that spread across her face, Valkyrie stepped in. The room immediately lit up with candles.

Like the study, the secret room was lined with shelves, and on those shelves were objects both alien and familiar. Among those she could categorise were ornate musical boxes, intricate statuettes, silver daggers and golden goblets. Before her was a table, and on that table was a blue jewel, nestled in a golden claw centrepiece. A faint light within the jewel started to glow as she stepped closer, and a man faded up from nothing on the other side of the room.

Portly. Wearing brown slacks and a matching waistcoat over a shirt with the sleeves rolled up to his forearms. Sandy hair that perched on top of his head like a loose bale of straw, shot through with grey. He turned and his eyes widened when he saw her.

"Stephanie," he said, "what are you doing here?"

She stared. "Uncle Gordon?"

Her dead uncle put his hands on his hips and shook his head. "What are you doing sneaking around this house? I always said you were far too inquisitive for your own good. Admittedly, it's a trait we share, but I for one am not above the occasional bout of hypocrisy to get my point across."

Valkyrie just stood there, mouth open. "Is that... is that really you?"

He stopped, like he'd been caught out in a lie, and then he started waving his hands and bobbing his head from side to side. "This isn't me," he said, "this is all a dream..."

"Stop that."

"Go back the way you came," he continued, drawing out his words, "and try to wake up. Remember, this is all a dreeeammmm..."

"I'm serious, Gordon; quit it." He stopped bobbing his head and dropped his hands to his sides.

"Fine," he said. "Then get ready for a shock. Stephanie: the world isn't what you think it is. There is magic here, real magic, and it is—"

"I know about the magic," she interrupted. "Just tell me what's going on. How are you here?"

"You know about the magic? Who told you?"

"Are you going to answer my question?"

"I suppose. What was it again?"

"How are you here?"

"Oh, well, I'm not. Not really. This isn't me. I mean, I am me, but I'm not. See the blue jewel? It's very rare, it's called an Echo Stone and generally it's used—"

"I know about Echo Stones."

"You do?"

"People sleep with the stone close by for three nights to imprint it with their personality and memories."

"Oh. Yes, you're quite right," he said, and looked a little disappointed. "It's generally used by the dying, and then given to loved ones to help comfort them through their grief. For me, however, it was more like a writing aid."

"A writing aid?"

"I imprinted my consciousness on to the stone. Or rather, the *real* Gordon imprinted *me* on to the stone. He comes in whenever he's stuck on a plot point or when he needs a new perspective on a story, or when he just wants a conversation with someone who can actually challenge him intellectually. We have some pretty interesting talks, let me tell you."

"That's... that's so..."

"Narcissistic?"

"I was going to say weird, but OK, we'll go with yours. How long do we have before it runs out of power?"

Gordon, the Echo-Gordon, shook his head and gestured to the centrepiece which held the stone. "When the Echo Stone is in its cradle, it's constantly recharging. I could stay out here forever – providing there was someone around, of course. It'd be pretty boring if it was just me.

"I have to say, Stephanie, while I welcome the chance to talk to you, and I would give you a hug only I'd pass right through you and that would be strange, Gordon himself is going to be a mite annoyed that you found your way in here."

"Um, actually... I don't think he will be. Do you remember the last time you spoke with Gordon – the *other* Gordon, the *real* Gordon?"

His eyes narrowed. "Why? Stephanie, what's wrong?"

She hesitated. "My name is Valkyrie."

"Valerie?"

"Valkyrie. With a K. Valkyrie Cain. You left this house to me in your will."

He stared at her. "Oh. Oh, no."

"Yes."

"Oh, my God I'm... I knew, I mean, I knew I might be in danger once I had the Sceptre of the Ancients, but, but... Tell me the truth, OK? Just be totally, brutally honest, just tell me flat out... Am I dead?"

"Yes." He covered his face with his hands.

She waited for him to look up. When he didn't, she searched for words to fill the silence. "I understand that this must come as a shock..."

Finally, he raised his head. "How did I die?"

"Nefarian Serpine killed you," Valkyrie said, as gently as she could under the circumstances. "Well, killed *Gordon*. Killed *you*, I suppose..."

"Serpine killed me? Then he has the Sceptre! Quickly, Stephanie, we have no time to lose—"

"Don't worry, he's dead. Skulduggery killed him last year."

"Oh," Echo-Gordon said, his impetus interrupted. "I see. You know Skulduggery then?"

"He's been showing me the ropes."

"And the Sceptre?"

"It's not a threat to anyone any more."

"Did you solve the clues I left? The brooch and the caves?"

"Yes we did. That was very clever of you."

"The riddle was my idea," he said proudly. "Gordon, the real Gordon, just wanted to leave clear instructions in case anything bad happened to him, but I convinced him to do it all in a riddle. It gives the whole thing an extra flair, don't you think?" His lower lip quivered for a moment.

"Are you OK?" asked Valkyrie.

"Not really. I'm the memories of a dead man. I'm struggling to find the purpose of my existence. Was there uproar? When I died, I mean? Was there a national day of mourning?"

"Uh... not a day, I don't think..."

He frowned. "But I was a bestselling author. I mean, I was *loved.* What about a minute's silence, observed throughout the country?"

Valkyrie rubbed her arm. "A minute? I'm not sure if, you know, if it was an *official* minute, but I'm sure I noticed that people were... quieter than usual..."

"What about sales?"

"Oh, well, your last two books went straight back into the top ten."

"What about my last book? What's happening with that?"

"The release date is three months away."

"That'll sell well," he said, stroking his chin. "Now that I'm dead."

"There were loads of people at your funeral," Valkyrie said. "Crying, saying how great you were, how much you'll be missed."

Echo-Gordon digested this and nodded. "I *will* be missed.

And I *was* pretty great." His face suddenly turned sour. "Was Beryl there?"

Valkyrie laughed. "Yes she was, and she was doing her best to squeeze out some tears and get all the sympathy."

"Never liked that woman. I always thought Fergus could do better. Not much better, mind you, the man has the personality of a wet towel. But anyone would be better than Beryl. Oh, Gordon left them a boat in the will, didn't he? How did they like that?"

"Fergus went all quiet and Beryl started squeaking."

Echo-Gordon laughed and clapped his hands. "Oh, I wish I could have been there. That would have certainly been something to see. We have *some* family, eh?"

"You're telling me. In fact, there's a family reunion tomorrow night."

"Really? Oh that's wonderful! Will you bring me?"

"Uh... what? Gordon, you're dead."

"Just put the stone in your pocket, then leave me in an empty room so I can gaze out at all the Edgleys and laugh. Or maybe I'll pretend to be a ghost and haunt Beryl."

"That's incredibly mature of you, but I don't think I'll be going. Saving the world tomorrow night, so..."

"Ah, of course. But if you change your mind..."

She grinned. "I'll bring you, I promise. So, what is this room? What are all these things?"

All of a sudden his chest puffed out. "These, my dear niece, are objects of great magical and historical relevance. The items you see on the shelves around you are so rare, many a collector would kill to get their hands on them. And I mean that, quite seriously. There is a woman—"

"China Sorrows?"

"You've met her then. Yes, China. If she knew about the existence of this little horde, she would stop at nothing to get it. So it probably wouldn't be a good idea to mention it to her. You know, I was in love with her for quite some time."

"Everyone's in love with China."

"Ah yes, but my love was stronger and true. I think she knew that, and I think, in her own way, she loved me as much as I loved her. Or loved Gordon as much as he loved... no, as much as I loved... she loved Gordon as much as I loved her. Or something."

"Are... are you sure you're OK?"

"Just having a small existential crisis, nothing to worry about." He paused, seemed to reflect for a moment and then brightened. "So Skulduggery has taken you under his wing, has he? You'll be safe with him. He's one of the good guys."

"Yes, he is. I'm learning all kinds of magic and he's teaching me to fight... It's dangerous, but I'm having a great time."

"I used to help him out on a few cases you know. Nothing big, just a few mysteries every now and then. I wasn't really a throwing-punches kind of action hero, though. I was more into the research, tracking down things, people. So what are you working on now?"

"We're trying to track down this nutjob who escaped from prison, Baron Vengeous."

"Vengeous?" Echo-Gordon said. "He's out?"

"We think he wants to bring the Grotesquery to life."

Echo-Gordon's eyes bulged. "The Grotesquery? That is quite unfair! I've been meaning to write a book about that whole thing and now I'm dead!"

"That *is* very unfair," Valkyrie said, nodding in agreement. "So do you know anything about it?"

"A little, I suppose. I don't have any books about it, but I know that it was put together from bits and pieces of some quite impressive creatures. I didn't think it was possible to bring it to life though."

"We're trying to figure that out too."

Echo-Gordon shook his head in awe. "Astounding. Genuinely astounding. It's got a stinger apparently, from a Helaquin, and parts of a Shibbach were grafted on. From what

I've read, Baron Vengeous had to rearrange its insides entirely, give it a whole new set of internal organs. The heart he gave it, from a Cú na Gealaí Duibhe, is on the right side, and lower than usual, about here." He gestured to his own ribs.

"If it does come back, would destroying its heart be enough to kill it?"

"Oh, yes. Kill it stone dead."

"Then... that's how we kill it, right? Simple."

"Not quite. Because most of it is comprised of a Faceless One, it will heal quickly. The stronger it gets, the faster it will heal until it suffers no injuries at all. It would take an awful lot to damage the Grotesquery while it's at full strength, I'm afraid. Have you found it yet?"

"No, we don't even know where to start looking."

"You should ask the Torment."

"Who?"

"A few years ago, I heard a rumour that a man called the Torment might know where the Grotesquery is hidden."

"*The* Torment? Not, like, Joey Torment or Sam Torment? An actual *the*?"

"An actual *the*, yes. He's probably dead by now if he even existed at all. It was just a rumour. You should ask Eachan Meritorious if he knows him."

"Um, actually, Meritorious is dead. So is Morwenna Crow. Sagacious Tome, too, but he betrayed the others, so I'm not sorry *he's* dead."

"Oh, dear. Meritorious and Crow? That's a lot of people dead. Is there anyone who *isn't* dead?"

"Uh... Ghastly Bespoke is a statue."

"Well, that's something at least."

Valkyrie glanced at her watch. "I better go. Tanith's waiting downstairs."

"Tanith?"

"Tanith Low."

"Oh, I've heard of her. Never actually met her, but I've heard of her. You know my tale *The All-Night Horror Show*, from my short story collection? That was inspired by something I heard about her."

Valkyrie smiled. "I think she'd be delighted to know that."

Echo-Gordon gazed fondly at Valkyrie. "You're suited to all this, you know. I helped Skulduggery for a time until I realised I didn't like putting my life in danger. Sometimes I regret taking a step back. But you... I always knew you'd be cut out for this adventuring lark. It's why everything was left to you in the will."

"Thanks for that by the way. It's... amazing."

"Think nothing of it. How did Serpine die, anyway?"

"Painfully."

Echo-Gordon grinned. "Oh, good."

The Bentley pulled up outside Gordon's house just as Valkyrie was closing the door.

"Are you all right?" Skulduggery asked as soon as he got out.

"I told you on the phone, I'm OK. Tanith arrived just in time to save the day."

Skulduggery looked at Tanith. "Thank you."

"Val had it handled," Tanith said with a shrug.

"How did your top secret sneaky business go?" Valkyrie asked, eager to change the subject.

Skulduggery hesitated. "This is a sensitive subject."

"We're all friends here, aren't we? So where'd you go?"

"Well, I... I broke into the Sanctuary."

"I'm sorry, you *what*?"

"What you were saying earlier, about how Thurid Guild is like a politician with people to please. It got me thinking. So I broke into his private chambers. I had a hunch."

Tanith stared at him. "That's... that's pretty dangerous, Skulduggery. If the Cleavers had caught you..."

"I know. It would have been an interesting fight. But I had to risk it, really. I was curious."

"About what?" asked Valkyrie.

"There may be reason to believe that Thurid Guild was involved in Vengeous' escape."

"Involved how?" Valkyrie asked, her eyes narrowing. "Is he a traitor?"

"My illicit investigation is just beginning. It's too early to—"

"Just like Sagacious Tome," Valkyrie interrupted. "And China!"

Skulduggery tilted his head. "China's not a traitor."

"But she used to worship the Faceless Ones, didn't she?"

"Well, yes, but we've all done things we're not proud of."

"Even you?" Skulduggery looked at her, but didn't say anything.

"How could a traitor be elected as the new Grand Mage?" Tanith asked, and he shook his head.

"These are my suspicions, nothing more. I liberated some files belonging to the Grand Mage—"

"*Liberated*?"

"—and I'll need some time to go over them. Until then, Thurid Guild is innocent until proven guilty. That said, obviously we still don't trust him. That would be silly."

"Sure," Tanith said.

"Absolutely," Valkyrie said.

"All right then, have either of you managed to turn up anything that will help us?"

Valkyrie looked at Tanith, who suddenly looked down at her boots.

"I've been... reading."

"Research?" Skulduggery asked. Tanith went a little red and Skulduggery tilted his head.

"You've been reading Gordon's book again, haven't you?"

"It's a white-knuckle roller-coaster ride," she mumbled.

He sighed and looked to Valkyrie. "And you?"

Echo-Gordon had asked her not to tell anyone about him, at least until he had grown used to the idea that he was the only version of Gordon Edgley left on the planet. Valkyrie had reluctantly agreed.

"I found something in one of Uncle Gordon's notebooks," she lied. "Apparently someone called the Torment might know where Vengeous hid the Grotesquery."

"The Torment?"

"I don't know if he's real or not."

"He's real."

"Do you know him?"

"No," Skulduggery said. "But I know someone who does."

10

THE ARMOUR OF LORD VILE

Billy-Ray Sanguine didn't like the Infected.

He looked at them as he passed, looked at their blank faces and dull eyes. Half of them dug, half of them cleared rocks and they never took a break. Dusk's command over them was absolute.

Sanguine left them to it. As he walked, he felt the knife in his belt. It was big and heavy and awkward. He much preferred his cut-throat razor, but that girl had taken it from him. He was looking forward to seeing her again.

The caves were big, and the lights they had rigged up barely made a dent in the darkness, through which Baron Vengeous now strode.

"The Infected have cleared the chambers to the east," Sanguine told him. "The armour ain't there. I've searched the caves to the west, didn't find anythin'. Tunnelled through a couple of collapsed passageways to the north, still nothin'. Looks like the armour, if it's here at all, is in one of the chambers to the south."

"It's here," Vengeous said with confidence. "Lord Vile died in these caves, I know it. What of my garments?"

In order to don the armour, Vengeous would need special garments to protect him from the Necromancer power within. It had been Sanguine's job to obtain these garments.

"They'll be ready by nightfall," Sanguine said, "as promised."

"They had better be."

Sanguine looked at him, but said nothing. The Baron was not a man to be trifled with, especially at a time like this. Someone else Sanguine didn't like was Dusk. He didn't like vampires as a rule, but he really disliked Dusk, especially the way he could sneak up without making a sound. Vengeous was the only person Sanguine had ever met who could hear Dusk approaching. Which was why, when Dusk spoke from right beside Sanguine, Sanguine jumped and Vengeous remained perfectly still.

"Baron," Dusk said. "We have found it."

Vengeous' eyes glittered in the lamplight. They followed Dusk deeper into the cave system. Water trickled down rock walls, made the ground slippery. They walked towards a pack of the Infected, who stood back to let Baron

Vengeous pass into this newly discovered chamber. Sanguine made his way to the front, and stood beside Dusk.

The lamps cast long shadows on the uneven walls. In the centre of the chamber was a large circular stone table and on that table lay the armour. It was dull, black and plain, without etchings or imprints. To Baron Vengeous, it must have been the most beautiful thing he had ever seen.

Lord Vile's armour.

11

THE TERRIFYING BRAIN-SUCKER OF LONDON

Vaurien Scapegrace sat at the table across from Skulduggery. Tanith stood directly behind him and Valkyrie stood in the corner beside the door, her arms folded.

Skulduggery looked up from the folder he was reading. "Vaurien, you haven't been very co-operative with your interviewers, have you?"

"Don't know what any of them are talking about."

"You are a known associate of a man they call the Torment."

He shrugged. "News to me."

"What is?"

"That I know him."

"Know who?"

"What?"

"That you know the Torment?"

"Yeah."

"Then you *do* know him?"

"Yeah." Then quickly, "No."

"You don't know him?"

"I, no, I, no. Never heard of him."

"I hate to say this, Vaurien, but that's astoundingly unconvincing."

Scapegrace shook his head. "Who is he? I've never heard of him. Torment who?"

"Do you recognise the pretty lady behind you?"

Scapegrace tried to turn in his chair, but the shackles meant he could only crane his neck. He looked back to Skulduggery and shrugged. "Should I?"

"That there is Tanith Low. Perhaps you've heard of her. Tanith is a renowned interrogator, known the world over for her one hundred percent success rate in getting the information she needs." Valkyrie saw Tanith arch an eyebrow, but she said nothing.

"Oh, yeah?" Scapegrace said. He was looking a little worried. "And how does she manage that?"

"Well, to put it delicately, she has the power to suck out people's brains."

Scapegrace stared and Tanith had to clap her hand over her mouth to stop from laughing. Valkyrie struggled to keep the smile off her face, and really wished she was anywhere but in Scapegrace's line of sight.

"She can't do that," he said. "That's illegal!"

"I'm afraid it's not. It's a loophole she's been exploiting for years. She sucks out the brain and swallows it, thereby digesting and absorbing the knowledge."

"But that's horrible," Scapegrace said weakly.

"You've left us with little choice. Tanith, if you wouldn't mind?"

From her position behind Scapegrace, Tanith held up her hands in a *what-do-you-expect-me-to-do?* gesture. Her hands dropped when Scapegrace tried to look back at her and she became deadly serious. The moment he took his eyes off her again she went back to helpless gesturing.

Scapegrace righted himself in his chair and made his hands into fists, and screwed his eyes shut. "You're not going to suck out *my* brains!" he yelled.

Skulduggery sat back and didn't offer Tanith any advice. She pointed a finger at him, wagged it slightly and then turned her attention to Scapegrace. She sighed, walked up beside him and held her hands over his head. His eyes were still screwed shut.

Tanith changed her mind about the hands thing and leaned over, putting her mouth next to his ear. His body went rigid. Her lips parted, and the barest sound of skin leaving skin made Scapegrace scream and jerk back and topple over sideways. He crashed to the floor.

"I'll tell you!" he squealed. "I'll tell you everything I know! Just keep her off me, you hear? Keep her away from my brains!"

"Is the Torment still alive?" Skulduggery asked, standing over him.

"Yes!"

"When was the last time you had contact with him?"

"Two years ago, I swear!"

"What was the nature of the meeting?"

"I just wanted to talk to him!"

"What did you talk about?"

Scapegrace peeked up, made sure Tanith wasn't about to start with the brain-sucking. "Nothing. He walked away. He wouldn't talk. I don't think he likes me."

"Why doesn't he like you?"

"I don't know. Maybe it's my smell."

"What do you know about the Grotesquery?" Valkyrie asked.

"Nothing, not a thing, honest."

"Tanith," Skulduggery said wearily, "suck his brains."

"No! Wait! I don't know anything, but *he* does! During the war – the war with Mevolent. He was tracking Baron Vengeous."

"Why?" Skulduggery asked.

"He was going to kill him. During that whole thing, the war, he was on *your* side. *I* was on your side too."

"I never saw you fight."

"I was somewhere near the back," Scapegrace said weakly. "But the fact is, we were all fighting the same enemy – that counts for something, right?"

Skulduggery tilted his head. "The enemy of my enemy is not necessarily my friend."

"The Torment, he told me once that he'd been watching Vengeous and he'd been about to strike when, when *you* showed up. You fought, and you took Vengeous away, and the Torment decided it was time to retire. He's an old guy. He was around long before Mevolent even arrived on the scene. But he told me, while he'd been watching Vengeous, he'd seen where he'd stashed the Grotesquery."

"Where?"

"Well, he didn't tell *me* that. Said something about me being unable to keep a secret or something."

"Where is he?"

Scapegrace looked up, eyes wide. "You swear you'll keep her away from my brains?"

"You have my word."

"Roarhaven," Scapegrace said after a hesitation. Valkyrie had heard of Roarhaven. It was a town of sorcerers, a dark little town that didn't take kindly to strangers. "He's in Roarhaven."

Scapegrace sat in the back of the Bentley, wrists and ankles shackled and a gag over his mouth. He had got into the car with the shackles, but the gag had been a recent addition. Skulduggery had grown tired of his conversation.

They drove east out of the city, left the streets for the suburbs, then left the suburbs for the countryside. After half an hour of driving along the narrow winding roads, pulling over occasionally to let massive tractors rumble by, they came to a small town beside a dark lake that shimmered in the early afternoon sun.

The Bentley came to a stop in the shade of a large tree that stood on the outskirts of the town, and Valkyrie and Skulduggery got out. It was warm and strangely quiet.

"No birds are singing," Valkyrie said.

"Roarhaven's not the kind of town to inspire song," Skulduggery responded. "Unless it's the dirge variety."

She could see people on the street, but they passed each other without a word.

Skulduggery pulled Scapegrace out after them and removed the gag. "Where do we find the Torment?"

"Give me a moment, OK?" Scapegrace said, looking over at the town. "I haven't been back here in years. I'm home again, you know? This is a big personal thing for me."

Skulduggery sighed. "Either you start being useful or we stuff you in the trunk and go looking ourselves."

"There's no need to threaten me," Scapegrace said, annoyed. "You're in a hurry, I get it. That's no excuse for being rude to me in my own home town."

"Are you going to be useful?"

Scapegrace glowered. "Yes."

"Good."

"But can you at least take my shackles off?"

"No."

"Even around my ankles? This is my first time home in twenty years – I don't want everyone to think I'm some kind of criminal."

"You *are* some kind of criminal," Valkyrie said.

"Yeah, but..."

"The shackles stay on," Skulduggery said.

Scapegrace muttered, but did as he was told. His shackles clinking as he walked, taking baby steps so he wouldn't trip over himself, he led them into town, staying away from the main street and sticking to the narrow alleys between buildings.

"Where does he live?" asked Skulduggery.

"Right over there."

Scapegrace nodded to the building right in front of them.

Valkyrie frowned. "In a pub? The Torment lives in a pub?"

"Not just any pub," Scapegrace snapped. "*My* pub. Well, it *was* my pub before I lost it. I took it as a sign, you know? A sign to move on, to see what else the world had to offer. Sometimes I regret it, leaving all this behind, going where I didn't have family, didn't have friends. There have been times when I've been so, so lonely..."

"It must have been awful for you," Valkyrie said. "Of course, maybe if you didn't go around trying to kill people..."

"I am an artist," Scapegrace said proudly. "When I kill, I make messy art."

They ignored him and came to the side door. Skulduggery hunkered down to pick the lock.

"Tanith could open that just by touching it," Valkyrie chided.

Skulduggery turned his head to her slowly, and a moment later the lock clicked and opened. He returned the lock pick to his pocket. "I like the old fashioned way better."

"Only because you don't have a choice."

"I'm an Elemental," he reminded her. "Tanith is an Adept. I'd like to see *her* throw a fireball."

Scapegrace coughed nervously. "She's not going to be here, is she? That Tanith woman?"

"Don't worry," Valkyrie said, "your brain is safe. For now."

Skulduggery opened the door and peeked inside, then gripped Scapegrace by the elbow and pulled him in. The pub corridor was dark and smelled of stale beer and wet towels. There were a few voices coming from the front.

"Where does he stay?" Skulduggery asked quietly.

"Underground," Scapegrace said. "I converted the cellar into a living space, then he made his own additions." They moved to the rear of the building.

"Back then," Scapegrace continued, "I was full of ideas. I was going to renovate the whole front of the pub, and extend out to the west, maybe get in a music system, a little dancefloor. In the end, I decided not to. Too expensive, you know. And, like, there was the fact that nobody wanted to dance, so..."

Valkyrie kept an eye out behind them, to make sure no one was sneaking up.

"But those were good times," Scapegrace said, his voice tinged with regret. "All the old crowd used to come and meet in my pub – Lightning Dave, Hokum Pete, Hieronymus Deadfall. We used to drink and talk and laugh. Back in the day."

Skulduggery tilted his head. "Vaurien, if you're trying to kill us, there are quicker ways than telling us your life-story."

"Less painful too," added Valkyrie.

"I just thought you'd like to know," Scapegrace said indignantly. "I thought it might help if I told you the history of the place and my relationship to it."

"Any particular reason *why* you think this knowledge would be helpful?" Skulduggery asked.

"If you'll let me finish, I'll tell you."

"OK then. Finish."

"The reason they frequented *my* pub in particular was because, in a town that's full of sorcerers, there weren't a whole lot of places you could get together and feel special, you know? But I took care of that. So while out in front the pub catered to the rest of Roarhaven's mages, there was also a private section just for me and my friends, to sit and talk and plan."

"Is that so?" Skulduggery asked as Valkyrie opened the door.

"Yep," Scapegrace said with a nod. "A private section right here in the back."

They walked in. Two men sitting at the bar. Two more playing pool on a ratty old pool table. A surly bartender and, standing in the corner, a giant, his balding head touching the ceiling. They all stopped and and looked over. Valkyrie and Skulduggery froze.

Scapegrace grinned. "Hi, fellas."

12

BARFIGHT

A fly buzzed loudly. It tapped a grimy window that looked out on to a dead tree. The bartender came out from behind the bar and the two men got off their stools.

"Scapegrace," said the bartender, chewing the name as he said it. "You've got some nerve showing your ugly face in my pub."

"*Your* pub?" Scapegrace said with a scornful laugh. "You won this place off me in a poker game and you cheated."

"So did you," the bartender said. "I just cheated better. Why're you back?"

"Couldn't stay away, could I? This town holds so many fond memories for me. Actually Hieronymus, I was hoping your sister might be around – is she here?"

Hieronymus Deadfall looked like he might explode. "Don't even *mention* her, you hear me?"

Scapegrace shrugged. "What you gonna do about it?"

"I think there's been a misunderstanding," Skulduggery tried, but he was ignored.

Deadfall stepped forward, fists bunched at his sides. "How about I finish what we started twenty years ago, how about that?"

Scapegrace scoffed. "You want to kill me, is that it?"

"Oh, it's not just me, pally. Anyone else in here want to kill this piece of scum, step forward."

Everyone took one step forward. "So that's how it is, is it?" Scapegrace said, acting upset. "After all that talk of friendship, after all those years, all that we've been through... you all want to kill me?"

"Kill you," said one of the pool players, "horribly."

"I'd love to help you out, fellas," Scapegrace said, holding up his hands and showing them his shackles, "but as you can see, I'm a little tied up at the moment. Still, I suppose if you manage to kill these two fine people who walked in with me, you might get your wish."

Deadfall narrowed his eyes. "Kill a little girl? Yeah, I think we could just about manage *that* momentous task. And what about you, skinny man? Who the hell are you?"

"We're really not looking for trouble," Skulduggery said.

"Then it'll come as a nice surprise," said the man to Deadfall's left. Electricity crackled in his open hand. Lightning Dave no doubt.

"We're here on Sanctuary business," Skulduggery tried.

The man on Deadfall's right bristled, and Deadfall grinned. "Hear that, Pete? They're with the Sanctuary."

Hokum Pete snarled. "I *hate* the Sanctuary."

"Oh," Skulduggery said.

"We *all* hate the Sanctuary."

"Ah. Then we're not here on Sanctuary business. I was just joking."

"Then you're going to die laughing," Deadfall sneered, "unless you tell us who you are right this second."

Skulduggery observed him for a moment then removed his disguise and laid it on the pool table. Eyes widened. Mouths opened. Backward steps were taken.

"The Skeleton Detective," said one of the pool players.

"I'm not going up against the *skeleton*," said his friend. "No way."

"What's wrong with you?" Deadfall barked. "This is *my* pub, you understand me? This is *my* turf. I'm the only one you should be worrying about in here. It's a dead man – what's the big deal? We can take him. There's six of us, there's one of him. Oh, and a little girl. That too much for you, tough guys?" The pool players glanced at each other nervously, then shook their heads.

"Well, there you go," Deadfall said. "We're agreed. We kill these two then we kill our dear old friend Scapegrace."

"This is gonna be fun," Scapegrace said, shuffling over to a booth and sitting down. "So how are you going to do it?"

"It's been a while since Brobding got himself some exercise," Deadfall said and the giant stepped forward.

Valkyrie glanced at Skulduggery. "You can have that one," she whispered.

"I'm gonna kill you," Brobding the giant said in a rumbling bass line of a voice. "Want you to know, it's nothing personal."

"That's good to hear," Skulduggery told him. "In which case, I'm going to knock you down and hit you with the pool table, and I want you to know, it's nothing personal either." Brobding laughed. They all laughed.

Skulduggery stepped forward and splayed both his hands, and Brobding the giant hurtled off his feet and slammed into the far wall. Valkyrie snatched a pool cue off the table and broke it off the first pool player's face. He went tumbling into the corner and the second player ran at her.

Hokum Pete ran forward and threw a punch that Skulduggery didn't even bother to block. He moved in past it and shoved, and Hokum collided with Deadfall.

Lightning Dave's whole body crackled with electricity, standing his hair on end and filling the room with the smell of ozone. He charged and Skulduggery kicked a bar stool. It hit Lightning Dave's legs and he cursed and fell.

The second pool player was trying to get his hands around Valkyrie's throat. She kicked his shin and poked his eye, and he cried out. He swung wildly and her block couldn't stop it, and his fist hit the side of her head. Skulduggery kicked Lightning Dave while he was trying to get up, and then Deadfall was on him. Skulduggery grabbed him and twisted, and Deadfall shrieked in a surprisingly high voice as he was hip-thrown to the dirty, sticky floor.

The pool player picked Valkyrie up and slammed her on to the table. The breath rushed out of her. He raised her up again and once more slammed her down. She grabbed the 8-ball, and when he raised her up a third time she smacked the ball against his ear. He bellowed in pain and dropped.

Skulduggery slammed his fists into Hokum Pete, then

twisted his arm and sent him facefirst into the wall. Hokum Pete slumped to the ground. Deadfall roared as Skulduggery turned to him. The bar owner strained, the muscles in his neck knotting. His face turned red, his fists grew and distorted and turned into sledgehammers. Spittle flew as he laughed in triumph.

Across the room, Valkyrie faced off against the pool player. He was rubbing his ear and he moved with a limp. He was squinting at her with one eye. "I'm gonna murder you," he threatened unimpressively. She still had the 8-ball in her hand so she threw it. It struck the pool player right between the eyes and bounced away. The pool player stood there, a look of puzzlement on his face, then he fell to the floor and went to sleep.

Valkyrie watched Deadfall slam one of those sledgehammer fists into Skulduggery's side and Skulduggery stumbled back to the wall. Deadfall swung for his head but Skulduggery ducked, and the fist hit the wooden panelling and went through. Deadfall tried pulling it out but his fist wouldn't budge. Skulduggery hit him. Hit him again.

Deadfall twisted and turned and swung his other fist. It hit the wood panelling and stayed stuck. "Aw, no," Deadfall whimpered.

Skulduggery took careful aim and punched. Deadfall's head

rocked back and his body slumped against the wall. He would have fallen in a heap were his sledgehammer fists not keeping him upright.

"Skulduggery," Valkyrie warned. Brobding the giant was getting to his feet, and he looked angry.

"Once again," Skulduggery told him, "nothing personal."

Brobding growled and Skulduggery ran at him and jumped, his body spinning and his right foot snaking out. His kick caught Brobding right on the hinge of the jaw. Skulduggery landed and Brobding whirled and fell to one knee. Valkyrie stared at Skulduggery.

"What?" he asked.

"You kicked him," she said. "But you don't *do* those kind of kicks. *Tanith* does those kind of kicks."

"You're impressed, aren't you?" He put both hands flat against the side of the pool table and shrugged. "I'm probably your hero."

"Oh, shut up."

Brobding the giant looked around then the air rippled and the pool table shot across the room and crashed into him. The pool table tipped over on impact, the balls flying through the air, and Brobding was sent sprawling. He didn't get up.

"Well," Valkyrie admitted, "you *did* warn him."

"That I did," Skulduggery said, leaving through the door they had come in through. A moment later he returned, pushing Scapegrace ahead of him.

"Hey, steady on!" Scapegrace yelled. "These shackles don't make it easy to walk, you know!"

Valkyrie looked at him. "You didn't get very far, did you?"

Scapegrace looked around at all the still bodies. "Oh, good," he said unenthusiastically. "You beat them."

"Nice try."

He shrugged. "Forgot Deadfall owned the place, honest."

"The cellar," Skulduggery said.

"Behind the bar," Scapegrace grumbled. Valkyrie went to the bar and peered over, saw the trapdoor. She nodded at Skulduggery.

Skulduggery shackled Scapegrace to a pipe that ran along the wall to stop him from shuffling away. Valkyrie opened the trapdoor and Skulduggery went first, drawing his revolver. Valkyrie followed him down the wooden steps, closing the trapdoor behind them.

The cellar was dimly lit and cold. The steps took them down into a badly wallpapered corridor. The carpet was worn, like a trail in a forest. One doorway led off to their right and another, a little further up, led off to their left. A small painting hung at an odd angle. It was a painting of a boat in a harbour. It wasn't very good. At the end of the corridor was a living room. Music played. *The End of the World*, by the Carpenters. Holding the revolver in both hands, Skulduggery took the lead.

The first room had a single bed and a set of drawers. Skulduggery stepped in, crossed to the bed and checked under it. Satisfied that the room was empty, he rejoined Valkyrie in the corridor. The second room had a toilet, a sink and a bath. None of these three were particularly clean, and there was nowhere for anyone to hide. They moved on towards the living room.

There was a lamp, and it was on, but the bulb was fading. The closer they got, the more Valkyrie could see. She could see that the carpet didn't match the wallpaper, and the curtains, which must have been added for aesthetic reasons because there certainly weren't any windows down here, didn't match anything.

Skulduggery had his back to the corridor wall and was sliding soundlessly closer. Valkyrie did the same thing on the opposite wall, allowing herself a view of the room that Skulduggery couldn't get. She saw two old-fashioned heaters, neither of which was turned on. She saw another painting, this time of a ship on a stormy sea. There was an armchair underneath the painting and a small table beside the armchair.

No sign of the Torment though. They stopped moving and she shook her head at Skulduggery. He nodded, and stepped into the living room, sweeping his gun from one corner of the room to the other. He checked behind the armchair. Nothing.

Valkyrie followed him in. On the other side of the room were a radio, a portable TV with a cracked screen and the record player that was playing the Carpenters. She parted the curtains, which led to nothing more interesting than a wall, and turned to tell Skulduggery that Scapegrace must have somehow warned the Torment, when she saw the old man glaring at her from the ceiling.

He had long dirty hair and a long dirty beard. He dropped from the rafters on to Skulduggery and knocked him to the ground. The gun flew from Skulduggery's hand and the old man grabbed it. Valkyrie threw herself sideways as he fired. The bullet hit the record player and the song cut off. Skulduggery twisted and pushed at the air, but the old man was already running through the corridor. Skulduggery scrambled up then stepped sideways as the old man fired twice more. Skulduggery peeked out to make sure it was clear and then ran after him.

Valkyrie wasn't entirely certain that her armoured clothes could stop a bullet. And what about her head? For the first time, she wished her coat had come with a hood. She ran after

Skulduggery, just as he ducked into the bedroom. She got to the bedroom, raised an eyebrow at the opposite wall which had parted to reveal a stone corridor, and sprinted through the gap. She could just make out Skulduggery ahead of her, moving fast in the darkness. She saw light flare up, saw his silhouette hurling a fireball.

Valkyrie ran on, aware that the ground was now slanting upwards. Her legs were getting tired. Her footsteps on the stone ground were uncomfortably loud in her ears. She couldn't see anything now. It was pitch black. She focused on the energy inside her then clicked her fingers and caught the spark. The flame grew and flickered in her palm, and she held it at arm's length to light her way. She didn't like the fact that it made her an easy target, but neither did she like the idea of falling into a pit full of metal spikes or something equally nasty. And then she came to a junction.

"Oh, come on," she muttered, in between gasps for breath.

She could go straight on or turn either right or left. She had no idea which direction Skulduggery had taken. She tried to stop herself from imagining lethal traps, or getting lost in a maze of corridors and dying down here, in the darkness and the cold.

Valkyrie cursed. She had to turn back. She decided to head up and look around the town, try and find where these tunnels would surface. It was better than standing around being useless, she figured.

It was at this exact moment that she heard a rumbling.

The path to the cellar was closing up. The walls were shifting back together. Right, left or straight ahead. She chose straight ahead and she *ran*.

13

ROARHAVEN

The walls were moving in, faster and faster. Valkyrie glanced back as the junction closed up. If she tripped, if she stumbled, the walls on either side of her would shift together with that terrible rumbling noise and squash her into something less than paste.

Her lungs burned like they used to do when she was swimming off Haggard beach. She liked swimming. It was much better than being squashed. And then, a light ahead of her, a flickering flame in the hand of Skulduggery Pleasant.

"It would be a tad redundant," he called out over the

rumbling, "to encourage you to hurry up, wouldn't it?" She let the fire in her own hand go out and concentrated on sprinting.

"Whatever you do," he continued loudly, "do not fall over. Falling over, I think, would be the wrong move to make at this moment."

She was close, close to Skulduggery, close to that wide open space he was standing in. The walls ahead of her shook and rumbled and started to close and she dove through, hit the floor and rolled to her feet as the corridor closed behind her and the rumbling stopped. She fell to her knees and sucked in air.

"Well," Skulduggery said cheerfully. "That was close."

"Hate..." she gasped.

"Yes?"

"Hate... you..."

"Breathe some more air; the lack of oxygen is making you delirious." Valkyrie got to her feet, but stayed bent over while she controlled her breathing.

"We better be careful," he advised. "The Torment may be old, but he's fast, and he's agile, and he still has my gun."

"Where... are we?"

"One unsavoury aspect of Roarhaven's chequered past was an attempt, some years ago, to overthrow the Council of Elders and establish a new Sanctuary here. We're in what was supposed to be the main building."

Valkyrie saw a switch on the wall and thumbed it. A few lights flickered on overhead. Most of them stayed off. Skulduggery let the flame in his hand go out, and they followed the corridor, then turned right and kept going. They walked through small patches of light and larger patches of darkness. The floor was covered in dust. He turned his head slightly. She knew him well enough to know when something was wrong.

"What is it?" she asked.

"Keep walking," he said quietly. "We're not alone."

Valkyrie's mouth went dry. She tried to read the air, like Skulduggery was doing, but even on her best day she couldn't sense more than a few metres in any direction. She gave up and resisted the urge to look around. "Where is he?"

"It's not him. I don't know what they are, but there are dozens of them, relatively small, moving as a pack."

"They might be kittens," she said hopefully.

"They're stalking us."

"They might be shy."

"I don't think it's kittens, Valkyrie."

"Puppies then?" Something scuttled in the darkness beside them.

"Keep walking," Skulduggery said. There was scuttling behind them now.

"Eyes straight."

And then they broke from the shadows ahead, into the light: spiders, black and hairy and bloated, as big as rats, legs tipped with talons.

"OK," Skulduggery said. "I think we can stop walking now."

The spiders emerged from cracks in the wall, moving across the ceiling, clacking as they came. Valkyrie and Skulduggery stood back to back, watching them close in. They each had three eyes, wide and hungry and unblinking.

"When I count to three," Skulduggery said quietly, "we run, all right?"

"All right."

The spiders clacked as they moved, closing in, drawing in tighter, the clacking becoming a din.

"In fact," Skulduggery said, "forget about the count. Just run." Valkyrie bolted and the spiders attacked.

She jumped over the spiders in front, landing and kicking out as one of them got too close. It was heavy against her boot, but she didn't wait to see if she had done any damage. She ran on as Skulduggery hurled fireballs. They swerved off course when the corridor ahead became alive with hairy, bloated bodies then ran into a room with a large conference table in its centre, the scuttling mass behind them quickly growing in size.

A spider scuttled on to the tabletop and sprang at Valkyrie as she passed. It struck her back and clung on, trying to pierce her coat with its talons. Valkyrie yelled out and swung round, stumbling as she did so, rolling and feeling the spider beneath her. She came up and the spider was still holding on. It darted up to her shoulder, towards her face, and she saw fangs. She grabbed it, tore it from her and flung it away. Skulduggery hauled her back and then she was running again.

They ran for the double doors ahead, and Skulduggery snapped out his hand, the air rippled and the doors were ripped from their hinges. They sprinted through and kept going, into a room that must have been the foyer. Skulduggery threw a few more fireballs and Valkyrie got to the main door, slammed her shoulder into it and burst into the warm sunshine. The light hit her eyes and blinded her momentarily. She felt Skulduggery beside her, tugging on her sleeve, and she followed him. She could see fine now, she could see the dark lake ahead and blue sky above.

They stopped running. They heard the spiders, the *click-clack* of their talons, the frantic scuttling in the doorway, but the spiders were unwilling to leave the darkness for the daylight and eventually the scuttling went away. A few moments passed and Valkyrie breathed normally and noticed for the first time that Skulduggery was looking at something over her left shoulder.

"What?" she asked, but he didn't answer.

She turned. The Torment was standing there, his long grey hair tangled in his long beard, with Skulduggery's gun pointed right at her.

"Who are you," the Torment said in a voice that hadn't been used in years, "to come after *me*, to disturb *me*, after all this time?"

"We're here on Sanctuary business," Skulduggery said. "We're detectives."

"She's a child," the Torment said. "And you're a dead man."

"Technically speaking, you may well be right, but we are more than we appear. We believe you have information that may aid us in an investigation."

"You say that as if I am obligated to help you," the old man responded, the gun not wavering. "What do I care of your investigations? What do I care of detecting and Sanctuary business? I hate the Sanctuary and the Council of Elders, and I loathe all they stand for. We are sorcerers. We should not be *hiding* from the mortals, we should be *ruling* them."

"We need to find out how to stop the Grotesquery," Valkyrie

said. "If it opens the portal and lets the Faceless Ones back in, everyone suffers, not just—"

"The child is addressing me," the Torment said. "Make her stop." Valkyrie narrowed her eyes, but shut up.

Skulduggery tilted his head. "What she says is true. You had no love for Mevolent when he was alive, and I'm sure you have no wish to see the Faceless Ones return. If you help us, there might be something we can do to help you."

The Torment laughed. "Favours? You wish to trade favours?"

"If that will make you help us, yes."

The Torment frowned suddenly, and looked at Valkyrie. "You. Child. You have tainted blood in your veins. I can taste it from here." She said nothing.

"You're connected to them, aren't you? The Ancients? I despise the Ancients as much as I despise the Faceless Ones, you know. If either race were to return, they would rule it all."

"The Ancients were the good guys," Valkyrie said.

The Torment scowled. "Power is power. Sorcerers have the power to run the world – the only reason we don't is weakness of leadership. But if the Ancients were to return, do you really think they'd make the same mistake? Beings of such power have no place on this earth. I had hoped the last of your kind had died out."

"Sorry to disappoint."

The Torment looked back to Skulduggery. "This information, dead man, must be worth a lot to you. And this favour you are promising – this too would be equally substantial?"

"I suppose it would be."

The Torment smiled and it wasn't a pleasant sight. "What do you need?"

"We need to know where Baron Vengeous has been keeping the Grotesquery since his imprisonment, and we need to know how he plans to raise it."

"I have the information you seek."

"What do you want in return?"

"My needs are modest," the Torment said. "I would like you to kill the child."

14

SPRINGING JACK

Jack couldn't spring. Even if he could, even if this cell, with its narrow bed and its toilet and its sink, was big enough, he still wouldn't have been able to spring. The cell was bound and dampened his powers.

Springheeled Jack sat on his bed and contemplated life without springing. He also contemplated life without killing, which was twisting him up inside, without his favourite foods, without dancing about on rooftops and without everything he loved. They'd throw away the key, he knew they would. The English Council, once they finally got the chance to put him away, wouldn't be lenient. His trial would be over in a flash and he'd be looking at hundreds of years in prison.

Jack lay down, resting his forearm over his eyes to block out that dreadful artificial light. No more open sky for him. No more stars. No more moon.

"You're uglier than I remember."

Jack catapulted off the bed. A man was standing in the cell, leaning against the wall and grinning.

"Sanguine," Jack said, his own mouth twisting. "Come 'ere to gloat, 'ave you? I'd like to say I'm surprised, but naw, that kinda behaviour is what I've come to expect from you."

"Jack, my old friend, your words, they sting."

"You're no friend of mine," Jack said.

Sanguine shrugged. "We may have had our differences over the years, but the way I see it, all that's behind us now. I'm here to help you. I'm here to get you out." He tapped the cracked wall. Loose chips crumbled and fell, trailing dust.

Jack frowned. "What gives?"

"I just want you to do a little favour for me, is all."

"Don't much like the idea of doin' *you* a favour."

"You'd prefer to sit in a cell for the rest of your life?" Jack didn't answer.

"Just a little favour. Somethin' you'd enjoy actually. I want you to cause some trouble."

"Why?"

"Never you mind. Think you'd be able to help me?"

"Depends. What kind of trouble?"

"Oh, nothin' much. Just want you to kill some folks."

Jack couldn't help it. He smiled. "Yeah?"

"Easy as pie for someone of your talents. You agree to do this, I take you with me right now and we scoot on outta here."

"Killin', eh?"

"An' lots of it."

"And that's all? Once I do it, we're even? Cos I know who you've worked for in the past, Tex, an' I ain't gonna start workin' for the Faceless Ones or nothin'."

"Did I mention the Faceless Ones? No, I did not."

"It's got nothin' to do with them?"

"Cross my heart and hope to die. So, you in?"

Jack put on his coat and picked up his battered top hat. "Let's go."

15

POINT BLANK

Bracing his left hand against the wall and gripping the chain with his right, Scapegrace heaved. The pipe was begging to give. He could feel it. He could hear it. Every other pipe in the place would have broken by now – he should know, he'd had them installed. Just his luck that the skeleton would shackle him to the only *secure* pipe in the building.

He gritted his teeth. His face was red from exertion and he really needed to start breathing again sometime soon. And then the pipe broke and Scapegrace went flying backwards, his *whoop* of triumph cut short when he hit his head on the floor. He lay there for a moment, free at last and trying not to cry, and then he got up, the shackle dangling from his wrist. There was nothing he could do about the shackles around his ankles, so he quickly shuffled to the door.

Making sure the skeleton and the girl weren't anywhere close, he stepped out. His steps were ridiculously short, and he probably looked like some sort of demented penguin as he made his way away from the pub. He'd find someone to help him, someone who could get these shackles off. After all, the *entire* population of Roarhaven couldn't want him dead, surely.

He came around a corner, near the Roarhaven Sanctuary, and froze. For a moment he was too stunned to even smile. But then the smile appeared and it brightened his day. The Torment was pointing a gun at Pleasant and Cain.

Chuckling, Scapegrace shuffled over. The skeleton's skull was as blank as ever, but the girl was looking at the Torment like she couldn't believe what he had just said. Nobody paid any attention to Scapegrace.

"You can't be serious," said Cain.

Scapegrace loved the way the Torment ignored her, and spoke only to the skeleton. "Kill the child," he was saying. "Shoot her, if you want. Set fire to her. Strangle her. I do not care." If Scapegrace had been able, he would have done a dance there and then.

"I'm not going to kill Valkyrie," Pleasant said.

"Dead man, what is one life compared to billions? And if the Faceless Ones return, billions *will* die. You know this."

"That may be so, but I'm not killing her."

"Those are my terms."

"There must be something else," Skulduggery said. "Something reasonable I can do."

"I'll make this easy for you."

The Torment tossed the skeleton's revolver back to him. The skeleton caught it and pointed it right between the Torment's eyes. Scapegrace lost his grin. Things had suddenly taken a turn for the worse.

"No one dies here," Pleasant said, "except maybe *you*. Where is the Grotesquery?"

"I am the Torment, dead man. Do you really think I fear death?"

For another few seconds, the gun didn't waver, but then Pleasant lowered his arm. Scapegrace could breathe again and the Torment nodded with satisfaction.

"You need my help," he said. "You have my terms. Kill the child."

"You can't just—"

"Time is running out."

"Listen to me, this is *insane*. She's done nothing—"

"*Tick*," the Torment said. "*Tock*."

The skeleton looked at the girl and Scapegrace saw the doubt in her eyes. She pointed at the Torment. "Beat him up. Beat him up or, or *something*. Shoot his foot."

The skeleton shook his head. "Threats won't work."

"*Empty* threats won't work, but if you *actually* shoot his foot—"

"Valkyrie, no. I've met people like him before. Everyone has a breaking point, but we don't have time." Pleasant turned back to the Torment. "How do I know you have the information I need?"

"Because I'm telling you I do," the Torment answered, "and you don't have the luxury to doubt me. By now, Baron Vengeous will have retrieved Lord Vile's armour. The time you have left is like sand clasped in a fist. It's sifting through your fingers, dead man. Will you kill the child?"

"He will not!" Cain said defiantly. "Tell him, Skulduggery!" Scapegrace's heart almost burst with joy when Pleasant remained silent.

Cain stared at the skeleton, and took one step away.

"Don't tell me you're actually *considering* this."

"Do you have your phone?"

"What?"

"You need to call your parents. You have to say goodbye."

A moment passed and Cain turned to run but Pleasant was too fast. He grabbed her wrist and twisted, and she fell to her knees in pain.

"Be brave," the skeleton said.

"Let go of me!" Cain shouted.

Pleasant looked at the Torment. "Give us a minute."

"A minute," the Torment said. "Nothing more."

Scapegrace watched as the skeleton pulled Cain to her feet, his hand still gripping her arm, and led her away. The words he spoke were quiet, and the girl shook her head and tried to pull away again. They got to the corner of the Roarhaven Sanctuary and finally the girl started nodding. She took out her phone.

"This is brilliant," Scapegrace said to the Torment.

The Torment turned his head to him and frowned. "Who are you?"

"I'm... sorry? It's *me*, it's Vaurien. Vaurien Scapegrace. I... built the cellar for you?"

"Oh," the Torment said. "*You*. Why are you back? I thought you were dead. It would have been nice if you were dead."

Although he had never known the Torment to make a joke, Scapegrace decided he was making a joke now, so he laughed.

"This is brilliant," he said again. "Making him kill Cain. I mean, it's just brilliant. It's *genius*. I'd never have thought of something like this."

"I know."

"Do you mind me asking, where do you get your ideas? Do they come to you in a dream or is it just, you know, instinct? I'm keeping a, like a journal, where I jot down all my ideas and my thoughts and—" The Torment looked at him again and Scapegrace shut up.

"You irritate me," the Torment said.

"Sorry."

The Torment went back to ignoring him. "Dead man," he said loudly. "Your minute is up."

Pleasant put his hands on Cain's shoulders. He spoke to her and went to hug her. She twisted and broke away, shoved him back. For a moment she was obscured from view, but when Pleasant moved again Scapegrace could see the tears in her eyes. Pleasant took her arm and they walked back.

"You will kill her?" the Torment asked.

Pleasant sagged. "Yes."

Scapegrace looked at Cain. She was standing silently, as

straight as she could, trying to be fearless despite the tears.

"Then by all means," the Torment said, "kill her."

Pleasant hesitated then took his gun from his jacket.

"I'm sorry, Valkyrie," Pleasant said softly.

"Don't talk to me," Cain said. "Just do what you have to do."

"That looks like protective clothing," the Torment commented. "Be sure to shoot into her flesh. You wouldn't want me to think you cheated after all."

Cain parted her tunic and Scapegrace smiled. He wished this entire thing was being recorded so he could play it back in the future, again and again. The moment when Skulduggery Pleasant killed Valkyrie Cain.

"Please forgive me," Pleasant said, then aimed the gun at the girl and pulled the trigger.

The gunshot hurt Scapegrace's ears. Cain's body jerked and her eyes widened. She stepped back then fell awkwardly to her knees, clutching the wound. Blood trickled from her fingers.

Valkyrie Cain fell forward, her face hitting the ground.

Pleasant looked down at her. "She was an innocent girl," he whispered.

"She had Ancient blood in her veins," the Torment responded, "and so was a fitting payment for the information you require. The Grotesquery is hidden in castle ruins, on the hill in Bancrook. Detective? Can you hear me?" Pleasant raised his head slowly.

"I wonder if you can get there before Vengeous," the Torment continued. "What do you think?"

"If you're lying..." Pleasant began.

"Why would I lie? I asked you to kill the child and you did. I keep my bargains."

Pleasant stood over Valkyrie Cain's dead body. After a moment he hunkered down and picked it up. "Scapegrace," he said. "Back to the car."

Scapegrace laughed. "What, do you think I'm nuts? I'm staying here."

"No. I'm taking you back."

Scapegrace grinned, and looked over at the Torment.

"Why are you looking at me?" the Torment asked.

Scapegrace's smile faded. "What?"

"There was nothing in our bargain concerning you."

"But I can't go back!" Scapegrace cried. "He'll put me in jail!"

"You seem to think I care."

"Scapegrace," Pleasant said, in a voice devoid of any human emotion. "Get back to the car. Start walking."

Scapegrace looked around desperately, but there was no

one to help him. Trying not to cry, he shuffled off.

"I wish to thank you, Detective," the Torment said. "I look around at this world, at what it's become, I look around at my fellow sorcerers as they huddle in shadows, and I realise now that I have been waiting. Do you see? I have been waiting for a reason to live again, to emerge from my dank and squalid cellar. I have a reason now. I have a purpose now. For years I have slumbered, but now I am awake. You have awoken me, Detective. And we shall meet again."

"Count on it," Pleasant responded. The Torment smiled then turned his back and walked away.

Scapegrace was betrayed. Let down. Abandoned. Pleasant walked beside him, carrying the dead girl in his arms. Scapegrace doubted he would survive the journey back to the Sanctuary. He had heard tales of the Skeleton Detective's fury, and there was no one else around for him to take it out on. Scapegrace couldn't reason with him, he couldn't bargain with him. There was no hope. No hope left.

They got to the car and Pleasant laid the girl's body carefully in the boot, then looked back at the town. The Torment was gone from sight and the town looked empty now, as night fell.

"Well, we did it," Pleasant said, sounding relieved. Scapegrace frowned, but didn't say anything.

"This has been a good day so far, all things considered," Pleasant continued. "I have the location of the Grotesquery *and* I got to kill Valkyrie, which admittedly is something I've been wanting to do since I met her. She can be incredibly annoying. Had you noticed that?"

"Um."

"She hardly ever shut up. I pretended to be friends with her, but honestly, I just felt sorry for the poor girl. Not the brightest, you know?"

"You're such a goon," said a voice from behind, and Scapegrace whirled around and squealed as Valkyrie Cain walked up, hands in her pockets and a smile on her face.

16

THE SWITCH

Valkyrie knew it was a bluff, she just knew it, and Skulduggery confirmed it when he uttered the code words.

"Be brave."

He was gripping her arm tightly. Her knees were sore from where she had dropped. Her performance was pretty impressive, she had to admit. Hopefully, it was also pretty believable.

"Let go of me!" she shouted.

Skulduggery looked over at the Torment. Scapegrace was

standing beside him, enjoying every second of what he thought was going on.

"Give us a minute," Skulduggery said.

"A minute," the Torment replied. "Nothing more."

Valkyrie let Skulduggery pull her to her feet and led her away. "Keep shaking your head," he said softly.

"What are we going to do?" she asked. "The only way he tells us what we want to know is if you kill me."

"I'm not going to kill you."

"Oh, good."

"I'm going to kill your reflection."

"What? How?"

"Where is it right now?"

"Half-day in school, so it should be at home."

"Call it, tell it to step back inside the mirror."

To keep up the act, Valkyrie tried, and failed, to pull away. When Skulduggery pulled her back to him, she continued. "But if you do kill it, what will happen? Will it, like, actually *die*?"

"It doesn't live," Skulduggery reminded her, "so it can't die. It will, however, *appear* to be dead. I think if we return it to the mirror afterwards though, it should be fine."

"You *think*?"

"This hasn't been done before. No one has bothered, simply

because sorcerers can tell a reflection from a real person with ease. The only way this will work is if the Torment is as out of practice as we're hoping."

They reached the corner of the Roarhaven Sanctuary and Valkyrie took out her phone. Skulduggery stepped behind the corner and hunkered down out of sight. He started to dig a hole with his hands.

Valkyrie dialled her home phone and it was answered after two rings.

"Hello," her own voice said.

"Are you alone?" Valkyrie asked.

"Yes," the reflection answered. "Your parents are still at work. I'm sitting in your room, doing your homework."

"I need you to step into the mirror, OK? We're going to try something."

"All right."

"And leave a note for Mum. Tell her I'm spending the night at a friend's."

"What friend?"

"I don't know," Valkyrie said impatiently. "Pick one."

"But you don't have any friends."

Valkyrie glowered. "Tell her I'm sleeping over at Hannah Foley's."

"Hannah Foley doesn't like you."

"Just do it!" Valkyrie snapped, and hung up. Skulduggery was scooping out handfuls of earth, making a shallow hole about a metre in diameter.

She hesitated. "It'll be OK, won't it? Once we put it back in the mirror, it'll come back to life, right? I know it's not '*life*' life, but..."

"Valkyrie, me shooting the reflection is just the same as me tearing up a photograph of you. There is absolutely no difference."

She nodded. "OK. Yes, I know. OK."

He smoothed out the base of the hole and with his finger he drew a large circle in the dirt, and in that circle he drew an eye with a wavy line through it.

"Are they looking?" he asked.

Valkyrie held a hand to her face like she was crying, and glanced back. "No, they're talking. The Torment is looking annoyed."

Skulduggery stood and held out a hand. The air around him became damp, and droplets of moisture began to form. A rainbow appeared in this mist and cloud, and abruptly vanished when Skulduggery drew it all in tighter and let it fall, as rain, into the hole.

He said, "Surface speak, surface feel, surface think, surface real," and then his fingers curled. The puddle became a mini-whirlpool that erased the pattern at its base. Skulduggery calmed the water and nodded to Valkyrie.

She stood directly over the puddle and looked down, then dipped her toe in the water. The puddle rippled, obscuring her view. And then a hand broke the surface. They watched the reflection, clad in the same black clothes Valkyrie was wearing, as it slowly climbed up, out of the puddle. No, Valkyrie corrected herself, it wasn't climbing out of the *puddle*, for she could still see the bottom of the hole. Rather, the reflection was climbing out of the *surface* of the puddle, and changing from a two-dimensional image into a three-dimensional person before her eyes.

Skulduggery took its hand and helped it out the rest of the way, and it stood there and didn't speak. It wasn't even curious about why it had been summoned.

"We're going to kill you," Valkyrie told it.

It nodded. "All right."

"Can you cry?"

The reflection started weeping. The sudden change was startling.

"Dead man," the Torment called. "Your minute is up."

Skulduggery rested his hands on Valkyrie's shoulders. "Push me away," he said.

He moved in to hug her and Valkyrie turned so that he blocked her from the Torment's view, and she shoved him back and switched places with the reflection. She pressed herself against the wall of the building and didn't move, expecting to hear a shout of alarm. But no shout came. They hadn't noticed the switch.

Skulduggery and the reflection walked back around the corner, and Valkyrie made her way to the cover of the trees. She moved quietly, keeping low, and she didn't once peek. At first, she reasoned that she didn't want to risk being discovered, but she knew it wasn't that.

The truth was, she didn't want to see herself being killed.

She flinched when she heard the gunshot. Her skin was cold and she had goosebumps. She rubbed her arms through her coat.

A few minutes later she heard Skulduggery and Scapegrace approaching. She watched them go to the Bentley. Skulduggery placed the reflection's body in the trunk. It looked so *limp*. Valkyrie took a deep breath. Tearing up a photograph. That's all it was. That's all.

The Torment had disappeared back into the town, having

suddenly lost all interest. Scapegrace probably expected Skulduggery to rip him apart, but Skulduggery was too busy teasing Valkyrie. She came out from hiding and strolled over, her unease fading. If he was joking, that meant the plan had worked.

"She hardly ever shut up," Skulduggery was saying. "I pretended to be friends with her, but honestly, I just felt sorry for the poor girl. Not the brightest, you know?"

"You're such a goon," Valkyrie said, a grin forming, and Scapegrace turned and squealed. She ignored him. "Did we get what we need?"

"Bancrook," Skulduggery said. "Vengeous probably has Vile's armour by now, but the Grotesquery should still be in Bancrook. We got what we need."

"You're dead," Scapegrace said in a small voice. "You're... you're lying in the boot."

"Sorry to disappoint you, but my *reflection* is lying in the boot."

"No," Scapegrace said. "No, I've seen reflections, you can *tell* if something's a reflection..."

"Not this one," Skulduggery told him. "She uses it practically every day. Over the past year, it's kind of... grown, so if I were you, I wouldn't feel bad about being fooled. If I were you, there's a load of other things *I'd* choose to feel bad about."

"Like how you could have got away," Valkyrie said, "if you'd just kept walking, instead of coming over to gloat."

"I could have got away?"

"Free and clear."

"And... and now?"

"Now we're going to Bancrook," Skulduggery said, "and we're dropping you off at a holding cell along the way."

"I'm going back to jail?"

"Yes, you are."

Scapegrace sagged miserably. "But I don't like jail."

Skulduggery snapped the shackles into place around Scapegrace's wrists. "Today is not a good day to be a bad guy."

17

GRAVE ROBBING

The remains of Bancrook Castle stood on the top of a small hill. Valkyrie followed Skulduggery through the gaping hole in the wall that acted as its doorway. The castle was dark and quiet, and most of the roof had fallen in. Above them the sun was setting, and a startling orange had bled into the sky.

They hadn't had time to stop off at Haggard after depositing Scapegrace at the Sanctuary, so the body of the reflection was still in the Bentley. It was a creepy sensation, looking in at it, seeing it lying there, cold and unmoving. Valkyrie kept expecting to see it breathe, or to see some flutter of the eyelids, like it was only sleeping. But it just lay in the boot, a thing, a corpse with her face.

Skulduggery held up his hand and read the air, then nodded with satisfaction. "No one has been here for a long time. The Grotesquery must still be around here somewhere."

They walked deeper into the ruins, clicking their fingers and summoning flames into their hands. The light flickered off the moss-covered stones that made up the walls. They took the steps leading down, and passed beneath ground level. It was cold down here and damp. Valkyrie pulled her coat a little tighter around herself.

Skulduggery hunkered down, examining the ground, looking for any sign that the Grotesquery was buried underneath, and Valkyrie went up to a section of the wall and scraped away at a covering of moss.

"Anything suspicious?" Skulduggery asked.

"That depends. Are we treating ordinary walls as suspicious?"

"Not particularly."

"Then I got nothing."

She abandoned the moss-scraping and glanced at her watch. Dinner time at home. God, she was hungry. She thought of her reflection, about all the times it had sat at the table, pretending to be a part of the family, eating Valkyrie's dinner and speaking with Valkyrie's voice. She wondered if her parents were starting to love the reflection more than they loved her. She wondered if it would ever get to the point where she would be a stranger in her own home.

She shook her head. She didn't like thinking those thoughts. They came regularly, unwelcome visitors in her mind, they stayed far too long and they made too much mess. She focused on the positive. She was living a life of adventure. She was living the life she'd always wanted. It was perfectly understandable, every now and again, if she missed the simple little luxuries that she didn't have time for any more.

She frowned and turned to Skulduggery. "It's probably a bad sign when you start to think of your parents as mildly distracting luxuries, isn't it?"

"One would imagine so." He looked up at her. "Do you wish you could go to the family reunion?"

"What? No, no way."

"Have you been thinking about it?"

"I haven't really had time, what with the world being in danger and all."

"Somewhat understandable. But still, these things are

important. You should try to seize the opportunity to reconnect with the people who matter to you most."

Valkyrie nearly laughed. "Are we talking about the same family here?"

"Family's important," Skulduggery said.

"Tell me, and be honest, did you ever have an aunt as bad as Beryl?"

"Well, no. But I did have a cousin who was a cannibal."

"Really?"

"Oh, yes. When they caught him, he ate himself to hide the evidence."

"He couldn't have eaten himself, that's impossible."

"Well, he didn't eat *all* of himself, obviously. He left his mouth."

"Oh, my God, would you shut up, you're being— car."

"I'm being *car*?"

"No," she whispered, letting her flame go out. "There's a car coming." Skulduggery extinguished his own flame and grabbed her hand. They sprinted for the steps, ducking back as headlights swept by, and then ran on. There was another set of stairs leading up, through the caved-in roof, to the top of the ruins. The steps were covered in moss and slippery, but these things didn't seem to matter to Skulduggery.

They emerged into the gloom of the evening, as the sun was finally melting into the horizon. They pressed themselves to what was left of the castle's battlements, and peered over. The black jeep was parked directly beneath them. They watched a white van approach and stop. Seven people got out, wearing blood-splattered clothing. The Infected.

Baron Vengeous and Dusk got out of the jeep. Vengeous still had the cutlass in his belt, but if he had found Lord Vile's armour, he wasn't wearing it.

Dusk spoke with Vengeous, then issued orders to the Infected, and they took a long wooden crate from the white van. Everyone but Dusk followed Vengeous into the ruins.

Valkyrie switched positions and peered down the crumbling steps into the castle. Vengeous approached the only wall that was still intact and she heard his voice, though she couldn't make out the words. Dust started to rise from the wall and it began to shake. The topmost stone came loose and fell. Within moments the wall was tumbling down, the stones falling on each other and rolling into the shadows, and the small room behind it was revealed. Valkyrie was too high up to see into this room, but she knew what it contained. Vengeous sent the Infected in.

She peered over the battlement at Dusk, who was leaning

against the Jeep, keeping look-out, then she turned to Skulduggery. "Sanguine isn't here," she whispered.

"Not yet, no."

"*Please* tell me it's time to call for back-up."

"It's time to call for back-up."

"Oh, good."

She dug her phone out of her pocket, dialled and waited. When the Sanctuary's Administrator answered the phone, Valkyrie passed the information on in hushed tones. She hung up and nodded to Skulduggery, and held up both her hands with her fingers extended. Ten minutes until the Cleavers arrived.

The Infected re-emerged, carrying a figure between them. It looked like a mummy, all wrapped in dirty bandages, but it was huge, and judging by the difficulty with which the Infected were moving, it was heavy. They carried it towards the open crate. One of the Infected lost his grip and the body of the Grotesquery nearly fell. Vengeous flew into a rage, threw the offending Infected to the ground and glared, his eyes glowing yellow for a moment. The Infected tried getting up, but something was clearly wrong. His body started trembling, shaking uncontrollably. Even from here, Valkyrie could see the panic in his face.

And then he exploded in a mist of blood and fleshy chunks.

"Oh, my God," Valkyrie whispered.

"Stay here," Skulduggery said and started moving.

She frowned. "Where are you going?"

"I have to delay them until the Cleavers arrive. We can't afford to lose track of them – not now."

"Well, I'm going with you."

"No, you're not. You're important to Vengeous and we don't know why – until we do, you're staying out of sight."

"Then I'll stay up here and, I don't know, throw stones, and when you're finished I'll go down and help out."

He looked at her. "In order to finish, I'll have to have defeated six Infected, Dusk and Vengeous himself."

"Yeah. So?"

"The Infected I can manage."

She frowned. "And Vengeous? I mean, you *can* beat him, right?"

"Well," Skulduggery said, "I can certainly try. And trying is half the battle."

"What's the other half?"

He shrugged. "Hitting him more times than he hits me." He moved to the battlement. "If things go wrong, I'll lead them away. Once it's clear, get back to the car. If you don't see me in five minutes, then I've probably died a very brave and heroic death. Oh, and don't touch the radio – I've just got it tuned right where I want it and I don't want you messing that up."

And then Skulduggery placed his hand on the top of the battlement, vaulted over it and disappeared.

18

OLD ENEMIES

Valkyrie edged up to the battlement, peeking down as Skulduggery landed gently. Dusk turned his head like he had heard something, but then looked the other way. Skulduggery crept up behind him, wrapped an arm around his throat and hauled him back. Dusk struggled, tried to release the grip, but Skulduggery was cutting off the oxygen to his brain and Valkyrie knew it would be over in moments. Once Dusk had gone limp, Skulduggery laid him on the ground. The entire thing had been done in complete silence.

Skulduggery crept to the castle entrance and Valkyrie

moved to the very edge of the collapsed roof, lying flat and peering over. The Infected had managed to place the mummified figure into the crate without dropping it again. Valkyrie saw their eyes narrow when Skulduggery walked up. Vengeous still had his back to him.

"Hello, Baron," Skulduggery said. She saw Vengeous stiffen slightly, then turn.

"Of course," Vengeous said. "Who do they send to try and take me down? Not even a man. Not even a monster. They send *you*."

Skulduggery gave a little shrug. "How've you been, Baron?"

"You taint me," Vengeous said, disgust in his voice. "Even being in your presence, it taints me. I can feel it in the air. Even these Infected, these half-Undead, even they are more worthy of my time than you would ever be."

Skulduggery nodded. "So, you married or anything? Do I hear the pitter patter of tiny evil feet?"

"I will destroy you."

"You're still upset about that time I made you explode, aren't you? I can tell."

"You never stop talking, do you?"

"I don't *have* to talk," Skulduggery said. "I can be quiet." A moment passed. "So, who've you got in the crate? Is it the shrivelled, lifeless, patchwork corpse of the Grotesquery? Am I right? Because if it is, I'm afraid I can't let you take it. I could, you know, give you its big toe or something, as a keepsake, but that's about it."

"What you are saying, skeleton, is blasphemous."

"You're the one who dug up your own god."

Vengeous started forward, taking his cutlass from its sheath. "I wish I didn't have to kill you now. I wish I could see the fury it would wreak upon you for this blasphemy."

"You do realise I've got no skin to cut, right?"

Vengeous smiled again as he approached. "This sword is woven razor, the same process they use to make the Cleavers' scythes. It will shear through your bones."

"Ah," Skulduggery said, taking a step back.

Vengeous was almost upon him. "What's this? No jokes? No taunts? Let me see how confident you are now, you abomination."

Skulduggery's hand went into his jacket and came back out with his revolver. He aimed it squarely at Vengeous' face. Vengeous froze.

"As it turns out," Skulduggery said after a moment's consideration, "I'm still pretty confident."

"Are you going to shoot me?" Vengeous sneered. "I wouldn't

be surprised. What would a thing like you know about honour? Only a heathen would bring a gun to a swordfight."

"And only a moron would bring a sword to a gunfight."

Vengeous scowled. "As you can see," he said, "you are vastly outnumbered."

"I usually am."

"Your situation has become quite untenable."

"It usually does."

"You are within moments of being swarmed by these filthy creatures of Undeath and torn apart in a maelstrom of pain and fury."

Skulduggery paused. "OK, that's a new one on me."

"Kill him!" Vengeous barked.

The Infected started forward, Valkyrie saw Skulduggery wave his arm and a gust of wind raised a cloud of dust to obscure her view. She glimpsed Vengeous backing up, shielding his eyes. There were gunshots, flashes of fire, and gutteral snarls of anger, and the Infected flew backwards through the air. When the dust cleared, only Skulduggery and Vengeous were left standing.

"Six shots," Vengeous said. "I counted. Your gun is empty."

"You're assuming I didn't reload in all the confusion."

"And did you?"

Skulduggery hesitated. "No," he admitted and put the gun away.

Vengeous took a moment to look around. "The girl," he said. "Cain. Where is she?"

"She had to stay home unfortunately. It's a school night, so..."

"Pity. I would have liked her to see me kill you." Vengeous laid his cutlass on the ground. "And I won't be needing a sword to do it." He strode towards Skulduggery, who raised his hand.

"Um, since you're not going to be using it, can I?"

Vengeous almost laughed. He punched and Skulduggery darted low and to the side, but Vengeous was expecting the manoeuvre and he brought his clenched fist down on Skulduggery's shoulder blade. Skulduggery tried to move in for a throw, but Vengeous shifted his weight slightly and stuck out his foot, and Skulduggery went tumbling. His leg hit the crate and he fell on to the Grotesquery.

Vengeous roared and reached in, grabbing Skulduggery and hauling him out. He sent out a right hook that cracked against the bone of Skulduggery's jaw. He followed it with a left cross, but Skulduggery managed to raise his arm in defence. The block turned to a strike to the throat, as sudden and savage as a snake.

Vengeous coughed and fell back, and Skulduggery kicked the inside of his leg.

Vengeous kept his guard close, protecting his head, but dropped it low when Skulduggery kicked for his ribs. The kick was a feint and turned to a step, and Skulduggery swung a punch, but Vengeous caught it, his left hand closing around the skeleton's right wrist. Vengeous surged upwards and in, his right elbow hitting Skulduggery's right shoulder like a bullet. Vengeous torqued his body and took Skulduggery off his feet and threw him to the ground, landing heavily on top of him.

Skulduggery's left hand came up to Vengeous's face, the fingers flexing, and Vengeous swatted the hand away before Skulduggery could push at the air. Vengeous punched, again and again, and grinned down at him.

"I'd hate to be you," Vengeous said. "A skeleton who feels pain. None of the advantages of a flesh and blood body, and all of its weaknesses. Whoever brought you back should have left you where you lay."

Skulduggery groaned. Some of the Infected were back on their feet and they looked at Skulduggery as he lay there. Vengeous stood and brushed the dust from his clothes. He picked up his cutlass.

"I'm going to cut you," Vengeous said, "into little tiny pieces.

I'm going to take a small part of your skull and turn it into some dice. Maybe I'll use the rest of you as keys on a piano. I wonder, skeleton, would you still be alive? Would you be conscious if you were dice, or keys on a piano?"

"Always wanted a life in music," Skulduggery mumbled.

Valkyrie couldn't watch any more. She got to her feet. "Hey!" Vengeous looked up to the collapsed roof and saw her.

"Heard you've been looking for me," she called out.

"Miss Cain," Vengeous said with a smile. "So you *are* here."

"That girl," Skulduggery muttered, "never does what she's bloody well told..."

"You want me, Baron?" Valkyrie shouted. "Come and get me!"

And then she stepped back and Vengeous started running up after her, and she went to the battlement and flung herself over.

19

ON THE RUN

T*his is so stupid*, Valkyrie thought to herself as she ran. Her foot hit a rock and she almost fell. She didn't know where she was going or what she would do. She had no plan at all, whatsoever.

She ignored the trail and ran deeper into blackness. She could hear her pursuers now, the commands being shouted to the Infected. She could hear the van and when she looked over her shoulder she glimpsed its headlights, bobbing like crazy over the uneven ground.

Then the world left her and she was falling.

She hit the side of the hill and started to roll. The ground levelled off and she hit a patch of briars that tried to get in at her through her clothes. The headlights came around the bend and she flattened herself, the briars tearing at her hands and hair. She dragged herself through as the headlights hurtled towards her.

Missing her by a hand's breadth, the van roared by. Valkyrie stayed a moment to catch her breath then ripped the briars away and got up. There were shouts from all directions. The Infected almost had her surrounded, and the only reason she was still free was because they hadn't realised it yet. She set off, limping slightly. There was a road ahead. If she could get to the pitch blackness on the other side, she might have a chance at escape.

But now there was another set of headlights. The black jeep. She had to get across the road before she was cut off. And then there was somebody standing in her way.

Dusk grabbed her and she tried to hit him, but he threw her down. "Finally," he said, as though he was bored of a game. He was about to continue speaking, but she saw his face twitch and his hand went to his belly. His fingers dipped into his coat, brought out the syringe.

This was her chance and she couldn't afford to mess it up.

Forcing the fear and the panic from her mind, Valkyrie

splayed her fingers. The air shimmered and the syringe flew from his grasp, vanishing into the darkness. He cursed, tried to run after it, but lost his balance and stumbled. Valkyrie was up, already moving fast in the other direction.

"That was a mistake," she heard him mutter. "That serum was the only thing keeping me under control..."

She glanced back as Dusk took hold of his human form and tore it off, like a snake shucking its skin. The vampire beneath the flesh and clothes, the creature within the man, was bald and alabaster white, its eyes black and its fangs jagged. She knew Dusk hadn't been lying: that *had* been a mistake. Valkyrie sprinted, and the vampire bounded after her.

The Infected were all around her and the black jeep had picked her out with its headlights. Baron Vengeous could plainly see her, but she didn't care. Vengeous would keep her alive until he decided it was time to kill her. The vampire, on the other hand, would rip her to pieces right there and then.

It was bounding after her and gaining fast. One more leap and it would be on top of her. She couldn't afford to try anything, couldn't afford to use her powers. Adrenaline was pumping through her system. Her powers probably wouldn't even *work*.

She took Billy-Ray Sanguine's razor from her pocket,

unfolding it as she ran. Over the sound of the oncoming jeep, she heard Vengeous trying to call off the vampire, but she knew the beast wouldn't listen. A vampire, after it's shucked its skin, has no master. Skulduggery had called them the most efficient killers in the world. The only thing a vampire cared about was blood.

The bounding stopped and she felt it in the air, felt it descending, and Valkyrie turned and lashed out. The razor opened up the vampire's face as she fell backwards. The vampire that had once been Dusk roared in pain, hit the ground and came at her again before she even had time to roll to her feet.

The jeep was still approaching, and it wasn't slowing down. It swerved and swung around in a cloud of dust and smacked right into the vampire, flinging it back. The passenger door opened.

"In!" Skulduggery yelled. Valkyrie jumped in and the jeep shot off.

"Seatbelt," Skulduggery said. Valkyrie reached for it as he turned the wheel and her head hit the window.

"Ow!"

"Sorry. Wear your seatbelt."

The van was right behind them, filling the inside of the jeep with yellow light. Skulduggery braked and turned, gunning the engine, and the yellow light withdrew sharply as the van missed the hidden turn. They left the van in their dust and followed a trail through the hills.

Valkyrie grabbed the seatbelt and tugged it a few times before she got it to work. She settled into her seat and clicked it in, just as Skulduggery braked.

"OK," he said. "Out." He opened his door and got out, hurrying to the Bentley. Cursing his name, Valkyrie followed.

The silence of the night was eerie. And then the ground ahead of them cracked and crumbled, and Skulduggery pulled out his gun as Billy-Ray Sanguine rose to the surface.

"Well, I do declare," Sanguine said with a smile. "The great Skeleton Detective, in the flesh – figuratively speakin', of course."

Skulduggery regarded him warily. "Mr Sanguine, I've been hearing so much about you."

"That so?"

"You're quite the little psychopath, aren't you?"

"I try."

"So tell me something – why wait eighty years before you helped your old boss escape? Why didn't you just bust him out the day after he was caught?"

Sanguine shrugged. "I suppose I had what y'all might call a crisis of faith and my faith lost. These past eighty years, goin' it alone, it's been good, but somethin's been missing, y'know?"

"You're under arrest."

"Speakin' of which, and I don't mean to be rude, but I just popped by to pick up the li'l darlin' there. I'll be out of your hair in a moment – again, figuratively speakin'." He passed down into the ground with a smile on his face.

"Oh, hell," Valkyrie said and Skulduggery reached for her, but it was too late. The ground exploded and Sanguine grabbed her, and Valkyrie didn't even have time to cry out before he took her down into the ground with him.

20

UNDER THE GROUND

Valkyrie gasped for breath as she plunged down into the darkness. The earth shifted around her. It scraped into her back and crumbled at her feet. Dirt flew into her eyes and the sound of a rockslide roared in her ears. She clung on to Sanguine as they moved.

"Scared?" he said in her ear. "What if I were to just... let go?"

He was right in front of her – she could feel his breath on her cheek – but she couldn't see him. It was impossibly dark, whatever tunnel they were making filling up above them as they moved. Her gut twisted as real, raw terror spread through her.

"I'll burn you," she said, but the sound of rockslide drowned out her small voice. "*I'll burn you!*" she shouted. She heard him laugh.

"You burn me enough you might kill me and then what would you do? You'd be stuck here, buried alive under the ground with only my corpse for comfort."

They slowed, the rockslide lessened, and they came to a stop. Valkyrie was shaking. Sweat drenched her. Panic caught at her throat.

"I can see you, you know," he said. "My eyes were taken, but my sight remains. And here, in the dark? I can see best of all. I can see the fear on your face. You can't hide it from me. So here's what's gonna happen. I'm gonna put some dainty li'l shackles on those wrists of yours and then we're gonna go pay a visit to Baron Vengeous. That sound like a nice way to spend the rest of your life?"

Valkyrie tasted dirt in her mouth, but didn't answer. It was too dark. She could feel the rocks all around her. Despite her loathing, she realised she was clinging tightly to Sanguine, terrified he was going to let her go and leave her here. She felt him move, heard the earth shift, and felt something cold and metal close around her wrists.

"Oh, one other thing," he said. "My blade. Where is it?"

"Coat pocket," she whispered.

His hand dipped into the pocket, removing the straight razor. "So good to have it back. It's like a part of me, y'know? Like a little piece of my soul..."

He could see in the dark, so she made sure he could see the contempt on her face. "Is there somewhere we need to go or are you going to keep us down here and bore me to death?"

He laughed, the rock shifted and they moved again, fast. She tried to work out how Sanguine did it, but it was as if the ground just parted for him then closed up when he'd passed. It was impossible to tell what direction they were going or even if they were headed up or down, and then suddenly the earth gave way and their momentum carried them through into the fresh air.

The moon, heavy and low in the dark sky. Trees and hedges and grass. Valkyrie fell to her knees, spitting dirt and sucking in air. The sweat that coated her body now chilled her, but the ground was solid and the roar was gone from her ears. She raised her head, looked back.

"Your chariot awaits, ma'am," Sanguine said, opening the door to the car that had been parked there. She tested the shackles, but they were on tight. She clicked her fingers, but no spark came. Her powers were bound.

Sanguine helped her to the car by gripping the back of her neck and forcing her in. Even if she managed to get away, there was nowhere to run. There were meadows in every direction. He closed the door, walked around the car and got in behind the wheel.

"Is it fun?" he asked suddenly. "Doin' all that detectin'? I always wanted to be a detective. I *was* one, for about a year. I liked the romance of it all. The suits, the hats, the dark alleys, the femme fatale, all that quick talkin'... But I couldn't stop *killin'* folk. I mean, they'd hire me, I'd try to solve their mystery, but halfway through I'd get bored and end up killin' them, and then the case'd be over and that'd be it. I solved one single murder that whole entire year, but I don't think that really counts, seein' as how I was the killer. I think that's kinda cheatin', in a way."

"Why are you doing this?" Valkyrie blurted out. "Why does he still want me? It's not like Skulduggery's going to back off just because I'm being held captive."

Sanguine stared. "Are you serious?" He laughed. "Li'l darlin', you ain't no *hostage*, you never were!"

"What?"

"This whole thing, everythin' that's happenin', it's *because* of you."

"What are you talking about?"

"You heard about the missin' ingredient, right? The one thing Vengeous couldn't get his hands on eighty years ago. You heard about that?"

"Of course. What's that got to do with me?"

"Sweetie, it *is* you. *You're* the missin' ingredient." She stared at him and his smile grew wider.

"You're a direct descendant of the Ancients, ain't you? What, you thought that little bit of information wouldn't get around? When I heard about that, I knew the time had come to set the Baron free."

"You're lying..."

"Scout's honour. The one thing he was missin' was blood with a certain type of power in it. Seein' as how he wasn't likely to get the blood of another Faceless One anytime soon, the next best thing is the blood of one of the guys who managed to *kill* a Faceless One. That was the last ingredient to the end-of–the-world-as-we-know-it cocktail he was brewin'. Must make you feel pretty special, huh?"

Valkyrie couldn't answer. She felt the colour drain from her face.

"This is good," Sanguine said, clearly delighted, as he started the engine. "This is *good*."

21

DONNING DARKNESS

It was time.

Vengeous felt its power, felt it pierce his skin and wrap itself around his insides. Even if he wanted to, even if he changed his mind about what he planned to do, it was too late now. It was pulling him forward. How could Vile ever have been beaten with power like this?

The Infected had laid out the armour on a table, in a small room at the rear of the church. From such humble beginnings, *Vengeous thought to himself, and smiled.*

He approached the table, reached out, but stopped, his hands hovering over the gauntlets. His fingers trailed in the air, moving over the chest-plate, the boots. The first piece of armour he touched was the mask. He picked it up carefully, held it, felt it change and shift beneath his touch.

The garments he wore – black and simple to the eye – were specially woven to ensure a successful binding. He would be wearing Lord Vile's armour – his body would need insulating against the raw power contained within, power that could sear his flesh and boil his blood.

By now, Billy-Ray Sanguine would have located the Cain girl and he would be bringing her to the church. The Baron himself had subdued Dusk, and injected him with the serum. By shedding his skin, Dusk had failed him, nearly cost him everything. But Vengeous would punish him later. For right now, all his dreams were about to come true.

As Baron Vengeous donned the armour, shadows rose from it like steam.

22

BLOOD AND SHADOWS

They drove deeper into the country, where the roads narrowed and twisted like snakes. Finally, they pulled up outside a dark old church and Sanguine got out, went around to Valkyrie's side and opened the door, then pulled her from the car. He took her arm and led her up the cracked, overgrown path. Vines clung to the crumbling walls and the small stained-glass windows were caked with grime and dust.

He pushed open the ancient double doors and guided her into the cold, dank church. There were still a few pews that hadn't rotted away, and there were hundreds of lit candles that sent the shadows dancing and pirouetting across the walls. The altar had been ransacked and cleared, replaced with a large slab, solid and proud, and upon that slab was the massive, bandaged body of the Grotesquery, covered in a sheet.

Baron Vengeous was waiting for them, clad in the black armour of Lord Vile. It was not what Valkyrie had expected. The armour did not clank or rattle, and it cast no sheen. It seemed to be alive, subtly moving and reshaping itself even as she watched.

There were others in the church, Infected men and women, the vampire virus working through their bodies, changing them every moment that passed. They stayed in the shadows as best they could.

She could see Dusk now. His human form had grown back, but it had kept the scar across his face. It was deep and ugly, and he was glaring at her with every ounce of hatred his blackened soul was capable of.

"Valkyrie Cain," Vengeous said, the mask distorting his voice into a rough whisper. "So nice of you to join us on this most auspicious of nights. The creature on this table will open the gateway for its brethren, and this world will be cleansed. The unworthy will be decimated and we will usher in a new paradise, and it's all thanks to you."

Sanguine took Valkyrie by the elbow and led her to the front pew, where he made her sit beside him, and they watched Vengeous lower his head, his hands raised above the body on the slab. Shadows started moving around him. The candles were flickering like a strong wind was blowing, but the inside of the church was deathly calm.

"The Grotesquery's gonna feed on you," Sanguine whispered, almost casual. "That good ole boy's been out for the count – he's gonna need your blood in his veins. Gonna have himself a slap up meal. You mind if I take pictures? Brought my own camera and everythin'."

"Knock yourself out."

"Thanks."

"No, really, run head first into the wall and knock yourself out because I'm telling you, you better be unconscious when Skulduggery gets here."

Sanguine grinned and sat back. "I can handle Mister Funnybones, don't you worry about that. Pay attention now, darlin', this is where it gets interestin'."

Valkyrie looked back at the altar just as the shadows bunched up behind Vengeous and descended on him like a shroud. He stiffened and his body jerked, as if he was being shot through with electric currents. The shadows started flowing out through his fingertips and down, passing through the sheet.

"Mr Sanguine," Vengeous whispered.

Sanguine pulled Valkyrie up and dragged her over to the slab. He grinned as he showed her his straight razor, then grabbed her wrist. She tried to struggle but he was far too strong, and she cried out as he ran the cold blade across the palm of her right hand. But instead of running off her hand and dripping on to the sheet, her blood drifted to the shadow stream, mixing with it, twirling through it and around it, being fed into the body of the Grotesquery.

And that's when the double doors swung open and Skulduggery Pleasant strolled into the church.

The Infected snarled and Valkyrie pulled her hand from Sanguine's grip. Vengeous looked up from his dark work and his armour grew angry spikes, as Skulduggery walked up to the end of the aisle and sat in the front pew. He crossed his legs, settled into a comfortable position and waved his hand in the air.

"Don't let me interrupt," he said.

Valkyrie frowned. Not quite the rescue she was counting on.

The Infected moved into the light, closing in on Skulduggery, who was acting like he'd just popped by for a chat. Vengeous sent the last of the shadow stream into the Grotesquery and then stepped back. Valkyrie saw him sag slightly.

Vengeous brought his hands up to his head and undid the latches on the mask, lifting it off. His face was pale and shiny with sweat. His eyes were narrow and cold.

"Abomination," he said. "You came here alone? No Cleavers with you? Mr Bliss isn't by your side?"

"You know me, Baron, I like to take care of things myself. Also, when you beat me up, you broke my phone, so..."

A smile now, cracking across Vengeous's lips. "Did you come here to witness the beginning of your end?"

"No, not really. I just came here to do this."

Skulduggery reached into his jacket, pulled out a small black satchel and lobbed it on to the slab. It landed on the sheet, over the bandaged chest of the Grotesquery. Vengeous gazed at it, reached out...

"Wouldn't do that if I were you," Skulduggery said, holding up a small device. "One push of this button and this lovely little church is decorated with bits of your god."

"A bomb?" Vengeous said, anger rising in his voice. His armour swelled and thickened protectively. "You think explosives could harm a Faceless One?"

"But that's not a Faceless One, is it? At least not a *whole* one. I expect it's a tad fragile actually, after spending all that time locked away in a wall. And I'm betting all this has taken a lot out of *you* too. That one little bomb could take you both out at the same time. Well, I say little, but it's actually about fifteen times more powerful than the *last* one I threw at you, and you remember how sore *that* was."

Sanguine pushed Valkyrie closer to the slab. "You'll kill *her* right along with all of us."

"I don't have to," Skulduggery said patiently. "I either press this button and foil your insidious plot and kill my friend while I'm at it, or I don't, and we leave, and you just wait another three years for the next lunar eclipse. It's up to you, Baron."

Vengeous observed him. "Take her."

Dusk stepped forward. "The girl must die!"

"Silence!" Vengeous roared. He locked eyes with Dusk until the vampire backed down, the flickering candlelight playing on his scar.

Vengeous looked back at Skulduggery. "Take the girl," he sneered. "You won't get far."

"We'll get far enough. Valkyrie?" Valkyrie held her hands out to Sanguine.

He glared at her, then put his straight razor on the slab and muttered. He undid the shackles and stepped back. Valkyrie joined Skulduggery as he moved into the aisle, but not before she snatched up the razor.

"Hey!" Sanguine shouted.

"Be quiet," Vengeous snapped.

"She has my blade!"

"*I said be quiet!*"

Sanguine shut up. Valkyrie folded the blade into its handle and stuck it in her pocket. She moved backwards, at Skulduggery's side, and the Infected moved with them.

"You're only delaying the inevitable," Vengeous said. "With this armour, I am the most powerful living being in this world."

"But are you *happy*?" Skulduggery mused, clicking the fingers of his free hand and summoning a flame. He cast the fireball behind them, at the ground near the doorway. The Infected hissed at the flames. Vengeous still hadn't moved any nearer to the satchel of explosives.

"I will take you apart, abomination."

"So at least I have that to look forward to," Skulduggery said. "You won't want to make any sudden moves until we reach the road – I'll know if you crazy kids disturb the air around the nice bag of explosives."

"Blow it up," Valkyrie murmured out of the corner of her mouth.

"Can't do that," Skulduggery replied in a whisper. He

moved his hand and the flames parted in the doorway and they backed through them, out into the night air.

"Why not?"

"Not a bomb," he replied softly. "It's a bag with a collapsible jack, for changing tyres."

"What about the remote?"

"It opens my garage door. Don't tell them, but it doesn't even have any batteries in it." He waved his hand and the flames came together again to block off the exit. They kept walking backwards to the Bentley, keeping eye contact with the Infected through the flames, making sure no one cheated and rushed out too early.

"Do we have a plan?" she asked as they backed away from the church.

"We need to get the Grotesquery away from the bad guys," he said, "so we'll have to split up. I'm going to leave, you're going to hide under the van, wait until they load the Grotesquery in there, and then you're going to drive off, right out from under their noses."

"*What?*"

"It'll be really funny, trust me."

"Skulduggery, I'm thirteen. I can't drive."

He looked at her. "What do you mean you can't drive?"

"Am I talking in code? *I can't drive*, Skulduggery."

"But you've seen others drive, haven't you? You've seen *me* drive. I daresay you've seen your parents drive. So you know the fundamentals."

She stared at him. "I know the big round thing sticking out of the dashboard turns the wheels. That fundamental enough for you?"

"The van over there is an automatic. You put it in Drive – you go. You press one pedal – you go fast; you press another pedal – you stop. Easy."

She stared at him. "Oh, bloody hell," she muttered and darted for the van, sliding beneath it as Skulduggery jumped into the Bentley.

The Bentley's engine roared, the tyres spun and it sped away from the church as a wave of darkness erupted from the doorway, extinguishing the flames. Dusk led the Infected as they poured out into the night, followed by Baron Vengeous, tendrils of shadows wrapping and coiling around him like angry snakes. He hurled the satchel to the ground and the jack bounced into the long grass. He whipped the darkness against an Infected woman, who was blasted off her feet by the impact and went sailing high through the air.

Valkyrie stayed under the van and kept very, very quiet. She saw Billy-Ray Sanguine walk up.

"She took my blade," he said. "*Again.*"

"I don't care about your *blade,*" Vengeous snapped. He turned to one of the Infected. "You. Move the Grotesquery into the van. This place will soon be teeming with Cleavers and I can't risk them damaging it."

The Infected hurried into the church then came back out, carrying the crate. Taking extra care, they loaded it into the van. They moved back towards the church, waiting for more orders, and Valkyrie slid herself from cover and got to her feet. She could hear Vengeous issuing commands from the other side of the van, and she took a deep breath and reached for the door.

It opened with a faint click and she got in slowly, keeping low. The key was in the ignition. She looked around to get her bearings, risked a glance out of the window at the bad guys and then turned the key. The engine came to life. Vengeous turned his head and frowned, moving to where he could see who was behind the wheel.

Valkyrie pulled the stick down to Drive and stamped her foot on the accelerator. She yelped as the van shot forward, fought to gain control of the steering. This was not fun. She wrenched the wheel to the right to avoid a tree, trying her best to keep the van on the narrow road. She saw the Infected running behind, but she couldn't afford to give them too much attention. It was seriously dark outside and she didn't know where the lights were.

She took one hand off the wheel long enough to flick a lever, and the wipers dragged themselves across the dry windshield. She went over a rock and bounced in her seat. She tried another lever and the indicator started blinking. Cursing Skulduggery, Valkyrie moved it up, down, to the side then tried twisting it, and the headlamps suddenly lit up the road ahead, just in time for her to cry out as the van swerved off the trail and hurtled over a hill.

Valkyrie was thrown around in her seat. Keeping one hand tight on the wheel, she clutched at the seatbelt, yanking it across her. She glanced down, trying to find the slot that the seatbelt clicked into. The bottom of the hill met up with the road again and she tried to steer on to it, but the van just kept going, and plunged down the next hill.

Valkyrie grabbed the seatbelt again, this time finding the slot, and the seatbelt clicked in and Valkyrie turned her full attention to driving, as the van hit a rocky outcrop, spun sideways and rolled. She smacked her head against the window as the world turned around her. She heard glass breaking and metal crunching. She protected her head as she pitched forward, and her arms slammed into the steering wheel, honking the horn. The van rolled on to another road and settled back on to its four wheels.

"Owww," Valkyrie moaned. She looked up to the cracked windscreen. Headlights. A car and a motorcycle were approaching, at speed.

Valkyrie pulled the door handle and had to hit the door with her shoulder to open it. She tried to get out, but the seatbelt wouldn't let her. She fumbled at the orange button and the belt retracted. Valkyrie stumbled out as Tanith's motorbike screeched to a halt.

The Bentley braked hard and Skulduggery jumped out, ran to her and caught her as her legs gave way. Words were exchanged, but Valkyrie couldn't make sense of most of them. There was a fuzz in her head as Skulduggery carried her to the Bentley. Her arm was hurting. She opened her eyes to see Tanith loading her bike into the back of the white van, beside the crate, then getting in behind the wheel.

Skulduggery said something in a faraway voice and Valkyrie tried to answer, but her tongue was too heavy and all the strength left her body.

23

ELEPHANTS AND BUNNIES

Kenspeckle poked her arm. "Does that hurt?"

"No," Valkyrie answered.

He nodded, scribbled something in his notebook. "Have you eaten?"

"One of your assistants brought me a burger for breakfast."

He sighed. "I meant, have you eaten *sensibly*?"

"I was very sensible while I was eating the burger. Didn't miss my mouth *once*."

He prodded her again. "What about that? Does that hurt?"

"Ow."

"I'll take that as a yes. Hopefully, the pain will teach you not to break yourself when your van crashes." Kenspeckle scribbled something else and Valkyrie looked around. There were no windows in here, but she could guess what kind of morning it was. Bright, blue skied, sunny and warm.

Kenspeckle closed his notebook and nodded. "You're making an excellent recovery," he said. "One more hour, the bone will be healed."

"Thanks, Kenspeckle."

"Think nothing of it."

"And, you know, sorry about what I said yesterday, about the salt water and the vampires..."

Kenspeckle chuckled. "Don't you worry about *me*, Valkyrie. I'm tougher than I look. Last night, when the nightmares came, they weren't so bad. I remember them being *awful*. Now, you just lie back there and let the muck do its work."

Feeling guiltier than ever, Valkyrie settled back on the bed. The mixture that coated her entire right arm was cold and slimy. It had to be reapplied every twenty minutes as its magical properties were absorbed through the skin.

She heard Skulduggery come into the medical bay. His fight with Vengeous had resulted in a fractured collarbone and a few cracked ribs. She looked over at him and laughed.

He stared at her. He was wearing a bright pink hospital gown, decorated with elephants and bunnies. It hung off him like a sheet on a hatstand.

"How come she gets the *blue* hospital gown?" he asked Kenspeckle.

"Hmm?" mumbled the professor.

Skulduggery's head tilted unhappily. "You said the only gowns you had left were these pink bunny ones, but Valkyrie is wearing a perfectly respectable *blue* one."

"Your point being?"

"Why am I wearing this ridiculous gown?"

"Because it amuses me."

Kenspeckle walked out and Skulduggery looked over at her. "The important thing," he said, "is that I can wear this gown and still maintain my dignity."

"Yes," she responded automatically. "Yes, you can."

"You can stop grinning any time now."

"I am so trying, I swear."

He walked over and when he spoke his voice had changed slightly, tinged with concern. "Feeling OK?"

"Yes."

"Are you sure?"

"Yes. No. I don't know. Whatever happens with the Grotesquery, it's my fault."

"Nonsense."

"But I'm the missing ingredient."

"That doesn't make it your fault, Valkyrie. However, if you insist on taking responsibility for something you never had any control over, you can use that to make you stronger. You're going to need all the strength you can muster, especially when Dusk catches up to you."

She frowned. "Why Dusk?"

"Oh, yes, something I should maybe mention. Dusk will be wanting to kill you. He has a history of vendettas. He holds a grudge and he doesn't let it go until he's spilled blood."

"And because I cut his face...?"

"You cut his face with Sanguine's blade, the scars from which do not heal."

"Ah. That'd... that'd make him pretty mad, wouldn't it?"

"I just thought you'd like to know."

"So what are we going to do about Guild? Since he's working with the bad guys and everything...?"

"Now, we don't know that. It's not fact. Not yet." Skulduggery was quiet for a moment. "Even so, it would be foolish not to take precautions. We will report back to Guild if and when we have to. At no time will we tell him what we're planning, where we're going or who we're hoping to punch next. Agreed?"

"Agreed. So he doesn't know we have the Grotesquery?"

"I may have forgotten to tell him. I *did* remember to tell Mr Bliss though, so he has organised three Cleavers to provide security. Any more than that, unfortunately, and it would come to the attention of the Grand Mage."

"I just hope you realise, after Sagacious Tome and now Guild, that I'm never going to be able to trust anyone in a position of authority ever again."

Skulduggery's head tilted. "You don't view *me* as an authority figure?"

She laughed. Then stopped. "Oh. I'm sorry. You were serious?"

"That's lovely, that is," he said as Kenspeckle wandered in.

"Detective, you will no doubt be happy to know that my assistants are moving the Grotesquery into my brand-new private Morgue, where it will clutter up the place just when I've finally managed to get everything in order."

Valkyrie frowned. "What would you need a private morgue for?"

"Experiments," Kenspeckle said. "Experiments so bizarre and unnatural they would surely make you vomit."

"Professor Grouse," Skulduggery said, "we brought the Grotesquery here not only because your facility is more advanced than the Sanctuary's, but also because you are the leading expert in science magic."

"Mm," Kenspeckle said gruffly. "It is. And I am."

"We need your help. We have a chance to dismantle the Grotesquery and hide the pieces all over the world so it can never be put back together, and we need you to do it."

"Fine," Kenspeckle said gruffly. "But you, Valkyrie, must rest. And you, Detective, must not place her in any danger for the next, oh, let's say an hour. Do we have a deal?"

"I can rest," Valkyrie said.

"And I can manage an hour," Skulduggery said.

"All right then," said Kenspeckle. "If you'll excuse me, I have a monster to take apart."

24

ARGUS

The old hospital was steeped in dead terror and stale tears. How many people had breathed their last while lying on those small beds? How many had spent their final nights in those tiny rooms, sleeping fitfully while their nightmares rampaged across the landscape of their minds? When Baron Vengeous walked these halls he fancied he could count every single one of them.

The psychiatric ward was the best. Here, even without the sensitivities brought on by his new armour, he could sense the echoes of fear, madness and desperation. But with the armour, these echoes soaked into him, making him stronger. He felt his armour flourish after all those years of neglect in that cavern.

This would be the perfect place for the Grotesquery to break down the borders between realities, open the portal and invite the Faceless Ones to return. Now all he needed was the Grotesquery itself – but that wasn't going to be a problem. For all his flashes of rage and his fearsome temper, Vengeous was a military man first and foremost. True, he had suffered a setback, but he had already initiated a plan to rectify the situation.

One of the Infected was standing further along the corridor and it opened the door as he approached. He could tell by its eyes that it was close to becoming a true vampire. He had already ordered Dusk to kill them all before that happened. Dusk, because of the serums he used, controlled the vampire part of himself, but the Infected would be far too unpredictable to keep around.

Vengeous focused on the armour, drawing it back in. He had been letting it writhe and revel in the collected anguish of the old building, but now it was time for business.

Billy-Ray Sanguine was waiting for him. There was a man shackled to an operating table, and when Vengeous walked into the room, the man's eyes widened.

"Impossible," he breathed. "You're dead. You're... it can't be you, you're dead!" Vengeous realised that with the helmet obscuring his face, the man thought Venguous was Lord Vile, *risen from the grave to exact a terrible revenge. He said nothing.*

"This is a trick!" the man said, straining against his shackles. "I don't

know what you think you're doing, but you've made a huge mistake! Do you even know who I am?"

"Sure we do," Sanguine drawled. "You're a lily-livered sorcerer who's managed to stay alive by runnin' from every conceivable fight. Why do you think we chose you?"

"Chose me?" the man repeated. "Chose me for what?"

"For a quick answer," Vengeous said, aware that the helmet even made him sound *like Vile.*

The man paled. He was sweating already. "What... what do you want to know?"

"As you can probably tell," Sanguine said, "I ain't from around these parts. And the gentleman who is makin' you mess your britches right now... well, he's been away for a time. So we need you, chuckles, to tell us where someone might go with the inanimate corpse of a half-god in order to, oh, I dunno, destroy it."

The man licked his lips. "And... and then you'll let me go?"

"Yeah, why not?"

Vengeous felt his armour coil. This man's fear was too potent to ignore. Vengeous narrowed his eyes, controlling the armour through sheer force of will.

"They'd go to the Sanctuary," the man said.

"That ain't what we're lookin' for," Sanguine responded. "We got people keepin' an eye on the Sanctuary and they ain't turned up there.

We're lookin' for somethin' a little more specialist, y'know?"

The man frowned. "Then... then maybe they've gone to Grouse."

"Kenspeckle Grouse?" Vengeous said.

"Uh, yeah. He does work for the Sanctuary. They'd bring anything weird to him."

"Where?"

"An old cinema, closed down now, the Hibernian. Are you going to let me go now?" Sanguine looked at Vengeous, and Vengeous looked at their captive.

"What did you do during the war?" Vengeous asked.

"Uh... well... not much."

"I know you, Argus."

"No. I mean no, sir, we've never met. I did some work for Baron Vengeous, but..."

"You supplied Baron Vengeous with the location of a safehouse, when he needed somewhere to lie low for a few days."

"I... yes... but how would you—?"

"Skulduggery Pleasant tracked him to that safehouse, Argus. The information you supplied led directly to his capture."

"That's not my fault. That's... it wasn't my fault."

"The safehouse was known to our enemies, but in your stupidity, you hadn't realised that."

"OK," Argus said quickly, "OK, I made a mistake and Vengeous got arrested. But, Lord Vile, what's it got to do with you?"

"I am not Lord Vile," Vengeous said. He reached up and removed the helmet, and it melted into his gloves and flowed into the rest of the armour.

"Oh no," Argus whispered when he saw Vengeous' face. "Oh, please, no."

Vengeous glared and Argus shook uncontrollably, and then it was as if his body forgot everything it had ever learned about how to stay in one piece. His torso exploded outwards and his limbs were flung to the corners of the room. His head popped open and his insides dripped from the walls.

Vengeous turned to Sanguine. "The Hibernian Cinema. We're leaving immediately."

The Texan brushed a piece of Argus' brain from his jacket. "And if we happen to encounter any dark-haired young girls along the way?"

"You have my permission to kill whomever you deem fit."

Billy-Ray Sanguine smiled. "Yes, sir. Thank you, sir."

25

A SMATTERING OF SLAUGHTERING

New York. 7:37 am

A man who wasn't there left the comfort of the shadows and strode after the three businessmen. He crossed Bleecker Street, followed them up Hudson, three steps behind them the whole way, and they never even sensed him. They were talking about Sanctuary business, slipping into code words whenever a civilian passed within earshot. They were sorcerers, these businessmen, and important ones at that.

The man who wasn't there followed them to the parking lot off West 13th Street, to their car, and when he judged the moment was right, he struck. The businessmen, the sorcerers, saw the air part and a figure blur, but it was too late to raise the alarm, and far too late to defend themselves.

Bologna. 10:51 am

Five of them: young, powerful and eager to prove themselves. They wore black clothes, leather coats and sunglasses. Their hair was spiked and their skin was pierced. They liked to think of themselves as goth-punks. No one argued. No one argued and *lived* anyway.

Italy in May. It was warm and sunny. The goth-punks waited around the statue of Poseidon, fighting off boredom by scaring the occasional passer-by.

One of them, a girl with no hair and wild eyes, spotted their target as he crossed the square. They moved towards him as a pack, grinning in anticipation.

He saw them and frowned, his step faltering. He started to back away. He worked with the Sanctuary in Venice – they knew he wouldn't be willing to use his powers out here, in full view of the public.

He started to run. They gave chase, the thrill of the hunt making them laugh.

Tokyo. 7:18 pm

The woman in the pinstriped suit sat in the hotel lobby and read the newspaper. The suit was deep navy, the skirt stopped just past her knees, and beneath the jacket she wore an off-white blouse. Her shoes matched her suit. Her nail varnish matched her lipstick. She was a very elegant, very precise woman.

Her phone, impossibly sleek and thin, beeped once, alerting her to the time. She folded the newspaper and placed it on the seat as she stood.

Two men, one old, one young, entered the hotel lobby. The woman appreciated punctuality.

She joined them at the elevator. The men didn't speak to each other. While they waited for the elevator to arrive, a young foreign couple walked up, in Japan for a holiday perhaps. The woman didn't mind. It didn't alter her plan one bit.

The elevator arrived, the doors slid open and they all stepped in. The young couple pressed the button for the eighth floor. The old man pressed the button for the penthouse. The woman didn't press any button.

The doors closed, the elevator started moving, and the woman's nails grew long and her teeth grew sharp. She killed everyone and painted the elevator walls with their blood.

London. 9:56 am

Springheeled Jack looked down at the man he was about to kill, and for the first time in his life he wondered *why*.

He wasn't suddenly struck by his own sins. He wasn't having an attack of conscience or anything pedestrian like that. He wasn't having one of those *epiphany* things. It was just a voice, that was all, just a voice in the back of his mind telling him to ask something. But ask what? He'd never had the urge to ask any of his victims *anything* before. He didn't know where to start. Did he just strike up a conversation?

"Hello," he said, as nicely as he could.

The man was a sorcerer, but not a very good fighter. He lay crumpled in the alleyway and had a scared look in his eyes. Jack felt uncomfortable. This was a new situation, and he didn't like new situations. He liked to kill people. Taunt them, sure. Maybe make a witty remark. But not... not *talk* to them. Not *ask* them something.

He blamed Billy-Ray Sanguine. Sanguine had taken Jack

out of his cell, taken him through the wall, through the ground and out into fresh air. He had talked a little, mentioned a hospital in Ireland called Clearwater, something like that, and then he had looked like maybe he'd said too much, so he'd shut up. Jack hadn't cared at the time. He'd been freed, after all, and all he had to do in return was kill someone. But the thought was nagging at him – *why*? Why had Sanguine wanted this bloke dead?

Jack tried to sound casual. "If someone wanted you dead, hypothetically, what do you think their reasons would be?"

"Please don't kill me," the man whispered.

"I'm not gonna kill you," Jack lied and gave a reassuring laugh. "Why would you think I was gonna kill you?"

"You attacked me," the man said. "And you dragged me into this alley. And, and you *told* me you were going to kill me." Jack cursed under his breath. This guy had a good memory.

"Forget about all that," he said. "Someone wants you dead. I'm curious as to why that may be. Who are you?"

"My name is—"

"I know your bloody name, pally. What do you do? Why are you so important?"

"I'm not important, not at all. I work for the Council of Elders here in London. I'm just, I help co-ordinate things."

"Like what? What are you co-ordinating now, for example?"

"We're... sending help to Ireland. Baron Vengeous has escaped from—"

"Damn it!"

The man shrieked and recoiled, but Jack was too busy being angry to bother attacking him. So Sanguine was working with that nutter Vengeous again, carrying out his orders as usual. Only this time, he'd tried to get Jack to do some of the dirty work.

"I been hoodwinked," he said. He looked down at the man. "If Vengeous is involved, that means all this is about the Faceless Ones, right?"

"Y-yes."

"I been hoodwinked. That's... unprofessional, that is."

"So are you going to let me go? You don't want to help the Faceless Ones, right? So are you going to let me go?"

Jack hunkered down. "I'd love to, pally. I really would. But see, I was sprung from jail an' I always repay my debts."

"But... but by killing me, you'll be helping them!"

"I'll just have to find some other way to get back at 'em, then. No hard feelings."

The conversation came to its natural conclusion with a bit more begging and then Jack killed the guy, so that stopped too.

Jack straightened his top hat and walked away. He still had a few friends, friends who could transport him where he wanted to go.

And it was such a long time since he'd been to Ireland.

26

MURDER IN THE NEW MORGUE

Stentor and Civet struggled to move the Grotesquery off the stretcher and on to the operating table. The Grotesquery was big and heavy and awkward, but most of all it was big and heavy. They had just managed to drag the top half over when the stretcher squeaked and moved, and the Grotesquery started to fall. Civet tried to grab it, but he went under and the Grotesquery dropped, very slowly, on top of him.

"Help!" Civet cried.

Professor Grouse stormed in. "What on earth are you playing at?"

"It, it fell," Stentor said, standing to attention.

"I can see that!" Grouse barked. "That specimen is a rare opportunity to study a hybrid form, you imbecile. I don't want it damaged."

"Yes, Professor. Sorry."

"Why were you trying to move it by yourself? Where's Civet?"

Civet managed to raise a hand. "Here I am, Professor."

"What on earth are you doing down there, Civet?"

"Trying to breathe, sir."

"Well, get up!"

"I would, sir, but it's very heavy. If you could maybe grab an arm or something..."

"I'm an old man, you fool. You expect me to lift that monstrosity off you?"

"Not by yourself, but maybe if Stentor were to help, then I could wriggle out. It really is getting difficult to breathe under here. I think my lung is collapsing."

Grouse gestured. "Stentor, help me lift."

"Yes, Professor."

Together, they pulled the Grotesquery back far enough to enable Civet to squirm out.

"I've never dropped a specimen," Grouse said as they

grunted and heaved. "I was never pinned by a corpse either, Civet. You remember that."

"Yes, sir," said Civet, as he finally managed to extricate himself.

Grouse hunkered down beside the Grotesquery, then took a pair of scissors and carefully snipped a few bandages away, revealing the scarred flesh beneath. "Astonishing," he murmured. "So many parts from different creatures, all merged into the one being. A being borne of impossible horrors."

Stentor nodded. "It'd be even more impressive if it *worked* though."

"Less talking," Grouse snapped, "more lifting. Lift it on to the table. And no more damage to it, you hear? I swear, you're lucky I'm so easy-going. Stentor. Bend your knees when you lift, you idiot."

"Sorry sir."

They strained and lifted, and suddenly Civet let go and jumped back. Stentor clung on, holding the Grotesquery half on, half off the table.

"What's wrong now?" Grouse demanded.

"Professor," Civet said nervously, "are you sure this thing is dead?"

"It's not a thing, it's a specimen."

"Sorry, sir. Are you sure this specimen is dead? I... I think it moved."

"Of course it moved. You moved it."

"No, sir. I mean, I think it moved on its own."

"Well, I don't see how that could be. The ritual to bring it to life was interrupted – only a small portion of Valkyrie Cain's blood was transfused."

Civet hesitated, then grabbed a massive arm and helped Stentor slide it further on to the table.

He leaped away. "OK!" he said loudly. "OK, that time I *definitely* felt it move!"

"A lot of energy was passed into it," Grouse said, frowning. "It may just be a residual spasm. The muscles may simply be reacting to stimuli."

"It wasn't a spasm," Civet said. "I swear."

Grouse looked at the bandage-wrapped body. It was big and cold and unmoving. "Very well," he said. "How many Cleavers are stationed here?"

"Three."

"OK, then. Boys, I want you both to go upstairs, tell the Cleavers to come down here, tell them we may have a—"

And then the Grotesquery sat up and Civet yelled and jumped back, but Stentor was too slow and it grabbed his head in its big hand and crushed it like a freshly laid egg.

27

RISE OF THE GROTESQUERY

Valkyrie opened her eyes. Was that a scream? She sat up and looked out into the corridor. The lights were flickering. She heard running footsteps. Then nothing. Something was wrong. Something was very wrong.

She got out of bed, her limbs protesting, her arm aching. Her bare feet touched the cold floor. She padded to the small wardrobe built into the wall, where she found her socks and boots. She pulled them on quickly in the darkened room, and she was just shrugging into her coat when she heard someone crying for help. Then a *thud* and the crying stopped.

Valkyrie poked her head out the door, looked up towards the morgue, and saw the figure moving through the dim corridor like some kind of puppet with half its strings cut. It moved in a jerky manner, stiff and uncoordinated, but even as she watched, it seemed to move a little more smoothly, like it was getting used to its own body. It stepped into a pool of light.

The Grotesquery. It was alive.

She saw the bandages – so old they might have turned to dust under her gaze – that had been used to keep it in one piece. She saw flesh between the bandages, and scars, and stitching. Its ribcage looked like it had been cracked and pulled open, so that now each rib punctured through its torso.

It had something that looked like a massive boil growing on the top of its left wrist and on the underside there was a thick ridge of flesh. Its right arm was huge, the muscles curling impossibly around one another, all the way down to its massive hand. Its fingers were thick, each tipped with a talon. The bandages covered its face completely, not even a gap for the eyes. Here and there black blood had soaked through.

Why was there no alarm? The Grotesquery was alive, but there was no alarm. Valkyrie stepped back, grabbed a chair and stood on it. She clicked her fingers but nothing happened. Her eyes narrowed. She focused, clicked her fingers again until she made a spark, cultivated it into a flame and held it up to the smoke detectors. After a moment the sprinkler system activated and the alarm pierced the silence.

She hurried back to the door as three Cleavers ran by. It was only when they got close to it that she realised how big the Grotesquery truly was. It towered above the tallest of them. They were used to dealing with serious threats. But they had never seen anything like this.

The Grotesquery batted away the swipe of a scythe and grabbed the first Cleaver by the throat. It lifted him high overhead as it swatted the second Cleaver into the wall. The third Cleaver swung his scythe and the Grotesquery swung his colleague's body into him. Valkyrie heard bones break.

Three seconds. The Grotesquery had killed three Cleavers in three seconds.

Valkyrie stepped back inside her room. The sprinklers were drenching her. She could run for it. Step out of the doorway, turn right, sprint the length of the corridor to the Research Area, then get to the stairs. She'd pass through the screen and be running from the cinema before the Grotesquery even saw her. It was still slow, it wouldn't even be able to catch her if it *did* see her. She could do it. So why wasn't she running?

Valkyrie backed away. She could see the shadow on the wall

outside her open door, getting closer. Her legs were unsteady and her arm still hurt. Fear coiled and thrashed in her belly. She felt the wall behind her and pressed herself to it. The darkness of the room didn't seem dark enough. It would see her. No, it didn't need to see her. It had no eyes.

And then it was too late to run, because the Grotesquery was passing the doorway, water running down its body. She could smell it now – it smelled of formaldehyde and mould. She held her breath and didn't move.

The Grotesquery stopped. Valkyrie readied herself. If it turned to her she'd launch herself forward, hit it with everything she had, hurl enough fireballs to send those bandages up in flames. Like that would be enough to stop it. Like that would be enough to save her.

Its head turned slightly, but not in her direction, as if the Grotesquery was listening for something, beyond the alarm. She suddenly thought of a radar that it could use to sense her, but a radar that had been unused for so long it wasn't as sharp as it could be.

She felt her muscles weaken and a coldness swept into her mind. Terror was robbing her of her strength. The thought that she'd be unable to move seeped in, grew and festered. The things she had learned meant nothing. The skills, the powers, the magic – to the Grotesquery she'd be even more ineffectual than the Cleavers it had just killed. Something less than a threat. Something less than an insect.

But it moved. It took another step, and another, and soon it was out of sight, moving on down the corridor. Valkyrie felt tears mix with the water that was running down her face. She blinked them back. She wasn't going to die. Not today.

She pushed away from the wall, balanced herself on shaky legs. She waited a few moments, then made her way to the door, her feet splashing slightly as she moved. She got to the door and peeked out, and fingers closed around her throat. She was yanked out into the corridor, her feet off the ground, gagging and spitting and trying to breathe.

The Grotesquery had its head raised, looking up at her with no eyes, examining her. Her hands were at its massive wrist, at those fingers, trying to pry them loose.

Something less than an insect.

She kicked, her boots slamming into the thing. She pelted her fists down on its forearm. It didn't make one bit of difference. Her heartbeat thundered in her ears. Darkness crept into her vision. She couldn't breathe. She needed to breathe. She was going to die.

She clicked her fingers, managed to summon a flame then

pressed her hand to the Grotesquery's bandages. The bandages instantly caught fire and then instantly snuffed out. No more tricks. She was done.

Then there was movement behind the Grotesquery – Skulduggery and Tanith, sprinting. The Grotesquery didn't need to turn. When they were right behind, it swung its left fist back. Skulduggery dodged under it and Tanith leaped to the ceiling, her sword flashing and now Valkyrie was dropping. Skulduggery swooped in, snatched her up and kept running, Tanith beside them.

The Grotesquery regarded its injured hand with something approaching curiosity. They stopped and looked back, as the flesh closed over and healed.

There was movement at the doorway beside them and Kenspeckle limped into the corridor.

"Stay behind us," Skulduggery ordered.

Kenspeckle grunted. "I plan to."

They felt the air pressure change and Valkyrie's ears popped. "What's happening?" she called out over the alarm.

"Its power is returning," Kenspeckle said grimly.

Skulduggery took his gun from his jacket. "This is our only chance to stop it before it becomes too strong."

He walked up to the Grotesquery, firing six times as he went, and six small explosions of black blood erupted against the Grotesquery's chest, barely making it stagger. Skulduggery put the gun away, clicked his fingers and unleashed two continuous streams of fire, turning the space between them to steam. The flames hit the Grotesquery but didn't catch.

Skulduggery pushed at the air with both hands and the air rippled. The Grotesquery was forced backwards. Skulduggery did it again and the Grotesquery fought to resist. Skulduggery went to do it a third time, and the Grotesquery reached out with its huge right arm and the arm unravelled. Long strips of flesh, each tipped with a talon, lacerated the air around Skulduggery. He cried out and fell back and the strips returned, wrapped around each other and reformed the arm. The Grotesquery smacked Skulduggery and he hurtled backwards through the air.

Tanith ran up, her hair plastered to her scalp and her sword darting out. The Grotesquery tried grabbing her, but she was too fast. She rolled and cut its leg then leaped up and slashed its arm. Both wounds closed over.

Its right arm unravelled again and she ducked and dodged, then jumped and flipped, and now she was upside down on the ceiling. She advanced, but the Grotesquery kept its distance. It raised its left arm.

Kenspeckle shouted a warning, but the fire alarm drowned

him out. The growth on top of the Grotesquery's left wrist, what Valkyrie had thought was a massive boil, suddenly contracted and a yellow liquid shot out. Tanith had to fling herself sideways to avoid it and she crashed to the ground. The liquid hit the ceiling and ate through it in an instant, leaving a gaping hole.

Skulduggery ran to join her and Tanith got to her feet, and even though the boil was now empty, the Grotesquery was still holding out its left arm. Skulduggery reached for Tanith, but he was a second too late.

A thin spike emerged from the ridge on the underside of the Grotesquery's wrist and jabbed into Tanith's side. She cried out and the spike retracted, returning to its sheath. Skulduggery caught Tanith as she collapsed. He backed away.

The Grotesquery looked at its hands and flexed its fingers, as if it was discovering what it could do with each passing moment.

Valkyrie and Kenspeckle ran up. Tanith was unconscious. Her veins were visible through her skin and they were a sickly green colour.

"She's been infected," Kenspeckle said. "Helaquin poison. She has maybe twenty minutes before she dies."

"How do we cure it?" Skulduggery asked.

The alarm whined and went silent, and the sprinklers cut off.

"I haven't seen this poison for fifty years," Kenspeckle said. "I don't have an antidote here. There is some at the Sanctuary if we can get there in time."

"I'll lead the Grotesquery away," Valkyrie said. "Meet you at the car."

Skulduggery looked up sharply. "What? No! You take Tanith—"

"Don't tell her this," Valkyrie said, "but she's too heavy for me to carry." And she ran before Skulduggery could stop her.

"Valkyrie!" he roared.

Her boots splashed as she sprinted. The Grotesquery held its arms wide, welcoming her. There was no way past it on either side and she didn't have Tanith's ceiling-running skills, so when the Grotesquery reached for her, Valkyrie dropped, sliding on the wet floor, between its legs. Once she was clear she scrambled up and ran on. She glanced back. The Grotesquery was turning, following her.

So that worked, Valkyrie thought to herself. *Now what the hell am I going to do?*

Just as she turned the corner, Skulduggery shouted something, something like *the vanity light*. She kept running. She passed the elevators, shut down because of the fire alert, and headed for the back stairs. The Grotesquery hadn't even reached the corner yet. She slowed, catching her breath, keeping her eyes on the corner. The vanity light. What had Skulduggery meant?

The Grotesquery came around the corner. The back stairs, the ones that joined up with the main stairs behind the screen, were right behind her and she readied herself to sprint if the patchwork monstrosity came up with any more surprises.

And then it disappeared, like it had been swallowed by the empty space around it. Valkyrie blinked. Another of its hybrid abilities, like the stinger and the acid and the unravelling arm. Teleportation.

Skulduggery hadn't said *the vanity light*, he had said *The Vanishing Night. The Vanishing Night* had been one of Gordon's earliest bestsellers. It had dealt with a creature, a Shibbach, that could appear anywhere, commit a very messy and overly-detailed murder then vanish and reappear a hundred kilometres away. She remembered Gordon now, the Gordon in the Echo Stone, telling her about the pieces of a Shibbach that Vengeous had grafted on.

Valkyrie didn't even have to look around to know the Grotesquery was behind her. She tried to run but her boot slipped on the wet ground, just as its right hand snatched at her. She fell sideways, glimpsed the Grotesquery's bandaged head and tumbled down the stairs. She sprawled to a painful stop, grabbed the banister and hauled herself to her feet. She was at the main stairs now, and she took them two at a time, going dangerously fast.

She reached the ground and sprinted for the screen, passed through and leaped off the stage. She ran for the exit, crashed through the door and the midday sunlight struck her like a fist.

"Valkyrie!" Skulduggery shouted. The Bentley was ahead, engine running, and beyond it Baron Vengeous was striding through the lane towards them, followed by Sanguine and Dusk and his pack of Infected.

The Grotesquery stepped out of thin air with a soft *whump*. Valkyrie dodged it and ran as the Bentley started moving. She jumped for the open window and Kenspeckle grabbed her and dragged her in as Skulduggery floored it. Tanith was in the backseat, still unconscious, and when Valkyrie righted herself she looked back and saw Baron Vengeous approaching the Grotesquery.

The Grotesquery turned its head, keeping its eyeless gaze fixed on the car.

"Seatbelt," Skulduggery said.

28

GOOD GUYS CONVENE

Bliss, flanked by Cleavers, was waiting at the rear of the Sanctuary. The Bentley pulled up sharply and Bliss yanked the door open, then lifted Tanith out. Her veins were sickly yellow spiderwebs that spread beneath her waxy skin, and she was barely breathing.

"Out of my way, out of my way," Kenspeckle muttered, shoving people aside. Bliss laid Tanith on the ground and handed Kenspeckle three different coloured leaves. He wrapped them around each other, tightly, then held them between his clasped hands and closed his eyes. A light shone from within, bright enough to almost turn his hands translucent. Valkyrie could see the bones of his fingers.

The light faded. Bliss took a clear tube and held it out, and Kenspeckle opened his hands slightly. He let a fine, multicoloured dust – the remains of the leaves – sift gently into the tube. Bliss added a few drops of a deep red liquid that smelled vaguely of sulphur, and Kenspeckle took the tube and shook it, mixing the contents. Bliss handed him a syringe gun and Kenspeckle loaded the tube into it.

"Hold her," Kenspeckle said.

Bliss placed his hands on Tanith's shoulders, Skulduggery held down one arm and Valkyrie pinned the other. The Cleavers secured her legs. Kenspeckle pressed the syringe gun to Tanith's neck and the gun hissed with compressed air. The concoction emptied into her bloodstream.

Tanith thrashed and Valkyrie lost her grip on her arm. She grabbed it again, struggled to press it to the ground, and eventually had to kneel on it to keep it in place. Tanith bucked and writhed as the antidote worked through her. The yellow veins surged red, and her muscles knotted and strained.

"Try to make sure she doesn't swallow her tongue," Kenspeckle said.

And then Tanith went limp and the veins were no longer

visible. Colour returned to her face.

"Will she be all right?" Valkyrie asked.

Kenspeckle raised an eyebrow. "Am I a magic-scientific genius or am I not?"

"You are."

"Then of course she'll be all right," he said. "Which is more than I can say for my assistants. Do you know how hard it is to get good assistants these days? Granted, neither of them were actually any good, but..." He brushed his hands off and shook his head. "They were fine lads. They didn't deserve to die like that." He looked at Skulduggery. "You'll stop it then?"

"We'll stop it."

"Fair enough." Kenspeckle stood up. "Let's get her inside."

Valkyrie was sore. Her arm was stiffening up and her body was covered in bruises. She had cut her lip without realising it and for some reason had a black eye, presumably the result of crashing the van or the tumble she took down the stairs.

Tanith was sitting beside her and she was sulking. Tanith always sulked when she lost a fight. After she had fought the White Cleaver last year she had spent most of her recovery time staring out the window, scowling.

The antidote had neutralised the effects of the Helaquin

poison, and the wound the stinger had made was already stitched up and healing. The moment she was able, Tanith had gone off and sharpened her sword. It lay on the table before them in its black scabbard.

They were in the Sanctuary meeting room. Mr Bliss was seated at the far end of the table and Skulduggery was standing against the wall, arms crossed and unmoving. The doors opened. Guild stalked in.

"Who do I blame?" he thundered. "Tell me, who? We had the Grotesquery in *custody*? We had it and I wasn't *informed*?"

"I take full responsibility," Skulduggery said.

"You do, do you? That would be quite noble if I wasn't blaming you *anyway*! You went behind my back, Detective. You requested the services of three Cleavers for guard duty and you didn't follow procedure. Where are those Cleavers now?"

Skulduggery hesitated. "They were killed."

"Well, that's marvellous news, isn't it?" Guild snapped. "Tell me, is there any part of this operation that you didn't botch?"

"Operation's not over yet."

Guild glared. "You're lucky I even let you in here, Detective. I don't know how Eachan Meritorious handled things, but your reckless behaviour will not be tolerated by the new Council!"

"Council of one," Tanith murmured.

Guild whirled. "I'm sorry? I didn't quite catch that. Could you repeat what you said so we can all hear it?"

Tanith looked at him. "Sure. I said 'council of one', referring to the fact that the Council is not the Council until it has all three members."

The Elder Mage bristled. "Your opinion is of little consequence in *this* country, Miss Low. You work for the Sanctuary in London, you shouldn't even *be* here."

"Actually I'm freelance," Tanith responded.

"And I requested her help," Skulduggery said. "It seems we could use it. Didn't you say we would be getting reinforcements?" Guild's face went red, but Bliss spoke before he could start shouting again.

"All the offers of international aid have been withdrawn. In the past few hours there have been attacks on personnel connected to practically every Sanctuary around the world."

"Distractions," Skulduggery said, "to keep everyone else busy. We've been isolated."

"Indeed we have."

"But who would be powerful enough to organise all this?" Valkyrie asked. "Vengeous?"

"This has taken a lot of planning," Skulduggery said. "Vengeous wouldn't have had the time."

"That's not what we should be concentrating on," Guild snapped. "We have to find the Grotesquery and stop it. *That* is our one and only concern."

"The lunar eclipse will take place at ten minutes past midnight tonight," Bliss said. "That leaves us with nine hours until the Grotesquery is strong enough to open the portal."

Guild laid both hands flat on the table. "So what are we doing about it? Please tell me we're not all sitting around just *waiting* for something to happen!"

"We have all the sensitives on alert," Skulduggery said. "Every psychic and seer we know is reaching out."

"And if they don't find anything, skeleton?"

Skulduggery, who was still leaning against the wall with his arms crossed, tilted his head as he looked back at Guild. "Then I recommend we work the case."

"What does that even mean?" Guild raged. "We are facing a global catastrophe that could mean the end of everything, and you're talking about *working the case*?"

"I'm a detective," Skulduggery said. "It's what I do."

"Well, you haven't been doing a very good job of it, have you?"

Skulduggery stood up straight now, hands down by his sides. "Working backwards," he said calmly. "Person or persons unknown have arranged to isolate us just when we need reinforcements to stop the Grotesquery. The Grotesquery is up and about because Vengeous finally got the missing ingredients he needed. Vengeous is out of his secret prison because Billy-Ray Sanguine broke in and freed him. Billy-Ray Sanguine knew where this secret prison was located because somebody in a position of power divulged this information."

"You're getting off topic again," Guild scowled.

"Somebody in a position of power," Skulduggery continued, "divulged this information, presumably for a big reward. Now, here's where I start speculating. It's possible that this same somebody only rose to this position of power because he promised that once he was there, he would find the location of the secret prison and pass it on. He would have made a deal with a powerful person or persons unknown, very possibly the same powerful person or persons unknown who have isolated us from the international community, but, very likely, he wouldn't have known who these mysterious benefactors planned to break out of that secret prison or, indeed, why."

Guild narrowed his eyes. "You better not be implying what I think you're implying."

Skulduggery nodded to a slim file on the table. "That file is a record of the meetings you've had with other councils across the world since you were elected Grand Mage. You have had approximately twice the number of meetings with the Russian Council as you have had with anyone else."

"These are official Sanctuary matters and are *none* of your business," Guild said, the veins in his neck standing out.

"Three of those meetings were about security concerns in the wake of Serpine's activities, where you would have been privy to confidential information including, but not restricted to, the location of various secret prisons in Russian territories."

Guild stalked up to Skulduggery and for a moment Valkyrie thought he might hit him. Skulduggery didn't move a fraction.

"You are accusing me of aiding a prison break?"

"Like I said, I'm speculating. But if I were to accuse you of anything, it would probably be more along the lines of treason."

"You're fired," Guild said.

Skulduggery tilted his head. "You can't afford to lose me."

"Oh, we can," Guild snarled, walking for the door.

"I have a job to do," Skulduggery said, "and I intend to do it. You may be a traitor, Guild, but you don't want the Faceless Ones back any more than I do."

Guild reached the door and turned, his lip curled. "Then do

it, skeleton. Stop the Grotesquery. Do your job. And once you're done, never set foot in here again." He left and nobody spoke for a while. Then Skulduggery nodded.

"I really think he's starting to like me."

29

PICKING UP A TAIL

They left the Sanctuary and drove through the narrower streets of Dublin. Skulduggery parked the Bentley once they reached the Temple Bar area, and they walked the rest of the way. Even though he was wearing his disguise, he was drawing all the usual looks from passers-by, who sifted in and out of the many pubs and restaurants.

They crossed the square, navigated between the hundred or so students who lounged around on the steps. Valkyrie liked Temple Bar. It was vibrant and packed, and there was music and laughter and chat everywhere. But if they failed to stop the Grotesquery, when this night was over, it could all be nothing but dust and rubble and screaming.

They reached a shop with a brightly coloured mural on its wall, and Skulduggery knocked on the door. From somewhere inside there came voices, and a few moments later the door rattled as it was unlocked. A man in his early twenties opened it. His eyebrows, nose, ears, lips and tongue were pierced, and he was wearing old jeans, a Thin Lizzy T-shirt and a dog collar.

"Hello Finbar," Skulduggery said. "I'm here to collect my belongings."

"Skul-man?" Finbar said, in such a way that suggested that befuddlement was his natural state of being. "Is that you? What's up with that hair and those gigantic sunglasses, man?"

"It's a disguise."

"Oh. Yeah, I get it. Nice. So hey, wow. How long's it been?"

"Since we last spoke?"

"Yeah. Must be years, yeah?"

"Last month, Finbar."

"Hmm? Oh, right. OK. And who's this you have with you?"

"I'm Valkyrie Cain," Valkyrie said, shaking his hand. He wore many rings.

"Valkyrie Cain," Finbar said, rolling the name around in his mouth. "Nice one. My name's Finbar Wrong. I'm an old friend of the Skul-man's, isn't that right, Skul-man?"

"Not really."

Finbar shook his head. "Nope, wouldn't call us *friends*, exactly. Associates, or... or... not colleagues, but... I mean, we know each other, like, but..."

"I'm going to have to hurry you along," Skulduggery said. "I gave you a small case to keep for me and I need it back."

"A case?"

"A black case. I told you I needed somewhere to keep some supplies, in case of emergencies."

"Is there an emergency?"

"I'm afraid so."

Finbar's eyes widened and his piercings glittered in the sunlight. "Oh, man. I'm not gonna die, am I?"

"I hope not."

"Me too, man. Me too. I got so much to live for, y'know? Hey, did I tell you me and Sharon are getting married? Finally, yeah?"

"Finbar, I don't know who Sharon is and I really need that case."

"All right, man," Finbar said, nodding. "I'm going to see if I can find it. It's got to be somewhere, right?"

"So suggest the laws of probability." Finbar wandered back into the shop and Valkyrie looked at Skulduggery.

"What's in the case?" she asked.

"My other gun, a few bullets, various bits and pieces, a spike bomb, an old paperback I've never read, a pack of cards—"

"Spike bomb?"

"Mm? Yes."

"What's a spike bomb?"

"It's a bomb with a spike in it."

"You gave a bomb to *that* guy? Is it safe?"

"It's a bomb, Valkyrie. Of course it's not safe. The case, however, is *very* safe. Whether he's been using it as a coffee table, a footstool or if he's simply spent the last few years throwing it down a flight of stairs, its contents will be in no way damaged. Providing he can *find* the thing."

Finbar reappeared. "I'm getting warmer, man, I know it. It's not in the front, so I'm thinking it's in the back, yeah? So I'm going to check out the back right now. You guys want to come in?"

"We're good out here," Valkyrie said politely.

"OK, cool. You sure? Skul-man? Sharon's in there, man. Why don't you say hi?"

"Because I don't know her, Finbar."

"Right, yeah, OK." Finbar wandered off again.

Valkyrie checked the clock on her phone. If she was home right now, living a normal life, she'd probably be figuring out what to wear to the reunion. Not that it would take long. She had one dress in her entire wardrobe, which she wore rarely, and with great reluctance. She figured that the Toxic Twins would have already started their beauty regime by this stage, applying eighty-four layers of makeup and figuring out which colour lipstick made them look the most trashy. Valkyrie was glad she had a reflection to go instead of her.

"Oh, hell," she said suddenly.

"What's wrong?"

"The reflection. It's still in the back of the Bentley."

Skulduggery's head tilted. "Oh. Oh, we seem to have forgotten about that."

Valkyrie closed her eyes. "If I don't go to the reunion, Mum'll go mental."

"Look on the bright side. If the world ends, none of that will matter."

She waited a moment without speaking, then he nodded. "That's probably not a great consolation," he admitted.

Finbar wandered back, holding a black case. "Found it,

man. Reason I couldn't see it, it was on the floor and there was someone sleeping on it. Y'know, for a pillow. It's good though. So, here."

Skulduggery took the case. "Thank you very much, Finbar."

"Absolutely no problemo, man. Hey, this emergency thing – it's serious?"

"Yes, it is."

"You need some help? It's been a while since I was, y'know, in the field or even out the door, but I still got it."

"I'm sure you do, but we can handle it."

"Oh, right. OK. Probably a good thing. I don't know if I got it any more, y'know? Don't know if I ever did, but... What were we saying?"

"We were saying congratulations on your upcoming wedding to Sharon."

"Oh, thanks, Skul-man."

"I'm sure you'll be very happy together."

"Yeah, me too. I mean, I've only known her three days, but sometimes you just gotta... get married... to someone..." He trailed off and looked puzzled. "I think."

"Well," Skulduggery said, "thank you for keeping this for me. Stay out of trouble."

"You got it. Hey, who's that with you?"

Skulduggery tilted his head. "This is Valkyrie. She introduced herself."

"Naw, man, not her. The guy in black." Valkyrie stiffened and fought the urge to look round.

"Where is he?" Skulduggery asked.

"Across the street, doing a pretty good job of keeping out of sight, but you know me, Skul-man. Eyes like a feathery thing. Whatchmacallit. Hawk."

"And he's watching us?"

"Yep. Wait, no. Not watching you. Watching *her*."

"What does he look like?" Valkyrie asked.

"Black hair, pretty pale. Ugly scar on his face. Looks like a vamp."

"You should get back inside," Skulduggery said. "Lock the doors."

"You got it, kemo sabe. I'll keep my crucifix close."

"Vampires aren't scared of a crucifix, Finbar."

"I don't plan to wave it at him, I plan to hit him with it. It's really heavy. I figure I can do some considerable damage to his head." He stepped back and closed the door.

Skulduggery and Valkyrie walked back through Temple Bar to the Bentley.

"Is Dusk still following us?" Valkyrie asked, keeping her voice low.

"I think so," Skulduggery answered. "This is the break we've been looking for. Dusk has a grudge against you. We're quite lucky in fact."

"Very lucky," Valkyrie agreed dryly. "Very lucky that a vampire wants to kill me. Are we going to lure him into a trap?"

"Indeed we are. But not here. He won't get close enough. He has to believe you're alone."

Valkyrie narrowed her eyes. "That sounds suspiciously like a suggestion that I should act as bait..."

"You have to go to the reunion."

"No no no..."

"You can't be around me, or Tanith, or any sorcerer. Dusk wouldn't risk it. He'll only strike when he thinks you're alone. That way he can take his time when he kills you."

"You're not making me feel any better about this."

"You're going to the reunion."

Valkyrie sagged.

"Tanith and I will wait nearby. The moment Dusk tries anything, we'll step in."

"But my family. My aunts and uncles and cousins and second cousins and..."

"We'll protect them."

"What? No, I mean my family is really, *really* annoying. When they're drunk, they all start dancing and that's just... that's just *wrong*."

"You'll have a wonderful time."

"I hate you."

"I know."

30

FIGHT

Springheeled Jack stood on the roof of Clearwater Hospital and looked down at the creature, admiring the beauty and the savagery, the sheer power he could feel, even from where he was standing.

"Quite a thing, ain't it?"

Jack wiped any hint of admiration from his face and turned as Sanguine strolled towards him.

"You lied to me," he said.

Sanguine nodded. "That I did. How'd you find us?"

"You told me where you were stayin', remember?"

"I did? Me an' my big mouth, I swear... So, you seen the critter down there. What do you think?"

"This all has to do with the Faceless Ones," Jack said and hit Sanguine. The Texan stumbled back, and he was straightening up when Jack kicked him off the edge of the building. Jack jumped, flipped and landed on the ground beside Sanguine.

"Ow," Sanguine said, flat on his back. His sunglasses had come off and Jack looked at the holes where his eyes should have been.

"I don't like being used," Jack said.

"If I'd apologised before, would you still have kicked me off the roof?"

"Probably."

"Figured as much."

Sanguine struck out with his leg, his boot cracking into Jack's knee. He rolled up and launched himself forward, forced Jack against the wall, driving in punches. Jack's hat fell.

Sanguine punched and Jack ducked. Sanguine's knuckles hit the wall and he howled. Jack shoved him away, giving himself enough room to manoeuvre, and he jumped and kicked, and Sanguine went sprawling.

"You can't beat me, Yank," Jack snarled.

"Yanks are from the North," Sanguine muttered, getting up.

"I'm a Southern boy." He came forward again and Jack ducked and dodged, flipping himself sideways. Sanguine growled in frustration. Jack smacked him and gave him another kick in the head, and once more Sanguine hit the ground.

Jack looked down at him. "So where is he? Where's Vengeous?"

"Ain't here right now," Sanguine said, not trying to get up.

"It's just you and him, is it? You and him and that thing?"

"We got vamps too. You know Dusk?"

"Met him in London once. He didn't realise the rooftops was *my* patch. We got into a bit of a scuffle, you might say."

Sanguine sat up and groaned. "Well, I'd love to watch you two kill each other, but he ain't around either. He's off on one of his vendettas, goin' after a girl in Haggard."

"You used me, Sanguine."

Slowly, Sanguine reached out, picked up his sunglasses and got to his feet. "You came all the way to Ireland to berate me, that what you did?"

"I came here to find out what you're up to."

"And then what?"

"If I don't like it? I'll stop it."

Sanguine's sunglasses were back on and he laughed. "That critter out there, *that's* what we're up to. You wanna stop that?

You go right ahead, my ugly little friend." The ground at Sanguine's feet started to crumble. "Go back to London, Jack. You can't do anythin' to hurt us here. We're too strong, buddy. What could you possible do to upset our plans?"

Sanguine grinned, and he lowered into the ground and disappeared.

31

THE EDGLEY FAMILY REUNION THING

Valkyrie checked that her parents had gone to the reunion and the house was empty, then she walked outside and waved. The Bentley drove up, Skulduggery got out, and together they lifted the reflection's body out of the boot and carried it into the house and up the stairs.

They positioned the reflection in front of the mirror and then let it drop gently forward. It passed through the glass, slumping to the mirrored room within. After a moment, the reflection stirred and stood up. It turned to them, its face placid and blank. Valkyrie fought down an irrational feeling of guilt for what they had put the reflection through. She started to imagine that it had a reproachful look in its eyes. She reached out, touched the glass and the reflection's memories swarmed into her mind.

She clutched her chest and took a step back. "Oh God."

Skulduggery steadied her. "Are you OK?"

"I just remembered what it was like to be shot."

"Was it fun?"

"Amazingly, no."

She stood up straighter. The reflection in the mirror was normal now. "I'm all right. I'm good."

"Then I shall leave you. You're going to have to walk to the golf club, I'm afraid. But don't worry, we'll be watching."

"What if I go to the reunion and Dusk doesn't fall for the trap? Then we're all just wasting our time."

"This is the only option we have, Valkyrie. Are you going to wear a dress?"

"Are you sure I can't go like this?"

"He'll be cautious enough as it is. You have to appear completely unaware."

"Fine," she growled. "A dress."

"I'm sure you'll look lovely," Skulduggery said as he left the room.

She called after him. "If anyone starts a sing-song at this thing, the world can fend for itself, all right?"

She heard his voice as he walked down the stairs. "That's fair."

Her eyes narrowed. The reflection's memories had mixed with her own, sidled into position like they always did, but there was something else now. A feeling. She shook her head. The reflection was incapable of feelings. It was a receptacle, a thing that absorbed experiences, ready to be downloaded. There were never any feelings, any emotions. Valkyrie wasn't even sure if this new thing *was* an emotion. It hovered in her mind just beyond her reach. Whenever she focused on it, it scattered.

No, it wasn't an emotion, but it *was* something. Something she couldn't pin down. A black spot in her memory. Her reflection had hidden something from her.

This, Valkyrie thought to herself, *is probably not a good sign.*

There were more here than she had expected. They filled the function room almost to capacity – people talking and laughing and shaking hands and hugging. Aunts and uncles and cousins of every degree, adding to the cacophony of chatter that came at Valkyrie like a wall of sound, slamming into her the moment she opened the door.

Most of these people she didn't know – she'd never seen them before, and would never see them again. It didn't exactly fill her with regret. She doubted she was missing out on anything spectacular.

Her dress looked nice, she had to admit. It was black and pretty, but she couldn't get comfortable. If Dusk *did* fall into the trap and try to attack, she'd regret not wearing trousers and boots, she knew she would.

"Stephanie?" She turned. The man was in his forties. His comb-over was neither subtle nor successful.

"It is Stephanie, isn't it? Desmond's daughter?"

Valkyrie drew a smile on to her face. "Yep," she said. "It's me."

"Ah! Wonderful!" the man said, grabbing her into a hug that lasted two uncomfortable seconds. He released her and stepped back. The sudden movement had dislodged his comb-over. Valkyrie thought it polite not to mention it.

"Last time I saw you, you were knee-high to a grasshopper! You must have been, I don't know, four? You were tiny! Now look at you! You're beautiful! I can't get over how much you've grown!"

"Yeah, nine years'll do that."

"Bet you don't remember me," he said, wagging his finger for some unknown reason.

"You're right," she said.

"Go on, have a guess."

"I have no idea."

"Go on, rack your brains, try to remember!"

"I don't know," she said, speaking slowly and taking extra care with the words in case he had missed her meaning.

"I'll give you a clue," he said, missing the point entirely. "Your grandfather and my father were brothers."

"You're my dad's cousin."

"Yes!" he said – almost cheered in fact. "Now do you remember?"

She looked at him and thought how amazing it was that he, like most of the people here, was the direct descendant of a race of super-magical Ancients, and yet it looked like he would have difficulty crossing the street without assistance.

"I have to go," she said, motioning over his left shoulder. He turned to look and she moved off to his right.

Valkyrie checked the time on her phone and found herself hoping that she'd get attacked by a pack of vampires sooner rather than later. This was a cruel and unusual ordeal she was going through, and if this turned out to be her last night alive, well then that just wasn't fair. She nodded to people she vaguely recognised, but walked right by before they had a chance to tell her how small she once was.

And then the Toxic Twins were blocking her way. Crystal's bottle-blonde hair was so straight it looked like it'd been ironed, and Carol's hair was hanging in ringlets that looked like a pack of worms trying to squirm to freedom.

"Thought you'd be here," Crystal said with much disgust.

"The family part of family reunion gave it away, huh?"

"Glad to see you didn't spend too long getting dressed up," Carol said and they both sniggered.

"Why are you even here?" Crystal asked. "It's not like we have any other rich uncles for you to suck up to before they kick the bucket."

"Oh, good, it's nice to know that you're finally over that."

The twins stepped in close and tried their best to loom over her. Not an easy task when they were both four centimetres shorter.

"You cheated us out of our rightful inheritance," Carol said, her lips curling unattractively. "That house Gordon left you should have been ours. Your parents had already been left the villa in France so *we* should have got the house."

"That would have been fair," Crystal snarled. "But he left it to *you*. You got everything. Do you expect us to just forget that?"

"Look at you," Carol said, flicking Valkyrie's shoulder with a finger. "You're a child, for God's sake. What do you need a house for? We're sixteen; do you know what we could do if we had that house? The parties we would have? Do you know how cool we'd be?"

"Do you even know how much that place is worth? We'd sell it and we'd be rich!"

"But we didn't get it, did we? You got it because you sucked up and you pretended to be the perfect little niece, and now you think you're so great."

"You're not great, you stupid little kid. You don't know anything, no one likes you, and look at you, you're not even that pretty!"

Valkyrie looked at them both. "You know," she said, "I'm trying to remember if there was ever a time when the rotten things you said actually affected me. I'm trying to remember if your amateur bullying ever actually worked, and you know what? I don't think it did."

Carol tried to laugh scornfully.

"Do you know why? Because I really and truly do not care. I don't have any feelings towards you at all, good or bad. To me, you're simply... *not there*. You know?"

They glared at her and Valkyrie smiled graciously. "Have a great night, OK?" And she left them there.

She moved through the crowd as best she could, squeezing

between tables and avoiding throngs wherever possible. She saw her mother and managed to get to her without someone trying to hug her.

"Steph," her mother said, smiling brightly. "You're here! Finally! How was last night?"

"It was good," Valkyrie lied. "Me and Hannah, you know, just stayed up chatting. Gossiping about, like, boys, and stuff." She faltered, suddenly realising she had no idea what girls her age talked about.

"And you wore the dress," her mother said. "It looks lovely."

"Lovely won't do me much good if there's a riot."

Her mother looked at her. "You are so odd sometimes. So when did you get here?"

"A few minutes ago. Where's Dad?"

"Oh, he's around here somewhere. You know what Edgleys are like. Any excuse to talk about themselves and they grab it with both hands. Having fun?"

Valkyrie shrugged. "Ah, it's OK. Don't know many people. What about you? Are you having a good time?"

Her mother laughed and leaned in close. "Get me out of here," she said with a brilliant smile.

Valkyrie blinked. "I'm sorry?"

Her mother nodded like she was agreeing enthusiastically. "I can't stay here one minute longer. I'm going to explode."

"You want to leave?"

Her mother waved to someone and looked at Valkyrie and kept the brilliant smile. "More then anything in the world. You see that lady over there?"

"The one with the strange-shaped head?"

"She'll talk about her dogs. All night. She has three. They're all small. What is it with small dogs? What's wrong with big dogs? I like big dogs."

"Are we getting a dog?"

"What? No. My point is, we should make up an excuse and leave early."

With Dusk and his Infected minions out there? Not bloody likely.

"We're here for Dad," Valkyrie said. "We've got to stay here and support him. He'd stay for *your* family reunion."

"I suppose..."

"It's only one night, Mum. After tonight you'll never have to see them again."

"I thought you'd be the first one bolting for the door."

Valkyrie shrugged. "I don't know. Sometimes I think I don't spend enough time with you guys."

Her mother looked at her and her tone softened. "You're

just growing up. I mean, yes, it would be fantastic if we could spend time together like we used to, but you need your space and your privacy. I understand that, love. Really."

"Do you miss the way it used to be?"

"I'd be lying if I said no. But I'll take what I can get. You spend a lot of time in your room and that's, you know, that's fine. You're distant sometimes, but that's fine too."

Valkyrie couldn't meet her eyes. "I don't mean to be distant," she said.

Her mother wrapped an arm around her shoulders. "I know you don't. And you're not *always* distant. At times like these, it's like nothing has changed. You're the same old Steph."

"But other times... I'm not, right?"

"Maybe, but I still love you no matter what. And your dad and me, we're just thankful that you're keeping safe. Other kids your age, they're out there getting into trouble, getting hurt, doing God knows what. At least *we* know where you are."

"In my room," Valkyrie said, trying a smile. She thought of the reflection, sitting on the sofa while her dad told a bad joke, or standing in the kitchen while her mother told it about her day. It made her feel rotten inside, all twisty, so she stopped.

After all, she had other things to be worrying about tonight.

32

SHADOW SHARDS

China walked quickly through the underground car park, her bodyguards on either side. It was quiet here and vast, and their footsteps echoed loudly.

One of her bodyguards, a man named Sev, stopped suddenly and looked back the way they had come. His eyes narrowed. "Something's wrong." His associate, a petite woman called Zephyr, took a gun from beneath her jacket.

"Miss Sorrows," she said softly, "please get behind me."

China did as she asked. The bodyguards were training their guns on a seemingly empty part of the car park. As far as China could see, there was absolutely nothing there that could pose any threat – but that was why she had hired them. They were good. They were the best.

Baron Vengeous stepped into the light. The armour looked to be part of him. Small trails of shadows danced at the seams, like they were still getting used to their new host. Vengeous wasn't wearing the helmet and his smile was cold. His cutlass hung from his waist.

Sev and Zephyr moved as one. The years they had spent fighting alongside each other had honed their skills, and when they were together there was no one who could stand in their way.

Until tonight.

Zephyr went to fire, but a shadow rose up. It struck her in the chest and she flew backwards, the breath rushing out of her. Sev got a shot off, and then the darkness sliced through him and he stiffened and fell. He was dead before he hit the hard ground.

Vengeous looked at China. "I *said* I'd be back for you. But tell me, before I have to hurt you, have you reconsidered your position?"

China's shoulders straightened and her voice became light, and she was suddenly as self-assured as always.

"You mean have I decided to come back into the fold?" she

said. "I'm afraid not. My reasons are both complex and varied, but can actually be reduced to something quite simple. I realised that you were all insane and highly irritating. You, in particular, annoyed me."

"You are a brave woman to be taunting me."

"I'm not taunting you, sweetie. I'm just really bored of this conversation."

The shadows moved at Vengeous's command and China twisted out of the way, the shadows skimming past and slashing into the car behind her.

Her laugh was birdsong. "If you want my advice, give it up. Lay down that ridiculous armour, put that Grotesquery thing out of its misery and walk back into that nice little cell they're keeping for you."

"I'm disappointed in you, China. The Faceless Ones are about to return and you could have been by their side."

Zephyr held out her hand and her gun flew into her grip and she fired, aiming for the head. The shadows became a cloud that covered Vengeous's face, soaking up the bullets and spitting them out again. When the gun clicked empty, the shadows settled.

"Please," Vengeous said, "tell me you have something more to offer."

Zephyr jumped up and clicked her fingers and a fireball rocketed across the space between them, but a wave of darkness reared up and swallowed it. Vengeous gestured and the wave smacked into her and she stumbled. She tried to push at the air, but a shadow closed around her wrist and yanked her off her feet. She slammed into a nearby car and the shadow flicked her, she hit the pillar and crumpled to the ground.

Vengeous turned back to China as if Zephyr had been nothing more than a pesky fly he'd had to swat. "Do you remember the stories we heard as children, about what the dark gods did to traitors? All of those stories will come true for you, betrayer. You will be my gift to them. You will have the honour of being the first life they consume."

China slipped off her jacket and let it fall. She breathed out and markings of the deepest black started carving through her skin. They spread over her bare arms, across her shoulders and neck, ran down her chest and trailed beneath her clothes. They carved into her face, twisting and settling into symbols, and she looked at Vengeous with those blue eyes, with those magnificent tattoos etched all over her body, and she smiled. Baron Vengeous smiled back.

China crossed her arms and tapped the matching symbols on her triceps. They glowed as she flung her arms out and a blue pulse shot at Vengeous, who deflected it with a shield of shadow. The shield turned sharp and it moved like a shark fin along the ground, and China intertwined her fingers and thrust out both palms. The symbols on her palms mingled and became a beam of dazzling light that burst through the fin, scattering bits of shadow.

Vengeous reached out with the darkness at his fingertips, wrapped them around a car. He stepped back and thrust his arms out and the car lifted into the air. China threw herself to one side. The car missed her by centimetres.

She moved forward, using the symbols on her body to hurl one attack after another, but Vengeous batted them all aside. Not once, but twice did he send a sneaky tendril of shadow to sweep her feet from under her, and each time she fell, he laughed. When he was close enough, Vengeous sent a slab of solid darkness smashing into her jaw. He grinned. He used the shadows to hit her again, and again she stumbled. The armour shifted, changed according to Vengeous's needs and intentions.

China's hair was a mess. Her make-up was smeared with blood and grime and her clothes were torn and dirty. Vengeous grabbed her and threw her, face first, into a pillar. She hit it and spun, dropping to the ground painfully.

Vengeous walked over, hunkered down, prodded China with

a finger. Her eyes flickered open, in time to see Zephyr rise up behind the Baron. The way she was holding her side, China knew the bodyguard's ribs were broken. But still she didn't give up. China allowed herself to admire her determination, as foolhardy as it was.

Zephyr charged at Vengeous, but the shadows turned sharp, and even as she was leaping they pierced her body from all sides.

She came to a sudden stop, suspended in the air by these shards of darkness that emanated from Vengeous' armour. China watched her try to take a breath, but her lungs were punctured, sliced through. Zephyr gagged on her own blood.

"No challenge," the Baron said. "No challenge at all."

The darkness convulsed and Zephyr's body tore apart.

33

THE CALM BEFORE THE STORM

Up on the dance floor, a portly man was throwing his wife around with gay abandon, twirling and twisting and having a ball, while his wife spent her time looking terrified. When she finally broke free she slapped his arm and went to storm off, but dizziness overtook her and she wobbled sideways and collided with another dancer, and it was like a glorious domino effect in slow motion, with extra squealing.

Something for Valkyrie to grin at, at least.

The band announced, in a loud muffle that was completely

distorted by the feedback on the microphone, that they were going to slow things down now. The band consisted of two gents in black slacks and blue sparkly jackets. One of them played saxophone, and he wasn't much good, and the other wore sunglasses and sang and played keyboard, and he didn't do any of those particularly well. That is to say, he didn't sing or play the keyboard particularly well – he wore sunglasses as competently as anyone who chose to wear sunglasses at night. None of this seemed to matter to a room full of drunken people who would dance to anything as long as they thought they recognised the tune.

There was a doorway leading to another room, presumably where all the tables and chairs were stored between functions. It was dark in here and Valkyrie didn't turn on the light. She put her coat on the remaining table and took a long box from its pocket. She laid the box next to the coat and opened it. She had asked Skulduggery to stop by Gordon's house on the way back. She'd told him there was something she had to pick up, and he hadn't inquired as to what that may have been. She was glad he hadn't asked. The Echo Stone glowed and Echo-Gordon faded up.

"Are we here?" he whispered excitedly.

"Be careful now," Valkyrie warned. "If anyone sees you..."

"I know, I know," Echo-Gordon said, inching towards the door. He peeked out. "Look at them all. It's been years since I've seen these people. I don't even know half of them." She stood beside him. He pointed.

"There's your mum. My, she looks beautiful. Will you tell her that?"

"Sure."

"And there's Fergus. And there's your dad. Oh, and Beryl. What's she doing? Her face looks strained. Is she having a stroke?"

"I think she's smiling."

He shook his head sadly. "Not a good look for her. And good God, where is that music coming from?" He moved slightly so he could see the stage and the two morons in blue. "Well, that's just... terrible. And there are actually people dancing? Horrific. I wouldn't be caught dead up there." He paused, thought about what he'd said and grinned.

Valkyrie moved to the window and glanced out, but it was too dark to see anything.

"Scared?" Echo-Gordon asked, his tone a little softer now.

She shrugged. "I don't like being bait for a vampire."

"There's a shocking piece of news," he said, smiling. "If you were to change your mind, Skulduggery would understand, you know. There's no shame in fear." She nodded, but didn't answer.

"I know him," Echo-Gordon continued. "He doesn't want to see you hurt, and I *certainly* don't want to see you hurt. Stephanie, or Valkyrie, or whatever name you go by. You are still my favourite niece and I am still your wise uncle."

She smiled. "You're wise?"

He pretended to be insulted. "So says the girl who's acting as vampire bait."

"Point taken."

She saw movement outside the door, someone coming in. She pointed and Echo-Gordon panicked, looked around for somewhere to hide and darted behind the door.

Carol and Crystal barged in, knocking the door open wider. It swung all the way until it was flat against the wall, having passed through Echo-Gordon completely. He now stood there in plain view, with his eyes closed. If Carol and Crystal were to look around, they'd see their dead uncle standing right behind them.

"Oh," Carol said, looking at Valkyrie. "It's you."

"Yes," Valkyrie said stiffly. "It is."

"Here with all your friends, are you?" Crystal said and the twins laughed.

Behind them, Echo-Gordon opened one eye, realised he

wasn't hiding behind the door any more and started to panic again.

"I'm just getting a break from everyone," Valkyrie said. "What brings you two in here?"

Echo-Gordon got on his hands and knees and crawled under the table, passing through the long tablecloth without disturbing it.

Carol regarded Valkyrie with half-closed eyelids, in what was presumably meant to indicate scorn. "We're looking for somewhere to light up," she said, producing the cigarette from her frightfully gaudy purse.

"You smoke?" Crystal asked.

"No," Valkyrie said. "Never really saw the point."

"Typical," Carol muttered and Crystal made a show of trying not to laugh. "We're going somewhere else then. Oh, and you better not tell on us, all right? You better keep your mouth shut."

"You got it."

The twins looked at each other triumphantly and walked out without another word.

Echo-Gordon stood up through the table and stepped out of it. "Ah, the twins. I'll never forget the day they were born," and his smile dipped as he added, "no matter how hard I try..." He noticed Valkyrie looking out of the window again.

He spoke kindly. "Fear is a good thing, you know."

"It doesn't feel good."

"But it keeps you alive. Bravery, after all, isn't the *absence* of fear. Bravery is the acknowledgement and the *conquering* of fear."

She smiled. "I think I read that on the back of a cornflakes packet."

Echo-Gordon nodded. "Understandable. That's where I get all my wisdom."

Valkyrie left the window, looked out of the door at her relations as they laughed and talked and drank and danced.

"I *am* scared," she said. "I'm scared of being hurt and I'm scared of dying. But mostly I'm scared of letting down my parents. Other kids my age, I can see it, they're embarrassed by their folks. Maybe the mother won't stop fussing or the father thinks he's funny when he's not. But I love my parents because they're good people. If we fail in this, if we don't stop Vengeous and the Grotesquery, then my parents—" and suddenly, unexpectedly, her voice cracked, "—will die."

The image of her uncle looked at her and didn't say anything.

"I can't let that happen," she said.

Echo-Gordon looked at her and she saw it all in his eyes, and he didn't need to say anything. He just nodded and murmured, "Well, all right then."

He looked back at the party, his broad smile returning, and he nodded. "It's time to put me back in the box, I'm afraid. You have things to do, don't you?"

"Yes, I do." She picked up the stone, placed it in the box.

"Thank you for this," Echo-Gordon said. "It was nice being around the family again. Reminds me just how much I don't miss them." Valkyrie laughed and closed the box.

"Be careful," he said and faded away.

She walked out to the function room. She saw her father talking with Fergus and another man. Her mother was sitting at a table, pretending to be asleep. Beryl stood alone, looking around like a startled heron. She spied someone she hadn't gossiped with and descended with alarming zeal. Carol and Crystal entered from another room. Carol was looking a little green and Crystal was red-faced with a coughing fit.

Valkyrie stepped through the glass doors, on to the small balcony, felt the fresh breeze and looked out over the dark golf course. Beyond the course were the dunes, and the beach, and the sea. Both hands resting on the balcony railing, Valkyrie took a deep, calming breath.

Something moved over the dark golf course. She blinked.

For a moment it had looked like a person, running and keeping low, but now there was no one there. Were this any other night, she might have been inclined to believe it was merely her mind playing tricks on her. But this wasn't any other night.

The vampire was coming.

34

UNFINISHED BUSINESS

Tanith sat in the Bentley and tried not to fidget. Her body wasn't used to sitting still and not doing anything. Skulduggery, sitting beside her, was a model of stillness and everlasting patience. She tried to relax, but every so often a shot of adrenaline would pump through her and her right leg would kick out involuntarily. It was very embarrassing.

They were parked on a slight bluff overlooking the putting green. From here they could see the golf clubhouse, but they were far enough away so that Dusk wouldn't recognise the car.

Once they saw anything suspicious, the Bentley would be able to speed down the narrow road and they'd be able to intercept the vampire before he even got *close* to the reunion. It was a good plan.

The moon was full and bright. Tanith checked her watch. The lunar eclipse was three hours away. Plenty of time to get what they needed to get and do what they needed to do. Hopefully.

Something hit the Bentley and the car shook. Tanith grabbed her sword and leaped out. Skulduggery was out the other side, gun in hand. An old man stood in the silver moonlight and looked at them. Tanith had never seen him before. He didn't look like one of the Infected. She started to relax.

"You lied to me," the old man said.

"You wanted to see the girl die," Skulduggery responded. "You got what you wanted." He wasn't putting his gun away. Tanith knew who it was now. She gripped her sword tighter.

The Torment's eyes were fierce. "It was a sham. I knew there was something wrong, but I had been in that cellar for so long I couldn't see it. It was a reflection, wasn't it? You did something to a reflection, improved it, so that it would fool me. You cheated."

"We don't have time for this. We've got a busy night ahead of us."

"Oh, yes," the Torment said with a smile. "You do."

He opened his mouth wide and a jet of black hit Skulduggery and knocked him back. Tanith tried to move away, but he turned to her and the stream of darkness struck her with such force it knocked her off her feet. She rolled, keeping her mouth and eyes shut. She heard the black stuff, whatever it was, splatter on the ground beside her. It was inky and foul-smelling, but it had substance and when she pulled it off her it came away in thick strips.

She opened her eyes, saw the Torment wipe his mouth and grin. She pulled away another strip of black, threw it down, where it joined the pool. And then the pool started to shift. It moved in on itself, bunched up and thickened and grew legs.

Lots of legs.

"Oh, hell," Tanith muttered as the black stuff formed into spiders and the spiders clacked.

Skulduggery clicked his fingers and hurled twin fireballs into the lake of scuttling blackness that was filling the ground before them.

Tanith's sword was out, slicing at the spiders as they leaped for her. The blade cut through their hard bodies and dark green blood splashed on to her tunic. She felt something on her leg and swatted at it, and another spider leaped on to her shoulder. She slammed the sword hilt into it and stepped back, stood on another spider that squished underfoot and she slipped. The ground went away and she was falling then she hit something solid and flipped over as she tumbled down the bluff.

Tanith rolled through long grass, burst through it to level ground, realised she was on the putting green. A few spiders had joined her for the trip and she looked up as they leaped for her. She fell back again, flicking her wrist, the sword-blade catching the moonlight. One of the spiders squealed. Tanith grunted with satisfaction.

She looked up at the bluff, to where the Bentley was parked, saw a wave of darkness blacker than the night spilling over and coming down towards her. Hundreds of spider legs clacking against stone and earth.

"I've got this," Skulduggery said from beside her right shoulder. She hadn't even heard him join her.

He stepped forward and raised his arms, like he was welcoming the wave of eight-legged killers. Tanith watched his fingers curl slightly as he took hold of some invisible thing, and then, ever so slowly, he moved his hands clockwise. The long grass swayed in the sudden breeze.

And then Skulduggery struck, his fingers tightening, his hands moving over each other in wide circles, and the spiders were lifted high off the ground. They spun in a whirlwind, more and more of them getting sucked in.

Tanith's sword dealt with the few that the whirlwind didn't trap, and then she stepped back and marvelled at Skulduggery's control. His hands moved faster and faster, in tighter and tighter circles, and the whirlwind narrowed and became a mass of churning black bodies. Then Skulduggery twisted his hands and the whirlwind folded in on itself, and the night was filled with terrible cracking sounds. Green blood, thick and heavy, spurted into the warm air.

Skulduggery dropped his hands and the mangled bodies of the spiders fell to the putting green.

"We have to get to Valkyrie," he said, turning towards the golf club. Tanith went to follow him, but stopped when he stopped.

The Torment was standing between them and the clubhouse, and the inky substance filled his eyes and rolled down his cheeks like tears. It ran from his nostrils and his ears and his mouth, and spread over his skin, in through his hair and his beard, covering his clothes and spreading further. His arms jerked, his hands becoming talons, and his shoes split as his legs grew and the blackness covered him completely. He arched his back and lifted his arms, and two pairs of giant spider legs burst from his torso, flexed and touched down. His limbs kept growing, and his body lifted off the ground as a third eye opened on his forehead and blinked.

He stopped growing. His eight legs clacked and his mouth was open wide and showing teeth. The Torment-spider looked down at them and chattered.

35

ATTACK OF THE VAMPIRES

Valkyrie walked from the party and went downstairs, passed the trophy cabinet and the golfing Wall of Fame, and as she approached the doors she saw someone standing just outside. The doors were glass, with stainless-steel handles, and the car park outside was supposed to be lit up – but right now it was in darkness. The lights must have shorted out.

The man wasn't moving. She could see his outline but not his features.

Valkyrie slowed. She could feel his eyes on her. The closer

she got, the more she could see. There were others out there with him, just standing there in the gloom. She stopped, looked at him through the glass.

The man reached for the handle and rattled the door, but it wouldn't open. This time of night, it was controlled by the door release button on the inside. If someone wanted to get in, they had to talk into the intercom, get a member of staff to come down and open the door. Dusk pressed his face against the glass door and looked at her. She could see his scar quite clearly.

She heard a window break somewhere else on the ground floor and she turned and ran back to the stairs, taking them three at a time. She burst into the function room, assailed by the music and the noise. She looked around for some way to secure the door, but there was nothing. There was no lock. She could barricade it, but how long would that last? And what would she tell everyone in here? What would she tell her parents? And where the hell was Skulduggery?

There had to be a way. Valkyrie needed to stop people from getting hurt, and she needed to do so without alerting anyone to the fact that they were in danger. She opened the door a crack.

The lights were out and the Infected were climbing the stairs. It was her they wanted. They'd ignore everyone else if they thought they could get her.

Valkyrie slipped out, making sure the door closed behind her and the people on the stairs saw her then she bolted for the staircase, heading up to the top floor. Footsteps behind her, running, and she reached the top floor and glanced around quickly, getting her bearings.

Her adrenaline was pumping. The air shifted and she felt someone almost upon her. She ducked down and spun, bringing her right arm around in a wide arc to slam into the Infected man's back and send him flipping over her straightened leg. Another grabbed at her, and she batted the arms away and snapped her elbow into his chest. Her attacker crashed back. The others tumbled over him and snarled.

She sprinted down the corridor and barged into a dark room, almost tripping over a chair. The patio stood out against the darkness along the far wall and she made for that, the Infected right behind her. She pulled open the balcony doors and she ran out and leaped over the railing.

Wind rushed in her ears.

Directly below her, the Infected stood outside the glass doors, waiting for their Undead comrades to flush her out. They looked up in surprise, and saw her flying over them.

And then the tarmac-covered driveway was coming at her and she used both hands, trying to manipulate the air. She did her best to cushion her fall but this wasn't the easy drop from her bedroom window, this was much higher, it was at an angle, and she hadn't taken into account the sheer velocity...

She landed and cried out in pain as she rolled, knees and elbows striking the driveway, her hip scraping as she tumbled, her skin torn and bleeding. She knew she should have worn trousers.

The world rocked to a stop, balanced itself out and she opened her eyes. The Infected were standing looking at her, and Dusk strode through them, his eyes narrowed and his lips curled in hatred. And then Valkyrie was up and running.

She was sore, she felt blood on her legs and arms, but she ignored the pain. She looked back, saw the mass of Infected surge after her.

She passed the club gates and took the first road to her left, losing a shoe in the process and cursing herself for not wearing boots. It was narrow, and dark, with fields on one side and a row of back gardens on the other. She came to a junction. Up one way she could see headlights, so she turned down the other, leading the Infected away from any bystanders. She darted in off the road, running behind the Pizza Palace and the video store, realising her mistake when she heard the voices around the next corner. The pub had a back door that smokers used.

She veered off to her right, ran for the garden wall and leaped over it. She stayed low, and wondered for a moment if she'd managed to lose the Infected so easily. Dusk dropped on to her from above and she cried out. He sent her reeling.

"I'm not following the rules any more," he said. She looked at him, saw him shaking. He took a syringe from his coat and let it drop. "No more rules. No more serum. This time, there'll be nothing to stop me tearing you limb from limb." He grunted as the pain hit.

"I'm sorry I cut you," Valkyrie tried, backing away.

"Too late. You can run if you want. Adrenaline makes the blood taste sweeter." He smiled and she saw the fangs start to protrude through his gums.

He brought his hands to his shirt, and then, like Superman, he ripped the shirt open. Unlike Superman, however, he took his flesh with it, revealing the chalk-white skin of the creature underneath.

Valkyrie darted towards him and his eyes widened in surprise. She dived, snatched the syringe from the ground and plunged it into his leg.

Dusk roared, kicked her on to her back, his transformation interrupted. He tried to rip off the rest of his humanity, but his human skin tore at the neck. This wasn't the smooth shucking she'd seen the previous night. This was messy and painful.

Valkyrie scrambled up. The Infected had heard Dusk's anguished cries, and they were closing in.

36

GIANT SPIDER MADNESS

The Edgley family reunion was taking up the main function hall, at the front of the building, leaving the rear of the golf club in darkness. That was probably a good thing, Tanith reflected, as she watched Skulduggery fly backwards through the air.

The Torment-spider turned to her and she dodged a slash from one of his talons. She turned and ran, but he was much faster. Tanith jumped for the side of the building and ran upwards, a ploy that had got her out of a lot of trouble in the past, but then, she had never faced a giant spider before.

His talons clacked as he followed her up, chattering as he came. She stepped over the ledge, on to the rooftop, then turned and waited for him to follow. The spider legs appeared over the edge first, then the head and the torso, and Tanith lunged. Her sword flashed, but hit one of the armour plates that protected the Torment-spider's underside. His leg swept in and crashed against her, and Tanith lost the blade, hit the rooftop and rolled. She reached for her sword, but a talon stepped on it.

Tanith backed away. The Torment-spider chattered once more then went quiet. His three eyes, devoid of any recognisable human trait, observed her. She knew he could strike and she'd never see it coming.

"Excuse me," she said as politely as she could, "I believe you're standing on my sword." The Torment-spider didn't answer. She briefly wondered if he *could* answer, if there was any kind of rational being left in there.

"I don't think this is entirely fair," she continued. "You're angry with Skulduggery because he didn't kill Valkyrie, but you and me, we've never even met. I mean, you have no *reason* to attack me. You don't even *know* me. If you got to know me, if you took the time, I'm sure you'd really like me. I'm a likeable girl. Everyone says so." The Torment-spider chattered in a short burst.

"Did you know, and this is a fact here, did you know that most spiders are really, really ugly? It's true. The women spiders have a really hard time of it. I saw it in a documentary. Why do you think the black widow kills the guys she mates with? Shame, that's why. I'm not saying *you're* ugly. Who am I to judge? I've only got two legs, right?" The Torment-spider advanced. Tanith took another step back.

"I didn't mean to insult you. Did I insult you? I didn't mean to. I'm sure, for a giant spider person, you're quite the catch. And, hey, looks aren't everything, yeah? You know what us girls really go for? A sense of humour. And you look like a guy who is ready to laugh. Am I right?" The Torment-spider chattered angrily.

"I thought so. So now that we've had this little talk, what do you say we stop beating around the bush, and you come and have a go?"

The Torment-spider went quiet again and Tanith smiled up at him.

"If you think you're hard enough."

A moment passed then the Torment-spider reared up, ready to strike, and Tanith sprinted towards him, dived between the legs that were still supporting his weight and snatched up her sword.

The giant spider scuttled around and Tanith slashed

upwards. Her sword raked across the armour until it found the space between the plates. The Torment-spider squealed and thrashed, and Tanith threw herself out from under him to avoid being crushed.

She felt a gust of wind and Skulduggery dropped on to the rooftop. He splayed his hands and the air pulsed, catching the Torment-spider on its underside and flipping him over. He landed on his back, his eight legs kicking and flailing. Tanith leaped in, landed on the spider's belly and stuck the tip of her blade in between the armour plates.

The Torment-spider stopped flailing instantly.

"Good boy," Tanith said.

Skulduggery walked around so he could see the Torment-spider's eyes. "I'm assuming, because you know when to stop struggling, that you're still capable of logical thought, so I'm only going to say this once. You either get in line or you get out of our way. We have a job to do tonight, and right now my partner is in danger and I have run out of patience. So what do you want to do – continue fighting or make a deal?"

For a second, Tanith didn't think Skulduggery would get an answer, but then that mouth opened and an old man's voice croaked from between those teeth.

"I'm listening."

37

TOOTH AND CLAW

Valkyrie sprinted for the next wall and leaped over it, into the garden. There was a higher wall ahead and she ran and snapped her hands out. The air rippled and she was propelled upwards, grabbing the top of the wall and hauling herself over. When she landed the garden was dark, the wall casting a deep shadow over the grass. She ran up by the side of the house and beyond.

She was on a narrow road now and turned left, her lungs burning with a fierceness she liked, the kind of fierceness she felt when she was swimming. She knew she could run forever with that fire inside her. She veered off on to an even narrower road, more like a lane than anything else. She could hear them behind her. The pack of Infected was more dispersed now, but the faster ones were steadily gaining. She passed her house.

The pier was just ahead and Valkyrie sprinted for it. The sea was rough tonight, she could hear its strength, and she knew this wasn't going to be easy, but she didn't have a choice. They were right behind her.

Did they know? Had Dusk told them about their vulnerability to salt water? A thought flashed into her mind. These weren't full vampires, they were only Infected. Would the water still have the fatal affect? She didn't have time to second-guess herself. This was the only plan she had and the only chance she had left.

Valkyrie ran to the edge of the pier and jumped, just like she had done on countless occasions when she was a child. She hit the water and it clutched at her and swallowed her completely. She kicked and shot back to the surface. She lost her other shoe. It was too dark for the Infected to see what was below them and they had no idea there was only one safe way to make that jump. Valkyrie heard sudden cries of pain mixed with sickening thuds as they landed, just like J. J. Pearl, smashing their bones on the rocks.

She'd never swum here at this time of night, however, and the waters were strong and strange to her. They pulled and pushed and threatened to drag her down, or away from the shore, but she fought them. More of the Infected came, splashing into the water all around her, and immediately they began to panic. She heard their cries, choked off by their rapidly constricting windpipes. One of them reached out in desperation, grabbing her and pulling her down.

Valkyrie's head went under and she twisted, prying the fingers from her arm and kicking the Infected person away from her. She lost sight of him in the cold blackness, but she was too far down and the water was too rough. She was going to drown.

An image flashed into her mind – the previous year, Skulduggery rising from the sea and walking across its surface. Her training. She needed to use her training. Skulduggery had taught her what she needed to know. She just had to calm down and focus.

Ignoring the pain in her lungs, Valkyrie brought her hands in close. She felt the current that was trying to drag her downwards, felt its strength and speed, but stopped fighting and let it take her, surrendering herself until she was a part of it. She hooked her fingers and for the first time became aware of the water as a mass of conflicting and opposing forces. She could feel these forces beneath her, above her and around her. She hooked into them and then she turned.

The current twisted behind her and now she was swimming, buffeted by the water. She passed the Infected as they flailed and she broke the surface, taking a deep breath. She thrust her arms out and caught the current again, went under, and for a terrible second thought she had misjudged this whole thing, but she regained her control, and guided the current as best she could towards the beach. She let go and the water around her turned gentle – relatively gentle – and she swam on until she could stand.

Gulping in lungfuls of air, Valkyrie looked back at the pier. It was hard to see because of the lights that faced her making everything before her one solid black mass. She dragged herself out of the sea. The tide was in so there wasn't much beach for her to stagger on to, but she managed to stumble on to the shore that remained. And then something came out of the shadows and struck her and she hit the sand.

She struggled and twisted, but someone else was there and a fist hit her face. The shape of a man, standing above her, crouching slightly.

Dusk.

The human flesh he had tried to remove still clung in places to his vampire skin, and it looked raw and red and painful. His right hand was tipped with talons, but his left was human and still had a watch strapped to its wrist. His face was the face of a man, a handsome man who now had a scar, but the fangs of a vampire had split his gums and torn his lips.

Valkyrie flexed her fingers, waited until her head was clear. Dusk wasn't moving. She thrust her hand out and now he did move, grabbing her wrist before she had the chance to push at the air. He hauled her up and spun her around, grabbed her from behind and exposed her throat. Valkyrie froze.

The vampire's laugh was guttural. "I'm not going to kill you. I'm going to turn you. You will be like I am."

She tried to speak, tried to say something, but her words had been taken from her. She felt his breath on her skin.

"Do you know who you're going to kill first, Cain?" he asked. "Do you know who you are going to rip apart, because the bloodlust will be the only thing that matters? Your parents."

"No," she breathed.

"For what you've done to me, for the scar you've inflicted and the pain you're causing me right *now*, I'm going to make sure that when the time comes, you'll be *begging* me to let you kill your own parents."

And then a voice. "Dusk."

The vampire turned and there was someone there, in the dark, leaping at them. Valkyrie felt an impact and fell forward. She heard the vampire hit the sand and snarl. She looked back as the two figures clashed.

The one who had saved her – she had thought it was Skulduggery, but saw now that it was not – was fast, as fast as Dusk. He wore a ragged old suit and a battered top hat.

Dusk swiped and the figure in the top hat ducked, his own fingernails raking across the vampire's belly, drawing blood. Dusk roared in anger and the figure flipped, driving a foot into his face. Dusk dropped back then suddenly lunged. He caught the newcomer in mid-leap, taking them both into the surf. Claws slashed and the man in the top hat cried out.

Valkyrie grabbed a stone, flat but thick and heavy. Dusk was on his feet, above the newcomer, and Valkyrie ran at him, slamming the stone on to the back of his head. Dusk dropped slightly and the newcomer kicked up, catching Dusk full in the face.

Valkyrie felt the air between them and she splayed both of her hands, hitting Dusk in the back and taking him off his feet. He splashed into the waves. The newcomer was on his feet, and suddenly sprang straight up, disappearing into the dark.

Dusk was rising out of the water, his human face contorted

with hatred. His mouth, which had been tightly closed against the salt water, opened in a snarl. He couldn't see the man in the top hat, but he glared at Valkyrie and moved towards her. At the last moment he looked up, in time to see the newcomer dropping down on top of him. The newcomer's heels slammed into Dusk's upturned face and the vampire crumpled into the wet sand.

Valkyrie watched the man in the top hat examine his wounds and mutter.

"Is he dead?" she asked.

"Naw," he answered, a little out of breath. "Just sleepin'." He spoke with a thick London accent. "Savin' people ain't normally my thing, but I figure since he was after you, you've got somethin' to do with Vengeous, am I right?"

"Well... I'm trying to stop him, yes."

"Good enough. See, they roped me into doin' 'em a favour. Didn't appreciate that. So here I am, doin' *you* a favour. That big guy, the ugly one? They're keepin' him at Clearwater Hospital. Don't know what you can do with that information, but if it messes up Sanguine's plans then I'm happy." He doffed his hat to her and started to walk off. She frowned.

"You're Springheeled Jack."

He stopped and turned. "Yes, I am, love."

"You're a bad guy."

His smile was unpleasant. "Right again."

She stepped back. "You're meant to be in prison. Tanith put you there."

Jack frowned. "You know Tanith Low?"

"Of course."

"She's... she's close?"

"She's somewhere around here, yes. She's with Skulduggery."

"Oh, bloody 'ell," Jack said, looking around nervously. "Oh, that's not good. 'Ave I just helped 'em?"

"I'm afraid you have."

"Oh, for... oh, for 'eaven's sake. Well that's just... That's just typical, that is. Don't tell either of 'em I was here, right? I saved your neck. Literally, your neck I saved. Promise me."

"Are you going to leave the country?"

"I'm leavin' now."

"Then I'll tell them tomorrow. If any of us are still alive."

"You're a right lady, you are. G'night now. And good luck."

And with a leap and a bound, Springheeled Jack was gone.

38

THOSE ABOUT TO DIE...

The earth's shadow was starting to creep across the face of the full moon. The convoy stopped on a quiet road. Engines were cut and headlights snapped off. The Cleavers jumped from the back of the trucks, making not one sound as they lined up and waited for instructions.

Valkyrie swung her leg off Tanith's bike and took off the helmet. She was nervous. Her palms were sweating and her teeth wouldn't stop chattering.

"Feeling OK?" Tanith asked, keeping her voice low.

"I'm good," Valkyrie lied. "I'm grand. We're just, you know, we're about to fight a *god*, like."

"Part of a god," Tanith corrected. "Parts of other things too."

Valkyrie looked at her and shook her head in wonder. "You're actually looking forward to this, aren't you?"

"Hell, yeah. I mean, fighting a *god*, part of a god, hybrid god, whatever. As you say, this is big. This is *major*. I've fought all kinds over the years, but... a god. Assuming I survive this, where do I go from here? What would top fighting a god?"

"I don't know," Valkyrie said. "Fighting two gods?"

The Bentley pulled up and Skulduggery and Mr. Bliss got out. Skulduggery took off his coat and scarf and left them in the car. He and Bliss approached and the Cleavers stood to attention. Valkyrie had to fight down the irrational urge to salute.

"Billy-Ray Sanguine and the Grotesquery are in a derelict hospital just north of here," Bliss said, addressing them all. "The vampire known as Dusk is currently in our custody, but the whereabouts of Baron Vengeous are still unknown. We can assume that he is on his way. He wouldn't want to miss the return of the Faceless Ones."

"I want you all to know," Skulduggery said, "that we are the first line of defence. In fact, we're practically the *only* line of defence. If we fail, there won't be a whole lot anyone else will be able to do. What I'm trying to say is that failure at this point isn't really the smart move to make. We are *not* to fail, do I make myself absolutely clear? Failure is bad, it won't help us in the short term and certainly won't do us any favours in the long run, and I think I've lost track of this speech, and I'm not too sure where it's headed. But I know where it started and that's what you've got to keep in mind. Has anyone seen my hat?"

"You put it on the roof of the car when you were taking off your coat," Valkyrie said.

"Did I? I did, excellent."

"We will attack in two waves," Bliss said, steering the briefing back into the realms of relevance. "The first wave will consist of Tanith Low, Valkyrie Cain, Skulduggery Pleasant and myself. The second wave will be you Cleavers."

"We're seizing our chance *now*," Skulduggery said, "before Vengeous returns and we have a battle on two fronts. The first wave will weaken the Grotesquery. We're going to hit it with everything we've got, and not give it any time to teleport away or to heal. Once we know that it is damaged, we'll call in the second wave. Does anyone have any questions? No? No one? No questions? You sure?"

Bliss turned to him. "There do not seem to be any questions."

Skulduggery nodded. "They're a fine lot."

Bliss gestured and the Cleavers divided into groups, and Valkyrie and Skulduggery strode away.

"I used to be so good at that kind of thing," Skulduggery said quietly.

"Well, my morale is certainly boosted," Valkyrie informed him.

"Really?"

"God, no. That was *terrible.*"

Tanith and Bliss joined them and they stepped into the trees. Valkyrie moved as stealthily as she could, but the others were moving in complete silence. She glimpsed Cleavers all around, their grey uniforms mixing with the gloom and the darkness until they became mere hints of people.

They stopped just inside the treeline. Ahead of them, past an old metal fence, was the main hospital building. The black jeep was parked outside and Sanguine emerged from the hospital doors, holding a phone to his ear.

"OK," Sanguine said, his voice clear in the quiet night, "I can hear you better now, go ahead."

As Sanguine listened to whatever was being said on the

other end of the phone, Valkyrie glanced at her companions, suddenly realising that Skulduggery was no longer with them. She looked back at Sanguine.

"So that's it then?" he was saying. "I just leave? Naw, that ugly critter is back there, standin' around and not doin' a whole lot."

Valkyrie narrowed her eyes, squinting into the darkness behind Sanguine. She saw something move. Skulduggery.

Sanguine continued talking, totally unaware of the Skeleton Detective sneaking up behind him. "I'm pretty sure the vampire's taken care of, we don't have to worry about him any more. And what about our friend the Baron?"

Valkyrie frowned. *Who* was Sanguine talking to?

"You sure?" he was saying. "You don't want me to...? No, no, I ain't questionin' you, I just... Yeah, I know who's payin' my salary. Hey, no skin off my chin, if that's the way you want it. I'm walkin' away now." He put the phone in his pocket and smirked.

"Have a nice life, Baron," he said softly, then turned and walked straight into Skulduggery's fist.

He staggered and went for his knife, but Skulduggery chopped at his wrist and his fingers sprang open, sending the knife flying. He swung a punch and Skulduggery caught him and smacked his head off the jeep. Sanguine slumped to the ground. Skulduggery picked up the knife and flung it away, then motioned for the others to join him.

They broke from the treeline. The large gate had already been blasted open and they moved through it, up to Skulduggery. He had Sanguine's phone in his hand and he was checking through it.

"Whoever that was," he said, "their number is blocked."

"Sanguine's been taking orders from someone else the whole time," Tanith said. "The persons in power you were talking about earlier, the ones who got Guild on to the council, the ones who took away all our support. He's working for *them*."

"And Vengeous doesn't know about it," Valkyrie said.

Skulduggery put the phone away. "That's a mystery for tomorrow," he said. "Providing there *is* a tomorrow."

He turned to Bliss and nodded. Bliss took a little run and then leaped, caught the edge of the roof and effortlessly pulled himself up. Tanith adjusted her centre of gravity and walked up the wall after him. Skulduggery held Valkyrie around the waist and the air shimmered as they shot upwards, gently touching down on the roof. Keeping very quiet, they crossed the rooftop.

There were four big, sturdy old buildings surrounding a large concrete courtyard. The courtyard had a small island of green where a spindly tree tried to grow.

The Grotesquery stood in the exact centre, unmoving. It was wearing a garment of sorts, made of thick, black leather that hung from its waist and gathered on the ground behind it.

Out here in the moonlight, the Grotesquery seemed even more wrong. Nothing this horrible should be allowed to exist on a night so beautiful. Its right arm glistened and the sac on its left wrist bulged with yellow acid. The silver light displayed its cracked and splintered ribcage in sickening detail, and black blood soaked the bandages covering its face.

Valkyrie and her companions crouched. The Cleavers took up positions all the way along the rooftop, surrounding the courtyard. Valkyrie's stomach churned. Her fingertips tingled. She needed to do something and soon. The anticipation, the excitement and the dread and the fear, were overpowering. Their first encounter with the Grotesquery had not ended well, but there were more of them now. They were stronger – but it was stronger too. She wondered if they were strong enough to kill it.

It was like Skulduggery was reading her mind. "This thing," he said softly, "the part of it that is a Faceless One, it died once. It can do so again." She nodded, but didn't speak. She didn't trust her voice.

Skulduggery looked over at Mr Bliss and he nodded, and then Mr Bliss stood, stepped off the edge of the roof and dropped all the way to the ground. Tanith ran down the side of the building, sliding the sword from its scabbard. Skulduggery and Valkyrie jumped, displacing the air beneath them to ease their descent. Valkyrie landed heavily, but managed not to stumble.

"I thought we were going to use the element of surprise," she said as they strode towards their target.

"We never had it," Skulduggery said calmly. "It knew we were here all along. It just doesn't care."

All four of them moved apart, coming at the Grotesquery from different angles.

Bliss didn't waste time with words, threats, vows or demands. He just walked right up to it and threw a punch. Valkyrie felt the concussion of the blow as it landed. The Grotesquery didn't even stagger. Instead it looked at Bliss through its filthy bandages, drew back its right fist and hit him. Bliss was launched backwards and crashed through the wall of the old building.

Skulduggery moved in and Tanith leaped, her sword flashing in the moonlight. The Grotesquery's right arm unravelled and its talons sliced towards Skulduggery. They cut his jacket then wrapped around him. He was picked up and swung towards Tanith. She twisted in mid-air and sprang off Skulduggery's shoulder, flipping over the Grotesquery's head. Skulduggery broke free and the Grotesquery reformed its arm and swung its massive fist. Skulduggery drew in the air to block it and Tanith slashed at the arm, which healed instantly.

Valkyrie clicked her fingers, turned the sparks to fireballs and threw them. The first missed, but the second exploded against the Grotesquery's side. Its stinger darted and Tanith ducked then lunged, her sword piercing its chest, but the Grotesquery smashed down on her arm and the bone snapped. Tanith cried out and was shoved away. The Grotesquery removed the sword and dropped it, and the wound healed.

Bliss extricated himself from the hole he had made in the side of the building. He dusted himself off, like being thrown through a wall was a mere minor inconvenience, but the first step he took was unsteady. He'd been hurt.

Skulduggery reached into his jacket, pulled out his revolver. Then he reached in with the other hand, to the other side, and pulled out an identical revolver. He thumbed back both hammers and fired. Twelve shots, hitting the Grotesquery with unerring accuracy, and then he dropped the guns and ran forward. Valkyrie saw something in his hand, a metal cylinder attached to a metal spike.

Skulduggery jumped, stabbing the spike into the area he'd been shooting. The Grotesquery took hold of him and flung him back, but the cylinder had a red light on top and it was flashing. The explosion sent Valkyrie to her knees, her ears ringing, spots dancing before her eyes. She looked back, hopeful, but the Grotesquery was standing there as if nothing had happened. A wound on its arm opened for a split second, enough for a drop of black blood to leak out, but then it closed. Was it weakening?

Tanith gathered her strength and sprang, but the Grotesquery batted her away. Her body twisted as she fell and when she hit the ground, she tried to get up again but couldn't.

The Grotesquery raised its left arm and Valkyrie dived. She held both hands out towards Tanith, felt the spaces between them, felt how they linked together, and when the stinger darted out she pushed and the air rippled. Tanith was sent skidding along the ground and the stinger missed. Valkyrie looked up, realising that she was now the Grotesquery's main focus of attention.

"The Cleavers," Valkyrie whispered. "Somebody signal the Cleavers..."

And then Bliss was there, standing between Valkyrie and the approaching Grotesquery. Instead of striking, Bliss pressed both hands to its chest and started to push. The creature kept walking. Bliss locked his body, but he was being driven slowly back. Valkyrie could hear him straining. Not even Bliss's legendary strength could stop it.

And then, amazingly, it faltered. Bliss gave another heave and the Grotesquery was actually forced to take a step back.

Tanith made herself get up on one knee and finally stand. The Grotesquery had stopped walking altogether and now seemed to be examining Bliss. It held up its left hand close to him.

"Tanith?" Bliss said through gritted teeth. His face was drenched with sweat. "If you wouldn't mind..."

Tanith looked quickly to Valkyrie. "Sword."

Valkyrie reached out, felt the air around them, used the air to close around the fallen sword and then she twisted her wrist and the sword flew from the ground into Tanith's left hand. Tanith was already swinging when the stinger darted, her blade intercepting it before it could reach Bliss.

The tip of the stinger fell to the ground. Valkyrie and Tanith stared down at it.

"I hurt it," Tanith said in disbelief.

"About time," Bliss muttered, drew back his right hand and let loose with an almighty punch that sent the Grotesquery reeling.

"Cleavers!" Bliss roared. "Attack!"

39

FACING VENGEOUS

The Grotesquery flailed and struck out and three Cleavers were flung away, but there were more to take their place.

Skulduggery and Valkyrie stood together. Tanith cradled her broken arm. Bliss had taken a step back to catch his breath. They watched the Cleavers attack and it was a sight to behold. They moved as a perfect team, silently and without the need for orders. They knew what they had to do, and they backed each other up, compensated for injuries, reinforced and provided distraction. The Grotesquery was not granted a single moment to recover.

Valkyrie saw the growth on its left wrist contract, spitting acid. It caught a Cleaver full in the chest and he went down, trying to tear his coat off, but dying before he was able. The Grotesquery's right arm unravelled again, and all five talons plunged into another Cleaver and then tore out. The Cleaver was thrown through the air like a rag doll.

A slice across the Grotesquery's tendon made it stagger. Another slice, across its back, splattered the ground with black blood. It lashed out wildly, struck nothing but air and stumbled to one knee. The Cleavers swarmed over it as it tried to heal itself.

And just when things were going right, everything went wrong. There came a voice from behind them – "*Heathens!*" – and they looked around. Baron Vengeous had returned.

He stood on the same rooftop they themselves had stood on, and the shadows whipped around him angrily. His armour shifted, became sharp, and when he walked forward, the shadows snaked over the edge and down to the ground. He strode on darkness and the darkness lowered him to the courtyard.

The Cleavers broke off their attack. The Grotesquery was on its knees. Its body was trying to mend the wounds it had suffered. It didn't get up.

"How dare you!" Vengeous thundered as he stalked towards them. "How dare you attack a *living god!*"

"It's not a god," Skulduggery said. "And it won't be living for much longer."

Valkyrie looked closer at the shadows around Vengeous. There seemed to be a clump of darkness trailing after him. Suddenly the darkness unwrapped and let its captive go and China Sorrows tumbled to the ground. Vengeous left her in his wake.

Bliss went to meet him. "You will go no further," he said.

"Then stop me," Vengeous snarled.

"That is my intention," Bliss said and punched.

Vengeous held up a hand, collecting shadows to form a barrier. Bliss hit the barrier and they all heard his knuckles break.

The armour shifted, reinforcing Vengeous's fist, and he smiled as he delivered a punch of his own. The blow caught Bliss beneath the chin, lifting him and sending him hurtling back.

Skulduggery lifted his gun and fired, aiming for the head. The shadows became a cloud that covered Vengeous' face, soaking up the bullets and spitting them out again. When the gun clicked empty, the shadows settled.

"Well, that didn't work," Skulduggery muttered.

"Cleavers," Tanith said, gripping her sword, "we have a new target." She ran forward and the Cleavers sprang. Vengeous held his arm out straight.

"Oh, damn it," was all Skulduggery had time to say before a wave of darkness erupted from Vengeous's hand and slammed into Tanith and the Cleavers. Skulduggery grabbed Valkyrie and dragged her down, the darkness passing above them. She glimpsed everyone else slump to the ground, unconscious.

There was a moment of stillness and then Vengeous reached out his arm, and a streak of shadow wrapped around Skulduggery and pulled him closer. Valkyrie felt something tighten around her ankle and then she was skidding along the ground, into the middle of the courtyard. The shadow released her and she rolled to a stop beside Skulduggery. Vengeous looked down at them.

"I am almost impressed. You actually managed to hurt the Grotesquery. I didn't think you'd be capable of such a feat."

"We're full of surprises," Skulduggery said and sprang. A sliver of shadows smacked him down. He groaned and rolled over. "That obviously wasn't one of them."

"None of you understands yet, do you?" Vengeous said. "You are no longer a threat. I am the most powerful sorcerer on this planet. When the Faceless Ones return, I will rule by their side. What hope do you have against me?"

Skulduggery stood and Valkyrie got to her feet by his side.

"Baron Vengeous," Skulduggery said, "I'm placing you under arrest."

Vengeous laughed. Valkyrie looked beyond him, at China, who was moving slightly. Her white trousers were slashed and torn, and her waistcoat was dirty and bloodied.

"Here we are at the end," Vengeous said, "and I'm wondering, have you, unlike China, learned your lesson? Are you ready to accept that the world belongs to the Faceless Ones? Are you ready to praise their name?"

"They're not here yet, Baron," Skulduggery said.

"But they're coming. You must realise that. The Grotesquery will call them and they will know the way back. And correct me if I'm wrong, but you seem to be out of reinforcements."

"Who says we need them?" Skulduggery asked and snapped his hand out. The air rippled and Vengeous stepped aside and flung back his arm. A wave of blackness hit Skulduggery and took him off his feet.

Valkyrie ducked under a return swipe and scooped up two small pieces of rubble. She brought her hands together, acting on pure instinct, and felt the air around them and *pushed*, and the pieces of rubble shot at Vengeous like bullets. He sent shadows to intercept them and they exploded in dry clouds of dust. He pointed at Valkyrie and the shadow slammed into her.

"So, so easy," he laughed.

The shadows were on her again, wrapping around her, picking her up and moving her back, slamming her against the wall. She felt the cold darkness seep through her clothes and tried to move, but couldn't.

Skulduggery hit the wall beside her, the shadows pinning him. "You're nothing without that armour," he said.

Vengeous smiled at his prisoners as he walked over. "Is this the part where you goad me? Where you insult my honour? This armour is a weapon, abomination. I'm hardly going to abandon my weapon right before the killing stroke, just so I can give my opponent a sporting chance. If my enemy is weakened then my enemy will be destroyed. Such is the way of the dark gods."

"Please don't kill me!" Valkyrie blurted.

"Valkyrie," Skulduggery said. "Don't worry, I'll get us out of this."

"He won't get you out of anything," Vengeous said. "You seem to have chosen the wrong side, my dear."

"Then I'll *change* sides!"

Vengeous smiled, amused. "Do you hear that, abomination?

Faced with the reality of the situation, your protégé has abandoned you."

Skulduggery shook his head. "Valkyrie, listen to me..."

"What?" Valkyrie snapped. "Are you going to tell me it'll be all right? Are you going to tell me to be brave? He's going to kill us! Baron, please, I don't want to die! Let me prove myself! Let me kill him for you!"

"You'd do that?" Vengeous asked. "Kill your mentor? Murder him in cold blood?"

"It's not murder if he's already dead."

Vengeous considered the proposal. "I suppose there is a certain poetry to it. Very well, Miss Cain. You get to be the one to kill him."

The shadows withdrew and Valkyrie dropped to the ground. She wiped her eyes with her sleeve and looked at Skulduggery, who was now hanging there quite limply.

"How do you intend to kill him?" Vengeous asked.

"I think I know how," she answered. "Something he said a while ago. Something about his weakness."

Vengeous motioned for her to come forward and she moved unsteadily to his side. She faced Skulduggery and raised her arms. "I'm sorry," she said.

Valkyrie closed her eyes, drew her hands into claws and

pulled her arms in close to her body, making the air shimmer around her, and then she twisted to Vengeous, but he smacked her arms away and grabbed her by the throat and lifted her off her feet.

"Did you really think I was that naïve?" he laughed as she kicked at the armour. "Such a clumsy attempt. If this is the best the abomination has taught you, you really should have asked for a better teacher."

Her hands closed around his wrist and she lifted herself, easing the pressure off her throat for a moment. "You're a military man," she managed to say. "You should recognise a feint when you see it."

"Oh, is *that* what this is? You distracted me long enough to get into the perfect position, is that it?"

"Precisely," she answered. "And now comes the moment when I launch the attack and beat you down."

He laughed again. "Well, pardon the expression, Miss Cain – but you and what army?"

Valkyrie gave him a smile, took one hand away from his wrist and pointed over his shoulder.

"That one," she said. He looked around as China Sorrows stepped up behind him.

40

FIGHT TO THE DEATH

China's whole body was covered in swirling black tattoos. Vengeous threw Valkyrie down and she watched China dodge an attack, tapping matching tattoos on her legs. They glowed green beneath her torn trousers and now she was a blur, weaving her way past Vengeous's shadows.

He snarled in annoyance and lashed out, but she was too fast, and now she was in close. Some of the tattoos glowed red as she grabbed him and punched, and Vengeous was taken off his feet.

His shadows curled around him and let him down gently then they shot at China. She clapped her hands together and the tattoos on her palms touched and mingled and a yellow barrier went up. The shadows struck the barrier and China grunted, but the barrier held.

The shadows around Skulduggery started to fade, as Vengeous' attention was focused elsewhere. Skulduggery broke free and dropped to the ground. He moved to Valkyrie, grabbing her arm.

"We have to get out of here," he said urgently.

"But we can help—"

"We can't stop him, he's too powerful."

"We're just going to retreat?"

"We're not retreating, we're advancing in reverse. Stick with me and stay low."

They sprinted for the main hospital building. Valkyrie looked over at the battle, saw a trail of shadows sneak around behind China, attack the barrier from there. The barrier was weakening. China dropped to one knee, her hands still flat against each other.

Valkyrie held on to Skulduggery, the air rippled and they shot up to the rooftop.

"We can't just leave her!" Valkyrie said as they ran.

"Agreed," Skulduggery said. "But we can't beat him when he's wearing that armour, that much we know. We need to find a way to get that armour off."

"What? But the only way we could do that is by getting in close, and we can't get past those shadows!"

"Exactly. So we need to cheat."

They jumped down the other side, landing beside the jeep, and found what Skulduggery was looking for.

"Ah," Valkyrie said. "Clever."

"Naturally."

Valkyrie crept across the rooftop. The battle was over. Unconscious Cleavers lay all around, the Grotesquery was still trying to heal itself, and China was hurt and on her knees. Baron Vengeous was standing behind her, gazing at his armoured hands.

"I can see why someone would choose necromancy," Vengeous was saying. "It has its limitations of course, but for the sheer *thrill* of using it against one's enemies... It's hard to beat.

"I fought alongside Vile during the war. I never liked him. He was... different. He had secrets. But I knew he was powerful. I just never realised *how* powerful. Nothing compared to the

Faceless Ones obviously, but still... potent. And now, that power is mine."

"You're not..." China muttered.

"I'm sorry? I didn't quite catch that."

Valkyrie stayed low and kept moving, getting closer.

"You're not in his league," China said, finding the strength to speak. "Vile... was extraordinary... You just wear his clothes."

"I wield his power," Vengeous said. "I wield the power of necromancy."

"It isn't yours," China said, and she laughed and it sounded brittle and painful. "You're right. Vile *was* different. He could have used his power to... to change the world... but you, Baron? You wouldn't know where to begin."

The victorious smile had drifted from the Baron's face. He gathered darkness in his hands. "I should have killed you years ago," he said.

The darkness hit China and flipped her over and then Billy-Ray Sanguine erupted from the ground behind Vengeous with Skulduggery Pleasant clinging to his back and holding a gun to his head.

Skulduggery threw Sanguine away and dropped his gun, grabbing Vengeous in a chokehold before he could even turn. Valkyrie leaped off the roof and displaced the air beneath her as Sanguine straightened up. She landed and focused, splayed her hand and he shot back off his feet.

Vengeous twisted violently, but Skulduggery held on. Valkyrie heard a small click amid all the curses and and she saw the armour's chest-plate open and a mist of darkness burst forth.

Vengeous screamed in rage and tried to pull away, but Skulduggery had a good grip on the chest plate. He threw it to the ground and Vengeous stumbled forward. Darkness leaked from the armour and dissipated in the night air.

Vengeous extended a hand and the shadows whipped for Skulduggery, but they were frail and slight. Skulduggery broke them and moved in, hitting Vengeous in the sternum with the heel of his palm. Vengeous gasped and staggered, tried again, but the shadows missed Skulduggery entirely this time, and the detective went low and to the side, raking an elbow across Vengeous's ribs and then driving it back and down into his kidney. Vengeous's knees buckled and he hissed in pain.

Something moved in the corner of Valkyrie's eye and she turned just as Sanguine rammed into her. He took her off her feet and she hit the floor. He was standing right over her, reaching down, and she punched the side of his knee. It hurt her fist, but hurt him more, and she rolled and got up, but he grabbed her again, hands on her throat.

She punched him in the gut, in the jaw, but he shook it off and grinned, fingers tightening. She punched him square on the nose and he howled and she grabbed his little finger and wrenched. He howled again and let go. She booted him in the groin and he gasped and reached for her then doubled over as the pain hit.

Vengeous got Skulduggery in some kind of lock that would have torn the muscles and sinew of a man with muscles and sinew. Skulduggery wriggled out of it and went to work with his elbows, slamming them like bullets into Vengeous's face and body.

Sanguine moaned in pain and went to get up, and Valkyrie grabbed him from behind, pressing his own straight razor against his throat.

"So that's where it is," he said, trying to pull back from the blade, but Valkyrie held him tight.

"Don't even try to do your disappearing act here," she warned him. "The moment I see the ground start to crack, you're dead."

The laugh that escaped his lips was dry. "You can't kill me, darlin'. You're one of the good guys. That'd be murder."

She pressed the blade in deeper. "See if I care."

She looked around as Vengeous snatched up his cutlass. The

blade flashed as Skulduggery held up his right hand to protect himself, and it sliced through his upper arm. He cried out and fell back, his severed arm falling to the ground, still wrapped in its sleeve. Vengeous kicked and Skulduggery went down, and Vengeous stood over him, cutlass raised.

"Baron!" Valkyrie shouted. He looked over, cutlass frozen in mid-swing. "Put the sword down."

Vengeous laughed. "Or what? You'll cut Sanguine's throat? Go ahead."

"I'm not kidding. I'll do it."

"I believe you."

"I'll do anythin'," Sanguine pleaded. "I'll go away, I'll never come back, I'll never see you again, I swear."

Vengeous looked faintly disgusted. "Try dying with some dignity, you godless wretch."

"Shut up, old man!" Sanguine shouted.

Vengeous laughed. "Look up, girl. It's almost time."

Valkyrie looked up at the clear night, at the full moon. The Earth's shadow had almost covered it.

"Can you feel it?" Vengeous asked. "The world is about to change."

Valkyrie felt a hand close over her own and suddenly Sanguine was twisting and she went right over his shoulder, landing in a tumble, the straight razor gone from her grip. She turned, ready to defend herself, but Sanguine took a look at the situation and then looked back at her, folded the razor into his pocket and sank through the ground.

Vengeous smiled at her then looked down at Skulduggery. "The eclipse is almost upon us, abomination. The Faceless Ones are coming. Everything I have planned, everything I have dreamed of, is being realised. You have failed."

"Not yet I haven't," Skulduggery muttered.

"What are you going to do?" Vengeous mocked. "Have you a clever surprise in store for me, up your sleeve? Be careful now, you only have one left."

"Then for my next trick," Skulduggery said and then faltered. "Ah, sod it, I couldn't be bothered thinking up something smart to say. Valkyrie."

Valkyrie clicked her fingers and hurled a fireball. It struck Vengeous in the chest, and the clothes he wore under the armour were set alight. Vengeous cursed and used the shadows to douse the flames. The revolver skimmed across the ground into Skulduggery's left hand and he fired.

The cutlass fell. Blood started to trickle from Vengeous's burnt chest. Vengeous could only stare down into Skulduggery's empty eye-sockets.

"But... but this isn't how I'm supposed to die," he said weakly. "Not... like this. Not by your hand. You're... you're an abomination."

"I'm a lot of things," Skulduggery said and dropped his gun.

Vengeous staggered back. He saw Valkyrie, reached for her. There was no strength in his grip. She pushed him and he fell.

Vengeous crawled to the Grotesquery. "Tell them I'm sorry," he whispered. "I've failed them..."

The Grotesquery moved its hand so that it touched Vengeous's face. It looked almost tender, until the hand gripped and wrenched and the Baron's head snapped to one side. The Grotesquery let go and the body crumpled.

The Grotesquery struggled to its feet. The last of the moon's brightness slipped into shadow. The Grotesquery stood, and although it looked unsteady, it didn't fall.

Skulduggery tried to rise, but couldn't. He snapped his fingers but no spark came. "Fireball," he said to Valkyrie. His voice was strained, sounded weak. "Shoot a fireball into the sky. It's our last chance."

She frowned, not understanding the request, but obeying nonetheless. Her thumb pressed to her index finger and they slid off each other with a *click*. The friction made a spark, she caught the spark in the palm of her hand and then it was a flame. She poured her energy into it, made the flame bigger, dipped her shoulder for the wind up and then threw. The fireball went straight up into the night, burning brightest at its peak, and then faded to nothing. She looked back at Skulduggery.

"That should do it," he mumbled and let himself collapse.

"What do I do now?" she asked, but he didn't answer.

She picked up Tanith's sword and looked over at the Grotesquery.

"Hey," she said. It turned to her and her mouth went dry. Everyone else had fallen. She was on her own.

"I overestimated you," a voice said and Valkyrie turned. The Torment approached, stepping over the prone bodies of the Cleavers. "I overestimated all of you. I thought you'd be able to manage this on your own."

The fireball. It must have been a signal, calling upon the last piece of back-up they had. Valkyrie briefly wondered what Skulduggery had had to agree to in order to enlist the Torment's services. She was pretty sure it wasn't anything cheerful.

"Leave," the old man said. "I don't like being this close to you. Leave me to take care of this creature."

"I'm not going anywhere," Valkyrie said, her words scraping from her throat.

"Then stand aside," he snapped, "and allow me to clean up your mess."

"*My* mess?"

"This monstrosity would not be alive if it wasn't for you and the blood that is in your veins. Your very existence is a threat to every living thing on this world."

It was an argument she didn't have the time nor the inclination to win, so Valkyrie backed off. She watched as the inky liquid leaked from the old man's eyes and ears and nose and mouth. She watched his arms and legs turn black and grow long, and the spider legs burst through his already-ripped shirt. She watched an eye open in the middle of his forehead and his torso lift off the ground, and she watched the Torment-spider look down at the Grotesquery with a pitiless gaze.

"Hello, monster," he said and vomited blackness.

The blackness hit the Grotesquery and it stumbled as the blackness grew and became spiders. The Grotesquery reeled, spiders all over its body, attacking as one.

The Grotesquery caught one of the spiders in its massive right hand, squeezed, and the spider burst. The Torment-spider scuttled after it, swiping with his front leg, catching the Grotesquery across the back. The Grotesquery hit the ground, bursting the spiders beneath it, and the Torment-spider stabbed downwards. The tips of two legs pierced the Grotesquery, pinning it where it lay.

And then it vanished and the air above the Torment-spider opened up. The Grotesquery dropped on to the Torment-spider's back. The Torment-spider reared up, trying to dislodge his attacker, but the Grotesquery had him in its grip now. Valkyrie saw the stinger dart out, but its point had been severed and it rebounded uselessly off the Torment-spider's armour plates.

The Torment-spider was cursing, the panic turning the curses into shrieks. The Grotesquery's right arm unravelled, the strands wrapping around his throat, pulling him back, making him rear up higher. The Torment-spider stumbled over the bodies of the Cleavers and the Grotesquery yanked back hard, and he tipped over. He landed on his back, his eight legs kicking in the air. The Grotesquery was slow to get up, but it was getting up nevertheless. The Torment-spider, however, was unable to roll on to its side.

"Help me!" the Torment-spider screeched.

Valkyrie felt the sword in her hand. If she could get to the Grotesquery before it stood, she might have a chance. But her legs wouldn't move.

The Torment was shrinking. His spider legs were retracting into his body, his own arms and legs reforming, the blackness absorbed through the pores of his skin. Valkyrie watched the race between the Torment, trying to reassert his human guise in order to get up, and the Grotesquery, who was now on one knee and struggling to stand.

The Grotesquery won the race by three seconds. It looked down at the Torment, now a pale and weak old man, helpless at its feet. Its huge right hand reached down, picked the old man up by his long hair, held him off the ground. The Torment moaned in pain.

Valkyrie looked down at her leg and willed it to move. One step. All she needed was to take one step, the first step, and the rest would take of itself.

Her leg moved. She took the step. The Grotesquery swung its arm and Valkyrie heard a tearing noise and the Torment was flung away.

The Grotesquery dropped the piece of scalp in its hand, turning to Valkyrie as she lunged, swinging the sword and cutting into its left arm. It grabbed for her but she ducked under and spun, using the sword the way Tanith had shown her, and the blade found the Grotesquery's side and opened it up.

Valkyrie skipped back, holding the sword in both hands, her eyes on the wound she'd just inflicted. She watched the parted skin try to reform, try to heal, then stop altogether.

The Grotesquery growled. Its right arm unravelled and came at her. One of the strips wrapped itself around her ankle and yanked her off her feet. She fell and the other strips darted at her. A talon ripped open her cheek and she felt her own warm blood splash across her face.

She reached forward and the sword sheared through the strip around her ankle. The Grotesquery recoiled, the strips snapping back, trying to reform the arm. The middle finger was missing.

Valkyrie jumped up, swinging the sword diagonally across the Grotesquery's chest, lopping off sections of splayed ribcage. Another swipe took the Grotesquery's left hand. It fell to the ground.

The Grotesquery backed off, flailing at her to keep her away. She waited for her chance and dived. The sword slid between the damaged ribcage and the Grotesquery stiffened. Valkyrie gripped the hilt with both hands and angled it downwards, towards its heart, and she rammed it in deeper and twisted. The Grotesquery screamed.

The scream hit her like a fist and darkness poured from the Grotesquery's injuries. It slipped into her and her legs gave out and she collapsed. She felt the darkness move within her, racking her body with pain. Her spine arched. Images flashed into her head, images of the last time she had felt such agony. Serpine, pointing at her, his green eyes starting to fade, his body turning to dust.

Her muscles started to spasm and she retched and gagged and tried to cry. And then the darkness left her and she opened her eyes, tears blurring her vision, watching the darkness rise from her, rise into the air and dissipate. She gulped in a breath.

"Are you OK?" she heard Skulduggery ask from somewhere far in the distance.

She raised her head. The Grotesquery was on the ground, unmoving. Little pieces of darkness still drifted from its body. She rolled over, up on to her elbow. "Ow," she groaned. "That was sore."

Skulduggery walked over slowly. He had picked up his severed arm and was now holding it out to her.

"Here," he said. "Let me give you a hand."

She decided not to respond to his terrible, terrible joke, and allowed herself to be helped to her feet. She touched a hand to her face, felt the blood that was still running from the wound. Her cheek was numb, but she knew that wouldn't last. The pain was about to hit.

"We didn't die," she said.

"Of course not. I'm too clever to die and you're too pretty."

"I *am* pretty," Valkyrie said, managing a grin.

"My, my," said a familiar voice from behind them. They turned.

"Look at what you've done," Sanguine said, shaking his head with mock severity. "You have foiled our insidious little plot. You have emerged triumphant and victorious. Curse you, do-gooders. Curse you."

"You don't seem too upset that you've lost," Valkyrie said.

He laughed and took off his sunglasses. He started to clean them with a handkerchief. "What, you think this is over? You actually think this is finished? Li'l darlin', it's only just *begun.* But don't fret, I'll see you both again real soon. Y'all take care now, y'hear?"

He put the sunglasses back on as the ground beneath his feet started to crack, and as he sank down into it, he blew Valkyrie a kiss.

After a few moments, when they were sure he wasn't going to pop back up, Skulduggery looked at her.

"So that plan worked out well," he said.

"Skulduggery, your entire plan consisted of, and I quote, '*let's get up close and then see what happens*'."

"All the same," he said, "I think the whole thing worked out rather beautifully."

41

BILLY-RAY SANGUINE'S ERSTWHILE EMPLOYER

Billy-Ray Sanguine sat in the shade and watched the pretty girls walk by. The square was alive with people, with chatter, with the glorious aroma of food. It was a beautiful day and he was halfway up the mountains in the walled town of San Gimignano, enjoying a fine cappuccino.

A pair of stunning Italian girls walked by, looked at him and giggled to each other. He smiled and they giggled again.

"Behave yourself," said the man sitting beside him.

Sanguine grinned. "Just admirin' the scenery."

The man put a thin envelope on the table, placed one manicured fingertip on top of it and slid it across.

"Your payment," he said, "for a job well done."

Sanguine looked inside the envelope and, quite unconsciously, he licked his bottom lip. He put the envelope in his jacket.

"It worked then?"

The man nodded. "Did Vengeous suspect?"

"He hadn't a clue," Sanguine sneered. "Guy was so caught up in himself he never imagined he was bein' played. Not for a moment."

"He used to be a fine ally," the man said sadly.

"Yet you had no hesitation in lettin' him take the fall for you and your little group."

The man raised his eyes and Sanguine forced himself to not look away. "The Diablerie needed to remain unseen," the man said. "We have too much at stake to risk being uncovered so soon. However, now that the Grotesquery has fulfilled its purpose, that need is coming to an end."

"You knew Vengeous wouldn't succeed, didn't you?"

"Not at all, and we did everything in our power to help him."

"I don't understand," Sanguine said, leaning forward slightly. "The Grotesquery didn't open no portal. It never got the chance to bring the Faceless Ones back. I mean... didn't your plan fail?"

"The Baron's plan failed. Our plan is quite intact."

"I don't... how?"

The man smiled. "It called to them. Its death-scream called to the

Faceless Ones. Our gods have been lost for millennia, barricaded outside our reality, unable to find their way back. Now they know where we are." The man stood, and buttoned his jacket. "They're coming, Billy-Ray. Our gods are coming back. All we have to do is be ready to open the door."

The man walked from the table and the crowd swallowed him. A few moments later, through a brief gap, Sanguine saw him standing with a woman, and the gap closed over and they vanished.

Sanguine let his cappuccino go cold. Once, he had worshipped the Faceless Ones, but eighty years ago he'd realised that if they returned and took over he wouldn't particularly enjoy it. Still, a job was a job, and he didn't let his own political or religious beliefs interfere, and besides, the Diablerie was a group who paid well. His hand drifted to his jacket pocket, to the slim envelope secreted there, and all misgivings fled from his mind. He stood and left the table, walking in the direction of the two pretty Italian girls who had passed him.

42

BAD THINGS

The heat broke and the rain came with the night. Valkyrie sat down by the pier, her coat slick and wet. It wasn't the black coat, the one that kept saving her life. This one was deep blue and it had a hood that she wore up. Her jeans were soaked. She didn't care.

It had been two days since they'd faced Baron Vengeous and the Grotesquery at Clearwater Hospital, and despite Kenspeckle's science magic, Valkyrie still ached. The gash on her cheek had healed up without even a scar, and all the other cuts and bruises had faded away to nothing, but her body was stiff and tired. She was alive though, so whenever something hurt, she didn't complain – she just felt glad that she was able to feel *anything*.

Haggard was quiet and sleeping. The sea came in against the pier and bucked against it, like it was trying to dislodge it, maybe grab it and pull it down into its depths. The air was fresh and she breathed it in, deep and slow and long. She didn't close her eyes. She kept her gaze on the water until she heard the car.

The Bentley stopped and its headlights cut off. Skulduggery got out, walked over to her, his coat flapping in the breeze. The rain spilled over the brim of his hat and dripped to his shoulders.

"Still keeping watch?" he asked.

Valkyrie shrugged. "Not all of Dusk's vampires were infected at the same time. There may have been one or two, freshly infected, that the water didn't kill. If nothing pops out at me by tomorrow night then I'll believe that they're all dead."

"And then you'll sleep?"

"I promise." She looked up at him. "How's your arm?"

He showed her his right hand and wriggled his gloved fingers. "Reattached and getting back to normal, thanks to Kenspeckle. We've had a rough few days."

"Yes we have."

"Did Tanith come and see you?"

Valkyrie nodded. "Came by earlier on her way to the airport. She told me Mr Bliss was taking care of the Grotesquery, taking it apart and stuff."

"Taking it apart, separating it into all its original components then chopping it up, cremating and scattering the remains. It's safe to say that the Grotesquery won't be returning. Or if it does, it'll be in really, *really* small pieces."

"And Vile's armour?"

Skulduggery hesitated. "Thurid Guild has it. Apparently, he plans to hide it away where no one can ever use it for evil again."

"Do you believe him?"

"I believe he plans to hide it away until he has a use for it."

Valkyrie got up so that she was standing beside him. "Are you still fired?"

"I am."

"But don't they see that it was *his* greed and *his* stupidity that helped Vengeous escape in the first place?"

Skulduggery's head tilted. "Who are *they*? There *is* no *they*. Guild is the Grand Mage, *he's* the one in charge. There is no one to watch the watchmen, Valkyrie."

"There's us."

He laughed. "I suppose there is."

There was a gust of wind that blew her hood down. She didn't fix it. "So what are you going to do?"

"I'm going to do what I've always done – solve crimes and save the world, usually with mere seconds to spare. Although granted, this time it was *you* who saved the world. Well done, by the way."

"Thanks."

"We'll get by. It won't be easy, operating without the Sanctuary's resources, but we'll manage. There is something larger at work here. It isn't over."

Valkyrie's hair was plastered to her scalp, and the rainwater ran in sheets down her face. "Sanguine's mysterious bosses."

"Indeed. Someone is working behind the scenes, keeping out of the spotlight as much as possible. But I fear that time is coming to an end, and we need to be ready for whatever happens next." He looked at her. "Bad things are coming for us, Valkyrie."

"That seems to be what bad things do, all right."

With the wind and the rain, she almost didn't feel it, but she saw the way Skulduggery tilted his head and so she examined the sensations that the air brought to her skin. The air currents twisted and writhed, but there was a space behind them that the air buffeted, in the same way that the sea buffeted the pier.

They turned slowly and saw the vampire. Its arms were sinewy and veins stood out against its wet, white skin. It was hungry, yet to feed, and it was having difficulty breathing. But it had survived and now it was looking for its first prey. It bared its fangs and its black eyes narrowed. Muscles coiled.

It came at them through the rain and Skulduggery was moving, taking his gun from his coat, and Valkyrie summoned a flame into her hand and prepared, once again, to fight.

The dead famous bestsellers:
out now in paperback